ANYTHING FOR LOVE

Sarah Webb worked as a children's bookseller for many years before becoming a full-time writer. She lives in Dublin with her partner and young family.

Writing is her dream job as she can travel, read magazines and s, watch movies and television (she's addicted to *Grey's my*) – all in the name of research.

er previous novels are *Three Times a Lady, Always the Brides-id, Something to Talk About, Some Kind of Wonderful, It Had to Be u, Take a Chance* and *When the Boys Are Away*.

Sarah also writes for children and her young teenage novel *y Green, Teen Agony Queen: Boy Trouble* has just been pub-ed.

Find out more and read Sarah's Launch Lizard blog on her website: www.sarahwebb.ie

Praise for Sarah Webb

'When the Boys Are Away is a fantastic read, filled with excep-tionally lovable characters that you'll hate leaving after the last page. Unputdownable' *Evening Echo*

'The story is told with Webb's characteristically light touch, so Meg's quirky take on life stops her running aground. Nautical ut nice' *Irish Times*

Meg is so cleverly drawn and easy to identify with. Hattie is efinitely more Samantha Jones than Charlotte York and she eps the "naught-ical" rather than nautical theme running through her quest (to find a rich husband). With the summer beckoning, girls' minds are turning to play and with this page-turner in your beach bag, the boys can stay away that bit longer!'
Irish Independent

'Sarah Webb is just getting better and better with every book'
Woman's Way

SARAH WEBB

Anything for Love

WITHDRAWN
FROM
STOCK

MACMILLAN

First published 2009 by Macmillan
an imprint of Pan Macmillan Ltd
Pan Macmillan, 20 New Wharf Road, London N1 9RR
Basingstoke and Oxford
Associated companies throughout the world
www.panmacmillan.com

ISBN 978-0-230-70975-1

A CIP catalogue record for this book is available from
the British Library.

Typeset by Intype Libra Ltd
Printed and bound in Great Britain by
CPI Mackays, Chatham ME5 8TD

Visit **www.panmacmillan.com** to read more about all our books
and to buy them. You will also find features, author interviews and
news of any author events, and you can sign up for e-newsletters
so that you're always first to hear about our new releases.

To my daughter, Amy-Rose,
Princess through and through

'Cheshire puss,' she began rather timidly . . . 'Would you tell me, please, which way I ought to go from here?'

'That depends a good deal on where you want to get to,' said the Cat.

'I don't much care where –' said Alice.

'Then it doesn't matter which way you go,' said the Cat.

' – so long as I get *somewhere*,' Alice added as an explanation.

'Oh, you're sure to do that,' said the Cat, 'if only you walk long enough.'

From *Alice's Adventures in Wonderland* by Lewis Carroll

Chapter 1

'How was your dirty weekend?' my sister, Grace, asked as I walked into the kitchen. She was sitting at the table, flicking through an old copy of *Grazia*.

I rolled my eyes. 'Don't ask. I'm giving up men for ever.'

'That good?' She smiled. 'Sit down for a minute. Adam's asleep; make the most of it. Besides, you always say that after a bad date.'

'This time I mean it.' I collapsed into a chair. 'It was a disaster. Barney is possibly the most annoying man I've ever met in my whole life, not to mention unbelievably tight. I ended up paying for everything and now I'm completely broke. I'll give you all the gory details tomorrow, I promise. Right now I just want to grab Adam and head home. Was he good?'

'Apart from the early mornings. Does he always get up at six?' She yawned to emphasize her point.

I grimaced. 'Sorry. He's only little.'

'It's OK. I had no plans this weekend. In fact, it helped keep my mind off things. I was going to tell you on Friday, but I didn't want to spoil your holiday. Me and Jason have decided to move things towards a legal separation. He's going to continue staying with his parents until everything's sorted out. So if you're still looking for somewhere to stay, I'd be happy to put you up for a while.'

'*What?*' I stared at her in disbelief. We'd been talking about my soon-to-be-homeless state before I headed off with Barney and she hadn't said a word. She had seemed a little distracted, but as Grace always had her mind on at least two things I hadn't thought much of it.

Three months ago Jason had gone to work and hadn't come home that evening. Grace had waited up all night, eventually phoning the guards at three in the morning in a terrible state, convinced he'd had an accident and was lying in hospital, comatose. The next day she was so distraught the doctor had to sedate her. By the time I got there, Grace was holed up in her bedroom, refusing to eat anything and sobbing her little heart out.

By day three when Jason finally rang to say he was fine, he was in London staying with his cousin, taking some time out, a spur of the moment thing, Grace was so relieved and then so furious she flung the telephone against the wall, denting the plasterboard. When he walked in the front door late that evening, she told him to move out immediately; she refused to have such a cruel and selfish man in her house. He'd been living in Glenageary with his parents ever since.

Grace flashed me a bright smile, crossed her knees and began to jiggle her top leg. 'Don't look so shocked,' she said, 'you know it's been on the cards. Would you like a coffee or a drink? A glass of wine?'

I shook my head. Eight years of marriage, and that was it? The end? 'Of course I'm shocked. It just seems so drastic. Are you sure?'

She shrugged, and then sat further back in her chair. 'I don't know what else to do. We've said unforgivable things to each other. And it's not just the London thing; his moods have been appalling. All the shouting – at me and at the boys. Horrible. I asked him to visit the GP, to see if he was depressed or anything. He went and there's nothing wrong with him. Jason says it's me that has the problem and if I can't deal with it, then we're better off apart.'

I put my hand on hers. 'Are you all right?'

She gnawed at the inside of her cheek, distorting her face. 'Most of the time. I'm keeping busy. I find the mornings the hardest, when the kids are at school. I rattle round the place a bit.'

'What about your plan to go back to work? You were thinking of doing something in September, weren't you? Why don't you just do it now?' It wasn't like Grace to be so despondent; usually she was full of beans and bubbling over with enthusiasm for some ambitious scheme or other. The last one had been setting up her own social-networking website for stay-at-home mums, listing part-time jobs and baby items for sale.

Her eyes dropped to the table and she drew circles on the pine with her finger. 'I know I had great plans but, to be honest, I don't have the energy at the moment.'

'Getting out of the house would probably help, Gracey. You can't sit around thinking about everything, you'll only drive yourself insane. What about marriage counselling? Have you tried that?'

She looked up. 'We went once. We spent the whole session picking at each other.' Tears sprung to her eyes. 'I'm not going again. There's no point. It was horrible. Look, I'm just about coping as it is. Let me deal with this in my own good time, and stop trying to fix everything, OK?'

'Fine.' I shifted in my chair. I was only trying to help. It was usually Grace jollying me along, I was just trying to return the favour. Except *I* didn't get all huffy when she gave me advice. I took her suggestions graciously and then promptly ignored them.

She gave me a limp smile. 'Sorry, I didn't mean it to come out like that. I know you meant well.'

We sat in silence for a moment, the only noise the drip, drip,

drip of Grace's tap and her sons shrieking in the garden. Shane, a stocky lad of five, was jumping on the trampoline, sending his three-year-old and much lighter brother, Eric, shooting up into the air, his curly brown hair billowing out like a dandelion seed head.

The tap gave a hearty belch of water and then went back to dripping again. Grace had asked Jason to replace the washer countless times, but he kept putting it off. I'd suggested she do it herself, she's brilliant at things like that, but she'd said it was a matter of principle and if Jason said he'd do it he was damn well going to keep his promise.

I looked round the kitchen; the once white walls were now grubby and crayoned. What had happened to Jason in the last few months? He used to be so house proud. And he'd never so much as raise his voice to Shane and Eric, let alone shout at them. In fact, Grace used to complain that he was far too lenient, leaving her to discipline them most of the time.

Grace stood up. Her eyes were swimming with tears. 'Tissue.' She grabbed a piece of kitchen roll and dabbed at her eyes. 'Sorry.'

'There's nothing to be sorry about. Stop apologizing. Is there anything I can do?'

'Yes. Move in and keep me company. You can have Eric's room, the boys can share. I'd love having you around. It would be like old times.'

I wasn't at all sure that was such a great idea. I liked living on my own. I'd got used to it and I didn't want to slip back to becoming dependent on Grace again. I knew she was only offering because she felt sorry for me. She couldn't really want a ratty single mum and her equally ratty teething baby in the house, could she?

I tried to stall her. 'It's all a bit sudden; I'll have to think about it.' I stopped for a moment, staring at her bare ring finger with a sinking feeling. Grace always wore her wedding

4

ring. Without it, her hand looked naked. 'But what about Jason? What if things change and you get back together again?'

'It's over. There's no going back.'

'Can't you give him one more chance? Aren't you rushing into things a bit? You can't break up your marriage just 'cause you're both unhappy. You've been together eight years. What about the kids? Compared to most of the men out there, Jason's a gem.'

'You have him, then, if he's so wonderful.'

'I'm only trying to help.'

She went silent for a few seconds. Then she said, 'Alice, I don't want him in this house again. He threw the remote-control at me.' She pulled back her hair. There was a long red mark and yellow and purple bruising on her neck, just beneath her ear.

I drew my breath in. 'Jesus.' I didn't know what else to say. No wonder she was so relieved to have him out of the house. Maybe she really did need me. Which was a first. Grace had been bailing *me* out all my life.

'Has he hit you before?' I asked gently.

'No, and he didn't hit me.'

'Throwing something at you in just as bad.'

'It only happened the once and I don't want to talk about it. Ever.' There was a fragile look in her eyes. I couldn't leave her to deal with all this on her own; there were obviously things about their marriage that I knew nothing about. And it was only temporary after all.

'I'll move in next week,' I said firmly.

'Thanks, Alice. It would really help.'

Adam started yelling from upstairs. Grace stood up. 'I'll get him. Coming, little man,' she called.

She came back downstairs with a red-faced Adam in her arms. 'He'd got his leg stuck in the bars of the cot, poor lad.

It'll be lovely having a baby around again. I can teach him his numbers and letters. And maybe some French.' She kissed the top of his sweaty head. 'Isn't that right, *mon petit chou*?'

'He can't even speak English yet,' I pointed out, but Grace was oblivious. She was blowing raspberries under his chin, making him squeal with delight. Maybe living together wasn't going to be so bad after all.

Chapter 2

As I drove back to Bray that evening, Adam fast asleep in his car seat, I thought about Barney, the twenty-seven-year-old would-be art photographer who worked in the local movie-rental shop. Only three days ago I'd been head over heels in love with the grubby-nailed man-boy. Was I mad? After the wash-out of a weekend in a damp B&B in Galway, with bang-bang-bang sex and a man whose only interests were taking photographs and watching movies, I was weary with disappointment. I felt grubby and low.

I shuddered. It was all my own stupid fault; I should never have handed him my mobile number along with my rental card in the first place. When I'd told Grace she thought I'd gone mad. 'No good will come of it, Alice,' she'd said, like a character out of a Jane Austen novel. 'You can't go asking men out; they'll think you're desperate.'

Unfortunately Grace may have been right. The thing is, I *was* desperate. I hadn't met anyone decent for months, apart from the rock-climbing dentist, Patrick Brewer, who had a near-death experience while scaling Dalkey Quarry and took up with his ex-girlfriend again, 'forgetting' to tell me about her for days, leaving me ringing him and ringing him, worried that something else had happened to him as he wasn't answering my calls.

And as for Dion Lanagan, a butcher who used to collect me

in his big white van which always stank of raw meat. When he traded me in for a rep from a condiments company I was actually relieved. He had terrible BO and liked to sleep with his arm round me. To combat the fruity armpit yang I used to wriggle about so my nose was safely away from the smell. Unfortunately this gave him funny ideas about my sexual preferences.

In fact Patrick and Dion were only the most recent in a long list of failures which included Adam's biological father. He went back to his girlfriend, too; or to be strictly accurate he'd never left her in the first place.

The thing is, when it came to men I wasn't unrealistic. I knew they all had their faults; I wasn't looking for Mr Right or for a surrogate dad for Adam; I just wanted someone kind, someone I could trust.

As I drove along the Bray seafront I wondered whether I'd blown my chance of ever meeting someone decent by having Adam. After all, a twenty-nine-year-old single mum isn't most men's idea of a dream date. But didn't everyone have some kind of baggage? And if mine came in the form of a blond toddler, was it really so bad?

I transferred Adam straight from his car seat into his cot and he was now sleeping soundly.

I sat down on my lumpy sofa and looked around my bedsit, thinking about Grace's offer. My curtains were thin and the street light was making the shabby Georgian room glow like a Hallowe'en pumpkin. I stared at the shower in the corner of the room, with the worst dribbling water pressure ever. Adam's yellow plastic baby bath sat in the shower tray, balanced on its end like a squat canoe. My single bed was pushed up against the wall, almost touching the tray. Adam's travel cot sat beside the sofa. And that was pretty much it: 11b St Belinda's Place, a huge sprawling four-storey Georgian house on Bray seafront which was literally falling apart. The landlord had finally been granted permission to turn St Belinda's into luxury apartments, and we were all out on our ear come the end of the month. I wouldn't be sad to leave. I had only ended up here because it was so hard to find a place I could afford that would also take a baby. You'd think it was the 1950s the way some of the landlords carried on.

But I did feel sorry for some of the other families in the building; many of them had been living there for years, like my next-door neighbour, Roz Gorski, who had become a good friend, and her two boys, and old Mrs Sutter who was in her eighties and had no family. At least I could always rely on Grace for help.

So you can see why I'd accepted Grace's offer. After all, she had a working shower, a warm bathroom and a back garden without a resident rat population.

But there was one major problem. I still hadn't told Grace about losing my job. – the magazine job she'd so kindly set up for me, pulling in old work favours. She was going to kill me.

Chapter 3

'Here's one.' Grace stabbed a buttery knife at the newspaper in front of her. She'd just dropped Eric and Shane off to playschool (he went three days a week) and big school respectively and was munching a piece of toast while reading the jobs pages of the *Irish Independent*. She seemed remarkably chipper for a woman whose marriage was on the rocks. I'd tried talking to her about Jason earlier, but she was clearly avoiding the subject, throwing herself into the appointments section with gusto. I sensed denial, but I kept my mouth firmly buttoned.

She'd taken the news of my sacking remarkably well. I'd broken it to her last week, the day before I moved in. I didn't want to pretend to go to work, like those sad men you hear about sometimes who are too afraid to tell their wives they've been made redundant and sit in the library all day in their suits, reading the newspapers.

'I did wonder how long you'd last,' she'd said. 'You're not really cut out for sales, are you?'

Charming! But seeing as she'd found me the job in the first place, I couldn't really say anything. Besides, she was right. Selling advertising space in an upmarket fashion mag was a bit of a long shot. I'd lasted just over two months before the sales manager, Rita, had had a gentle word with me. She said I wasn't meeting my sales targets and had actually lost the magazine two of their regular advertisers. We agreed that it was probably best to call it a day. She was terribly nice about it but I felt such a failure.

'This sounds interesting,' Grace continued. 'Assistant-Fund Raiser for St Jude's Hospital. Excellent organizational and communicational skills a must. Office skills and some experience of event management are also essential. Salary level 32,000 to 38,000 euro per annum depending on experience. Not bad. Might even get you that mortgage.'

The thing is, I'd fallen in love with a house in Bray: Rosewood Cottage, a two-bedroomed cottage with a small garden out the back that was currently covered in concrete slabs. It was completely run down and the pocket-sized front garden was a mess, littered with old plastic bottles sticking out of the scutty grass. But it had potential.

It was round the corner from St Belinda's Place and I'd spotted the 'For Sale' sign while I was out walking Adam in his buggy a few weeks ago. 'Two hundred and sixty thousand euro, priced to sell,' the estate agent had said when I rang. I'd made an appointment to visit. It stank of cat pee, but when I closed my eyes I could see Adam playing on the freshly laid grass in the back garden while I pottered in the kitchen, and climbing roses over the front door. I had a good feeling about the place; I knew we could be happy there, me and Adam.

The only problem was the mortgage. Grace had bullied me into visiting a mortgage advisor when I'd first got back from London. He'd told me I'd be looking at a mortgage of about 180,000, based on my realistic projected salary. I had some savings and Grace had promised to help me as much as she could. Mum had left us equal shares of the proceeds of the family house sale after the mortgage and the bills had been paid off; that would help. But here was the catch: I had to have at least three months' worth of pay slips from a permanent job in Dublin. Hence my increasingly frantic job hunt.

Grace stopped reading the St Jude's ad for a moment and looked at me. 'Hey, didn't you work for an events company in London?'

I lifted my head and rolled my eyes. All this work talk was depressing. I'd been studying some luscious shoes in *Grazia*, trying to bolster my rather damp mood. I'd spent all morning on monster.ie and jobs.ie and it made sobering reading. There were plenty of jobs for 'Inbound Customer Service Reps' and 'Casual Accommodation Assistants' (otherwise known as chambermaids) and even cashiers in betting shops in some rather dodgy areas of Dublin, but nothing remotely appealing.

I wanted to do something interesting, ideally in radio. I'd worked in a radio station in London so it wasn't all that far fetched. I'd adored working at Live 95, it had been my last temping job before I came back to Ireland. The radio station's offices and studios were always bustling, full of people, all yakking into mobiles, powering in and out of the place clutching furry blue microphones with the Live 95 logo on them. One of my jobs as receptionist was to scour the dailies for any mentions of the station. I had to cut them out and file them. Complete waste of time; no one ever looked in the clippings file unless there was a board meeting coming up.

So I'd also typed 'media' into Google, ever hopeful, but the only jobs on offer in Dublin were for a Finnish Online Editor of Yahoo, an intern on a business magazine, and a Telesales Executive on *Buy and Sell*. And as I'd just proven, telesales wasn't really my thing.

If I had to work – and let's face it, as a single mother there wasn't much option unless I wanted to manage on the single mother's allowance, and live in rented kips for the rest of my life – I wanted to find a job that meant something. For the first time in my life it wasn't just about rent money. I wanted Adam to be proud of me.

'Alice, concentrate,' Grace said. 'This is important.'

'OK, OK, I worked in an events company. For a whole two weeks. They organized trade fairs for logistic companies and truck manufacturers. It was hardly very glamorous and I don't think they were the kind of events that crowd are talking about.'

Grace's eyes lit up. 'Events are just big parties. I'm good at parties, I could help you, and you're great with people. You'd make a wonderful fund-raiser.'

'You're very kind. But fund-raising is just sales by another name. I'd be hopeless.'

'Don't be so defeatist. Think of the money. Good for your CV too. And you might even enjoy it. What do you think?'

I snorted. 'Yeah, right. I don't know a thing about organizing balls. Or managing anything for that matter. I have no interest in auctioning off one of Westlife to do your ironing in the buff.'

'See, that's a great idea, you're a natural! I've always rather fancied that Shane. Or the cute blond fellow. What's his name?'

'Kian.' I smiled. 'You live a very small life, sis.'

'Don't I know it? But you're the one who can name all the Westie boys.'

'True. But only because you've been buying all these celebrity gossip mags.' I cracked the spine of *Grazia* in her face.

Only months ago, Grace was an avid reader, whipping through everything from Marian Keyes to Anne Enright and devouring the book pages in the *Sunday Times*. Now she didn't even read that newspaper's 'Style' supplement. In fact, the captions below the glossy photographs in *Hello!* or *Now* were about the extent of her reading these days. She'd also become quite the telly addict, watching all the afternoon chat shows. She'd completely given up reading a newspaper or listening to the news on the radio; it was all very perplexing.

Grace winced. 'Don't remind me, it's a sad addiction.

Anyway, back to the St Jude's job. I know it's a bit of a long shot; you're not exactly qualified. But if you get an interview, sorry, think positive, *when* you get an interview, they'll see how amazing you are. Even if you don't get the job it might lead to something. You never know.' She shrugged. 'It's worth a try.'

I knew my despondency was beginning to irritate her. To diffuse the atmosphere I stood up and flicked on the kettle. 'Want a cup?'

She shook her head.

I made a cup of instant and then opened the cupboard and pulled a biscuit out of the striped ceramic barrel.

'Want one?' I asked, proffering the open jar.

Her back stiffened. Was I overstepping the mark? Maybe I shouldn't be helping myself to her coffee and biscuits.

'No thanks, I'm fine.' Her voice was a little clipped.

I was right, I *was* getting on her nerves. It really was time to get a job.

I sat back down at the table. 'I'm sorry it's taking me so long to find work. I feel such a failure.'

'Don't be silly. Something will come up.'

'I hope you're right. I can't live here for ever.'

'You're welcome to stay here as long as you like. You know that.'

'Thanks, but I won't feel properly settled until I have my own place with a whopping great mortgage. Even if it is a smelly hovel in Bray.' I squeezed her hand. It felt cool under mine. 'But I do appreciate it. You're always looking after me.'

'That's what sisters are for.'

But Grace had done much more than any normal sister. From the age of ten she had been responsible for dragging me out of bed, making sure I ate something and getting me to school on time. And when Mum died, she was all the family I had left.

When I'd come back from London to have my baby, six months pregnant and just starting to show, she'd taken one look at me at the airport and started to cry.

'Why didn't you tell me?' she'd asked, staring down at the inch of taut white skin peeping out from under my over-stretched jumper.

'I didn't know how. I feel like I've let you down.'

She'd just thrown her arms around me and hugged me close, her tears trickling down my neck.

I'd stayed with Grace and Jason until Adam was three months old. Grace had insisted. It had been quite a squish, camping out in the living room, me on the sofa, Adam in Eric's old travel cot, but we'd all managed.

Now, I was so eager to get some caffeine into my system I almost burnt my tongue off. Adam, currently playing happily with some plastic bricks at my feet, was teething again and my energy levels were brushing the floor low. If I had my own place at least I could leave him to cry a little. Here I was always nervous of waking the whole household. When Adam niggled I'd been popping him in beside me in Eric's bed and cuddling him until he dropped off. I so needed that mortgage, but first I needed a job.

'I hate to say this,' I began glumly, 'but Mum was right. I should have gone into the bank. I bet they have part-time work and job sharing in the bank. Do you think they'd take me now?'

Grace's eyebrows lifted. 'With your maths? No offence, but I don't think so. Why don't you apply for that St Jude's job? There's nothing else in the paper and no one's exactly chomping at the bit to hire you.'

Ouch!

She ripped the large ad out and handed it to me. 'Your CV isn't bad if we just give it a few tweaks. I'll help you with the application letter. I can give you a mock interview if you like.'

She lifted a strand of my hair. 'You might need your highlights topped up, though. They're looking a bit rock chick.'

'You can stop right there.' I got the feeling I was about to be bamboozled into doing something I'd regret. 'There's no way I'm applying for that job.' Adam started to grumble, pulling at the leg of my jeans. 'Thanks for all your advice, but I'm sure something will come up soon.'

I didn't want to sound ungrateful; Grace *was* trying to be helpful. I whipped Adam onto my knee and gave him a hug. 'I'm going to take this little fellow to the park. I wouldn't even get an interview for the St Jude's job; I'm not cut out for anything like that, but thanks for being so supportive. You're the high flyer in this family, Gracey, not me. I'll try the temping firms first thing tomorrow. I'll just have to wave Rosewood Cottage goodbye.'

I blame myself for what happened next, but how was I to know that Grace would take my parting words as a challenge? I should learn to keep my mouth shut when my big sister is around.

Chapter 4

Two weeks later I heard a strange creaking noise in Grace's back garden. It was just after ten on Monday morning and she and Eric were at their mother and toddler group. I peered out of the bedroom window, my heart hammering in my chest. A tall dark-haired man was crouched over, trying to pull something out of the overflowing garden shed. Jason's bike. He was trying to steal it. I whipped out my mobile to ring the guards but then the front wheel came off in the man's hand and he fell backwards. I recognized him instantly.

I reefed open the window and yelled down ,'Jason! What are you playing at?'

Adam stared up at me in surprise. He'd been pottering at my feet while I attempted to tidy up our small room, which meant moving heaps of clothes from one surface to another.

Jason shaded his eyes with his hand. 'Alice? Is that you? What are *you* doing up there?'

I opened my mouth to explain, but then thought better of it. Grace wouldn't want her business shared with the whole estate. In Angel's Grove the houses were built criminally close to each other and the neighbours – mostly stay-at-home mums like Grace – loved a bit of a gossip to spice up their day. Grace had already warned me about telling anyone about Jason; the official line was that he was 'away working'.

'I'll be down in a second.'

I clicked the window closed and went downstairs, Adam on my side like a hip extension. Sometimes I forgot he was there at all.

I glided open the sliding door at the back of the kitchen. Grace had doctored it with WD-40 at the weekend and it moved like a dream.

Jason stepped forward but I stood in his way.

'You can't come in,' I squealed, feeling rather stupid. Grace had changed the locks and warned me if Jason tried to force his way into the house I was to stop him.

'But it's my house. And my key doesn't seem to work.' He looked at me with hound-dog eyes and my heart softened. 'Please? I just have to get a few things.'

This was all so difficult. Jason was the big brother I'd never had. We'd all grown up together, playing on the green, hanging out at the basketball nets. Later on, he used to look after me when Mum was working at the nursing home and Grace was out with one of her boyfriends.

From her mid-teens, Grace had a steady stream of boyfriends. Mum used to call her the serial monogamist. I think she was a bit jealous. She was always moaning about being abandoned by Dad, having to drag up two teenagers on her own and having no real social life. Dad left when I was six and Grace was nine. He now lived in Florida with his 'fancy woman' as Mum used to call her and we didn't have any contact with him. It can't have been easy for Mum, but she made such a song and dance about being on her own that it used to annoy me.

I was about to stand back when I remembered the remote control incident. 'Jason, I can't let you in. Not after what you did to Grace.'

'The London thing? That was so stupid.' He ran his hand through his short cropped hair. 'But this is all just temporary. Grace will come to her senses soon. I'm just keeping out of her way at the moment. Listen, I'm supposed to be on a job. Can I just run up and get some clothes? Please?'

I softened a little. It was Jason after all. He was clearly delusional about Grace giving him another chance, but I didn't have the heart to set him straight.

I looked at him closely, checking his pupils weren't dilated. Grace hadn't said anything about drugs but you couldn't be too careful. But apart from his flushed cheeks and the bruise-coloured shadows under his eyes, he looked normal. 'OK, but be quick. Grace will be back any minute.'

But of course, the way my luck was running, Grace arrived back while Jason was still in the house. I thought I'd better come clean as soon as she pushed Eric's buggy into the hall.

'Jason's upstairs.'

She swung around. 'What?'

'He's just getting a few bits.' When I saw the black look on her face I chickened out. I did have to live with her after all. 'It wasn't my fault. He practically forced his way in the back door. He was rummaging in the shed for his bike. I thought he was a burglar.'

'Was he now?' She unclipped Eric, strode into the kitchen, swung him into the high-hair and handed him a rice cake. He threw it on the tiles and she handed him a digestive biscuit instead. She put her hands on her hips and stood at the bottom of the stairs. She took a deep breath and bellowed, 'Jason! Get the hell out of my house.'

He appeared at the top of the stairs. 'It's my house too, Grace.'

She narrowed her eyes. 'Don't even start.'

Just then the phone rang. 'I'll get it,' I said.

But something flickered across Grace's face. 'No, I'll get it.' She rushed towards the kitchen but I was too quick for her and I whipped it up.

'Go and deal with Jason,' I hissed, my hand over the mouth-piece.

'Hello,' I said into the phone.

'I'm sorry, is this a good time?' I didn't recognize the male voice.

'Oh, yes,' I said cheerily. 'It's an excellent time. My sister and her husband are just trying to kill each other. I presume you're trying to sell me something. Go on, give me your spiel. Or are you in marketing? I'm actually one of those weird people who likes answering questions, even quite personal ones. I'm unemployed at the moment so I don't have anything better to do.'

'That's what I wanted to talk to you about. I'm Jack Wise-heart, Director of Fund-Raising at St Jude's. You applied for a job here. You have a most interesting and may I say a most entertaining CV. We'd like to interview you next week.'

I dropped the phone.

It spun on the floor and, as I crouched down to pick it up, Adam, who was in his usual spot on my hip, acted like a dumbbell, giving my hamstrings a nice old work out.

I could hear Jack's voice on the other end of the line. 'Alice? Are you still there?'

'I'm so sorry,' I gabbled into the receiver, my mind spinning. 'There seems to be something wrong with the line. I'll ring you straight back.'

I cut him off and marched into the hall. 'Grace, that was some guy called Jack from St Jude's. He wants to interview me. How did he get my CV?'

Grace stopped yelling at Jason and looked at me defiantly. 'From me. I emailed it in for you. You got an interview? Hey, that's great.'

I was outraged. 'How could you? I never said I was apply-ing for that job. And he said my CV was *entertaining*. What the hell did he mean?'

She winced. 'I may have embellished it a little.'

'Grace, show me what you sent him.'

'I'll just get rid of Jason first.'

'But you've already done that, haven't you, Grace?' Jason said, glaring down at her. 'And from the sounds of it you've moved on to bossing Alice around instead. She's welcome to it. You'll be hearing from my solicitor in the morning; I want my legal share of this house. And if you think I'm going to pay for you and your sister to live here in the lap of luxury, you have another think coming.'

'Lap of luxury.' Grace snorted. 'Don't make me laugh. I'm still waiting for you to fix the shower: how long has that been? Let me see, ah yes, two years. And you still haven't put that trellis up on the back wall, the tap in the kitchen's still dripping and—'

Jason walked down the stairs, a large black travel bag in his hands, and pushed past her rather roughly.

'And you're not taking that bag,' Grace screeched, grabbing at the handle. 'It's mine.'

'Let go,' he said in a low, threatening voice.

He swung it away from her and the handle ripped off the bag.

'Now look what you've done,' Grace said.

'What *I've* done?'

I'd had enough. 'Just stop it the pair of you. Jason, please leave. I have a few things to sort out with Grace. And if you need to collect anything in future, it's probably best to ring Grace first.'

He scowled at me like a teenager. 'But she slams down the phone every time I ring.'

'Then text or email her.'

'I'm not emailing my own wife,' he said.

'Ex-wife,' Grace said icily.

Jason stared at her and opened his mouth as if he was about

to say something, then decided against it. 'Fine by me,' he muttered and then stalked out of the front door, slamming it loudly behind him. Eric began to cry and Grace bustled into the kitchen. I ruffled Adam's hair and kissed the top of his head. 'It'll always be just you and me, buster. It's easier that way.'

When I walked into the kitchen Eric was munching away on another biscuit and Grace was sitting at the table, staring out the back window. Jason had left his bike propped up against the garden shed.

'He forgot his bike,' she murmured. 'He loves that bike.' I was still angry with her but I softened a little when I saw the tears in her eyes. She wiped them away with her knuckle. 'I guess that's it then. I'd better get myself a lawyer.'

I thought she already had. She'd obviously been having second thoughts. 'I suppose so,' I said gently. 'If you're sure that's what you want.'

'Positive. And I'm sorry about the St Jude's thing. I was only trying to help.'

'I can find a job myself, Grace. You don't have to mother me all the time.'

She gave me a look. Really? It said. And even though she was still crying I felt a sense of irritation bristling. She always thought she knew best.

'Are you going to ring the St Jude's man back?' she asked.

In all the drama I'd forgotten. 'Yes. It's a shame, he sounded nice.'

'What do you mean a shame? You have an interview.'

'I didn't get that interview, *you* did.'

'It's your CV.'

'I thought you said you embellished it.'

'Only a little. I just gave it a little more oomph. Hang on a second.' A minute later she handed me a clear folder. I pulled out several A4 sheets and began to read.

'Alice Devine, Pitch for the Assistant Fund-Raiser's Job at St Jude's', the front page read in large navy-blue letters. I read on. I smiled when I realized what Grace had done. It must have taken her hours.

CV: Alice Devine

Date of Birth: 18/2/1978
Nationality: Irish
Marital Status: Single **[no mention of Adam I noted]**
Tel. (Mobile): 086 1958818
Address: 12 Angel's Grove, Delgany Glen, Delgany, Co Wicklow

WORK EXPERIENCE
[this is where Grace's editorial skills came in handy]

Sales Executive at Harmony Media, Dublin　　　*Jan to May 2008*
short-term contract
[Grace had talked to Rita, who kindly said she'd gloss over the fact I was fired if they rang her. She also told Grace she owed her big time.]
Office Angels Recruitment Agency　　　*Oct 2000 to June 2007*
Relevant posts include:
Office Manager at London Live 95FM Radio　　　*2006 to 2007*
[True!]
Assistant Event Organizer at Events Logic, London　　　*2006*
Promotions Manager, Harcourt Events, London　　　*2005*
I was in charge of several large accounts including Triple X Beer and Smashing Cider.
[I used to do beer promotions for these guys, trooping round the Irish pubs, giving out scratch cards, and free caps and T-shirts. Luckily the company, run by two wide-boy Greek brothers, went bust so there was no chance the guys at St Jude's would actually be able to contact them.]

Grace had also added some of my other temping jobs, in newspaper offices (free sheets), and a transport consultancy (a taxi company). Even I was impressed. She'd also added:]

As you can see, I have a wide range of experience in various positions. As one of the prized temps in Office Angels Recruitment, I was in great demand. Many companies offered me full-time positions, but I remained loyal to my company and always declined their generous offers.

EDUCATION

Excellent Leaving Certificate
[For me, passing *was* excellent!]
Diploma in Business Studies and Media Studies from Dublin Business School **[True!]**
Private PR tuition from a top account executive – Grace Silver of Pemberton PR
[Grace added this – she used her married name – she said this gave me a real edge and showed I was a serious player. I wished she hadn't put it in, but it was too late now. She said if I'd listened to her at all over the last few years, I would have picked up more than most college PR students. And she did bang on about her job a lot, so maybe she was right.]

INTERESTS

I enjoy going to the gym, swimming and hockey.
[Not that I've actually done any of the above in the last, oh, ten years.]
I also like travelling, music, theatre, books.
[That's all true. Except for the theatre bit. Grace put that in. It would make me sound cultured, she said. And she told me to say I'd adored Ralph Fiennes in *Faith Healer*, and was a huge Beckett fan if they asked. (As if!) She said no one really understood Beckett's plays and they were all about dreary things like

death and mortality and the futility of life, and one of them was about men in flowerpots, or compost bins or something. She originally included opera but changed her mind and deleted it – thank goodness. Theatre was bad enough.]

I am very interested in voluntary work and have been involved in many different flag days and fund-raising efforts for various organizations.

[For this read – I once did a sponsored fast in school and sponsored Josep Gorski in his school's Readathon. I gave him twenty euro too! Oh, and I used to be in the Girl Guides and once bag-packed in the supermarket to raise money to go youth hostelling on the Isle of Man.]

OTHER QUALIFICATIONS

Languages: Fluent Polish, some French, Slovakian and Czech
[I asked Grace was this a joke. She said no. I do have some Polish, courtesy of Josep and Roz. Plus she said Polish, Slovak and Czech are very similar languages and being able to talk to our new European neighbours shows initiative and forward thinking.]
Full Driving Licence
[After failing the test three times.]
Computer Skills
[Very, very basic.]

REFEREES

[Grace had put her best friend, Petra, and her husband as my referees, but I laughed when I read their titles:]
Petra Almquist, Image Consultant, 49 Maple Lawns, Delgany, Co Wicklow.
[Petra is Swedish but has lived here for years. She used to work as a freelance stylist, but gave it up to look after the twins, Linn

**and Pippi, 3, and Nils, 7. Now she runs a shop in the mornings
while the twins are at playschool and, in Nil's case, big school.]**
*Davey Hannigan, Chef-Patron of Davey's Restaurant, Grand Canal
Dock, D1.*
**[This is Petra's husband (she kept her own name). And as
Davey's is a burger joint, although a rather upmarket one, I
don't think he'd describe himself as chef-patron, more general
dogsbody.]**

'Grace, some of this CV's pure fiction.' Not that it actually mattered. There was no way I was doing that interview.

Grace smiled. 'Don't worry, we can tweak it a bit for the next
application if it makes you uncomfortable. Besides, everyone
exaggerates on their CV. So are you going to ring the St Jude's
man back or will I?'

I took a deep breath, my cheeks filling up like a hamster's,
and then blew it out noisily. 'I'll do it.' I had no idea how much
my life was about to change.

Chapter 5

'You'll want to know exactly what the job at St Jude's entails, I'm sure,' Jack said when I rang him back, apologizing profusely for the delay and the chaos earlier.

I was about to tell him not to waste his time. I had it all planned in my head: 'Thanks very much for your time, but something has come up and I'm not interested in the job after all.' But I didn't want to be rude so I listened patiently as he listed the duties of the Assistant Fund-Raiser, which sounded rather all-encompassing. He mentioned something called the Ladies' Guild a few times.

'What exactly is the Ladies' Guild?' I asked.

He laughed. 'Sorry, good question. It's what we call our ladies' committee. They do a lot of voluntary fund-raising work for the hospital, lunches, fashion shows, balls, that kind of thing. One of the Assistant Fund-Raiser's jobs is to back them up, do some of the admin work like sending out the invitations and taking notes at their meetings, plus a few other bits and pieces like collecting dry cleaning; it's all very straightforward.'

I was surprised. 'Collecting dry cleaning? Is that standard?'

Jack hesitated for a moment and gave a little cough. 'To be honest, no. But I think it's best to warn you in advance: the chair of the Ladies' Guild can be a little, how can I put this delicately?'

'Lazy?' I suggested, instantly regretting it.

He just laughed. 'Busy. You'll meet her at the interview. Her name is Maud Hamilton-O'Connor.'

The name rang a bell. I was sure I'd read about her in one of Grace's glossy mags.

He added, 'She can be a little intimidating, but her heart's in the right place.' Then he gave another cough, aware that he'd been rather indiscreet. 'As I said, the Ladies' Guild do amazing work. Now, did I mention the flag day?'

Just after I'd said goodbye to Jack, Grace walked into the sitting room. She'd obviously been lingering outside the door.

'Well?' she said.

'The interview's on Thursday at ten.'

'You'll go?'

I shrugged. 'I've nothing to lose. And Jack was so nice; I didn't have the heart to tell him I wasn't interested.'

'Jack?'

'The Director of Fund-Raising.'

She gave a whoop. 'That's my girl! This calls for a celebration. A glass of wine in the sun? We may as well make the most of it.'

I grinned at her. 'Why not? Any excuse.'

Sitting outside, I told Grace what Jack had told me about the St Jude's office and the Ladies' Guild. 'They run all kinds of things to raise extra funds for the hospital,' I explained. 'Balls and charity auctions and stuff; it all sounds very glitzy. Apart from the dry cleaning bit. Apparently there's some woman called Maud and I have to collect her dry cleaning.'

Grace looked confused. 'Who's Maud?' she asked.

'Maud Hamilton-O'Connor. She's the head of the Ladies' Guild. She'll be on the interview panel on Thursday.'

Grace's mouth dropped open. 'That's Boothy Hamilton-O'Connor's wife.'

'No! I knew I recognized the name.' I sat up, sloshing some

of my wine onto the deck. Even I knew Boothy. He was one of Ireland's richest men. He was all over the news on a regular basis. In his mid forties, he was strikingly good-looking with intense dark brown eyes and salt and pepper hair, the kind of George Clooney type who only improves with age. He also had a larger than life personality with fantastic, controversial expressions for everything from SUVs ('Dublin Dumptrucks') to the bin charges ('Sin Bins'), and he was always giving 'state of economy' soundbites on the telly and the radio. His recent claim to fame was the sale of his Slainte site, an Irish social-networking site – Facebook with a begorrah twist – which he'd recently sold to Google for a reputed fifty-three million euro. He also presented *Business with Boothy*, Irish television's answer to *The Apprentice*. Boothy *was* business in Ireland.

Grace whistled. 'Talk about big guns. From what I've read about her, Maud's pretty intimidating.'

I stopped for a moment and looked at Grace, the reality of the situation was finally sinking in. My stomach felt jittery. 'Grace, help. The interview! Maud will be expecting someone really glam and well connected. It'll be a disaster.' I groaned and banged my forehead against the table. 'What was I think-ing?'

She stroked the back of my head. 'You'll be the most pre-pared interviewee ever. I promise. Trust me.' She went inside and came back a moment later with her smart brown leather Filofax and flicked it open. She sat down and rattled a pen against her bottom teeth. 'We don't have much time. We'll rope in Petra to style you. Here's the plan . . .'

Chapter 6

'Have you seen the new Beckett at the Gate?' Maud asked. 'Isn't it divine?'

I gulped. Maud Hamilton-O'Connor tilted her head and framed it with her long, pale hands, one on the side of her face, the other supporting her chin, both pointy elbows resting on the green leather-topped conference table in front of her. She looked like she was posing for the back of a literary novel. Her gold half-rimmed glasses only added to this effect.

I had no idea what to make of her and so far I'd spent most of the interview staring at her extraordinary rope of hair, perched on top of her head and held in place by what looked like two wooden knitting needles. She was wearing a floaty white cashmere cardigan with delicate gold and turquoise embroidery up the sleeves, and a matching skirt. Her ivory chest was flecked with gold freckles and she had no breasts to speak of and hadn't bothered with a bra under her white silk vest. Her pert nipples were rubbing against the material. It was all very disconcerting.

'Well?' she demanded.

Up until this moment the interview had been going fine. I'd managed to answer all the questions thrown at me, including one or two curve balls from Jack, who was pretty sharp. Maud kept calling him 'Dear boy'. which was rather amusing as he was at least thirty-five, with strong, square shoulders, dark brown hair, which was greying a little at the temples and laughter lines fanning each eye. Hardly a boy. In fact, he was very attractive in a wiry John Cusack kind of way, if you didn't mind the slightly crooked nose that is. (I didn't!)

As Maud had started rapping her silver pen on the notepad in front of her I decided I'd better answer the question.

Channelling Grace, I heard myself say, 'Beckett. Such an original voice and so ahead of his time. I adore Billie Whitelaw's interpretation, don't you? She just compliments his genius. Have you seen her version of *Not I*? Incredible. I was watching it on the internet only last week.' Grace had made me sit through twenty minutes of *Not I*. I couldn't make head nor tail of it, but from the look on Maud's face, it did the trick.

Her eyes opened a little, the sharp hazel tones reminding me of a goats'. 'No, I've never had the pleasure. On the internet did you say? How interesting.'

'I watch a lot of cultural things on the internet,' I said. 'Like, um, ballet.'

'You're a fan?' Her eyebrows arched. She was clearly surprised.

Uh, oh. Grace had covered a lot in her three-day-long interview crash course, but not ballet. Think, I told myself. Think! 'I just adore Monica Loughman,' I improvised. 'Isn't she amazing? Such talent. And so young.' Luckily I'd caught the end of an interview with the Irish ballerina on the telly while I was clearing up after breakfast yesterday.

'Quite,' Maud said. 'I saw her dance *Giselle* with the Tchaikovsky Perm State Ballet; we travelled over especially to see her. Have you ever been to Perm, Alice? What an adventure. And the art—'

'We'd better get back to the business side of things,' Jack interrupted. As I was quickly discovering, Maud liked to be centre stage.

'You wanted to ask Alice about her event ideas, Koo,' he said.

I looked at Koo. Apart from shaking my hand at the beginning she hadn't contributed to the interview. Koo was another member of the Ladies' Guild. With her head of springy blackberry curls, heart-shaped face and Bambi eyelashes, Koo had presence.

'Koo was most interested in the haunted house event,' Jack said pointedly. 'Weren't you? Koo!'

Koo's oversized sunglasses had slid halfway down her nose and her mouth gaped open flabbily. She was clearly having a nap.

Maud coughed loudly. 'Koo, darling.'

Koo shook her head a little and sat up in the chair, wiping one side of her mouth with a knuckle. 'Sorry, did I miss anything?'

'Glasses,' Maud hissed under her breath.

Koo levered them up, resting them in her wild hair, rolled her head twice, making it click rather frighteningly, and then looked at me. I almost recoiled. Her eyes were emerald green and there was so much emotion there, I wanted to dive in and take a look around.

Koo blinked and I realized I'd been studying her openly. She narrowed her eyes and glared at me. Acid rose into the back of my throat, making me cough and splutter. Jack passed me a glass of water. I smiled gratefully at him, took a sip and then proceeded to cough again, spitting water all over the desk in front of me. I wiped at it with the sleeve of Petra's jacket. 'I'm so sorry,' I murmured.

I could feel Maud's eyes widen and I fixed my own on the top of the desk. Maud's nails were long, perfectly oval, and French polished. If they weren't real they certainly looked it. Koo's were short but congealed-blood red.

'You were interested in the haunted house event, Koo,' Jack prompted.

'Was I? It does sound fun.' She scanned the page in front of her, running a pen down my list of event ideas and stopping in the middle of the sheet. 'And what about the toy boy auction? Very original.'

'You do like your toy boys, don't you, darling?' Maud trilled. 'It's always been your downfall.'

I looked at Jack. He gave me a look, a smile lingering on his lips. He was obviously used to Koo and Mauds' banter.

'At least they still fancy me,' Koo said. 'I'm not a withered old hag yet.'

'What are you implying?' Maud demanded. 'That I'm past it?'

'You started it.'

It would have actually been quite entertaining, if it wasn't supposed to be a job interview.

Jack put his hands in the air. 'Ladies, let's continue with the interview.'

'Apologies,' Maud said, clearly flustered and throwing Koo a daggers look. 'Do continue, Alice.'

'To be frank, I think bog standard charity balls have been done to death,' I said, playing Grace's trump card. 'What you need are innovative events, something a little different, but not too different, of course. Events that get people talking, and catch the imagination. That's why I thought a mums' and daughters' ball might work. How many little girls would love to go to a proper ball with their mums? Hundreds I'd say. Or a celebrity handbag auction. To find good homes for all those last-season bags.' I began to talk animatedly about my ideas, well Grace's more accurately. I'd only come up with three of them. I watched Koo read through the seventeen event suggestions, nodding a little. Did that mean she liked them? God, I hoped so. And what about Maud?

'Yes, yes,' Maud cut in, 'but how exactly would you go about getting media coverage? It's all very well organizing exciting events, but we need bottoms on seats. The right ones too. Especially when it comes to the charity auctions. We need to attract the right people. I see you've been trained by Pemberton. A very prestigious firm, I know them well. So tell me exactly how you would publicize our events?'

Yikes. The one area Grace knew back to front, PR, and the very one she'd forgotten to cover. It was on my CV and everything. It was probably second nature to Grace, like breathing, so she hadn't thought to go over it, but it wasn't second nature to me.

My palms felt sweaty and I could feel a hot flush creep up my chest and neck, towards my face. I took a couple of deep breaths through my nose, hoping it didn't make me sound like a horse. I had to say something. Maud, Koo and Jack were all looking at me expectantly.

'I have a lot of media contacts,' I began hesitantly. 'Especially in radio. I wouldn't like to mention any names of course, it's important to be discreet, don't you think? Let's just say some big names. Very big names. Especially in radio.' Damn, was I repeating myself? I hadn't done an interview for so long and my nerves were jangling like cut electric cables underneath my clammy skin. Lies, all lies. I had no radio contacts outside London. I needed to come up with something good, and fast.

Hang on a second. Grace's job, what did Grace do every day in her job? She'd told me about it so many times, some of it must have rubbed off, if I could just remember. In a flash it came to me. Celebrities!

'For a big event like a ball or an auction I'd find celebrities to endorse the event and do interviews to publicize it. Try and find a new angle for the press. There's a huge appetite for celebrities these days and we should tap into it.'

'Go on,' Maud said.

I racked my brains. What did Grace do next?

'Then you'd write a press release,' Jack prompted.

I nodded and smiled at him gratefully. 'I'd write a press release and make sure I sent it out to the right people. No point bothering if it doesn't hit home.'

'Absolutely,' Jack agreed, putting his hands together and pressing the tips of his fingers against his lips. His full, firm lips. I tried not to get distracted.

'And then a few weeks before the event I'd do a lavish mini event, maybe a photo call with some celebrities or models. Animals and babies, the press love animals and babies.' Oops, that was for politicians, but they didn't seem to notice and it was a maternity hospital after all.

'Then I'd invite a select group of journalists to a special lunch and tell them all about our event and why they should support it. And hit them with our killer angles.' I remember Grace saying it was all about angles. I'd quipped 'Like right angles and obtuse angles you mean?' and she'd crossed her eyes at me.

'What kind of angles?' Koo asked, sitting up even further in her seat, her ample chest jiggling with the exertion.

Smiling, I stopped myself saying right angles. 'It would depend on the event. For a toy-boy auction I'd try to rope in a boy band, get them to have a topless pillow fight in a hotel room, feathers everywhere, sticking to their oiled chests; for an Italian ball, a gimmick like baking a giant pizza in St Stephen's Green Park, or building a blue grotto like the one on Capri.' (I remembered Grace had been there with Jason years ago and had loved it.) I was on a roll. 'A family science day with a huge bubble factory on Grafton Street, with giant bubbles floating up into the sky. For the flag day, lots of celebrity babies—'

'I'm not sure about a science day,' Maud cut in. 'Isn't that a bit geeky?'

'I love it!' Jack enthused. 'Our whole research department is built on science. And it's one of our main drives this year, Alice. Funding the research department.'

'You seem to have plenty of ideas,' Maud said, wrestling control back. 'As long as you can implement them, there shouldn't be a problem. And can you really speak Polish?'

'*Tak*,' I said. '*Na zdrowie*.' Which meant 'yes' and 'cheers'.

'How useful. My housekeeper is Polish. You're clearly a girl who likes a challenge,' Maud said.

I wasn't sure about the girl bit. Maud wasn't that much older than me. Thirty-seven, maybe, or thirty-eight. Still, it was as close to a compliment as she'd given me all morning.

'I love a challenge,' I said with gusto. 'And I really want this job. It sounds ideal for my particular skills base.' I had no idea what I'd just said. It was one of Grace's phrases. Convince them you want the job, she said. Tell them how committed you'll be.

'I'd be very committed,' I added.

I just about stopped myself begging: 'Please give me this job. Please, please. I really need the money and Jack is really cute.' Not that that should make any difference, of course. Knowing my luck he was probably married, or gay, or both. Then suddenly I had a thought. This seems to be going well. What if they do offer me the job? What about Adam? A huge lump of guilt played dodge ball in the pit of my stomach. I *couldn't* work full time. It wasn't right. I was a terrible mother.

'So, have you any questions, Alice?' Jack asked.

'Yes!' I piped up. 'Could I do a four-day week? Or work from home one day a week? I have a baby you see, Adam. And I'm on my own. But I can do the job, it's just I'd feel so guilty being away from him all week. I'd work better . . .' I tailed off. What the hell had I just said? Stupid, stupid, stupid. They hadn't even offered me the job yet. And they sure as hell weren't going to now. How unprofessional can you get? Goodbye St Jude's. Goodbye Rosewood Cottage. I sat there glumly, staring at my hands in my lap. I felt like crying.

'We'll take that into consideration,' Jack said kindly. 'Thanks for being so honest.'

I shuffled out the door, too ashamed to look at Koo or Maud.

As I collected myself outside, taking deep breaths, tears pricking my eyes, I heard Maud's voice ring out.

'A four-day week indeed. Who's next on the list, Jack?'

'Hang on a second.' It was Koo. 'I liked her. And you have to admit, Maudie, she has some great ideas. It's not easy being on your own. You know that.'

'What are you implying? I'm not on my own, I have Boothy.'

Koo snorted. 'The invisible man?'

'Ladies,' Jack intervened. 'Let's discuss this rationally. Alice's interview I mean.'

I knew I shouldn't be listening but I was transfixed. They obviously had no idea I was still in earshot.

'What did you think of her, Jack?' Koo asked.

'I think she's ideal,' he said. 'I know her outburst at the end was a little unconventional.'

I winced.

'But at least she was being honest,' he continued. 'And maybe she could do one day a week from home. She's the best candidate so far by miles.'

'What about Poppy?' Maud said. 'She was darling. And so well dressed.'

'But allergic to hard work I bet,' Koo protested. 'I'm not having another of those trust-fund idiots who can't type a letter to save their lives. I like Alice.'

'I don't!' Maud said strongly. 'She's too pedestrian. She'd turn up at a ball in a Coast dress for heaven's sake.'

'That's what I like about her,' Koo said. 'She's normal. And for your information, her suit was Armani.'

'I know that! Armani 2007,' Maud countered. Then she gave

a short laugh. 'Second hand,' she added witheringly. How the hell did she know that? The woman obviously had special powers. Sadly she was right; I had no business even being in the same room as her.

I sloped away, feeling wretched. Walking towards the train station, my head hung low, I rang Grace.

'How did it go?' she said eagerly.

I told her about the interview and how I'd blown it at the end. 'I'm not going to get it, am I, Gracie?'

'No,' she said calmly, 'but you did your best. You should be proud of yourself. And the next interview won't seem so intimidating. Think of it as a trial run.'

My heart sank. Grace was right of course. But just for once she could have lied. She could have said, 'Of course you'll get it, after all that preparation and effort. Have a little faith in yourself.' She was far too honest and sometimes it hurt.

But she wasn't *always* right.

Chapter 7

I opened my eyes. What was that strange giggling noise? It stopped and I looked at my watch. Half past three. I'd put Adam down for his nap after lunch and I'd crawled in beside him for a little rest. It was grey and miserable outside and I had feck-all else to do. This whole job-hunting thing was so depressing.

Two beeps. Ah, my mobile phone. Grace had sent me a new ring tone, a baby giggling. I sidled out of the bed, careful not to disturb Adam, crept outside and listened to my new message.

'Hi, this is Jack Wiseheart. From St Jude's. Please ring me back as soon as you can. I have good news.'

Good news? Did that mean he was offering me the job? Oh, no. There was no way I could face Maud Hamilton-O'Connor again, job or no job. My heart began to race.

'Is everything all right?' Grace was standing in front of me, a bundle of dirty washing in her arms.

'Perfect. Just going to the loo.'

She looked at me suspiciously.

I slid into the loo and locked the door behind me before she could ask any more questions. Living with Grace was becoming more and more claustrophobic. I'd forgotten how nosey she was. I waited until I heard her walk down the stairs and then, before I could change my mind, I rang Jack back.

'Hi, Jack, this is Alice. Alice Devine.'

'Alice. I have good news. I want to offer you the job.'

I must have made a startled noise because he asked, 'Are you all right?'

'Are you serious?'

'Yes. You're the best person for the job.'

'But what about Maud? She didn't seem all that thrilled with me. I don't think I'm posh enough for her. And she's terrifying.'

There was silence for a moment. Was it my imagination or could I hear muffled laughter. 'Don't worry about Maud,' he said eventually. 'She'll grow on you.'

'Like a fungus?' I suggested. Oops, had I just said that out loud?

He laughed heartily. 'Like a fungus. Alice, please take the job, I'm begging you. I desperately need someone normal in here. I've even persuaded Maud to let you work from home on Mondays. And because of your experience we're willing to offer you 38,000 euro per annum.'

I sat down on the side of the bath. 'Thirty-eight? Really?' An image of Rosewood Cottage floated in front of my eyes. I took a deep breath. Come on, Alice, you're a big girl now, you can cope with Maud. 'OK, I'll do it,' I said firmly. 'When do I start?'

As I waited in Greystones Dart station for the commuter train into town I gulped down the butterflies that had risen in my throat and opened and closed my palms. Yes, decidedly sweaty. My armpits were sticky too. I was glad Petra had chosen a black top for me. A Joseph top with a daring slash down the front, showing my newly bronzed cleavage and the plain silver Tiffany butterfly necklace she'd also lent me. 'Neat and tasteful,' she'd said.

Even down the phone I could hear Petra bristle when I told her what Maud had said about the interview suit.

'Stupid cow,' she clipped, 'but accurate, I'll give her that. I should have put you in the Prada suit. But I love the buttons on the Armani.' She paused and gave a click of her tongue. 'We obviously need to up our fashion game. Leave it to me.'

I was very, very nervous. And Petra's rather cutting-edge first-day outfit wasn't helping. At least she'd let me cheat. I was allowed wear a pair of ballet pumps with black Swarovski crystal trim at the toe and heel for travelling in. But she'd made me promise to squeeze my feet into the half a size too small Christian Louboutin courts before I put a foot in the office.

My bag was bulging from the shoes, a large make-up kit, a notebook and two pens. I'd tried to tell Grace they'd have pens in the office, but she was insistent.

'It looks professional to carry a pen and a notebook at all times,' she said. 'And pens run out. Bring two.'

Everyone seemed to have good advice for me. And in each case it seemed to add to the weight of my handbag, a dark green Birkin (vintage). I was a walking ad for Petra's shop.

Even Jason had advice. He'd rung me on my mobile last night

'I can't talk to you,' I hissed, scurrying into the bathroom and turning the tap on full in case Grace had suddenly been granted super powers, and could hear me through the wall. 'Go away.'

'I have to talk to someone. I really miss the kids. Grace won't let me see them after the thing in the hall.' First it was the London thing, now the thing in the hall, it sounded like an ongoing series of horror movies – next we'd have the thing in the swamp or the thing from outer space.

'You should have thought of that before you shouted at her. Thanks a bunch for getting me involved.'

Silence. A breathy sigh and finally he said, 'Look, I just want to see the kids. I'm dying without them. I patted a toddler on the head in the supermarket the other day, he reminded me of Eric, and his mother hit me with a cucumber and told me I should be ashamed of myself. She thought I was some sort of child molester. I need to play with them; I'm having withdrawal symptoms.'

It was on the tip of my tongue to point out that his idea of playing with the kids sometimes meant handing them a packet of crisps each and ducking and diving while trying to watch Sky Sports over their heads.

'Are you insane?' I asked instead. 'Grace would kill me for even talking to you.'

'What am I supposed to do? I can't sleep, I've no appetite, my hair's falling out. I made so many mistakes at work yesterday the lads sent me home. They said I'd cut my hand off or something. I don't know what's wrong with me.'

I softened a little. He did sound in a bit of a state.

But then he added, 'She has no right to make me suffer like this.'

Suffer? I thought about Grace, sobbing herself to sleep most nights, just about managing to keep it together in front of the children, and spending all her savings on food. Jason hadn't put any money into the current account for two weeks. She'd put a small amount away every month as soon as she'd started working, long before she had children, to pay for the best schools and colleges, and it irked her to have to dip into her children's education fund. But she didn't have any other choice.

'I'm not taking sides here,' I said, 'but you have to give Grace some money for food. I think what you're doing is disgraceful.'

Silence again.

Eventually he said, 'You're probably right. But—'

I'd had it. 'Just put some money in the damn account. She

has enough to worry about at the moment without you being mean about money.'

'If I do, will you talk to her about access? That's not right either.'

'Fine,' I conceded. 'But I'm not promising anything.'

'Thanks, Alice. So how are you? Any news on the job front?'

'Actually, yes.' I felt a surge of pride puff into my chest. I sat up a little straighter on the toilet seat. 'I'm the new Assistant Fund-Raiser for St Jude's Hospital. I start tomorrow.'

'Is that the job Grace got for you?'

Instant deflation. '*I* did the interview. She just sent in the application.'

'Don't forget to bring a spare pair of tights.'

'What?'

'You know, in case you get a ladder. I heard about it on the radio.' Jason was addicted to morning chat shows. It was a wonder he did any work at all.

'Thanks for the advice,' I said drily. But I had bunged a spare pair into my bag in case.

I'm a smart, confident fund-raising assistant, I told myself, willing the train to hurry up. I rolled a stone backwards and forwards under the thin sole of my ballet pump, trying to keep my mind off my nerves. I patted my sheet of sleek newly mink-blonde hair courtesy of a very eager student, and great value for thirty euro even if she did drone on endlessly about her rubbish boyfriend.

Grace was also delighted about the job. And surprised, although she tried to hide it.

'I can help you with the PR side of things,' she'd said. 'It'll be nice to use my brain again, it needs a serious work out.'

With Grace on my side, I felt a lot more confident. I could save all the PR work for Mondays, if possible. That way she could help me. Things were slotting into place nicely. And in exactly twelve weeks time, all being well, I'd apply for my first mortgage.

I'd rung the estate agents the very same day Jack Wiseheart had given me the St Jude's job. They said Rosewood Cottage was very much still on the market. 'It's probably the smell of cat pee,' I'd suggested. I'd put down the phone feeling a lot more positive than I had for a long time. Now I just had to hold down the St Jude's job for twelve weeks. And really, how hard could that be?

I slipped my fingers into my handbag and double checked the moleskin notebook Grace had given me for good luck. It was still there. I stroked its mousy grey cover like a comfort blanket. 'It'll be fine,' I whispered to myself. 'What could go wrong? It's only my first day.'

I held on to the railings outside the National Gallery and slipped my feet into the Louboutins. Although they squeezed my toes, they were actually reasonably comfortable thanks to their clever padded insoles. Honestly, rich people have no idea how lucky they are. I lifted my foot and admired the silky red soles.

'Hey, nice shoes,' a passing courier shouted.

I looked up, all ready to smile until I realized he was laughing at me, while weaving flamboyantly in and out of the traffic.

'Show off,' I shouted back, quickly putting my foot back down and brushing the front of my black pencil skirt self-consciously. It had a habit of riding up my legs, and I was determined to be careful. I didn't want to scare anyone with my wobbly thighs. Petra had convinced me to wear black fishnets.

'Very now,' she'd insisted. But I was already having doubts. I got the feeling she was using me as a mannequin, and had forgotten I was a real woman with a real job to go to and a real boss to impress. Too late to worry about that now.

The fund-raising office was in the administration block at the back of the hospital, an old Victorian building that had been added to over the years and was now a mish mash of extensions.

As I clicked my way through the corridors that smelt of bleach, and up the tiled stairs towards the fund-raising office on the fifth floor, I cursed my heels. I shouldn't have listened to Petra. I was getting a lot of funny looks from the patients – red-faced puffing women in slippers and short nightdresses, dressing gowns ineffectually pulled across their huge bumps.

Finally I found the right door and took a moment to steady my breath. I raised my hand to give a firm, authoritative knock but the door was flung open and I rapped Maud Hamilton-O'Connor's bony chest, right in the middle of her ribs. She was too shocked to say anything. She brushed her chest with her right hand and murmured what sounded suspiciously like 'For God's sake' under her breath. She clutched at the door jamb. I saw to my horror that her chest was red and angry where I'd hit it.

What do you do when you've assault someone like Maud? Well, you don't stand there and open and close your mouth like a goldfish, like I did, or stagger on your new heels and fall down at her feet like a clown.

'Here, let me help you,' a male voice said.

I looked up, cringing with mortification. Maud was staring at me, pity and contempt in her steely eyes. Jack held out his hand and I took it gratefully. He whisked me to my feet and I brushed down the back of my skirt.

'Some entrance.' He smiled at me. 'Welcome to St Jude's, Alice.'

Maud stared at me, regaining her composure. 'Yes, indeed. And I'll see you tomorrow, Alice, in Shelbourne Lodge. Jack will fill you in. Bright and early please.' With that she took one last look at me and walked away, holding her head up regally.

'I'm so sorry,' I said to her disappearing back.

She turned, bent her fingers a little at me, as if I didn't deserve a full wave, and then strode off.

'She hates me,' I said glumly.

'No, she doesn't,' Jack said kindly. He put his hand on my back and pushed me towards the doorway. 'Would you like a coffee?'

'Got anything stronger?'

He laughed. 'I wish.'

We walked inside. I was a bit disappointed to tell the truth. No wonder they'd held the interview in a hotel, the office was tiny. Daylight was bravely trying to shine through the grubby, fly-splattered sash window. An old beige roller blind hung limply from the top of the window frame, and a wilting fern sat in a white plastic tub on top of a large grey filing cabinet. Two desks sat face to face across the room. One was littered with sheets of paper, an untidy tower of metal letter trays, and a mug with no handle holding a leaky biro and some leadless pencils; the other was completely empty except for a spotless (and obviously new) phone.

'Home sweet home.' Jack waved his hand around the room and perched on the edge of the messy desk. 'It's not exactly glamorous. When Maud's not here I work from the café down the road.' He winked at me conspiratorially. 'Or from home. As long as the job gets done.'

I put my bag down on the empty desk. 'I guess this one's mine.'

'Yep. I'll show you over the hospital in a minute. Then I'll fill you in on exactly what you'll be doing in St Jude's and give you a swift crash course on Maud Hamilton-O'Connor and the girls before tomorrow's comedy meeting.'

'Comedy?'

'Sorry, I mean committee. The St Jude's Ladies' Guild, to give it its official title. Otherwise known as Maud's committee. She's the queen bee; she also does most of the work. If you learn how to play her, your job will be easy. If you don't.' He whistled. 'Floss was a nice girl but she didn't last long.'

'Floss. Is that a person or a dog?'

He smiled. 'A person. Your predecessor. She went off to do a cookery course in the country. Said her nerves were shot and at least raw ingredients don't condescend.'

I bit the inside of my lip. That didn't sound good.

He looked me up and down, taking in my outfit. 'You know something, I think you'll be well able for Maud. It's time for the guided tour. Are you ready?'

I pulled my ballet pumps out of my bag and slipped them on. 'I am now.'

'Very resourceful.' Jack smiled. 'I prefer the heels though.'

'Do you now?' I smiled back and raised my eyebrows. Was he flirting with me?

Something flickered across his face and he added, 'Someone I know has the same pair. I bought them once for her birthday.'

'Nice present,' I murmured, feeling utterly foolish. Of course he had a girlfriend; of course he wasn't flirting with me. My heart sank a little, but as I followed him down the corridor and towards the wards, I told myself it was probably for the best. It made things less complicated. Jack wasn't good-looking in the conventional sense, but as I watched his firm buttocks move beneath his dark denims, I have to admit I was disappointed.

Jack turned around and I whipped my eyes off his bum and tried to concentrate.

'The labour wards are in there,' he said. He waved his hand at double swing doors. I cocked my ears for screams but it all seemed quite peaceful until two midwives bustled through the doors in surgical greens, chatting and laughing. They brushed past us, nodding at Jack and ignoring me.

'This is the Ross Ward where all the premies are looked after.'

I stared through the thick glass at the little plastic-covered cots inside. They reminded me instantly of the incubator we had at primary school to hatch chicken's eggs.

One of the plastic pods had two babies in it. Two tiny babies with heads the size of apples, tubes coming out of their mouths, wires attached to their gently rising and falling red-pink chests. They were wearing the smallest nappies I'd ever seen. Looking at them made my heart sting, they looked so fragile.

'Why are there two in that one?' I asked, still staring at them. I couldn't take my eyes away. I'd seen premies on *Grey's Anatomy* and *ER*; in fact Grace and I were addicted to medical dramas, but seeing the real thing was shocking and so affecting.

'Sometimes twins do better when they're in the same incubator. The doctors don't know why exactly, but I guess they get lonely on their own after spending months together in the womb.'

A nurse who was studying a heart monitor beside one of the babies looked over at us and gave Jack a smile.

'A lot of our funding goes on machinery for this department,' he said. 'It's incredibly expensive and we have to keep bang up to date. The technology changes all the time. There are a lot more multiple births these days and a lot of babies born way before their time. But if they're strong, they have a good chance of survival. Most of them are little battlers. These two fellows are nearly out of the woods, they'll be home in a few weeks.'

I felt a wave of relief. After having Adam, anything to do

with babies or children made me emotional, but crying on my first day probably wouldn't be such a great idea.

'Why are there so many multiple births?' I asked with interest.

'Some of it's because of fertility treatment. But it's mainly because women are leaving it later to have children; twins are much more common with what they call an elderly primigravida, a mother over thirty-five. Medically, it's not ideal.'

'Maybe they haven't met the right person until then,' I said, slightly irritated by what he'd just said. The way things were going, I might be well into my late thirties before Adam had a sibling. 'Maybe their husband or boyfriend won't commit,' I continued. 'There are good reasons for these things you know.'

He put up both his hands. 'Hey, I'm just stating the facts. And I agree, life doesn't always work out the way we'd like it to.'

He looked at me, his gaze soft. 'Anyway, let's get back to the office. I'll go through the various computer packages we use and the different phone extensions. Sometimes people ring us in a panic looking for a doctor or the labour ward. We have to know exactly where to redirect them.'

I must have pulled a face because he added, 'Not exactly thrilling I know, but it is important. And tomorrow will be a little more interesting, I can promise you that.'

At lunchtime I grabbed a sandwich and walked to the park in Merrion Square. I needed some fresh air after being in the stuffy office most of the morning and Jack had rushed off to a lunchtime meeting with one of the sponsors of the upcoming Ladies' Lunch. It was all sounding deliciously glitzy already.

Jack had explained the phone and the computer system in-between taking calls, typing up a progress report for the board, and quickly filling me in on the main St Jude's fund-raising events, including the Ladies' Lunches, the annual ball, the Flag

Day, the Charity Auction, the Winter Fashion Show and the Christmas Card drive.

'There seems to be an awful lot of work for two people,' I said when he'd finished reading out the full list.

'I haven't even mentioned the fun run or the women's art project. Or the day-to-day press requests. If someone's doing fund-raising for the hospital, sometimes they ask for some publicity backup. Say if a book's been published, they might like us to help them organize a launch or a special signing event.'

I must have looked worried because he grinned at me. 'I won't lie to you, it's busy. I'm rarely home before seven and I work most weekends, but I love it. When you see what the extra money can do in the hospital, how it helps the medical staff and the research teams,' he shrugged, 'it makes it all worthwhile. And Maud is a power house. She has the Midas touch when it comes to raising money. Look at the Hamilton Wing. Old Boothy never would have coughed up if she hadn't twisted his arm for a whole eighteen months. That and the new government tax breaks. He pumped millions into the project.'

My jaw dropped. The Hamilton Wing, Maud *Hamilton-O'Connor*; of course. I had been in London at the time, but even I remembered the hoo-ha about the glitzy, state of the art private wing.

Jack smiled at me. 'Don't underestimate old Maudie. You'll see just how much work she does tomorrow.'

'Tomorrow?'

'You'll be spending the day with her. Taking notes at one of the Ladies' Guild meetings. Best just to listen. If they ask you anything, say you'll get back to them and run everything by me. And don't make any promises.'

'You won't be there?'

'No. I have meetings all day. Just to warn you – and I think

I mentioned this before – Maud may need you to do the odd personal thing for her; so think of yourself as her PA or Girl Friday as well as my assistant fund-raiser. Maud and the girls are your responsibility now.' Was I imagining it or did his eyes twinkle when he said this.

'Don't look so worried, Alice, it'll be fun. Tomorrow's your first day in Shelbourne Lodge.'

'Shelbourne Lodge?'

He smiled. 'Maud's house. Amazing place. All white marble floors and chandeliers. Her housekeeper's called Magda. She's quite a character. She'll answer the door to you. Tell her I said hi.'

Marble floors? Housekeepers? Acid rose in my throat. I was already horribly out of my depth.

Chapter 8

I stood on the pale yellow gravel and stared up at Shelbourne Lodge in Ballsbridge, Dublin's most exclusive leafy suburb. I felt completely intimidated. This wasn't just any old house, it was a Hollywood hunk of a house. An elegant Victorian three storey over basement, red brick, with a Giant's Causeway block of granite steps leading up to an enormous shiny black door. It even had its own marble fountain bubbling away in the middle of the enormous gravel drive.

The dramatic ivory damask curtains framing the huge first-floor bay window were open and I peered in. The room was straight out of *Homes and Gardens*. A crystal chandelier dripped down from the ceiling like an ice sculpture, and there was an ornate white marble fireplace, complete with a gold-framed mirror over its gravestone-sized mantle. The glass looked a bit cloudy and mottled, but it was probably an original Louis XIV antique.

A figure passed in front of the window and I jumped back in fright. A pale, moon-face stared out at me. It certainly wasn't Maud, thank goodness. It had to be her housekeeper, Magda. I gave what I hoped was a friendly wave and the woman pointed to her left and walked off. A few seconds later the front door swung open with such force the lion's-head knocker gave a brassy rap all by itself.

'Hello?' I said a little uncertainly as there didn't seem to be anyone there.

'Come in,' a voice said from behind the door. I peered around it. A tiny woman was holding the higher than average door catch, standing on tiptoes to reach it.

I stepped into the hall and she closed the door behind me, one of her slim hips giving it a good whack. Then she tucked her dark wispy hair behind her miniature ears and stood up straighter. 'I Magda. You Mees Devine. Mees Hamilton-O'Connor expecting you.'

'Are you Polish?' I asked.

She narrowed her eyes. 'Do I look Polish?'

I gulped. 'Sorry. I didn't mean anything by it. Are you Ukrainian? Or Slovakian? I have Polish neighbours you see. Sorry, *had* Polish neighbours. Lovely family. The Gorskis. Roz and I are great friends. The landlord threw us all out with very little notice. It was really disgraceful you know and it's so hard to find—' I stopped mid sentence because Magda was jumping from foot to foot. She probably had better things to do than listen to my accommodation woes. And if she was Slovakian I'd probably insulted her. They have a funny kind of relationship, the Slovaks and the Poles.

'Yes, I Polish. Slovak, pah!' She gave a small snort, turned on her heels abruptly and tripped off along the white marble tiles. She muttered something to herself and then said, 'Follow me.'

'Sorry,' I said to her back, not knowing quite what I was apologizing for and feeling like a child. '*Dziekuje*,' I added, remembering some of the Polish the youngest Gorski boy, Josep, who was a bit of a brain box had taught me. I taught him Irish geography and history (he loved war stories, the bloodier the better, and was mad about the Easter Rising) and he gave me Polish lessons.

She spun around looked at me a little crookedly. 'What you say?'

'*Dziekuje*,' I repeated nervously. 'I'm so sorry. I'm sure my pronunciation is terrible. I was taught by a seven-year-old.'

'No, you say it right.' She looked at me rather suspiciously. 'I never hear Irish lady say Polish. You Irish?'

'I am, but I guess I have a funny sort of accent. I lived in London for a few years.'

'And you really have Polish friend?' Her eyes narrowed and she rolled her lips in, making them as thin as a reed.

'Magda?' Maud's voice hammered down the stairs. 'Is that Alice? Show her to the study, please. I'm just getting ready.'

'Yes, Meeses Hamilton-O'Connor.'

Magda looked at me curiously. 'And *you* Maud's new PA?'

'I suppose so.' It wasn't technically my job description but I thought it best not to quibble.

'Good luck to you.' She leaned in towards me and hiked her thumb up the stairs. 'She a beetch.'

I gave a shocked laugh.

She wiped back some stray wisps of hair with the ball of her hand. 'Sorry, I just have bad day.'

The poor woman did look wrecked. Her shining skin was tinged with buttercup yellow and there were dark shadows in the carved cups under her eyes. I realized with a start that going by the smoothness of her skin she was younger than she looked.

'Alice! Alice, are you still down there?' Maud's voice rang out and her head appeared over the first-floor banisters. 'I must apologize, Magda's English is appalling; you won't understand a word she's saying. But you have some Polish, don't you? Now, I don't want you speaking Polish to Magda when I'm around. I won't understand what you're saying.' She gave a wry laugh. 'You might be talking about me.'

'Control freak,' Magda muttered.

'What was that, Magda?' Maud said sharply.

'Noth-ink,' Magda said, breaking the word into two distinct syllables.

'Good. Alice, I want you to wait up here in my study. I'm nearly ready for you.' Maud's head disappeared and I heard her climb the stairs to the third floor.

Magda's eyebrows crept up her forehead. '*Kurwa*,' she muttered under her breath, which I knew was pretty rude as Josep used to amuse himself by teaching me Polish swear words. 'This way, Mees Devine.'

'Alice, please. And you stay where you are. I'll go on up myself.' I stared up the staircase, which swept regally up the eggshell-blue wall. 'Which floor?'

'Third floor. First door on the right. Study of Maud. You wait there for her. She getting dressed.' She leaned towards me. 'She take hours.' She rolled her eyes dramatically. 'You sure? I bring you up; no trouble.'

'Yes, you stay here. It'll save your legs.'

'Good. Hate damn stairs. Why not bungalow? Reech enough for bungalow. Have shark. Reech enough for farm.'

'Did you say *shark*?'

'In kitchen. In big tank. Called Pussy Galore and Honey Ryder. Stupid name for shark I tink.' Magda rolled her eyes. 'Idea of Nick. You meet Nick?'

I shook my head.

'He Maud husband. You lucky. Tink he movie star or something. Stoopid man. Ver vain.'

'Alice!' Maud was clearly getting impatient. 'Study. Now!' She clearly didn't like her 'staff' chatting to each other.

'On my way.' I smiled at Magda. 'See you later. Nice to meet you. *Do zoba* . . . um, *da zobie* . . . *da zombie*—' I stumbled, then shut my mouth, giving up. I couldn't remember how to say see you later. Clearly Josep's rather haphazard lessons were wearing off.

'*Da zobaczenia*. Hey, Irish girl, I like you.' She patted my shoulder firmly and I almost fell backwards. 'You funny. Welcome to hell.'

I laughed, praying she was joking.

The stairs were steeper than they looked and by the third floor my heart was thumping in my chest. I stopped on the top landing to catch my breath and then pushed open the first door on the right and walked in.

'Get out!' a voice shrieked from a rectangular bathtub the size of a Mini Cooper.

Maud sat up sending a wave of frothy bubbles splashing onto the Travertine marble floor. She was wearing a 1950s style pink silk shower cap. Luckily the bath was so alive with bubbles I couldn't see a thing.

'I'm so sorry,' I stammered. 'Magda said—'

She glared at me frostily and pointed at the door, her other arm held rigidly across her neat chest. 'Out!'

'Just going.' Outside the door I buried my head in my hands. She was so going to feed me to the sharks.

Chapter 9

After my idiotic mistake, I sat trembling in Maud's study, trying to erase the memory of seeing her practically naked from my mind. I wondered idly where she'd got her rather nice pink shower cap, but I knew I couldn't ask.

I still wasn't sure if Magda had set me up or not but, although I was sorely tempted to find her and ask her, I was in enough trouble with Maud as it was without being caught skulking round her house. I'd already tried to open a locked door, the room beside this one. In fact, my hands were shaking with nerves just thinking about what Maud was going to do to me. Maybe she'd fire me on the spot.

I stared gloomily at the pile of glossy magazines on the low glass coffee table. I'd managed to find Maud's study; the first open door on the left, not the right like Magda had said. It looked safe enough to enter, and I hoped to goodness I wasn't in Maud's private boudoir or something. It was a long, rect-angular room with a sash window at one end looking out at a chestnut tree, its leaves swaying in the breeze, fluffy white flowers on the end of every bough, like candles on a Christmas tree.

An off-white French writing desk was pushed up against the window. Someone had obviously been swinging their legs a little too vigorously as there was a scuffed, darker patch under the desk on the otherwise immaculate woodwork panel.

I stared at the overflowing brown leather in-boxes stacked to the right, and a matching pen holder holding lots of very posh-looking silver and gold pens. At the centre of the desk a pile of envelopes spilled over the surface.

Curiosity got the better of me and I sat very still on the stiff sofa for a moment and listened. Nothing. I knew Maud had left the bath as I'd heard it empty with a loud, horror-movie gurgling noise. I figured the elephant-sized bath probably had several sets of plug holes to deal with the amount of water it had to drain away.

I was a bit obsessed with baths to the honest. I hadn't had one since Adam had been born and it was beginning to get to me. Grace said she hadn't had a bath alone for three years. I'd raised my eyebrows at this and grinned, but she'd said rather tetchily that it wasn't Jason she was talking about, it was the boys. If they heard a bath running they always hopped in, whether she was in it or not. She couldn't lock the door. The bathroom contained the only toilet in the house and although the boys seemed perfectly happy to pee in the garden when she had guests over; when she was in the bath they always seemed to have some sort of toilet emergency. She'd resigned herself to the fact that she probably wouldn't have a solo bath until about 2012.

I crept over to the desk. I stared at the doorway and listened again. Still nothing. A stray leaf slapped against the window-pane and I jumped. My poor heart. Once I'd calmed myself, I stared down at the envelopes. I'd never seen such an interesting bundle in my life. And they sure as hell weren't bills. In fact, if my hunch was correct they were all invitations. Very special invitations. They were mostly in shades of cream and ivory, with the odd pale blue or green. One yellow one had petals embedded in the web, the largest one was a heavenly shade of creamy gold. The envelopes were thick and luxurious, the kind that were lined with silky tissue and I wondered if they felt as good as they looked. I'd just have a little touch and see. No one would ever know.

I lowered my hand slowly and stroked a cream envelope on top of the pile. I was right. It was super-velvety, like posh toilet paper.

'What the hell are you doing now?'

I whipped around, catching one of the envelopes with my hand and sending the whole pile fluttering down onto the carpet. Maud was standing at the doorway, her hands on her bony hips, glaring at me. At least she was dressed this time, in a white crinkled silk dress that almost touched the floor.

'I was just tidying your desk for you,' I stammered. I bent down to pick up the envelopes.

'Leave it. I'll need you to RSVP them all anyway. Send my humble regrets, a prior engagement, blah, blah blah.' She waved her hand in the air, as if brushing a fly away from her face. 'Except for the St Malachy's Hospital Ice Ball. I think I'll send Jack. Always good to know what the opposition are up to, don't you think?'

St Malachy's was another Dublin maternity hospital, newer and rather glossier, although it didn't have a premie ward or anything like that. Babies in distress were transferred to St Jude's, Jack had told me this yesterday, rather proudly.

St Malachy's tended to attract all the WAGS and pop stars and even I'd heard of its glam celebrity-laden charity balls. Last year at their X Ball they'd helicoptered in an *X Factor* hunk and some of the male cast of *Hollyoaks* for the night. It had been in the papers.

Maud sat down on one of the sofas and gestured at the one opposite her. 'Now, tell me, are you simple or just accident prone?'

Charming. She hadn't mentioned the bathroom incident,

for which I was pathetically grateful, so I suppose it was a fair question in the circumstances. I scuttled over and sat down, clutching my hands together in my lap in case they took on a life of their own and jumped out, causing even more damage.

'Just a bit accident prone,' I said honestly. 'But only when I'm nervous. Normally I'm quite safe to have around.'

'Hum.' She didn't seem all that convinced. 'You weren't my first choice for the job, you know. Saffron Foxwood would have been ideal. Her mother's a dear. But the silly girl's taken herself off to Africa to work with Aids orphans.' She gave a deep sigh. 'Bob Geldof and that Jolie woman have a lot to answer for. It's Africa this, Africa that. Makes raising money for our own little Irish mites frightfully difficult, I can tell you. And don't get me going on tsunamis and earthquakes. What a nightmare!' She rolled her eyes. 'Anyway, let's get started. You're au fait with mail merge I presume? I have hundreds of invitations that simply must catch the post today.'

Yikes, labels. I'd had numerous label disasters over the years. And mail merge was a darned sight more difficult than it sounded. I'd have to ring Grace and coerce her into helping me over the phone.

'Yes, of course,' I said, my voice surprisingly calm considering my stomach felt like a milk churn. 'What kind of computer do you have?'

Maud waved her hand at the desk. A wafer-thin chrome laptop had been hidden under the forest of invitations.

'Windows or Mac?' I asked, praying she'd say Windows. I know Macs were supposed to be super-duper easy, but I'd never taken to them.

'What?' she barked.

I winced. 'The operating system. Is it Windows by any chance?'

She gave a bored sigh. 'Lord, I have no idea. Floss dealt with all that kind of thing. I just dictated everything to her.' She twisted her engagement ring round and round on her finger, the diamond the size of a gooseberry. 'Nick's been on at me for weeks to send out invites to our drinks party. I really don't see why his secretary can't do it, but Nick—' she stopped abruptly and gave me a tight-lipped smile. 'It's simple. Find the file called drinks party and send an invitation to everyone on the list.'

'That's the title,' I asked, not wanting to make yet another mistake, 'drinks party?'

'Yes, yes.' She stood up and pointed at the built-in cupboard behind me. 'The box of invitations and the matching envelopes are all in there. And do make sure you use the cream envelopes with the gold-coloured lining, not the silver lining. Gold is this year's theme, silver was last year's. Understand?'

'Gold lining, no problem.' I nodded a little over-zealously, feeling like one of those dogs you sometimes see on the back shelf of cars. 'And the invitations are cream?'

'No!' she snapped. 'Gold! Matt gold. In a brown box. Oh, for goodness sake.' She strode over to the cupboard and whipped open the doors. 'That's the box,' she pointed at a long rectangular dark brown box with a gold card taped to its lid, 'and those are the envelopes.' She pointed at another matching box which had a cream envelope – turned backwards to show the lush gold lining – also taped to its lid.

No wonder she thought I was a simpleton.

She glanced at her watch. I peered at her wrist to see if it was diamond encrusted but darted my eyes away when she caught me at it.

'You have one hour,' she snapped. 'I want them all labelled and ready by the time I come back. You can pop them into the post office on the way to the committee meeting. You have a Dictaphone with you I presume?'

'No, sorry.' I wanted to say I left it at home with the Philips screwdriver and the can opener, but thought better of it.

'Never mind. Just use a pen and paper. But for heaven's sake don't forget it next time. There's one in the office. Our meetings are very intense. You might miss something.'

Intense? I was instantly filled with dread. Jack had done his best to fill me in on the committee's politics but I could see now he was only fire fighting. No wonder Floss had had a nervous breakdown, poor girl.

'And don't swing your legs at the desk,' she added, walking out and leaving the door wide open behind her.

A few minutes later I was settled at Maud's desk, staring at the generously sized screen of her top-of-the-range laptop. I was in luck, it wasn't a Mac. I rang Grace on my mobile and pinned it to my ear. I'd found the file called 'Drinks Party', and I'd opened the document labelled 'Invitation List Gold'.

'Grace,' I hissed as soon as she answered, 'it's an emergency. You're going to have to talk me through doing address labels again. I'll explain later.'

'No problem. I'll just shut myself in the loo.' I heard her yell, 'Take that grass out of your mouth, Eric,' and belt up the stairs.

'Where's Adam?' I asked nervously.

'On my hip. He's been good as gold all day. I'll have to be quick; Eric's in the garden in the travel cot and I don't know how long he'll stay there without screaming the place down. Labels. Right, first check . . .'

Ten minutes later Maud's industrial-sized printer was chugging away, spitting out reams and reams of address labels. And I was feeling quite pleased with myself. I took the boxes out of the cupboard and put them on the coffee table. Now, did Maud want the labels centred in the middle of the envelope or to the right? I looked at some of her post which I'd tidied into a towering pile in the top in-box. It seemed to vary. I'll ask her, I decided. Better to get it right.

I walked into the hall. I could hear the murmur of voices from a room in front of me. The door was ajar and as I got closer I recognized Maud's scouring-pad-on-steel tones. There was another male voice, tinny but strong. As I listened, I realized Maud was talking to someone on her speaker phone.

'I said no, Maud. You're not flying the whole way to Somerset. He'll be fine.'

'But he's upset. He's only seven. Surely—'

'It happens all the time. Sand in your jocks, head down the toilet, it's all just boarding-school stuff. Nothing to worry about.'

'But he's being bullied!'

'He's just going to have to learn to stand up for himself. Fight back. Those boxing lessons I've organized should sort things out. Look he wasn't buggered by a prefect or anything, like in my day, lighten up.'

There was a deathly silence.

'Anyway, what have I told you about ringing me at work?'

'But Nick—'

'I don't really have time for this.'

'Don't be like that. I'm upset. I just thought—'

'Don't think! Leave that to me. I'm sorry, I have to go. Don't wait up. I'm working late.'

'But we're supposed to be going—'

The phone went dead.

I waited for a respectable amount of time and then knocked on the door.

'Go away, Magda. I'm busy.'

'It's me,' I called, still outside the door. 'Alice.'

The door flew open. 'Yes?' Maud's eyes looked flat and glassy. 'You've broken the printer, haven't you?'

'No. I have a very quick question. Do you want the labels in the middle of the envelope or to the right, only—'

'I don't give a rat's ass where you put the labels. Just get on with it. Now, if you'll excuse me.' With that she closed the door in my face.

Chapter 10

Two hours later I was chasing down the West Pier in Dun Laoghaire after Maud and her friend Gunella, a horsey-looking woman in her mid-thirties with flaxen-blonde hair and teeth the size of piano keys. Koo was a little way behind us.

'Do try to keep up, Koo,' Gunella said, pumping her arms with every step.

Koo's arms were thrust deep into the pockets of her cashmere coat and she was having trouble negotiating the uneven surface in her spindly-heeled boots.

'So everything's in place for La Grenouille next week?' Maud asked, with an impeccable French accent. The St Jude's Ladies' Lunch was being held in an upmarket restaurant in the middle of town. It was one of the few Dublin restaurants with a Michelin star and I'd always wanted to eat there. It looked like I was finally going to get my chance.

'Pretty much,' Gunella said. 'I'm still waiting for Gucci to deliver the perfume for the goody bags.'

Maud's nose twitched. 'We used Gucci last time. Isn't there anyone else we can try? This is a very select event after all.'

'I'll see what I can do,' Gunella said. From the way she gnashed her large teeth together I don't think she was too thrilled at the prospect.

'Are you getting all this, Alice?' Maud said.

'Doing my best.' I was running a little ahead, stopping to jot down notes, lagging behind and then catching up again. It was like being in the airport. Maud and Gunella were on one of those travellators and I was on the flat, just trying to keep up.

'Why are you having your meeting outside?' I asked Koo as I lagged behind yet again.

'Gunella's obsessed with fresh air.' Koo tossed her head at Maud and Gunella, pulled her coat round her body and adjusted her sunglasses, which had slipped down her nose. 'Can't see the attraction myself.'

Maud put her arm out to stop Gunella in her tracks and wheeled round.

'What was that, Koo?' Maud asked.

'Nothing. Hey, Gunny, I've been meaning to ask you, what's with the orthopaedic shoes?'

'They're MBTs,' Gunella said, looking down at her chunky grey shoes. 'They're designed by Masai warriors.'

'Really?' Koo didn't look impressed. 'Are they supposed to make your bum stick out like that?'

'Koo,' Maud warned. I looked down at Maud's feet. She was wearing a matching pair in pristine white.

'And what's wrong with your shoulders, Gunny?' Koo continued. 'You're walking like a duck.'

'It's my yoga belt.' Gunella smiled at her smugly. 'It's holding my shoulders back. My yoga teacher recommended it for my posture. Look.' She unzipped her purple Juicy Couture hoody and flashed it open. Her shoulders were trussed up like a turkey's wings, a white canvas belt digging into her flesh. She looked like something out of Opus Dei.

Koo gave her a withering look and wrapped her arms tightly round her own ample chest.

'Let's press on, shall we?' Maud said. 'At least some of us are interested in our physiology, Koo. I know you were up all night, but do please try to be civil.'

'I'm freezing my tits off and these boots are not designed for this.' Koo shook a leg in the air, almost falling over. I held out a hand to steady her. 'Thanks,' she said. 'Look, I need a drink. Is there anywhere around here that does a decent Martini?'

Maud glared at her, and then walked on.

Koo said, 'Maudie, don't be like that. I'm joking, I'm joking, OK. But I could murder a coffee. Take pity on me. We could go to the Belgrave.' Koo skipped over yet more dog poo. 'Alice could check out the dining room. We often use it for smaller lunches,' she told me. 'Go on Maud, we can brainstorm over an early lunch. You know you're hungry.'

Maud relented. 'Fine. But you need to focus, Koo. You've been less than useless all morning.'

Koo poked her tongue out.

'You might want to get that seen to,' Maud said drily. 'It's not supposed to be green.'

'Super,' Gunella squealed, oblivious. 'I do like the Belgrave's oysters. And can we do a St Jude's event with dogs? I know, I know – a dog show. I could enter Bunny and Charlie Boy.'

'We'll see,' Maud said, surprisingly kindly. She frowned at Koo and gave a tiny shake of her head.

'Wait till you meet Gunella's gun dogs,' Koo whispered to me. 'Stinky, incontinent old things. Heads like lump hammers. Their breath will knock you out. Rather like her old man's. Although his stinks of port and garlic, not rotting meat.'

Twenty minutes later Koo and I were lounging on a plush grape-coloured velvet sofa in the very swish and very quiet bar of the Belgrave Club, an impressive Georgian building in Monkstown overlooking Dublin Bay. Maud was in the hall taking a phone call on her Blackberry.

'Looks like something's wrong,' Gunella said, pointing at Maud through the glass panels of the door. Her friend's lips were pinched and from the wicked step-mother look on her face, someone had just said no to her.

'Brace yourself.' Koo swigged back her champagne cocktail and slammed the glass down on the low table in front of her. She'd changed her mind about the coffee. 'She's coming back.'

'They've just made Aoife Hearty the face of Newbridge Silver,' Maud said without preamble. 'She has to fly out to Brazil on Monday for a photo shoot. For a whole flaming week.' Aoife Hearty was a popular television presenter and a supporter of the hospital.

Gunella squealed. 'But what about our lunch? She's supposed to be our guest speaker.'

Maud flopped into a leather armchair. 'Obviously she can't do it. We'll have to find someone else.'

'Talk about late notice.' Koo leaned forwards. 'Any ideas, Maud?'

'Alice, you're supposed to be taking all this down,' Maud barked.

I whipped out my notebook and poised my pen. I could feel my cheeks redden.

'Maud,' Koo said evenly, 'Alice is doing her best.'

'Yes, yes, I know but I'm under a huge amount of pressure. All this is *your* job, you know. I shouldn't have to deal with logistics.' I presumed this was directed at me. My head was down and I was trying not to snap back. Maud was just plain mean. Rosewood Cottage, I whispered to myself, like a mantra.

Maud continued, 'Chasing celebrities, organizing the venues, finding gifts for the goody bags, all your department, Alice. And we're miles behind with plans for the ball in October. We've been filling in while Jack found a new assistant fund-raiser. As it's your first week, I'll let you off, but I need you to take a fully proactive role in organizing the ball and the charity auction. We have a brainstorming weekend coming up for the ball and you'll be expected to join us. We must decide an original theme for it, and fast. And nothing to do with Mardi Gras, or fire-eating or any kind of circus act. Something classy. We're thinking Italy, aren't we, Koo? Or maybe Greece. But not Venice, masked balls have been done to death. Amalfi, Positano, Capri.'

Proactive role, I scribbled. Brainstorming weekend. Original themes. Balls! I underlined this twice. Although in my head it was prefixed with the word bloody. And hang on – Capri? Wasn't that one of Grace's ideas?

'Now back to the lunch,' Maud said. 'How about Paulie O'Hara?' Paulie was the very popular captain of the Irish rugby team.

'Had him last year,' Koo said. 'Not literally, Alice, in case you're wondering, although he is quite cute.' She winked at me. 'Anyway, I thought we wanted a woman this time.'

'Barbara Woodhouse,' Gunella piped up.

I stifled a laugh. Maud and Koo just ignored her.

An hour later and things weren't looking good. Maud and Koo had already rung several of the personalities on my scribbled wish list with no luck.

As I was jotting everything down my mind was ticking over. What on earth had I taken on? I didn't recognize half the celebrity names they were rattling off; let alone how to contact them. And as for original themes for balls? I was way out of my league. My stomach lurched and I felt dizzy.

I jumped to my feet. 'I'm just popping to the loo.'

'Left at the end of the corridor,' Koo said.

'She really is most ineffectual,' I heard Maud say in my wake. 'And you'll never guess what she did this morning. I was in the bath . . .' I didn't hang around to hear any more.

I rang Grace from the safety of a locked cubicle.

'It's a disaster,' I wailed. 'I should never have listened to you. I can't do this.'

'Calm down and tell me what's wrong.'

'I have to find celebrities. And presents for goody bags. And go on a brainstorming weekend. Maud's so horrible to me. Her celebrity speaker has just pulled out of the charity lunch next week and she's in a foul mood. I can't do this. Where do you find celebrities, Gracey? They're hardly in the phone book. Do you pounce on them in nightclubs, or sit outside RTE waiting for them? I don't fancy getting arrested as a stalker.' My eyes were filling up. This was all so overwhelming.

'Alice,' Grace said firmly, 'start by taking a few deep yoga breaths. Can you do that? In through your nose, out through your mouth. In, out. In, out.'

I followed Grace's voice. The breathing helped calm my nerves all right, but it also made me feel even dizzier. I closed the toilet seat and sat down.

'Now, this is what you'll do,' she said. 'You'll take it day by day. First, you'll impress them by finding a wonderful celebrity for their lunch. When is it exactly?'

'Next Thursday.'

I could hear Grace suck her breath in through her teeth. 'Tricky one. Leave it with me. I'll find someone for you.'

'You will? A proper celebrity?'

'Yes, I promise. So are you OK? Crisis averted?'

'I suppose so.' My palms were still sweaty but my tears had stopped. 'Thanks, Grace.'

'Hang in there, sis.' There was a loud noise and then a shriek. 'Oops, have to go.'

As I clicked my mobile off I realized I'd forgotten to ask about Adam. I'd been too busy all morning to miss him, but now the mere thought of him made my stomach ache.

Five minutes later I walked back into the bar, my head held high. While I'd been hiding in the loo, dreading having to face Maud again, Grace had rung back with news.

'Maud thought you'd fallen in.' Gunella giggled.

'I have someone for Thursday if you're interested,' I began, my voice faltering. 'A celebrity.' What if Grace had got this all wrong? They wanted someone glitzy, high profile; what the hell was I doing? I felt a lump of gloom pressing into the pit of my stomach.

Maud said, 'Do spit it out. And sit down for goodness sake. You look as if you're about to faint.'

I clutched at the arm of the purple sofa and sat down beside Koo.

'Well?' Maud demanded.

My throat felt tight. I swallowed, then said in a small voice, 'Peggy Baker.'

Maud narrowed her flinty eyes. 'And who exactly is Peggy Baker?'

I could feel the blood drain from my face.

But then Koo said, 'She's only the most exciting up-and-coming chef in the country. You must know her, Maudie. She has her own show – *The Soup Dragon*. She's like an Irish Nigella Lawson.' Koo winked at me and gave a click with her tongue. 'Good on you, Alice. How did you find her?'

I had no idea. I thought it best to say something resembling the truth. 'Through my sister. She has a lot of friends in the media,' I added for effect.

'Always good to have contacts.' Maud gave me a curt nod. 'In that case, I'll expect exceptional press coverage for the ball and charity auction.'

My heart sank. Why couldn't I just keep my big mouth shut?

Chapter 11

'Where are you going?' I stared at Grace on Saturday morning. If it was Grace. If you didn't look too closely at her face, she'd pass for a twenty-five-year-old. She was wearing a red cotton shirt dress, straight-legged jeans with a chunky turn up at the ends, and white beaded flip flops. Her hair was swept back off her face with a thick black plastic hairband and she was wearing a pair of oversized Jackie O sunglasses. I was impressed. It was certainly an 'outfit'. Not like my thrown together T-shirt and denim skirt.

'I'm bringing Shane to soccer practice.' She brushed down her dress. 'What do you think? I went shopping with Petra yesterday afternoon. We popped the older kids into the crèche for a couple of hours and brought Adam with us in his buggy. I hope you don't mind. He seemed happy enough.'

'Course I don't mind. And you look great. I hope you don't mind me asking, but does this mean Jason lodged some money into your joint account?'

'Yes, finally!'

'Good.' I was relieved yet slightly worried. He'd kept his promise, so it was only a matter of time before he came looking for me. Jason was the kind of man who followed things through.

She looked at me for a moment, sensing my unease. 'Did

you have anything to do with it?' Her eyes narrowed. 'Have you seen him?'

'No.' Technically I hadn't. 'I didn't know Shane was a soccer player,' I added, eager to change the subject.

'He's just starting today. And you'll never guess who the coach is.' Her eyes were dancing. I began to get a little suspicious.

'Who?'

'Arvin Hudson.' She grinned.

I gave a laugh. 'No! *Your* Arvin?' I hadn't heard Arvin's name in years. A tall and stocky Canadian, they'd been quite serious in college until Grace had given him the 'It's not you, it's me' speech. Or so she'd said.

I'd never understood why she'd dumped him. He was handsome and kind and I'd thought she was mad. At the time she'd brushed off my questions, saying he was too intense, but I knew for a fact that since then she'd always been curious about him. Often, when I used the computer directly after her, I'd find *Arvin Hudson* still framed in the Google search box.

She nodded. 'Small world. He's working for Dell over here now. Head of European marketing no less.'

'Have you talked to him?'

'No. I read his profile on Friends Reunited. He said he coached soccer in Bray and I did a bit of research. For Shane of course. I'm sure Arvin's the best football coach there is.'

'Did he play in college?'

She looked a little sheepish. 'No, but he was a great rugby player. It's all the same, isn't it?' She waved her hand in the air vaguely and gave me one of her chippy smiles.

It all began to click into place. The new clothes, the make-up, the sunny mood. And the sudden interest in Shane's burgeoning soccer career.

'Grace, do you really think it's such a good idea? You broke

Arvin's heart, remember? He might not be all that thrilled to see you.'

In his turn, Arvin had broken Grace's bedroom window, chucking stones at it late one night, trying to get her to come out and talk to him. And I'd always suspected that Arvin was behind all the heavy-breathing phone calls that Mum had eventually reported to the local garda station.

She waved her hands in the air again. 'That was years ago. I just want to catch up with an old friend, that's all. And he was always so good-looking,' she added rather wistfully.

I stared at her. 'Gracey, are you sure you're quite ready for another relationship?' I said carefully.

She just laughed. 'Who's talking about a relationship?' She leaned in towards me and hissed, 'It's sex I'm after.'

I nearly jumped out of my skin. This wasn't the Grace I knew, the Grace who channel-hopped during Samantha's more raunchy *Sex in the City* scenes and was firmly against showing too much cleavage. 'Are you serious?'

She shrugged. 'Why not? I'm sick of being just another mum, worrying about Rice Krispies stuck to the walls, obsessing about things like potty training and strange bum rashes; I want my life back. I used to be fun you know.'

'You're still fun, Grace.'

'But I'm bored with myself, and I'm sick of my own company in the evenings. You're OK, you're working; you get out of the house every day. And you get to wear grown-up clothes and flirt with your new boss.'

'I don't flirt with him.'

'If you don't, you should. He sounds lovely.'

'But he has a girlfriend, remember. Why don't *you* get a job,' I suggested. 'Something part-time.'

'What about the boys?' She shook her head. 'No, what I need is a social life. I need to start again. Petra's no use, she's always knackered and she hates pubs and nightclubs. I need some adult company. I just thought someone like Arvin would make a nice distraction. Don't go getting all judgemental on me, Alice. You're no saint, handing your mobile number to strange men in shops.'

'Hey, that's not fair! Barney wasn't strange.' I hesitated. Actually he was a bit strange, but not in the way Grace meant.

She lifted her eyebrows, but said nothing. 'I just need to cut loose a bit, that's all.'

I smiled at the thought. Grace had never been a 'cut loose' kind of girl. I had to save her from herself.

'Why don't I come with you?' I said. At least that way I could keep an eye on her.

'No.' She obviously saw straight through me.

'Please, Grace. I'm feeling a bit vulnerable at the moment, what with Maud and everything. I don't want to be on my own today.'

Grace squirmed. She found it hard to say no when I played the vulnerable card. 'It'll be really boring. Standing round watching lots of little boys get muddy.'

'Adam would love it,' I said firmly. 'He's due a walk anyway.' I linked my arm through hers. 'And there might be some cute single dads there, who knows? At the very least I can watch Arvin and the other grown-ups. I always find the sight of men running about in shorts rather cheering.'

'Where's Arvin?' I looked the pitch. There were dozens of muddy boys of all shapes and sizes chasing balls and bumping each other, like under-walked puppies. Two lads in their mid-twenties were trying to keep things under control, but there was no sign of Arvin.

Grace shrugged. She leaned the top of her stomach against the white wooden barrier and sighed. I couldn't see her eyes through her sunglasses, but I could tell she was disappointed. 'I must have made a mistake. Maybe there are two Arvin

Hudsons.' Shane was still standing glued to her side, staring at the other boys.

'Why don't you go and join them?' Grace suggested, ruffling his hair.

He whipped his head away from her hand and scowled at the ground. 'Don't wanna.'

'Shy,' Grace mouthed to me. She straightened up. 'I'd better go and find out who's in charge.'

A tree trunk of a man lumbered along the sideline towards us. His stomach wobbled under his over-tight navy T-shirt.

'I'll ask this guy,' she said.

I cocked my head. He looked vaguely familiar. His pink cheeks were swimming with sweat. His arms were wrapped round a bundle of red and yellow bibs and a stack of miniature orange traffic cones.

But I would have recognized those china-blue eyes and the strong, square jaw anywhere.

'Hey, Arvin,' I shouted without thinking.

Grace gave me a huge dig in the ribs. 'Don't be daft, that's not Arvin,' she hissed.

The man came to a shuddering halt in front of us, hugging the cones to his chest. He pushed his wire-rimmed glasses up the bridge of his nose and blinked a few times. For a few awkward seconds no one said a word.

Shane pulled on Grace's hand. 'Mum, I'm bored. Can we go home?'

'Alice?' Finally the man grinned, his teeth lighting up his face. He always did have film-star teeth. 'Hey, what are you doing here?'

I heard Grace give a tiny squeak.

'Is that your baby?' Arvin nodded down at Adam, who was snoring away in his buggy, oblivious.

I nodded. 'That's Adam.'

'And this young man looks like he's here to play.' He gave a nod in Shane's direction. 'Is he yours too? He certainly looks like a football player to me. What's your name, sonny?' He put the cones onto the muddy grass and crouched down.

Shane turned his head away and buried his face in Grace's legs.

Arvin stood up again and smiled at Grace. 'Sorry about that—' He stopped mid sentence, staring at Grace, who had just lifted her sunglasses and rested them against her hair-band.

'Hi, Arvin,' she said gently. 'This is my lad Shane. It's his first day, he's a bit nervous.'

Arvin stared at Grace, a dark red blush rushing up his solid neck and into his already flushed cheeks.

'What a coincidence,' I trilled. 'Are you one of the coaches, Arvin?'

'Yeah,' he said, his eyes still glued to Grace's face. 'You look exactly the same,' he told her, shaking his head. 'Shawks, you look even better. How can that be? It must be what, ten years?'

'Thirteen,' Grace said.

Arvin's eyes widened. 'Is that so?' He whistled. 'And this is your boy?'

She nodded. 'I have two sons, Shane's the eldest.'

Arvin smiled. 'Two boys. Isn't that something?'

A dark-haired man sprinted over – a ball cradled in the crook of his arm – and slapped Arvin on the back. He had the intense, hypnotic eyes of a young Roy Keane. 'Hey, Arvey. Are you ready to get started? The kids are going a bit wild.' The man looked at me, his eyes sparkling mischievously. 'Hi, girls. Here to play?'

'Depends who's asking,' Grace said sassily.

I stared at her. He was twenty-six at most. What the hell was she doing? Poor Arvin. But he didn't seem all that bothered.

'This is Gary,' Arvin said. 'Gary, Alice and Grace. Old friends of mine.'

'Less of the old,' Grace said, resting the tip of her tongue on her upper lip.

Shane suddenly perked up and stared at Gary, 'Are you a real football player?' he asked.

Gary nodded. 'I used to play for Shamrock Rovers.'

'Really?' Grace and Shane asked simultaneously. I don't know which of them was more impressed.

'Coming?' Gary ran off, throwing the ball down, dribbling a little and then passing it back to Shane.

Shane let go of Grace's leg. 'OK.' He ran off, kicking the ball back to Gary.

We all watched Shane running up the field after his new hero.

'He's got a real way with kids,' Arvin said.

'How did you get into all this?' I asked him, nodding at the pitch. 'I thought you were a rugby man.'

'Margaret,' he said. 'She's been involved with the club for years.'

'Who's Margaret?' I knew Grace was dying to know, but was far too polite to ask.

'My wife. She's Irish.' He gave a laugh. 'Always did like the Irish girls.'

'Where did you meet her?' I asked.

'Alice!' Grace hissed, but I could tell she was as curious as I was.

Luckily Arvin didn't seem to mind my mini-interrogation. 'In Toronto. She was nursing and we met at a charity ball for the hospital.'

'Really?' Grace smiled. 'How funny. Alice has just started working as a fund-raiser for St Jude's Hospital.'

'Is that so? And how about you, Grace? Are you running the country yet?'

Grace gave a laugh. 'Not yet. I work in PR but I've taken a career break to look after the children.'

'How long have you been married?' he asked.

Grace leaned forward on the barrier and rested her arms on it. 'Actually, I'm separated.'

It was the first time I'd heard her say it out loud and I have to say it sounded strange.

Arvin's face dropped. 'I'm sorry.'

She gave him a half smile and turned her palms up to the sky. 'These things happen.'

A whistle blew in the middle of the pitch and Gary yelled over, 'Arv! Are you set?'

'Sure.' He smiled at us. 'Sorry, I have to run. Maybe you guys could swing by our place for a barby or something. Bring the kids. Margaret loves kids. Be swell to catch up properly.' His eyes lingered on Grace.

'Thanks,' Grace said, clearly taken aback by his warmth. 'That would be nice. Maybe in a few weeks. Things are a bit up in the air for me at the moment.'

'I understand.' Arvin loped off and Grace watched his back, a strange expression on her face.

'He's still a lovely guy,' I said.

'I know. He was always a sweetheart.' She pressed her lips together tightly and then bit the inside of her lip. 'Do you think he was pleased to see me? He didn't seem all that interested.'

I understood how she felt. It was good to have someone to daydream about, it made you feel alive, even if nothing ever came of it. But she'd just had those hopes dashed. I wished I had someone to think about. Jack was seriously starting to grow on me, but he was already taken.

I nudged Grace with my shoulder. 'He's still mad about you. Did you see the way he blushed?'

This seemed to cheer her up a bit. 'He did, didn't he? Shame he's got so heavy.'

'And so married,' I added.

A moment later Gary appeared in front of us. 'Shane's

jumper,' he said, handing the navy hoody to Grace. 'They have a habit of disappearing if you leave them on the sidelines.'

'Thanks,' she said, taking it from him, her hand lingering on his for a second longer than was strictly necessary.

He stood still for a moment, smiling at her. He seemed reluctant to leave.

Adam started to grizzle. I bent down and stroked his cheek, willing him to go back to sleep. But it was no use. He started crying loudly.

'Back in a minute,' I told Grace. 'Nice to meet you, Gary.' I flicked off the brake and wheeled Adam down the sidelines. He gave a loud burp and then nodded off again.

When I got back there was a huge grin on Grace's face.

'He asked me out.' She ran her hands over the barrier.

I stared at her. 'Really?'

Her eyes slid away from mine. 'OK, OK, I asked *him* out. He said 'yes' straight away, no messing around. Just a straight, "Yeah, cool. How are you fixed tonight?" I've never asked anyone out in my life. It's very liberating. I can see why you're addicted to it.'

'Once, Grace! I did it once, and are you mad? He's so young.'

'Barney was young. And it's only a bit of fun. As you say, there aren't that many decent guys around; you have to grab opportunities when you can.'

'I don't think it's a good idea, Gracey. You're still pretty raw after all the Jason business. You'll have to tell him you can't get a babysitter. And what about Arvin? They seem to be friends.'

'What do you mean?' She pushed her hands into her hips. 'Arvin won't mind. He's happily married. It's only for a friendly drink.'

'I thought you said you were after a quickie.'

'Shush!' Grace looked around her. 'I never said that!'

'Yes, you did.'

'I'm not arguing about it here.' She stopped for a second. 'Anyway, so what if I did? I have needs you know.'

I tried not to laugh. 'Where are you meeting him?'

'Dalkey.'

'Where *exactly*?'

'Ivory.'

I snorted. Ivory was a popular, busy pub with loud music and televisions. Grace would hate it.

'What?' she said.

'You're going to come home complaining about the noise and the price of drinks. I guarantee it.'

She ignored my dig. 'Will you babysit?' she asked. She pressed her hands together. 'Please? I really need a night out.'

I shook my head. 'I don't approve you know.'

She snorted. 'Alice! Stop being such an old granny. I just want to have a bit of a laugh. Nothing's going to happen, I promise. OK? I'll be back by midnight.'

'Fine,' I said grumpily, a little jealous. He was gorgeous, and more my age than hers. 'Can I invite Roz over?' I wanted to tell Roz all about my new job. I knew she would have some good advice on dealing with Maud.

'Have whoever you like.'

Hang on a second. Grace just said I could invite whoever I liked. Suddenly I had an idea. I'd have Roz over some other time; this was far too good an opportunity to miss. I gave a theatrical sigh. 'I'll babysit. But you owe me.'

I rang Roz anyway. We hadn't talked for ages and I wanted to tell her all about my early experiences with Maud Hamilton-O'Connor.

'She's scary, Roz,' I said. 'And you should see her house, it's like a palace. Huge. I feel sorry for the poor housekeeper. Josep's lessons are coming in useful by the way; she's Polish.'

'Maud's Polish?'

'No, her housekeeper. Magda.'

'Ah. Figures. Speaking of Josep, he'd love a word. He's hopping up and down beside me, dying to talk to you. Do you mind?'

'Course not, put him on.'

'*Czesc*, Alice.'

'*Czesc*, Josep.'

We had a little chat in rudimentary Polish before Adam started to niggle.

'Josep, I have to go now, will you put your mum back on?'

'OK. Hey, our new house is cool, but there's no one to play with. It's a bit boring. At least in St Belinda's I could talk to you if I was desperate.'

'Thanks, Josep, I'll take that as a compliment.'

'I heard that,' Roz said, coming back on the line, laughing. 'He's a little charmer, isn't he? When things are a little less hectic for us both, we must meet up. Good luck with Maud. And stand up for yourself, Alice, don't be a pushover, do you hear me?'

'I'll try.'

'*Da zobaczenia*, my friend.'

'*Da zobaczenia*, Roz.'

'Nice accent, Alice, keep practising with Magda.'

Chapter 12

That evening I sat on the sofa, nervously tapping my feet, waiting for Grace to leave. I'd put Adam to bed early. He was exhausted from crawling after Eric in the garden all afternoon, so he hadn't protested. Eric was sitting at my jittery feet playing with random bits of Brio train track and mismatched trains and carriages. Shane was watching *Grease*, slicking back his wet just-out-of-the-bath hair with his hands, and wiggling his hips in his Bob the Builder pyjamas. We both love *Grease*, I must have seen it dozens of times, but it still makes me smile.

'He shouldn't be watching this,' Grace said, staring at the screen. John Travolta was strutting his 'Summer Lovin'' stuff, throwing in some pretty agile pelvic thrusts. 'It'll give him ideas.'

'I like it,' Shane said. He put his hands on his hips. 'Wella, wella, wella, uh.' His voice was choir-boy innocent.

Even Grace had to laugh. She smiled at him. 'Eric's going up now and then you have twenty more minutes, understand?'

He nodded, his eyes glued to the screen.

'I'll put Eric to bed,' I said. 'You go on.' I picked him up and followed her into the hall.

She kissed her hand and blew it at me. 'Thanks, you're a doll. I'll be back before midnight.'

'OK, Cinderella. And your skirt's far too short by the way.'

She was wearing a long, white gypsy skirt which almost swept the ground, hooped gold earrings and a denim jacket. Once again, she looked great. The new clothes took years off her.

She grinned at me. 'Yes, Mum.'

It was good to see her in such high spirits. Meeting up with Gary was insane, and I'm sure she knew it in her heart, but maybe that was part of the attraction.

I closed the front door behind her and listened as she climbed into her car and pulled away from the drive, leaving a hurl of loud guitar music behind her. I shook my head. Grace hated loud music; she was obviously having some sort of early mid-life crisis.

As soon as the coast was clear I popped Eric on the sitting-room floor and keyed a quick message into my mobile. 'The pigeon has flown the coup. Repeat, the fox has left the lair.'

Ten minutes later Jason's jeep tore into the drive and screeched to a halt, scattering the gravel with its chunky tyres. Shane ran to the window and screamed, 'Daddy!', jumping up and down with excitement. Jason waved and grinned from behind the windscreen and then swung his long legs on to the path.

'Da?' Eric crawled over to the window and pulled himself up Shane's legs, almost pulling down his brother's pyjama bottoms in the process. For once Shane didn't swat him away.

'Daddy's here,' Shane told Eric. 'See, he does love us.'

Tears pricked my eyes. Bloody hell; out of the mouths of babes. I instantly began to feel less guilty about inviting Jason over.

Jason's arms were almost pulled out of his sockets with plastic shopping bags. He pushed the jeep door closed with his back, and rested his shoulder against the door bell.

I rapped on the window and put my finger to my lips. 'Adam's asleep,' I mouthed.

'Sorry.' He was hopping from foot to foot with impatience.

'Quick, quick, open the door. I think he's got sweets,' Shane said, his voice squeaky and his cheeks flushed. 'And presents. Oliver at school is always getting presents from his dad. He says if your dad doesn't live with you, you get more presents. Is that right, Alice?'

I wasn't sure how to answer that one, so I said nothing. Shane ran past me, followed by Eric. Shane tried to reach the latch by jumping up, like a puppy going after a stick held aloft.

'Calm down,' I told him, 'and stand back.' He was hyper with excitement. I shoved him gently out of the way with my hip and opened the door.

Shane threw himself at Jason's legs. 'Daddy!' he screeched. 'I missed you!'

Eric jabbered, 'Dada, dada,' and then started to cry, overwhelmed.

He was joined by a loud screech from upstairs. 'That's Adam,' I told Jason. 'Into the living room, all of you. And keep the noise down.'

Eric was still wailing. Jason dropped his bags – which as Shane had suspected were crammed full of sweets, crisps and cheap plastic Tesco's toys, the kind Grace hated with a passion – and whisked Eric into his arms.

'It's OK, little man,' he said, brushing away Eric's tears with the back of his hand. 'Daddy's here now.'

Eric clung to Jason. 'No go, Dada. No go.'

Jason looked at me, his eyes dark with emotion. 'You see what she's doing to them.'

Adam roared again. I didn't like Jason's tone. He knew as well as I did that their marital problems were as much his fault as Grace's, even if she was being as stubborn as all hell now. But I knew Jason was feeling truly miserable about being separated from the boys, and seeing Eric in such a state can't have been helping.

'We'll talk later,' I said, nodding at Eric. 'You spend some time with the boys. And keep it all, you know, normal. Don't go talking about—'

'G-R-A-C-E,' he spelled out.

I nodded.

'Understood.'

As I sat on my narrow bed, feeding Adam yet another bottle, I wondered what Grace was up to. And then I had a horrible thought. What if she decided the pub was too jammed, or too dirty; what if she came home early? I heard a peel of rather girly laugher from downstairs. Shane. Jason was singing 'Greased Lightning' for him; I could hear his baritone voice rumbling up the stairs. I smiled to myself. Whatever Jason had done to Grace, the kids adored him.

At ten Eric was slumped over Jason's knee, fast asleep, a vertical indent on his face from the seam on Jason's denims. Shane was still going but, like a Christmas toy running out of batteries, he was starting to fade.

'Ten more minutes,' he begged Jason, his hands pressed together, a gesture that was pure Grace. 'Please, Dad. I miss you.'

'You've already tried that one, you charmer,' I said. 'No, it's really late. Look how dark it is outside. Bed time.'

'Dad!' he protested.

'Alice is right. I'll read you one story and that's it.'

Shane put three fingers up, cocked his head to one side and gave a cheeky grin.

Jason smiled. 'Two, and that's my final offer.'

I peeled Eric off Jason's knee and put him straight to bed.

Twenty minutes later I was curled up on the sofa, sipping a glass of much needed white wine from the fridge and chomping down cashew nuts.

Jason perched on the arm of the sofa and smiled at me.

'What kept you?' I asked him.

'I ended up reading six books.'

'Sucker.' I laughed.

He sat down on the armchair opposite me, winced, then leaned forwards, pulled out a plastic gun and put it on the coffee table.

'Are you going to tell Grace I was here? If not you'll have to hide all the evidence.' He pointed at the gun.

I shrugged and then blew out my breath. 'I don't know. I understand the boys need to see you, but it's all so raw still. For the moment, take them home with you just in case.'

He nodded, knelt on the rug and began to put the toys back in the plastic bag, along with their cellophane wrappings. 'Where is she, anyway?'

Yikes! 'Out with Petra,' I lied rather smoothly.

He looked at his watch. 'It's late enough. I suppose I'd better get going. I'm sure you have things to do.'

I was disappointed. I had been looking forward to some adult company; even if it did mean discussing Grace and the boys all night. 'Not really. Would you like a glass of wine?'

'Better not. I'm driving. I'd love a cup of tea though.'

Ten minutes later we were sitting on the deck, staring up at the stars.

'Aren't we fierce European sitting outside all the same?' Jason said.

I gave a laugh.

'Do you mind if I ask you something?' he said.

Here we go, I thought. I knew it was just a matter of time until he started asking about Grace. 'Fire ahead.'

'What really happened in London?'

I sat up. Talk about blindsiding. 'London?'

'Grace said you broke up with Adam's dad. That he wasn't interested in being a part of Adam's life. He must be some bastard to desert his kid like that, whatever happened.'

Ah, now I saw where he was coming from, but I really wasn't all that happy talking about it. 'Some men aren't into

87

kids,' I said and then quickly added, 'So, how are you coping at your parents' place? Is your dad still driving you up the wall?'

Jason ignored my question. 'Why won't you talk about what happened in London?'

'It's in the past. It's all irrelevant now, my life's here. I got pregnant, Ned wasn't interested, we broke up. End of story.'

'Ned? Is that his name?'

'Yes, now can we move on to something else? Please.'

'Fine.' He seemed a bit miffed.

'I'm sorry, it's all a bit complicated and upsetting and . . .' I paused, not knowing what else to say. 'He had someone else, OK? Betty. But she was living in Barcelona and I'd never met her, so I managed to persuade myself that it wasn't anything serious, that I meant a lot more to Ned than she did. People did try to warn me, but I was mad about him. He was a DJ at the radio station and he was—' I stopped. I was about to say seriously sexy. 'Very charismatic,' I said instead. Sexy sounded so pathetic; like I was some sort of slave to my hormones. Which I was at the time. The sex! I'd never experienced anything like it. Just thinking about it made me come over all funny.

'I haven't even told Grace the full story,' I continued. 'Please, just leave it.' I started to feel brittle as Ned's angular face and slightly crooked nose floated in front of my eyes. I put a finger up and touched the bump on my nose, remembering what he used to say in his deep, honey-toned voice. 'We must be soul mates, Alice. We have matching nose bumps.'

I blinked back my tears. Damn it!

I hadn't thought about Ned for, oh, most of the evening, which was an improvement. I thought things would be easier in Dublin, that his grip on my heart would weaken, and it was getting better, gradually. I no longer cried myself to sleep, my heart heavy with what might have been. I still ground my teeth when I thought of Ned with Betty, who was tiny and slightly grubby and not at all the sex goddess I'd imagined her to be, which made it even more depressing, but it really was getting easier day by day.

Jason sensed my distress and backed off. 'I'm sorry, I didn't mean to upset you.'

'S'OK.' I didn't trust myself to say much. 'It was my own fault. I should have known better. He told me they were on a break and I believed him. But she was actually away doing some research in Barcelona for a few months for her MA. As soon as she got back to London he pretty much dumped me, apart from one drunken night when she was away at a hen party. I guess he broke my heart. But I should have known better,' I said again.

Jason opened his mouth and I quickly added, 'And don't go singing that stupid song, Jason. It won't help.' He had a habit of breaking into awful 1980s songs at inopportune moments. 'I know you too well.'

He opened his mouth again and belted out the chorus of 'I Know Him So Well'.

I screwed up my face. 'Please, I'm not in the humour.'

He laughed and put his hands up in defeat. 'You win. I was just trying to lighten the mood. And if you do want to talk about Ned, I'm here.'

'Thanks.' It wasn't part of my life that I was particularly proud of. I already felt bad enough about everything without dragging it all up again.

We sat in silence for a moment.

'Listen, Jason, I know you've being going through a rough time, but I have to ask you something. Did you mean to hit Grace with the remote control?'

He winced and stared down at his hands. 'She told you about that?'

'Yes.'

'I'm not proud of it. I wasn't myself that day. I just felt so angry, so out of control, but she threw it at me first.'

'She didn't tell me that bit.' Now I didn't know what to think. Things obviously weren't as black and white as they seemed. 'Grace said you'd gone to the GP. What did he say?'

'That it sounded like stress, that I should look at my diet and go and see a counsellor if it all got too much for me. Oh, and I have high cholesterol.'

'That's it?'

'Yep. But I've been putting on a lot of weight recently, too. And my hands are freezing sometimes.'

'Your hands?'

'I know, it sounds nuts.' He shrugged. 'If I could just control the mood swings, maybe Grace would take me back. What do you think?'

'You should talk to Grace about that. I'm keeping well out of it.'

'But she *won't* talk to me, that's the problem. Dad says I should come down heavier on her; tell her she's not taking this marriage seriously. Let her know who's boss.'

I snorted. 'Did he now? I'm sorry, but your dad's nuts. Is he living in the dark ages? Your poor mother.'

Jason smiled wryly. 'I know. But maybe he has a point; maybe I do need to be stronger with her.'

'Whoa there, he man. Let's focus on the boys for a second and forget about Grace. I think you're right, they need to see you.'

'Good. Will you please tell her that?'

I snorted. '*Tell* her? This is Grace we're talking about? I can try suggesting it.'

Jason's eyes flashed. 'I have a right to see my boys. She can't stop me, you know. I'll get a lawyer. Sue her sorry ass.'

'What are you on about? This isn't *The Sopranos*. Calm down.'

'Sorry. But I have to do something. I miss them so much. It's like someone's sawn my arm off. Without them I'm only half alive.'

I looked at him in surprise. It wasn't like him to be so emotional. In fact, Grace was always complaining about it. She said it was like he'd forgotten how to have fun. He used to whisk her away for dirty weekends in the country, now he always insisted on bringing the boys with them. Sharing a family room, however big, with two bouncing boys wasn't exactly conducive to romance, she complained.

Maybe that was the problem; all the romance in their marriage had dried up. No wonder she was out with a younger man, she was obviously looking for the kind of attention she clearly didn't get at home. If I could just help them rekindle that romance, maybe there was hope, but I'd have to tread softly.

'What about Grace?' I asked gently. 'Do you miss her too?'

He ran his hands through his hair, making it stick up on end like a pineapple. 'Every minute.' He shrugged. 'But what can you do? She won't talk to me, won't answer my calls. And you know how stubborn she is.'

'Surely there's something you can do?'

'Like what?'

'Maybe you should try making some sort of dramatic romantic gesture to grab her attention. Fill the living room with roses, dress up as Superman and climb up the side of the house, whisk her off to Rome on a private jet, like in *Pretty Woman*; hell, do something.' I started to get quite riled up. 'Fight for her dammit!'

Jason stared at me. 'Do you think it would work?'

'I don't know, but isn't it worth a try? At the very least, it might make her think twice about this whole separation thing.'

He stood up. 'You're a genius.' He held my head between

his two hands and kissed my forehead. 'What time is Grace due back?'

'Midnight I think.' My heart sank. OK, maybe tonight wasn't the ideal night for a grand romantic gesture. In fact what was I thinking? It was a bad idea, a very bad idea. 'Actually she's staying at Petra's tonight.'

'Petra's?' His face fell. 'But she'll be in tomorrow night?'

'I think so.'

'If I organize something, will you babysit? Maybe if take her out to dinner, somewhere really nice, she'd at least talk to me.'

I smiled at him. 'It's worth a try. Of course I'll babysit.'

'Thanks, Alice, you're a star.'

He was as jittery as a may fly. 'I'm going to run. Things to do. Romantic gestures to plan. As you say, it's worth a try.'

I gave him a hug. I wanted to say 'break a leg', or 'go get her, Tiger', but I didn't want to raise his hopes too much. After all, there was no telling how Grace would respond, even to a private jet.

In fact, it was just as well I'd put him off as Grace didn't appear until four a.m., staggering into the hall, knocking a spider plant off the console table and waking Adam.

After I'd settled Adam (yet another bottle; at least the child wasn't going to be calcium deficient) Grace's mobile rang. I climbed out of bed to hush her and couldn't help but hear her giggle down the phone as I pulled my dressing gown round me at the top of the stairs.

'Yes, I'm home.' Hiccup. 'No thanks to you. What? Now! I can't. Well, OK. Just for a minute. I'm taking off my skirt, it's falling to the floor. Oops, I've forgotten my pants, must have left them in your car. They're good ones too. Keep them for me, will you? The fridge? Yes. Why? Oh!' Grace gave a shocked laugh.

She moved from the stairs where she was sitting into the

kitchen and I heard the bottles in the fridge door rattle as she opened it. I strained my ears to listen. 'No, no cucumbers. How about a Frube? What? It's a yoghurt stick; the kids eat them. Oh, yes. Soft.' She giggled. 'Not very bright, Grace. But I have some in the freezer. Hang on. You want me to what? Where? Are you serious? That's not very hygienic, Gary! I'll have to wash it first.'

Yuck! I'd heard more than enough. I jumped back into bed, put my fingers in my ears and tried very hard not to think about what my sister was doing in the kitchen. Grace had clearly turned to the dark side.

I had a sudden thought. Jason! I'd have to get her back on the straight and narrow by this evening. But I was too scared to venture into the kitchen.

I took my fingers out of my ears.

'Yes, yes, yes, yes!' she squealed. 'Is that good, Gary? Sorry? Oh, right, I'll try. Oh, give it to me harder, you bad, bad boy. What was that? Oh, OK. You're so big. The biggest, baddest boy in the world. You're a sex machine. A sex god. Harder, harder . . .'

Dear Lord. I shoved my fingers back into my ears and started humming 'Summer Lovin'' to myself.

Chapter 13

At seven o'clock the following morning the house phone rang. I was in the kitchen with Adam and whisked it off the receiver before it woke Eric and Shane.

'Grace, it's Petra. You'd better get over here pronto.'

'Petra, Grace is in the shower, it's Alice. Is everything all right?'

'Not really. Davey is less than thrilled; we only had the lawn laid last week, but hopefully we can clear it up. Or get that gombeen Jason to do it. He blasted us with "You're the One That I Want" at midnight. He's got quite a powerful voice. Davey had to go down and ask him to be quiet. I still don't understand why he thought Grace was staying here.'

Uh, oh. It was the last time I watched *Grease*, I swear. It was obviously a catalyst for all kinds of nonsense. 'Clear what up?'

'He only went and covered the whole bloody lawn with rose petals. I think they probably spelled out Grace's name or something, but now it's just one big soggy mess.'

'I'm so sorry, Petra. It's all my fault. I told him to try making a romantic gesture to get Grace back. But I didn't think he'd do it at your house. Grace was out with her toy boy last night, that's why I said she was staying at your house.'

'Toy boy? What toy boy?'

'I'll let her tell you herself. Best not to say anything about Jason's shenanigans. I'll explain later.'

Grace came down the stairs, looking amazingly perky for a woman who'd had less than three hour's sleep. Maybe she was still drunk. Then I remembered the Frube incident and tried not to shudder.

'Who's on the phone?' she asked.

'Petra.'

'And what *about* Jason's singing?' Grace asked suspiciously. She has brilliant hearing; she should have been a spy. She glared at me and pointed at the phone. 'Hand it over. Now, Petra, full details please.'

I watched as her eyes widened. 'Rose petals? "You're the One That I Want"? Isn't that all a bit teenage?'

And this was from the woman talking dirty to a slip of a thing and re-enacting *9½ Weeks* with frozen yoghurt sticks?

I heard Grace giggle. 'Toy boy? Alice is naughty to tell you. Gary. Yes, yes, he's divine.' She stroked her hand down her thigh, and I winced. She gave a throaty, Joanna Lumley laugh. 'I know. That bit between the waist and the hip. I never thought I'd see it again either. Except in *Sex and the City* and that Aero ad. Yes, he is a bit like him if you squint your eyes up.'

That's it, I was getting out of here. I went upstairs to dress Adam. I switched on my mobile to ring Jason and it immediately juddered and beeped into action. Four new messages.

Number one – 1 a.m.: **Where is Grace? Petra knows nothing about her staying over.**

Number two – 1.30 a.m.: **Grace's car is not outside our house either. Why did you lie to me?**

Number three – 2.33 a.m.: **I'm still here. And still no car.**

Number four – 2.35 a.m.: **Who is he? I HATE YOU!**

I'd really done it now.

I tried to ring him, but his mobile was switched off. I needed to calm him down before he got to Grace and made things even worse between them. I texted him, my thumb punching in the message: **Jason, calm down. G was just at an all-night party. There's no one else.**

Later he texted back: **All-night party? She has 2 young chil-dren. What was she thinking? Sorry 4 all the texts and 4 being so paranoid. It's not your fault. Jx.**

I felt really low.

To make matters worse the following day a black jeep pulled up outside the house and a spotty guy in a baseball cap ran up the drive and thrust a flyer advertising a new pizza-delivery service into the letter box.

'Is it Daddy again?' Shane asked, spotting the jeep. He jumped down from his chair and flew into the hall.

Grace followed him out. 'What do you mean *again*?'

By the time I got there from the kitchen, it was too late.

'Daddy was here on Saturday night,' Shane said innocently. 'I wasn't supposed to tell you. Isn't that right, Alice?'

Grace glared at me. 'Alice! How dare you? Shane, get into the kitchen and close the door behind you.'

'Can I live with Daddy?' he asked her. 'He brought us sweets. I miss him.'

'No!' she said sharply. 'Now get into that kitchen.'

'Grace, he's only five,' I said. 'He doesn't mean—'

Her eyes were sparking. 'Are you telling me how to raise my kids?'

'Calm down. I'm just saying—'

'I can't believe you let Jason into this house after everything he's done.'

'If you'd just listen for one minute—'

'And I can't believe he just called in like that without any warning. I thought I'd made it clear that he wasn't to do that.'

'Actually . . .'

She narrowed her eyes. 'What?'

'I invited him.'

'You *what?*'

'I'm sorry, but the boys need to see him.'

'I'll decide what they need and don't need, understand?'

I put my hands on my hips. 'I hadn't realized you ran this house as a dictatorship.'

'I am *not* a dictator.' Grace was getting very flustered. Angry red spots were appearing on her cheeks and I knew I shouldn't have said that, but she had to listen to someone about the boys.

'Look,' I said calmly, 'I think you and Jason should see some sort of marriage counsellor, get some proper access sorted out for the boys.'

She put her hands on her hips. 'Do you now? And what makes you the great expert? Your son doesn't even *have* a father.'

I gasped. It was plain mean and not at all like Grace. Tears sprung to my eyes. 'You think I don't beat myself up about that every single day? I'd love Adam to have a dad like Jason. You don't know how lucky you are. Stop being so blind.'

'Have you quite finished?' she asked me icily, reminding me of Maud for a second.

I nodded. She walked up the stairs, clinging onto the hand-rail.

I sat at the bottom of the stairs until I heard Adam calling. Everything was such a mess. I had to do something, but what?

Chapter 14

On Tuesday I was sitting in Maud's hall, waiting for her permission to go home. I wasn't allowed to leave the house without checking with her first and she was upstairs doing something vital with her stylist. (Stylist? Who has a stylist?) Maud told me she'd only be a minute, but that had been twenty minutes ago and I was starting to get very impatient.

I'd had a pretty boring day to be honest and I was dying to get out of the place. I'd spent most of the afternoon cooped up in the study, RSVPing all Maud's invitations. She'd colour coded them – a red cross on the ones I was to decline quickly and politely, a blue cross on the ones I was to decline with a personally written note saying how sorry she was to have a prior engagement on that particular evening, and how she hoped to see them at the ball in October; and a green cross on the ones I was to accept graciously.

I then had to log them all on an Excel sheet and finish dealing with Maud's dozens of new emails. For someone who didn't work, she was amazingly busy. I had to hand it to her, she was remarkably organized when it came to St Jude's. She'd left a long 'to do' list for me to work through, all written in her spidery handwriting.

I was about to hike upstairs and find her when I heard a loud wailing noise coming from the basement. I'd only been in the basement once, looking for Magda. She'd shooed me upstairs pretty quickly. I hadn't thought much of it at the time, Magda was always a bit odd, but afterwards I wondered what she was hiding down there. Maybe she had a secret boyfriend Maud didn't know about. Maybe her whole family was living in the enormous wine cellar.

There were two kitchens in Maud's house, the vast, state of the art show kitchen on the ground floor, and the real kitchen in the basement where food was actually prepared; not that Maud and Nick ever ate in from what I could make out. In the upstairs fridge, there was just champagne, strawberries, blueberries and cherries in cut-glass bowls on the spotless shelves. Maud said her body was a temple and she only snacked on fresh fruit, but I'd seen her cram her mouth full of chocolate digestives from a secret stash in her desk drawer when she thought I wasn't looking.

The show kitchen was also home to Pussy and Honey, the sharks, who I'd become quite fond of. Magda told me there was over 2,000 gallons of water in the shark tank and they'd had to build a network of steel girders under the floor to hold the extra weight. Every day she brought me a sandwich and a mug of coffee in the kitchen. And every day she cleared up after me. I watched the sharks circling in their electric-blue tank as I ate my lunch, perched on a stool at the white granite island and trying not to spill crumbs on the immaculate surface. Maud always went out for lunch, leaving me to chat to Magda when I could get her to stay still for more than a few seconds; she was always cleaning or polishing something.

When I heard the wail, I went down the steep wooden stairs to the basement to investigate the noise. Another wail. Coming from the right. The real kitchen.

Another scream and a woman's voice, saying something in Polish I couldn't quite make out. I walked in. A robust-looking toddler was strapped into a white plastic designer high chair that looked like an eggcup lined with lurid-orange felt. He was

kicking his chubby pink legs and straining against the reins to get out.

She spoke to him again in Polish. I caught, *'Prosze,* Josh.' Please, Josh.

I was so taken aback to find a child in the house I was dumb-struck. I just stood and stared at the girl who was trying to shovel a spoon of mashed-up food into the toddler's mouth. He looked bigger than Adam, maybe eighteen months old. He kept trying to pull the spoon out of the girl's hand, perhaps he didn't like what she was trying to feed him, or perhaps he wanted to feed himself. I opened my mouth to say something to the girl when I felt a hand on my shoulder.

'What *you* do here? Out, out, out.' Magda spun me round with her strong arms.

'Hey! I want to help—' I began. But she was having none of it. She pushed me out of the door. 'Back up the stairs. No say anything to Maud. Understand? Or I be—' She drew a finger across her throat and made a throaty gurgling noise. She accompanied me towards the stairs.

'But the baby,' I said, horribly curious, 'is it yours, Magda? And who is the girl? She looks a lot like you.'

'She no look like me. She just Polish. You people. You all same.'

'Give me some credit. That's not fair.'

'You tink you so great having Polish friend? I say show me dis Polish friend. I tink you just vole for Maud.'

'Vole?'

'Vole! Spy girl!' She jabbed her finger at my collar bone.

'Take your hands off Alice,' Maud's voice rang down the stairs.

We both looked up. She was staring down at us from the landing. 'What on earth is all this noise?'

The toddler gave an almighty scream and then there was a clatter. I looked through the doorway. He'd kicked his bowl out of the girl's hands and it had skidded across the terracotta tiles and came to rest against one of the dark green farmhouse kitchen presses.

Maud didn't budge an inch. I looked at her suspiciously.

'Upstairs,' she said to me a little dejectedly. I was completely unnerved. What on earth was going on here?

'Magda, is Josh all right?' Maud asked, her fingers touching her forehead.

'Yes. Josh ees good. Just no like his tea. Nothing to worry about.'

'Good.' She looked at me, arched her eyebrows and walked back up the stairs.

Magda gave me a little push, but I wasn't budging.

'Is Josh your baby?' I asked her.

Magda sucked her teeth. 'You very annoying girl. Ask her.' She tossed her head up the stairs. 'I cannot tell you.'

'Can't or won't?'

'Just go! Now!'

I followed Maud into the living room. She was staring out the window with her back to me.

'Who is Josh?' I asked immediately before I chickened out. 'Is Magda hiding one of her relations and her baby down there? Do you know about this, Maud? Are they illegal immi-grants?'

'Honestly, Alice! Of course they're not. Josh is my son,' she said, her back still to me. 'Janny looks after him. She's Magda's cousin or something.' Then she swung round. 'Kindly don't concern yourself with other people's affairs. Do you under-stand?'

I met her gaze. This wasn't right. Why was she hiding her son away below the stairs? Was there something wrong with him? Was he like the crippled boy in *The Secret Garden*, hidden away for years until Mary found him and dragged him into

101

the sunlight? Was that it; was Josh sick? Was Maud ashamed of him?

Her face crumpled. 'Please don't ask. It's all a bit difficult.' She gripped the top of one of the mahogany chairs so hard her knuckles went white. 'I know what you're thinking, but I do love him.' She swallowed. 'Very much. Too much probably. Nick says—' She broke off abruptly and cleared her throat. 'Anyway.' She pressed the tips of her fingers against her mouth and then something flickered across her face and she said, 'Please excuse me,' and rushed past me. I heard her run up the stairs.

I went downstairs again to find Magda. This was all very perplexing. She was in the kitchen, scrubbing a kitchen cupboard.

She held up the brown-streaked cloth. 'Banana. So sticky.' She stood in front of me and brushed her hair out of her eyes with the back of her wrist. 'So?' she said sharply, but her eyes were soft.

'Maud told me about Josh,' I said.

'She tell you about Nick?' She pretended to spit on the ground. 'He biggest pig ever. Not natural, taking baby from mother like that. Maud sad, that's all. Never meant to hurt Josh.'

My eyes widened.

'She no tell you about Nick?' She sucked her teeth again. 'Oh, Magda, you very stupid voman. Ignore me.'

'Magda,' I pleaded.

She beckoned me towards her. '*Dobrze*. But no say I tell you. Promise?' She crossed her heart with her finger. 'Promise on your life.'

'*Dobrze*.' I crossed my heart too, trying not to smile. I hadn't done that since primary school.

She kicked closed the kitchen door and pulled me towards the corner of the room. 'Dees top secret, yes?'

I nodded eagerly.

She sighed. 'Is sad story. Maud tell me she have post-nature depression. After Josh. Very bad.'

'Post-natal?'

'Yes, yes. And he slip in bath. She supposed to watch him, but she crying and took her eye off him. He cough up water for ages.'

I gasped.

'Get worse. Then she leave him in shop. Go in to buy magazine. Put him down in leetle car seat and drive off.'

I sucked in my breath, remembering something. 'I left the house when Adam was asleep in bed once. Completely forgot I had a baby. I was like a zombie from the lack of sleep. It's so easy to do when they're little. Was her baby all right?'

Magda nodded. 'Yes, fine. Lady in shop look after him. Maud remember quick and drive back. But when Maud tell Nick he say it all her fault; he say it final straw after bath.'

'Poor woman.'

'Get worse. He say she no fit mother. Say he not want to lose baby. Take Josh off her and say she never to look after him again. Only au pair.'

'No! But it was a mistake. It could happen to anyone.' Could Maud's husband really have been so cruel? But after hearing him on the speaker phone, I didn't find it all that hard to believe.

Magda crossed her heart. 'Yes. True. I swear. I look after Josh for three week before Janny come over. Janny have very good English, but like to tell Josh Polish. Maud not know Janny speak English, so say nothing. Janny not have to deal with Maud that way. I get Janny. She like to meet you.'

Janny turned out to be charming, if a little cocky. And Magda was right, her English was excellent. In fact, as she'd picked a lot of it up from watching old DVDs of *The OC*, she sounded Californian. She corroborated Magda's story and made me swear again not to let on to Maud that I knew anything about Maud and Josh. There was something not quite right about the whole story, something missing, but I couldn't quite piece it all together at the time.

It had been quite a day.

Earlier that afternoon I'd the pleasure of meeting Maud's husband in the flesh. Although I'm not sure 'pleasure' is quite the right word.

I'd been standing on the third-floor landing when Maud's bedroom door swung open and out strode Nick, tucking his blue and white striped shirt into his pin-striped trousers, and zipping up his fly. He was even more handsome in the flesh, with huge, manly hands, and hypnotic dark brown eyes. Energy and drive practically buzzed through his skin. I was rooted to the spot.

He stared at me. 'Who the fuck are you?'

'Alice Devine,' I stammered. 'Maud's new assistant fund-raiser.'

He looked me up and down, his eyes lingering on my modest cleavage.

'Not bad,' he murmured.

I blushed deeply and stared down at the carpet.

'Nick!' Maud ran out the door in a white silk dressing gown, her hair tousled and her lipstick smudged. As soon as she saw me, she pulled the belt on her dressing gown tighter and folded her arms across her chest.

'Alice, you're supposed to be in my study,' she said icily. 'I see you've met my husband, Mr Hamilton-O'Connor.'

Nick grinned at me. 'Call me Boothy; everyone else does. I was just giving Maud a quick how's your father. She loves it in the afternoon, don't you, Maudie? Can't get enough of my—'

Maud looked mortified. 'Nick!' she snapped. 'That's quite enough. Must you be so crude?'

He just laughed. 'What's the matter, woman? I'm sure Alice isn't as innocent as she looks. Maybe she'd like to join us next time. Are you up for it, Alice?'

I squirmed, horrified at the thought.

'Only joking.' He snorted. 'You should see your face, girl. It's a picture.'

'I'm just going to finish the emails,' I murmured, scurrying back into the study. I closed the door behind me, but I could still hear Nick's voice booming out through the wood.

'What?' he said. 'Don't look at me like that, Maudie. It was only a bit of fun.'

'I won't have you making me look foolish in front of yet another assistant, Nick. How could you?'

'You're the one who wanted me home this afternoon.'

'I haven't seen you properly in days, and I wanted to talk to you.'

'Well you've seen me now. All of me. Come here.'

'No!'

'You know you want me,' he growled.

'Nick, you promised we could talk. Let's go downstairs. Are you hungry?'

'Only for you. My car's not coming for a few more minutes. Come on, Maudie, don't be such a tease. It won't take long, I'm hard already. Feel.'

'Ow, Nick, let go of me.'

'That's not what you said a few minutes ago. You were quite happy to wag your bony ass at me then, weren't you? Always looking for attention, that's your problem. But only on your terms. Get back into that bedroom. Your girl can probably hear us.'

'But Nick—'

A door slammed and everything went silent.

I let out my breath. What an appalling man. No amount of money was worth being married to such a pig. I started to feel a little sorry for Maud.

Chapter 15

'Maud's lunches should be renamed lunch marathons,' Jack said in the office on Wednesday morning. The fan behind him made a noisy splutter and he gave it a whack with the side of his hand. It shuddered back into action. 'They usually go on well into the night. Last time I didn't get home till after two. I had to take Koo home in a taxi and lift her up the stairs and into bed. Thank goodness I'm off the hook this time.'

My stomach lurched. 'Tell me you're going to be there, Jack.'

'Sorry. I have to go to a first Holy Communion.'

I stared at him. 'Maud gave you the day off for that?'

He smiled. 'It's my godchild. Maud can surprise you sometimes.' The fan shuddered again and went into overdrive. He slapped his hand down on the stack of A4 sheets that were lifting off his desk. 'Don't look so worried, you'll be fine. Koo will be there; just try to keep her off the drink. And Maud seems to like you—'

I tried to protest but he put his hand up. 'Stop. Forget about hitting her and the bath thing.' He grinned. 'Anything else I should know about?'

I bit my lip. 'There is one other thing. I thought Magda was harbouring a Polish baby and his mum in the basement. Maud was appalled I thought her baby was an illegal immigrant. But how was I supposed to know she had a baby?'

He grinned. 'So you met Josh, I take it?'

I nodded.

'Cute, isn't he? What did Maud say exactly?' I could tell he was trying not to laugh.

I told Jack the whole story, starting from when I heard Josh crying. Not the bit about Maud and the post-natal depression, or Nick being such a pig; I wasn't sure how much he knew and I had promised Magda and Janny after all.

'Anything else you want to confess?' he asked when I'd finished.

God, I hoped not. I shook my head. 'Nothing I can think of.'

He smiled at me again. 'You're doing grand. The girl before Floss only lasted a week. Maud didn't take to her. Said she was a ninny.'

After all my mistakes, including my latest one, I wondered what Maud called me behind my back. But really, how was I supposed to know who Josh was? I'd been working for her for days and she hadn't mentioned anything to me about a baby. I only knew about her son in boarding school because of that eavesdropped phone call.

But luckily Jack seemed to find the whole thing hilarious. Jack and I had been getting on brilliantly all week. He'd even attended another Ladies' Guild meeting with me, to give me some moral support. I'd begged him. After the last meeting in the Belgrave Club when I'd cried in the loo, I needed all the back-up I could get.

At the meeting, they toyed with calling the autumn ball the Caprese Ball, but Koo thought it sounded too much like a salad. Jack had suggested Amalfi, and they'd all agreed it sounded far better, very exclusive. Then Maud had suggested an Italian fact-finding mission to make the ball more authentic. And Gunella had immediately suggested a few days in Positano in her parents' villa.

'Bring it on,' Koo said, rubbing her hands together. 'I love Italian men. And I haven't had a good shag in weeks.'

Jack started to look nervous.

'Don't worry, Jack,' Maud said wryly. 'I'll chain her up at night.'

'How are you fixed the weekend after next, Alice?' Koo asked me, after scowling at Maud. 'Can you arrange babysitting?'

I was surprised. 'Are you sure you really need me?'

'Yes. To take notes,' Maud said firmly. 'You're coming.'

And that was that.

Jack winked at me and whispered. 'Don't look so worried. It's a beautiful part of the world. I once spent a week in Sorrento with my wife.'

'Your *wife*?' This just got better and better.

He just put his finger to his lips. 'Shush. I'll tell you about it on the plane. We'll have loads of time.'

This week I'd collected Maud's dry cleaning, the weight of which had nearly taken my arm off; collected some satin peep-toe pumps she'd ordered from a designer shoe shop in town in three different colours – red, emerald green and golden yellow; booked her hairdresser to visit on Thursday morning instead of Wednesday (Maud never did her own hair, she got a professional blow dry every second day); and bought a birthday present for Nick: a gold Montblanc pen with the inscription 'To My Darling Husband XXX Maud.' It had an eighteen-carat gold nib with platinum inlay according to the man in the shop – he said he only sold two or three a year and my husband was a very lucky man indeed. As if.

I tried to help Janny with her transitive verbs – she went to English classes twice a week and was very advanced; and taught Josh how to blow raspberries – Magda said Maud would be 'trilled' – I think she was being ironic.

I also spent a very happy afternoon with Jack planning the rest of the year on the very large wall planner – Grace's idea.

He said looking at it made him *feel* very organized, even if he wasn't. The man worked so hard. It was only when I studied the wall planner that I realized just how much was heaped on his plate. And how much extra work the Ladies' Guild piled on top of it.

Between January and May (when I started) he'd already organized a Valentine's Day Lunch, found an Artist in Residence for the hospital, overseen a redesign of the St Jude's website, organized a golf classic, and dealt with all the day to day phone enquiries and never-ending emails (a good chunk of which were probably from Maud!).

Although I was enjoying the job – at least I think I was, I was too busy to tell – I was wiped by Thursday, and I hadn't slept properly all week. My spiralling stress levels, Grace's moods and Adam's teeth, were all keeping me awake. Most nights I just lay there, while my mind went into overdrive, thinking about all the terrible things that had happened and *could* happen in Maud's house. Grace told me to stop worrying so much. To just take it day by day. But *she* wasn't the one dealing with mad Maud, not to mention worrying about running into Nick again. Plus worrying about making a fool of myself in front of Jack. And *her* children weren't teething. I was in tatters.

Chapter 16

Thursday meant the St Jude's 'Oui Care' Ladies' Lunch and I was petrified. 'Oui' because the venue was the French restaurant, La Grenouille; 'Care' because it was in aid of buying a new incubator for the special care unit at St Jude's. The 'Oui' bit was Maud's idea. She could be quite clever when she wanted to be.

Grace wasn't helping my nerves. She'd been unnaturally quiet all week. I overheard her arranging to meet Gary on Friday, a huge mistake if you ask me, but when I confronted her she said she needed a night out after the week she'd lived through and was I going to begrudge her every little scrap of joy for the rest of her life? I thought it best not to ask if 'Little Scrap' was her nickname for Gary.

She'd also emailed Jason a document setting out terms of access. She showed it to me first, not for my opinion I think, but to show me how grown-up she was being. The tone was painfully formal and controlled. Mostly.

```
Jason
I have spoken to the boys and they would like
to see you. I will allow this, with the fol-
lowing conditions: you must collect them every
Saturday morning at twelve (Shane has soccer
```

practice before that) and drop them back by half past four. Please make sure you are punctual as Eric needs his routine. And don't fill them full of junk food. By prior arrangement you may take them on a Sunday instead of Saturday. Please give me at least three days' notice.

Here is a list of suggested activities:

1/ The zoo – you may need to do this on a Sunday and start out early to avoid the crowds. Watch Eric with the monkeys. They have very sharp teeth and carry Ebola and I don't trust that monkey island they have in the middle of the lake. Surely monkeys can swim?

2/ If wet – the play centre in Bray. Do not let Shane on the dodgems. He is not old enough and they are very bad for the neck.

3/ The aquarium in Bray. The concrete floor gets very wet and slippery underfoot. Hold Eric's hand tightly at all times.

4/ If you must, bowling in Stillorgan, or the cinema. No fast-food joints please. The toilets in those places are rarely clean. Goodness knows what the kitchens are like. I will need to pass the film for suitability. Remember the time you let Shane watch *Jaws*? He had nightmares for weeks. I rest my case.

Please do not let them just sit around and watch television or play video games. The boys need their time to be properly planned and structured, with adequate arrangements made for rest, meals and both athletic and mental stimulation.

Grace

Shortly after Grace sent the email, Jason texted me.

Is G for real? How anal can u get? Of course I'm not going to let Shane on the dodgems. I will pick up boys at 12 on Sat and we will go to the aquarium. Can you pass this with Stalin?

Back at the lunch, Maud grabbed my arm as I rushed past her.

'Alice, do stop running around like a headless chicken. Have some decorum. I need you to run an errand. It's a delicate matter, so do try and be discreet. Pop out to the convenience store and buy some tampons, please. Keep the receipt. Jack will refund you tomorrow.'

Halleluiah, I thought, despite all the money, Maud's a mere mortal. I felt a smile coming on, but I pressed my lips together to stop it.

'What kind?' I said in my best discreet voice, praying I had enough to cover it in my wallet.

She just looked at me witheringly, threw her eyes skyward and said, 'For God's sake, Alice. Whatever they have.'

Scanning the shelves I wondered what would be more insulting, super plus, normal or mini? I bought a box of each and when I tried to hand Maud the large brown paper bag she hissed, 'They're not for me, Alice, *really*, they're for our guests. I like to cover every eventuality. Leave them in the bathroom. Put them in one of those baskets they use for the hand towels.' She looked me up and down. 'And do please get changed. Our ladies will be here any minute.'

Change? I had nothing to change into. It was my plain black dress or nothing.

Just then, as if summoned by Maud's words, the first guests appeared in the open doorway, three glossy, perfectly groomed women in their forties or early fifties (they were so well preserved it was hard to tell), each in a wrap dress. It was obviously the-ladies-who-lunch uniform as Maud was also in a wrap dress – a vintage Diane de something or other Koo had told me earlier. Maud's subtle cream and chocolate-brown dress was now joined by a Swedish-looking poppy print, a rather loud black and white striped affair with an elaborate twist at the front, and my favourite, a striking petrol-blue dress.

The women flapped their hands about excitedly and chattered to each other, like a flock of exotic parrots. Maud made a faint purring noise under her breath, pulled herself up and strode towards them before I had the chance to say anything.

'She lives for these events,' Koo said, appearing at my side. 'Watch her. I've never seen anyone work the room like she does. She's amazing.'

There was pure admiration in Koo's eyes as she watched Maud welcome the women and guide them towards the bar area. 'Chloe's wearing Issa,' Koo said. 'She's the blonde who looks a bit like Meg Ryan. Six hundred quid a pop those dresses. And she still looks like a pregnant zebra.'

I laughed. 'Koo!'

'She does. Has she never heard of control knickers? Lord knows what she'll look like after her lunch. Just look at that flabby ass wobble.' She smiled. 'But at least she eats. Watch the guests over lunch. Most of them just move the food round their plates and knock back the wine. Probably scared of bursting their gastric bands.'

As a tall, raven-haired waiter offered the group champagne on a silver tray, Maud smiled at him suggestively, then leaned towards Chloe and whispered in her ear. The woman hooted with laughter, slapped Maud's hand, and said, 'Maud, you are naughty.'

When I looked back Koo had disappeared. I was alone. Help! Maud was staring at me, so I pointed at the paper bag in my hands and dashed towards the loo.

I put the boxes of tampons into a basket, then pressed my hands down on the cool slate slab which held the sink, and closed my eyes. My heart was hammering in my chest and bile was rising in my throat. Yet again I was hiding from Maud in the loo, how pathetic. What a nightmare. I thought I'd be so busy all morning running round the place for Maud that I'd need comfortable clothes and footwear. So I was wearing a neat black jersey dress and flat black riding boots. What was I thinking? I should have talked to Petra. Tears pricked my eyes. What the hell was I going to do? I wanted to go home.

The door of a cubicle swung open. It was Koo. Koo looking amazing in her tight burnt-orange dress teamed with towering snake-skin wedges. She put her hands on the slate, almost touching mine, and lurched towards the mirror, jutting out her chin, her straightened hair falling round her face like a cloak.

'Bloody blackheads,' she muttered. She began to press and pick at her skin with her fingers, leaving red marks on the porcelain surface. 'I had a go at them only last week, I even bought a blackhead remover on the internet. Piece of shit. I should send it back.' Then she looked over and noticed my eyes which were now swimming with tears. 'What's up?'

I was mortified. This couldn't be happening. Of all the people to find me crying in the loo.

I blinked back the tears. 'New mascara. I think I'm allergic.'

Koo turned around, hopped her curvy bottom onto the slate, and swung her legs like a small child. 'Happens,' she said evenly. She looked at her watch. 'Ten minutes till kick off. Has your cook turned up yet?'

My stomach churned. I was very, very worried about 'my cook'. I knew from talking to Grace and Petra that Peggy had an incredible story to tell, but it was the first time she'd be talking about it in public. It was a risk. It could all backfire if she didn't engage with the audience. But Grace said it was worth the gamble.

'Yes,' I said. 'Peggy's outside having her picture taken with Odette Cunningham and the sponsors.' Odette was a curvy ex-weathergirl turned celebrity 'reporter' for the *Irish Daily Star* and was a regular guest on the afternoon chat shows. She was stunning in an obvious kind of way, perfect film-star blonde hair, big boobs and a huge Bratz-doll head, your average nightmare.

Koo snorted. 'Odette gets everywhere. Literally. Can't stand her. But Maud won't let me kill her.' She gave a twisted smile.

'The sponsors love her,' I pointed out, 'and that's all that really matters, isn't it?' I was getting used to Koo's strong opinions and knew to take them with a pinch of salt. Grace's advice was to stand up to her. She said women like Koo admired other strong women. Roz had said pretty much the same thing – to stand up for myself. It wasn't easy. Koo was so confrontational, but I was doing my best. In fact, I was starting to rather enjoy it.

Koo rubbed her lips together to even up her lip gloss. 'You're right. So what's with the funeral outfit?'

My face dropped. I ran my hands down my dress. 'I was wearing a Ghost dress but my son, Adam, puked on it.'

She laughed. 'What age is he?'

'Nearly one.'

'Cute age. Can't be easy doing it all on your own. Does he see his dad much?'

I gulped. Talk about direct. 'No. He lives in London.'

She just rubbed her finger over her teeth, wiping away a lipstick stain. 'You're probably better off. Most men are more trouble than they're worth.' She looked at me for a moment. 'Who minds him when you're at work?'

'My sister, Grace. She has two of her own and she's far better with him than I am.'

'I'm sure you're a great mum. Don't beat yourself up so

much.' She stared down at my feet. 'Hey, what size shoe do you take? Your feet look kinda big.'

I tried not to take offence. 'Six.'

'Me too. You're in luck. Stay right there.' She jumped down and strode out the door. I stared after her in astonishment, too startled to move.

Ten minutes later I was wearing a pair of stretchy red boots with high wedge heels. I checked out my new reflection in the mirror. Koo had worked wonders: smoky eyes, toffee-coloured lips and tousled hair, complete with thick black hairband. Dramatic red bead choker round my neck, waist clinched in with a thick red leather belt.

Koo had an arsenal of accessories in a plastic bag in the back of her car, plus a silver box which opened out like the Tardis, crammed full with layers of glittery Mac eye shadows, cute Benefit boxes, clusters of lipsticks and lip glosses, dozens of pencils and chubby sticks, Mac and Clinique foundation, and scary-looking steel eyelash curlers. It was surprisingly tidy, each rectangular compartment clean and orderly.

'Thanks,' I told Koo who was watching my reaction, a smile on her lips.

'For nothing. Us mums have to stick together.'

'You have a child?'

Koo grinned and flapped her hand in front of her face. 'Na. It just feels that way sometimes. I'll tell you about Mac some other time. Now, ready to be bored?'

'Koo!' I gave a laugh. She was starting to grow on me.

She jostled me gently with her shoulder. 'Only joking. I'm sure Peggy will be just scintillating.'

The meal went by in a blur. The lunch had been meticulously planned, right down to the colour of the linen napkins (baby blue and baby pink), the tiny strings of blue and pink paper Chinese lanterns hanging from the restaurant's low ceiling, and the goody bags at every setting, including a fab shell-pink leather-covered notebook embossed in silver with a discreet J, a tiny baby cradled in the hook of the letter – the St Jude's logo.

I'd given my seat to a last-minute guest, which suited me as I was far too nervous to sit down and eat. I spent the entire meal hovering by the door, admiring the dresses and shoes, and eavesdropping on the most incredible snippets of conversation.

'Three million euro he's after.' A bronzed woman in a white trouser suit gave a throaty laugh. 'He can forget it. We were only married a lousy eighteen months.'

'I keep telling James I need a Lexus jeep. All the girls swear by them. But he says there's nothing wrong with my Range Rover.'

'Do you think his wife knows? She's just over there. Is she looking at me?'

If the hum of animated conversation and shrieks of laughter were anything to go by, the women seemed to be enjoying themselves. But when the lunch finished and Maud stood up to introduce Peggy, my nerves starting jangling again.

I stood at the back of the room and tried to keep out of the way of the ultra-efficient staff who were bustling about with silver pots of tea and coffee, and clearing away the mostly untouched dessert plates – what a waste. Three tasters: tiny profiteroles, miniature banoffee pies, and dinky lemon-meringue pies, all carefully selected by Maud and Koo.

Koo appeared beside me and handed over a plate and a dessert fork. 'I've been watching you. You've haven't eaten. Here.'

She walked away wordlessly before I had a chance to thank her. I tried one of the mini profiteroles. The pastry felt dry in my mouth but I swallowed it down and sipped on the bottle of lukewarm water cradled in my hands. Once the sugar began to hit my system I started to feel a little more hungry and I quickly polished off the whole plate.

Maud tapped a glass with a fork to get everyone's attention. 'I hope you all enjoyed your lunch.'

The crowd clapped and one woman with a fab 1970s *Charlie's Angels* hair-do whooped, twisting her arm in the air. Maud frowned at her like a Victorian headmistress and I stifled a giggle.

'And now we have a special treat for you,' Maud continued, after the applause. 'Peggy Baker. Baker by name, baker by profession. I'm sure you all know Peggy from her hugely successful *Soup Dragon* television show and her cookery books. But I was talking to her over lunch and she has quite a story to tell. So without any further ado, I'd like to introduce the one and only Peggy Baker.'

The room erupted into applause and I closed my eyes. Please make her OK, I pleaded. Please.

Peggy looked around the room, making eye contact with several people. She was a petite woman, with cropped jet-black hair and piercing blue eyes. Her plain navy silk dress hugged her womanly hips and her peacock-blue velvet high-heeled boots gave her extra height. When she opened her mouth to speak, a surprisingly big, slightly husky voice flowed out.

'I'm here today for two reasons,' Peggy said. 'Number one, I do appreciate a good lunch and Dermot the chef and his kitchen have done themselves proud. Here's to the La Grenouille team.' She brought her hands together and the whole room joined in. As the applause died down she said, 'On a more serious note, I want to thank the St Jude's team for all they do for mums and babies. I am personally so grateful to them for taking such good care of me over the last few years. I haven't spoken about this before, but I've decided it's time.

Maybe telling my story will make other women who have had a similar experience feel a little less alone.'

She stopped for a moment, composing herself. The room was completely silent. All eyes were glued on Peggy.

'Two years ago I had a baby,' Peggy began. 'Ella. She was born at twenty-eight weeks and she lived for ten days, hanging on to life like a tiny bird with twiggy arms and a downy head as small as an orange. Her lungs weren't able for it in the end. Collapsed. All the life sucked out of her in one sudden moment. I was there when she slipped away and I felt like a part of me had died too. She was so innocent, so small, and I'd failed her. I couldn't hold on to her. Couldn't save her. I felt useless, washed up, a failure as a woman.'

She stopped for a moment and took a few breaths. 'Sorry,' she murmured, 'this isn't easy for me.'

Maud, who was still standing at her side, put her hand on Peggy's arm.

There was a lump in my throat. Although Peggy had told me some of her story and Grace had filled in the gaps, hearing it again was heartrending.

Peggy continued, 'Incompetent womb they said. "We'll have to stitch you up the next time," a nurse told me. I'm sure she didn't mean to be cruel but her words almost cut me in two. Next time. Like losing my baby was nothing. Just one of those things. Like I'd forget Ella and move on. Anyway, I made a scrapbook, to remember her by. I put the tiny white cotton hat she wore in the incubator between the cover and the first page. It looked like a doll's hat. My heart was shattered. But six months later, I started to feel a little differently. I felt in my heart that Ella would want me to move on with my life. So we tried again for a baby. And again and again. But nothing happened. And I resigned myself to being childless. After Ella, I just couldn't face IVF and all the tests and hospital visits it would involve.

'I told myself I was luckier than most. I had a great career, a wonderful husband. And I tried to hold on to that thought. It wasn't always easy: I had a lot of black days. And then the summer after I lost Ella I became an outreach mum for St Jude's, visiting teenage mums who needed some advice or just needed a friend. I wasn't a mother myself, but I was a sister and an aunt and I thought I could give young women some support, some comfort maybe. At the very least I could teach them how to cook.' She smiled.

Gentle laughter rippled around the room.

'It was my husband's idea, to be honest. He'd seen a notice looking for volunteers while we were in the waiting room, for yet another check up. He managed to persuade me, telling me I'd be a brilliant help to young mums; that giving something back would make me feel better, make me feel useful. And you know, he was right. And now his mum and sister also volunteer. It's a family affair. And it's been nothing but a blessing in all our lives. The teenage mums have taught us so much. Especially the ones whose babies are sick, just like Ella was. It really is a privilege to work with them. They have taught all of us to appreciate what we have – our family, each other – and to take each day as it comes, and to support each other no matter what. Just before Christmas we had another baby, Noah. He's five months now and a little darling.'

There were lots of aahs, then a round of applause.

Peggy smiled. 'Thank you. So I guess I'm here today to say two things. First, you never know what's round the corner. We have so much in this country, so much. Be good to each other and count your blessings. And second, there is something you can do to make this world a better place. You can help St Jude's by supporting the work they do for mothers and their babies. Today they are raising funds to buy a new incubator for the special care unit; the unit which was so good to my little Ella.' Her eyes welled up and she blinked back them the tears and touched her hand to her mouth. 'Sorry.' She took a deep breath and then continued, 'I know you each have envelopes by your places; please do give generously. Every little helps.

'I raise my glass to the St Jude's staff, especially the nurses. They do an amazing job. And well done to Maud and her team for all their hard work in making today such a success. And thanks to Alice for inviting me here. And most of all, thank you for listening and for supporting the hospital.'

I nearly keeled over with relief. Peggy was inspirational, and from the rapturous applause, everyone else thought so too. I slipped outside to ring Grace and tell her the good news.

'Sorry for doubting you.' Koo was outside the front door, sucking heavily on a cigarette. 'I had no idea Peggy was one of those volunteer mums. How did you know about her baby?'

'I didn't. It was just luck I guess.'

'Beginner's luck,' Koo said.

A chill ran down my spine. Had Koo seen through my doctored CV? I looked at her but her face gave nothing away.

'Anyway, not bad at all,' she said. 'The lunch I mean. Almost not boring.' Koo gave me one of her rare, wide Julia Roberts smiles. 'Want one?' She flipped opened her packet of Marlboro Red.

'No, thanks.'

She lit a fresh cigarette off the old one, and ground the spent stub into the pavement. 'So how are you finding the job so far?

I considered this. 'Interesting,' I said.

She nodded. 'I'd say it is. *Interesting*.' She gave me a knowing smile. 'So you're not leaving us?'

'Of course not. I need the money.'

She laughed. 'Is your bikini packed for Positano? Gunella has a killer pool. One of those infinity things.'

My heart sank. My saggy baby belly certainly wasn't bikini material.

'Don't look so gloomy, Alice. It'll be fun. And Maudie's a howl on holidays. A regular party animal.'

'Maud?'

'Sure. She'll be on the tequila slammers in no time. You just watch.'

This I had to see.

Chapter 17

When I walked into the St Jude's office the following Tuesday morning, Jack was violently slapping the side of the printer.

'What on earth are you doing?' I asked him.

'The toner's practically gone. If you move it round a little in the cartridge it sometimes prints a few more sheets.'

'It might be easier to take the cartridge out and shake it. Be careful you don't get black powder all over yourself. I did that once in London.' I remembered it clearly. Luckily I had been wearing a black top at the time, which had hidden the sooty powder stains, but I'd spent the morning with a black smudge on my nose, like a chimney sweep. It was only when Ned sat on my desk after his morning show and said, ''Allo, Bert, been up chimney again?' in his best Cockney accent that I'd figured out what all the sniggering was about and rushed to the loo to wash my face.

Jack smiled. 'Good idea. Where have you been all my life, Alice?'

I turned away and hung my jacket on the back of the door to hide my blushes. I knew Jack was married, but I couldn't help it.

Luckily he didn't seem to notice my pink cheeks. 'I just need one copy of the Mini Marathon Press Release,' he said. 'I can photocopy the rest. We have to be in the Shelbourne for the press launch in less than an hour. Yippee-eye-eh.' He groaned.

He'd told me last week he'd rather have his chest hair pulled out with tweezers than go to another press launch. He also hated public speaking; luckily Maud and Koo did most of that.

'You mean Maud's house?' I asked, suddenly feeling rather leaden and exhausted. Even though I was supposed to be working from home on Mondays, I'd spent yesterday running errands for Maud.

Namely:

1/ Picking up the flight tickets for the Positano trip. First class for Maud, Gunella, Koo and Gunella's half-sister Jessica, who was coming along for the ride, lucky girl; mere mortal class for me and Jack.

2/ Collecting two Hermès swimsuits from Brown Thomas department store in the city centre.

3/ Collecting wads of special white acid-free tissue paper from Maud's dry cleaners so Magda could pack Maud's clothes for the trip.

4/ Getting a taxi *back* to the city centre to pick up some exclusive 'no wrinkles' sun cream from a small beauty shop on Wicklow Street. I won't tell you how much it cost; I nearly fainted.

5/ Booking her beautician for a bikini wax. Booking her hairdresser for a pre-holiday trim . . .

It really was endless. Hence, I'd had it up to here with Maud Hamilton-bloody-O'Connor.

I was heartily relieved when Jack said, 'No, the Shelbourne Hotel. Maud's busy. Said something about buying new swimming costumes for Positano. I wasn't really listening. She wanted you to go with her to carry her shopping bags, but I said it was out of the question.'

'Bloody cheek. Carry her shopping bags?' I gave a rather horsey snort. 'Who does she think she is, Victoria Beckham? I collected two new swimsuits for her yesterday. How much swimming can one woman do?'

Jack gave a laugh. 'The only time Maud's suits so much as sniff aqua is in the washing machine. If they ever make it that far. She's such a dry cleaning addict she probably ships them off there too. She never, ever swims. Says it ruins her hair.' He pretended to flick his hair back and I giggled. 'She sits at the side of the pool under an umbrella with a big sun hat on. And heels. Wait till you see her in Positano. It's quite something.'

The Positano trip was just over a week away, and the mere thought of it was frightening the life out of me. I was convinced Maud would take one look at me in my swimsuit and pack me off for a swift Italian tummy tuck.

'Let's not talk about it,' I said. 'It's making me feel a bit queasy.'

Jack laughed. 'At least it's free. The flights are courtesy of some friend of Boothy's in Aer Lingus.'

He pressed a key on his computer and the printer chugged into action. 'According to Koo, Gunella's villa is like something from a movie. I, for one, am very glad you'll be there; it'll make the whole trip a lot more bearable. It's usually just me and the girls, and I spend most of the evenings holed up in my room pretending to work in an effort to avoid them. They all get a bit frisky when they're on holiday.'

'Frisky?' I gave a snort. 'I'm sorry but I just can't see Maud being frisky.'

He smiled knowingly.

'How often do you go on these trips?' I asked.

'I've only been on two. Maud and Gunella go all the time. Koo, not so often. Last autumn we went to Cascais.'

'Cascais?'

'It's in Portugal, just down the coast from Lisbon. Nice place, quite upmarket, lots of expensive boutiques and seafood restaurants. I was bored out of my tree. The girls just wanted to sun themselves by the hotel pool all day.' He stopped for a second. 'Mostly. Think of Positano as a free holiday.'

'Maud's been at pains to remind me it's no such thing. We have to bring the Dictaphone, notebooks, the laptop and—'

'Pay no attention. Once she gets to Italy she'll loosen up. She's a different gal when she's away.'

'Koo said exactly the same thing. You both make her sound like some sort of werewolf.' I held up my top lip with my finger, bared my teeth at him and gave a growl.

He laughed, pulled a sheet out of the printer, scowled at it, balled it and threw it into the large green recycling bag. Then he thumped the side of the printer, hard, and pressed print again. 'Maybe she is.'

He pulled out the freshly printed press release and studied it. 'I'll have to go over the telephone numbers with a black pen, but I hope no one will notice. At least the photo of the baby has come out all right this time. Speaking of babies, how's Adam? Is he walking yet?'

'Almost. He's pulling himself up on the furniture and wobbling around on his feet like a little drunk.'

'One of my nephews is about the same age. One and a bit.' He put the sheet on his desk and doctored it with a black pen. 'Karl.'

'How many nieces and nephews do you have exactly?'

'Eleven last count.'

'Eleven?'

He smiled. 'Big family. Six of us.'

'Where do you come?'

'Second youngest to the twins. The only boy.' He studied the document once more and then placed it under the lid of the photocopier. 'It'll have to do. Can you pull out some folders and put a hospital information sheet in each? I'll add the press release in a minute.'

'No problem.' I walked over to the metal shelving where the

stationery was arranged in shallow plastic baskets, each basket carefully labelled. It was one of the first things I'd changed in the office, on day two, and it had already made a big difference. I'd like to take the credit, but it was actually Grace's idea. When I'd described the office after my first day, she'd rolled her eyes heavenward and said, 'First, get the stationery in order. It'll make your life so much easier, and Jack will be dead impressed. Men are useless at that kind of thing.'

As we made up the press packs together, Jack told me about his siblings. Sheila was the eldest, an accountant who lived in Putney with her architect husband. 'They're big into walking,' he said, 'they go on a trek every year in a different country. It's the Himalayas this time.'

Maeve was next in line, a public health nurse who lived in an old farmhouse just outside Bantry in County Cork. She kept chickens and cows and made her own farmhouse cheese. She was separated with three kids and from the way he fondly described her, she sounded lovely. The next sister, Caroline, the bossy one, lived in Clontarf with her husband and four kids, including Karl.

'And finally,' he said, 'there are the twins, Clare and Anne-Marie, two kids each. They're turning thirty in a few weeks' time.'

'So you're what? Thirty-five, thirty-six?'

'Thirty-two.'

I was surprised. He looked and seemed a lot older. And it wasn't just the slightly receding hairline. He was the kind of man you felt you could trust; if you asked him to do something, he'd do it. He had this air of experience; as if he knew something about the world that other people didn't. I'd only known him a short time, but I was already so comfortable around him.

'Five sisters,' I whistled, 'that's quite something.' No wonder he was so good with Maud and the Ladies' Guild.

'I know. Blessed art thou amongst women and all that. My dad died in his fifties, Mum lives with Maeve now on the farm, helps out with the kids. I lived in a very oestrogen-driven house for many years. Didn't do me any harm. Juliette said it was the making of me.'

'Juliette?'

'My wife.'

Juliette. So that was her name. He never talked about her in the office and I didn't like to pry. One morning last week he'd walked in the door half an hour late, looking pretty exhausted. When I'd said 'Big night last night?' he'd just run his hands through his hair and replied, 'Something like that.' But as he'd dumped his bag under his desk and got straight to work I knew the subject was closed.

I said nothing, waiting for him to elaborate, but he didn't. Instead he handed me the last of the press releases. 'Now, we're almost ready. I just need to bash out a few quick emails.' He sat down behind his desk and stared at the computer screen.

He seemed a little preoccupied with something and I was about to ask him whether everything was OK when the door swung open and in strode Koo. She sat down on the edge of his desk, her bare calves hanging over the side. She was wearing an uncharacteristically sombre outfit: a stylish beige on-the-knee skirt with ivory-coloured buttons down the front, elegant cream Chanel sandals, and a crisp white cotton shirt. 'How's my favourite boy?'

Jack shifted nervously in his seat.

'I love the skirt,' I said, trying to distract her. I knew he had work to do and besides, she always had to grab Jack's attention; it irritated me. 'Where did you get it?'

She jumped down and smoothed her hands down the side of the skirt. 'Maud. I know it's a bit fusty. But there will be so much flesh on display today, I thought I'd cover up for a change.'

'It suits you.' I meant it. Even with the heavy make-up and big hair, quiffed on top of her crown, the back rolled into a chunky chignon and fastened with a long silver clip, she managed to look elegant.

She flashed me a grateful smile. 'Thanks. So are we all set?'

'Why don't you two go on?' Jack said. 'I'm just sending out some extra details to the *Irish Times*. Everything else is covered.'

Koo nodded. 'Great idea. This place is like an oven. Don't know how the pair of you stick it.' She fanned her face with her hand. 'We'll see you there.'

I picked up the press folders and put them in a St Jude's canvas bag.

'Hey, like the bag,' she said. 'Very "I'm Not a Bag". Can I have one?'

'Of course.' I peeled one out of its plastic wrapping and handed it to her.

She put her brown Chanel bag inside it, and swung it onto her shoulder. 'What do you think? Très green.' With that she powered out of the office.

'I'll be about ten minutes behind you,' Jack told me. He lowered his voice. 'Watch Koo with the vino. She loves a free bar.'

Great, that was all I needed. Babysitting a tipsy Koo.

As we walked up a bustling Kildare Street, towards the Shelbourne Hotel, Koo explained that every year invited 'celebrities' ran the Women's Mini Marathon in aid of St Jude's.

When Jack arrived I asked him about the models. 'What's their motivation for running in case anyone asks? Is it just for the publicity? Or are they really interested in the hospital?'

'Shush!' He looked round, but none of the journalists were

listening. They were all huddled in the corner, riffling through the sponsors' goody bags. 'The girls are vital,' he said. 'They're each sponsored to the hilt: two mobile-phone companies and Ford. It's our best year yet.'

'But they're practically page-three models.'

He grinned. 'How could you say such a thing? Marsha Heart is an ex-Miss Ireland. And Trinity Curley is married to one of the Guinness family.'

'They're all going to give themselves black eyes,' I said a little grumpily. With their glossy manes and gravity-defying breasts they were making me feel very inadequate. 'They're not wearing anything under those running vests.'

Jack grinned. 'I'm sure they will during the race. Trinity ran marathons in college. Her lad, Alfie, was in our premie unit for almost three months and we used to chat in the canteen. He's fine now, but it was touch and go for a while. That's why she's running.'

I groaned and hit my forehead with my hand. 'I'm a horrible, judgemental person. Take me outside and shoot me.'

Jack handed me a headshot of a pretty blonde with oversized scarlet lips. 'Karen Vickers hasn't arrived yet. She's always late. She'll rock up in spray-on shorts and flirt with the cameramen. During the race she'll forget the name of the hospital and she'll collapse halfway around the course and have to be taken away in an ambulance.'

I laughed. 'Why did you ask her then?'

He shrugged. 'I didn't. She offered. She's a friend of Marsha's. Anyway, she's actually good fun and the tabloids love her.' He looked around. 'Speaking of ambulances, where's Koo?'

The photo call in St Stephen's Green Park was rather wind blown, but the two girls had gamely lined up for 'a start' behind a rope held by two men in suits from Ford. Jack was right, Trinity turned out to be a lovely girl with beautiful manners, and a genuine interest in the hospital; Marsha was polite but a little stand-offish. As the girls posed for the photographers Koo's mobile rang.

'Sorry, sorry,' she told Jack, walking away from the scene to take the call.

Seconds later she came back, her face white. 'It's Mac. He fell out of bed. May says he's very upset and asking for me. I have to go. Sorry, Jack.'

'I'll order you a taxi,' he said immediately.

'S'OK, I have the car.' She was slurring her words a bit. Her eyes were hidden behind huge Chanel sunglasses, but it was obvious she'd enjoyed her pre-lunch tipple.

'You're far too upset to negotiate the roads,' Jack said diplomatically. 'Alice, can you drive?'

'Yes, but my car's—'

'Would you mind driving Koo home?'

'Jack!' One of the photographers called over. 'Where's Karen?'

'On her way.' He leaned towards me. 'I'm so sorry to do this to you, but Koo needs company. Mac's—'

'Jack!' Another photographer shouted. 'Can you move the St Jude's banner to the right?'

'Just a second,' he told him. He held both my shoulders gently. He was so close I could smell his lemony aftershave. 'Are you OK with this?'

'What if I say no? I didn't sign up to be Maud and Koo's lap dog, you know.'

His face dropped and I gave him a reassuring smile. 'I'm joking. Poor Koo. I'd be happy to. And I think Karen's just shown up.' A buxom blonde came tottering down the path as fast as her high-heeled Posh Spice runners would allow. In fairness to her, she looked fabulous, the tiny vest straining to constrain her pneumatic chest, her pink shorts cut high to show off her shapely nut-brown legs.

'Sorry I'm late, boys,' she trilled at the photographers. 'The seat of my other shorts ripped halfway up Grafton Street. I had to pop into Top Shop to buy another pair. Otherwise I'd be flashing my bare bum to the world.' The photographers lapped it up.

'Let's go,' I said to Koo, who was looking more and more agitated by the second, pacing the path and scratching at her arm, a screaming red patch appearing in the crook of her elbow.

The next thing I knew, I was driving down Baggot Street in Koo's gold two-seater Mercedes SL, trying not to crunch her gears, paranoid I'd crash it. Koo's head was pressed back against the headrest so hard the muscles in her neck were tense and wiry. My knuckles were white from my ultra-tight grip on the steering wheel. We must have looked a right pair, two lunatics on the run.

I had tried to tell Jack that my car was an automatic, but I'd got distracted. If we were stopped by a guard for dangerous driving, I hoped, in the circumstances, he'd be understanding.

'Who's Mac?' I asked Koo as soon as we got underway.

'My husband.'

'I didn't know you were married.'

She gave a wry smile. 'He doesn't go out much. At all in fact. He had a stroke nearly eight years ago. May comes in two days a week; she's a nurse; and my mum helps out sometimes. He goes into a nursing home when I need a break or if I'm going away. But most of the time it's just me and Mac. Jack didn't tell you?'

I was too gob-smacked to speak.

'Obviously not.' She gave a dry laugh. She put her sunglasses on top of her head, screwed her eyes closed, then opened them again. Her eyes were red and puffy, as though she'd been attacked with pepper spray. 'Jack's very discreet. I guess he didn't tell you about *us* either?'

If we hadn't been stopped at traffic lights I think I would have crashed the car. 'You and Jack?'

'Yep. Started in Cascais. Silly, really. I should have known better. Fucking the staff and all that. Even if he is rather cute.'

I said nothing, so she continued, 'Jack and I have an understanding. At home it's all strictly business, but away,' she smiled lazily. 'Let's just say I can't wait for our little trip to Positano.' She gave a throaty growl and I tried not to grimace. 'I don't know why I'm telling you all this,' she added. 'Must be the wine. I'm a terrible drunk, Alice. I shoot my mouth off. Pay no attention to me.' She closed her eyes.

I concentrated on the road. This was turning out to be quite a day for revelations. It made me wonder about Jack. Wasn't Koo a bit obvious for him? And what about his wife? And poor old Mac? But maybe Koo didn't know about Juliette.

'Is Jack single?' I asked a little testily. Luckily Koo didn't seem to notice the tone.

'I guess so.' She shrugged. 'He's pretty tight lipped about his private life. He didn't say anything about a girlfriend; but you never know with Jack. He keeps himself to himself most of the time. He was for ever making phone calls home when we were away, so maybe he does. I wouldn't have pegged him as the cheating type, but you never know with men, do you?'

'No, you certainly don't. But what about Mac?' I blurted out, unable to keep it in. 'Doesn't he mind?'

Koo said nothing for a moment. 'Alice, he's been paralysed for eight years. Most days he thinks he's six or seven. I read him *Biggles* and *Just William* stories; he likes those. I love him. But he's not the man I married.'

'I didn't mean to sound so judgemental. It can't be easy for you.'

'Easy?' Koo snorted. 'My whole life's been on hold since his stroke. At first they gave him six months to live. I can do that, I thought, I owe it to Mac. So I took him home, learned how to nurse him myself. How to change a catheter, how to feed him intravenously. They said he'd never get his swallow back, but he did. He sips tea now and he can eat normal food as long as it's fairly soft. And at Christmas and on his birthday he has a little sip of whiskey. Sometimes he recognizes me and smiles. Sometimes we can even talk for a few minutes. That used to be enough. But now I'm just so tired; I want my life back.' She gave a deep sigh and rapped her fingers on the dashboard. 'Boring, boring. Enough about my sad little life. What about you? Boyfriend?'

'No. But I'm looking.'

'Be careful. Love has a way of disappointing you. After the initial honeymoon phase, most marriages are a sham.'

Cheery thought. I didn't know what to say to that so I said nothing.

As we passed University College Dublin, Koo said, 'Thanks for driving me home. I'm sorry if I'm a bit of a moan sometimes. With Mac and everything it's—' she broke off and stared out the window. I realized she was crying. We drove on to Cabinteely and she directed me into the Park, a modern estate. We pulled up outside her house, a detached dormer bungalow, and I switched off the engine and sat in the car, wondering what to do.

Tears were rolling down her cheeks and she was doing nothing to wipe them away. I reached into my bag and pulled out a fresh packet of tissues. Grace always had buckets of them, and I was glad she'd made me take one this morning, along with baby wipes. 'You never know what you'll need at a photo shoot,' she'd said. I handed it to Koo.

She took it off me and stared down at the packet. Eventually she pulled out a tissue and dabbed at her eyes. 'Thanks.' She stared straight ahead. 'Sometimes I just wish he'd just get on with it and die. Isn't that awful? Other times I wonder what I'd do without him. It's so hard to let go.' She gave an almighty sob and dipped her head, her chin flat against her chest.

Without stopping to think about it, I put my arm around her and squeezed. 'I'm so sorry,' I murmured. I held tight as the tears fell down her cheeks and landed on her lap, leaving dark blotches on the linen. Her shoulders heaved, and her hands were balled into tight fists. Her breath was laboured, coming in gulps in between the heaving sobs. We sat in silence, the cars windows steaming up at the edges, the interior filled with Koo's sorrow.

Eventually she stopped crying and lifted her head. 'I must look a state.' She flipped down the passenger mirror and stared at her panda-eyed reflection. 'Yuck!' Then she licked the edge of the tissue and wiped away the mascara, pulling at the delicate skin under her eyes, which made me wince. Respectable again, she hid her eyes behind her sunglasses. 'Sorry about all this. The crying and everything.'

I gave her a gentle smile. 'I was crying in the loo at La Grenouille last week, remember? And that was just over a dress. You have every reason to be upset. I can't imagine what it must be like for you. If there's—'

'Thanks.' She cut me off. I realized she wasn't being rude; she just didn't want to start crying again.

'I'd better go in,' she said. 'How are you going to get back to the office? Will I order a taxi?'

'I'll come inside with you first.' I wanted to make sure she was all right before I left her alone.

'You don't have to.'

'I want to.'

'But what about Jack? Isn't he expecting you back?'

'He'll understand. Look, my mum had a stroke, I do understand what you're going through.'

'How is she now?'

'Unfortunately she had a second stroke; she died six months later.'

'Sorry.'

'It's OK. It was a long time ago.'

Walking into Koo's house, I thought about mum. When she had her first stroke and lost the use of most of her right side, I had just finished my final school exams, so I took over, doing all the shopping and the cooking. Grace was in her final year of college and almost failed her exams because of the stress. To this day she bristles when anyone asks about her degree. She feels she was robbed of the first that was rightfully hers.

Then Mum had her second stroke, which pretty much wiped out her entire system and she had to go into a home, St Mary's. It was always far too hot, like a greenhouse. I often think it would have been better for all of us if she'd died immediately. Grace hated visiting the place; she said it smelt of urine and was full of old people sitting and gazing into space, or staring at the front door, dreaming of escape.

I didn't mind St Mary's, it was peaceful there and some of the nurses were really nice to me. I used to sit with Mum for hours, just holding her hand and chatting to her. She couldn't talk; she could barely move her eyes, but it didn't bother me. I painted her nails, brushed her hair, rubbed hand cream into her withered hands and read her Enid Blyton stories. Grace always said I would have made a brilliant nurse if only I'd stuck at the exams long enough.

Koo's house seemed so ordinary. After Maud's palace, I'd been expecting something equally dramatic. There were black and white photographs of beach scenes on the walls in wooden IKEA frames, a small iron and glass console table littered with post, a plain beige carpet running up the stairs.

As Koo dumped her bag under the table a Filippino woman with apple cheeks opened the door to the right. A waft of warm air blasted us – moist and slightly fruity – the air of a sick room.

'May,' Koo said, 'this is Alice from St Jude's. I wasn't feeling great, so she kindly drove me home.'

'Hi.' May gave me a warm smile, showing tiny, child-like teeth. 'You OK now, Koo?'

'Much better, thanks.'

'I so sorry to call you. I know you busy today but Mac's not good.' May's dark eyes were full of compassion. 'I don't know what happen. I was in the kitchen and bang, I hear noise and Mac groan. I run in and Mac on floor. I not secure side of bed properly. I so sorry. Is all my fault.'

Koo squeezed May's shoulder. 'Don't be silly. I've done it myself a few times. The catch is a bit knackered; I should get it replaced. And Mac's stronger than he looks; and quite determined when he wants to be. Do you think he's broken anything?'

'No, he just got a fright.'

'Listen, you go home, May,' Koo said kindly. 'I'll see you in the morning.'

A few minutes later I was sitting beside Mac's bed. I'd persuaded Koo to pop upstairs, have a shower and change while I kept an eye on him. I stroked his hand, his skin was papery beneath my fingers.

'Who are you?' he asked.

'Alice, Koo's friend. Remember?'

He gave me a nod and smiled. 'Friends. Friends are good. I have friends. Si and Jumbo. They're my best friends. Jumbo has a catapult, you know.'

'Lucky boy.'

Then Mac went silent and turned his head away from me, staring at the wall. I looked around. From the brass chandelier, the built-in bookshelves and the fireplace I figured this was once the sitting room. The floor was dark blue linoleum, toning in with the sky-blue walls and midnight-blue velvet curtains. Mac's chunky metal hospital bed was the main focus of the room. To the left of the bed was a small table holding a plastic jug of water and a squat tumbler, a tray with brown and clear bottles of medicine, Vaseline, tiny containers of nasal drops with white plastic tops, like baby bottles for a doll, and an old-fashioned round metal tub of jelly sweets.

Koo walked in. She'd changed into a black velour tracksuit and her hair was scraped back into a ponytail. Without make-up, she looked years younger. I realized she was probably the same age as Grace.

'Koo.' Mac looked up at her and beamed. 'Don't you look lovely today? Are you going running?' His face lost its slight flabbiness and I got a hint of what he must have looked like in his prime, like Richard Gere, his long slightly hooded, sexy blue eyes twinkling, his cheekbones sharp and defined, his temples sprinkled with grey. Now his face had collapsed and his hair was white.

Koo smiled at him. 'No, Mac.' She smoothed down the blanket on his bed and tucked in the edges. 'You love running, don't you? Mac's done seventeen marathons and an Iron Man, haven't you? He even got me into running at one stage. We used to do the West Pier together, didn't we?'

Mac stared at Koo, his face blank again.

'It's Koo,' she told him gently, 'and this is my friend, Alice.'

'I have friends,' he murmured. 'Si and . . . and Jumbo.'

'That's right,' Koo said. 'You do. You have lots of friends. Lots of friends.'

At that moment, I remembered Mum and I could see her bewildered post-stroke face so clearly that tears sprung to my eyes.

'He's not in any pain,' Koo said, misinterpreting my tears.

I shook my head. 'It's not that. I was just thinking about my mum. You're so good to nurse him at home, Koo. It's an incredible thing to do. And I'm sure you don't get much help from the government.'

She snorted. 'Tell me about it. I'm up to my tonsils in debt. We used to live in a three-storey red-brick, near Maud. This is more suitable for Mac. Besides, I needed the money. Nurses don't come cheap. But sometimes I wonder if I did the right thing.' She gazed at Mac, stroking his hand. 'He was such an active man; so fit. Maybe he would have been better off in a nursing home.'

'I doubt it. He seems very content,' I said. 'And the way his eyes lit up when you walked through the door, that has to be worth something.'

'It is,' she agreed. 'Sometimes the old Mac is there for a few minutes and it makes everything worthwhile. But at what cost?'

'Tea?' Mac said softly, his eyes meeting Koo's. 'Whiskey?'

Koo laughed. 'He's always trying it on. Aren't you?' She stroked his head. 'No whiskey today, Mac. It's not your birthday yet.' •

Chapter 18

On Wednesday morning I found a text message from Moira, Jason's mum, asking me to ring her urgently.

'Do you mind if I make one quick personal phone call?' I asked Jack as soon as I got into the office. 'My mobile's out of credit.'

'Course not. Fire ahead.' He gave me a warm smile and there was such kindness in his eyes I almost started to cry. I'd been up all night, my head spinning with all kinds of things – Mac, my mum, Ned, even Barney – and I hadn't got much sleep.

I keyed in Moira's home number.

'Alice,' Moira said as soon as she recognized my voice, 'thanks so much for getting back to me. I have to be quick. Frank's out spraying the roses and he won't be long. I'll come straight to the point. I'm really worried about Jason.' Frank was Jason's dad.

'Oh.' My heart sank. I thought as much.

'He can't stay here for ever,' Moira continued. 'Frank's nerves won't take it. They've been having the most terrible rows. Now Frank's retired he's got all this time on his hands. Fixing Jason's marriage seems to be his top priority. And Frank's blood pressure is appallingly high, Alice, I can't tell you. When is Grace going to see sense and take him back? I know Jason has his faults but he's a good boy at heart.'

'Aren't they all,' I muttered.

'Sorry?'

'Nothing. I don't really want to get involved, Moira. Grace is my sister and she's been very good to me.'

'I understand, really I do. But I don't know how much more of this Jason can take. His moods are yo-yoing all over the place. And all this business with the heating—'

'The heating?'

'Yes, one minute he's freezing, the next he's boiling. It's playing havoc with the thermostat, I can tell you. I'm worried that there's something seriously wrong with him but he refuses to go to the GP again. Says it's a waste of time and money.'

'I'll try talking to him; it's the best I can offer.'

'Thank you, Alice. You're a good girl. I know you'll do your best.'

I put the phone down and rubbed my temples. I could feel a whopper of a headache coming on.

'Everything all right?' Jack asked.

'Nothing a sawn-off shotgun couldn't deal with.'

'That bad?'

I'd already told Jack a little about the whole Grace and Jason situation, mainly so he understood why they both rang me so often at work. He didn't seem to mind; in fact, he was very sympathetic.

'Just the usual Devine family dramas,' I said. 'That was Grace's mother-in-law. She thinks there's something wrong with Jason; he has the oddest symptoms.'

'Like what?'

'Mood swings, hair loss, getting hot then cold.' I stopped. 'I shouldn't be boring you with this. It's hardly work.'

'Don't worry about that.' He thought for a second. 'That hot and cold thing is interesting though. Sheila has an under-active thyroid; hypothyroidism it's called. Basically her

142

thyroid is shot. She used to complain all the time about being hot and cold. Your thyroid has something to do with regulating your body temperature apparently.' He shrugged. 'It might be worth getting your brother-in-law checked for it. At least they could rule it out.'

At lunchtime I rang Jason. I'd spent my lunch hour googling hypothyroidism and the more I read, the more I became convinced that Jack was on to something. It all fit: the mood swings, the tiredness, the dry skin, the wonky body thermometer.

I told Jason about Jack's hunch. He didn't seem all that impressed but he did say, 'My granddad had some sort of thyroid thing. Hang on, I'll just ask Mum.' I heard him shout 'Hey, Mum, did Granddad Finney have a thyroid problem?'

'Yes, yes, he did. Heavens, I hadn't thought of that. Who are you talking to, Jason? The doctor?'

'No, Alice.'

The next thing I heard an excited squeak and then Moira came on the line. 'Alice, you're a genius. Thank you, thank you. I'm sure you're right; this will change everything. I'm so grateful.'

I smiled to myself. At least someone appreciated me.

Jason rang me just before five. 'I went to see my GP this afternoon. There's a chance you're right. I'll get the results of the blood test on Friday. I'm sorry I snapped at you, Alice.'

'That's OK. As long as you get better, that's the main thing.'

There was a pause and then he said. 'Do you think Grace'll take me back; once I start feeling a bit more like myself again? It's such a relief; I thought I was going mad.'

'What happens if your blood test comes back negative?'

'I hadn't thought of that. I just want everything to go back to normal as quickly as possible. I want my old life back. I know I've been impossible to live with, but when Grace hears about the thyroid thing, I'm sure she'll be sympathetic.'

This was all such bad timing. If only Jason had had the blood test weeks ago, before Grace had met Gary, then things might have been different.

I had to stall him. 'Best not to rush things. You both have a lot of talking to do.' Surely in the circumstances she'd give Jason another chance? Or was I being naive? And what about Gary?

He sighed. 'I suppose you're right. I'll be over on Saturday to see the kids so I'll talk to her then. And thanks, Alice, you've been great. I don't know what I would have done without you. You've been my rock.'

When he found out about Gary, I doubt if he'd be so impressed with me. Maybe there was a solution although Grace was very attached to Gary; it was unlikely she'd let him go easily. But, hang on, what if Gary got rid of *her* before Saturday. Maybe Jason would have some chance.

But how? Appeal to Gary's decent streak? Ask him to keep away from Grace for the sake of the marriage? Somehow I didn't think that was going to work. Unless. Arvin! He'd always been such a nice guy. Maybe he'd talk to Gary for me, put pressure on him to do the right thing. There couldn't be that many Arvin Hudsons in the phone book. I'd call over to him this evening after work and ask for his help.

I knocked on the yellow front door. Arvin lived on a leafy street at the back of Bray town. He must be doing all right, I thought, as I stared up at the Victorian town house. I heard a noise from inside and my stomach clenched. I steeled myself to repeat the lines I'd been practising over and over in the car. 'Hi, Arvin. I hope you don't mind me calling in, but I need your help. It's about Gary Costello.'

The door swung open and a dark-haired woman stared at me. 'Hello? Can I help you?'

'Hi. I'm looking for Arvin. Is he in?'

'No, but he should be back soon. I'm his wife, Maureen.'

I stood there dumbstruck for a few seconds. Maureen was petite, and with her olive skin and short hair, she reminded me of Demi Moore. She was also at least fifty, a good ten years older than Arvin and she looked strangely familiar.

'I'm Alice,' I managed eventually. But what on earth was I going to say next? Think, Alice, think. Then I had it. 'My little boy plays with St Pat's. That's why I'm here. To talk to him about my son.' I smiled at her, relieved.

She seemed to accept this. 'You must know *my* son then, Gary. Gary Costello?'

I stared at her. 'Gary is Arvin's son?' I felt dizzy.

'Stepson.' She gave a laugh. 'They're more like best friends. Thick as thieves those two.'

Stepson was a little better; at least they weren't blood relations.

'Would you like to come in and wait for Arvin?' she asked. 'He won't be long.'

'It's fine, I'll catch him on Saturday. I was just passing. No need to bother him. Thanks anyway.'

She looked at me a little quizzically and then nodded. 'Nice to meet you. I'm sorry, I didn't catch your last name.'

'Devine,' I said. 'Alice Devine.'

'Devine?' She stared at me and then her eyes narrowed a little. 'You're not related to Grace Devine, are you?'

I opened my mouth to say yes, but something in the way she said Grace's name warned me not to. Instead I shook my head and said, 'No, no relation.'

'Good. She was a nasty piece of work. My Arvin nearly fell apart after . . .' She stopped herself. 'Anyway, it doesn't matter.

It's all ancient history. Nice to meet you, Alice. I hope your son's enjoying the soccer.'

'Oh, he is. Nice to meet you too.'

As I walked away, I felt horribly uneasy. If Arvin and Gary really were as close as Maureen claimed, did Arvin already know about Gary and Grace's fling? As I drove back to Grace's, I started to worry. There was trouble brewing, I could feel it, but as I was off to Positano first thing in the morning, it was out of my hands. I could hardly tell Grace about Gary and Arvin and then skip the country. I'd just have to hope nothing happened in the meantime. I was only going to be away for three days after all. What could happen in three days?

Chapter 19

'There's something I should tell you,' Jack said as we sat in the packed departure lounge at Dublin Airport waiting to board the flight to Naples. Maud, Gunella and Jessica were in the first-class lounge and Koo was meeting us in Italy the following day because the nursing home didn't have a bed for Mac until then.

'I'm not great at flying,' he said.

'Just as well you're not the pilot then,' I said breezily. 'He's Italian. He walked past a few minutes ago. Cute too.'

He smiled patiently. 'I'm just warning you. As long as there's not too much turbulence I should be OK.'

'You're serious?'

He nodded. 'You'll have to keep my mind off it. Think you can talk the whole way from Ireland to Italy?'

I grinned. Now there was a challenge. 'I'll give it a go.'

As soon as we sat down in our seats Jack started to fidget. I'd given him the window seat because he said it made him feel marginally less claustrophobic. As the passengers filed into the plane, Jack kept glancing out the window at the dull Irish sky and then staring straight ahead at the seat in front of him. Then he took the laminated safety instruction card out of the blue netting nestling against his knees and started to read it. The card shook in his hands.

'Are you OK?' I asked.

He nodded, then said, 'It's a bit cloudy, do you think there'll be turbulence?'

'I don't really know. Would you like a mint?' I passed him my fresh tube of Polos. He nodded and started to pick open the tin foil at the end; his hands were shaking so badly it took him ages.

When the seatbelt lights pinged on he fastened his lap belt, opening and closing the buckle several times to check the clasp was working properly. In fact, his increasingly neurotic behaviour was starting to worry me. We hadn't even taken off yet.

He just about held it together during take-off, gripping my hand until my skin went white.

He gulped. 'I heard a noise. A bang.'

'It's just the wheels locking away,' I said. 'Nothing to worry about.'

'Are you sure? I think I can hear a rattling noise. Oh my God, maybe we're going down.'

I needed to distract him, and quick.

'Tell me about your wife,' I said, clutching at straws. 'Is she cute?'

He smiled at me gently. 'She died a few years ago, but she was cute, very cute.'

She was dead? OK, now he'd floored me. Dear God, Jack's single, I immediately thought. Appalling, I know. I tried to put it to the back of my mind and concentrate on what he was saying.

'I'm so sorry,' I said. 'I had no idea.'

'Maud didn't say anything?'

I shook my head. 'No. We don't really have that kind of relationship. It's more of a master and slave kind of thing.'

He gave a laugh. 'I guess she's not the warmest of women at times. Anyway, it was a long time ago, nearly six years now.'

'What was her name? If you don't mind talking about it.'

He paused for a moment and then said, 'Juliette.'

Of course. Juliette. 'Pretty name.'

'Yes. When I first met her I was completely tongue-tied. She was so beautiful. She reminded me of Audrey Tautou, the French actress, fragile-looking, but strong inside. I fell in love with her instantly.'

'Ahhh,' I said. I couldn't help it, it was so sweet. 'Where did you meet?'

'At work. We were both traders. She was far better than I was of course, made far more money too. Spent most of it on shoes. She had a thing about black stilettos. She always said you could wear any old clothes as long as you got the shoes right.' He gave a short laugh. 'She kept them in their boxes; all stacked up at the bottom of the wardrobe. They're still there in fact; I hadn't the heart to throw them away and now,' he shrugged. 'I've got used to them, I suppose. She never even got to wear some of them.'

An image flashed in front of my eyes. Jack taking a pair of pristine black stilettos out of a box and holding them up, admiring them, the curve of the instep, the dagger-like heel. His fingers running over the shiny leather. I felt a lump in my throat and I just nodded. 'I like shoes too,' I said softly.

Then he stared out the window. His eyes were moist and I felt bad for upsetting him.

'It must be hard for you,' I said. 'We can talk about something else.'

He blew out his breath noisily. 'I like talking about her,' he said simply. 'I miss her. When she died she took part of my heart with her.'

My eyes filled up and next thing I knew tears were pouring down my cheeks. 'I'm so sorry,' I murmured, mortified, wiping them away with my fingers. 'She must have been very special.'

'She was. But she was also a complete workaholic and she couldn't cook to save her life, even though she was half

French. And she had a terrible temper. She used to get these rages; they'd just swoop down out of nowhere. One minute we'd be talking about something banal like the electricity bill and the next thing she'd be accusing me of being a stingy bastard and not understanding how much good clothes cost. She'd storm out of the house in a rage.' He stopped. 'But none of that mattered. Do you know what the hardest part of losing someone is? All the unfinished business. We'd had a fight the night before she died. I never got a chance to say sorry.'

'What happened?' I asked softly. 'Sorry, ignore me if—'

'No, no, it's OK. She had an aneurism. It was all very quick; there was nothing the doctors could do. I told her she was pushing herself too hard, in fact that's what we'd been arguing about. It was all too soon after . . .' he paused for a moment. 'Anyway she was always very driven. Going in early to get her paperwork done, staying late to catch the American market. In the end her system just couldn't take it. One of her work colleagues found her in the company car park, slumped over the wheel of her Audi. It was only eight in the morning; she'd left the house at half six to beat the traffic. She must have been there for—' he broke off. 'Anyway, they rang me immediately, said Juliette had been in an accident, and told me to jump in a taxi immediately, not to drive. I think they were afraid I'd crash on the way there.

'When I got to the office there was an ambulance outside the building with its lights flashing, no siren, just lights, and the ambulance men were loading a trolley into the back. There was a blue blanket pulled up over the face, but as soon as I saw the blanket I knew it was Juliette under there. Then I just shut down. I collapsed on the pavement and they brought me into St Vincent's with her body. I hugged her the whole way there, apparently, wouldn't let her go, but I don't remember any of it. I don't remember a thing until about two days later. Mum and Maeve came up from Cork to help with everything. Then Caroline took over and ended up doing most of the funeral arrangements. She's always been good in a crisis. I don't know what I'd do without her. I stayed with her for a few weeks and then I went to France for two months to stay with Juliette's granny. I needed a rest and she lives in this tiny village in the Dordogne, somewhere I can't pronounce – Lanquissey or something.' He gave a laugh and then shrugged. 'I'm hopeless at languages. Anyway, she has this old stone farmhouse with a small pool. It was just what I needed. I swam and read paperbacks and magazines, anything to keep my mind occupied, and did very little else. She's a brilliant cook and she got me eating again. And then I came back to Dublin and started looking for a new job. I couldn't go back to the office, it would have killed me. The charity work was Caroline's idea. She thought helping other people might help me too. She's never had much time for the trading to be honest. As I said, she's pretty good at taking control.'

'So you started working for St Jude's?' I said.

'No, I worked for Word Focus Ireland for a few years. They support Aids Orphans in Uganda. I went out to visit the project a few times which was an eye-opener, but the travel started to get to me. I needed to be at home more. And then Caroline spotted the St Jude's job in the paper, and the rest is history. I've been working for them for two years now and it seems to be going OK. At least Maud hasn't fired me yet.'

'Surely it would be up the board to fire you?' I said.

His face dropped a little.

'Sorry, sorry,' I said quickly, 'that came out wrong. Of course they're not going to fire you, they're lucky to have you. What I meant is, does Maud really have that much power?'

'Yes and no. But let's not talk about old Maudie and work. It's far too depressing.'

The plane lurched a little. Jack moaned under his breath and pressed his head against the back of his seat. He closed his eyes and beads of sweat popped out at his temples.

'Did I tell you about my sister's husband?' I said quickly. 'You were right. About the thyroid disorder. But it's all a bit of a mess now because of her affair.'

Jack's eyes were still screwed closed.

'She has a toy boy,' I said, louder. 'And they're at it like rabbits. With food and everything. Like in *9½ Weeks*, only worse.'

Jack opened his eyes. 'What did you just say?'

I grinned. 'I thought that would get your attention. She met this football player, Gary. But it turns out he's her exboyfriend's son.'

'Son? What age is he?'

I laughed. 'Don't look so horrified, he's not that young. I'll start at the beginning.' An hour later, after the whole story and more, we were descending over Naples.

'Look at the sea,' I cried, leaning over Jack's chest and staring out the window. 'It's so blue. Isn't it beautiful? Look, is that a castle?'

Jack just laughed. 'You're like a six-year-old. When was the last time you were on a plane?'

As we sat in our seats waiting to disembark, Jack let go of my lower arm and I shook it. He had quite a grip.

'Sorry,' he said. He took my arm in his hands and started to rub it gently, his warm fingers lingering over my bare skin. I shivered a little and drew it away.

'That flight can't have been much fun for you,' he said. 'Thanks for talking me through it.'

'Any time.'

'And I'm sorry about your sister and everything. I hope it all works out for the best.'

I looked at him and smiled. His eyes were kind and honest. I could feel myself blushing and I looked away, embarrassed.

'Thanks,' I murmured, then busied myself with putting my water and unread magazine back into my handbag.

Jack was single. It was all I could think about. It made this holiday a much more interesting prospect.

Chapter 20

There was a large black limousine waiting for us outside the airport. I'd suggested getting the bus from Naples to Positano, but Maud had looked at me as if I was crazy. She'd probably never been on public transport in her life. So limo it was.

Jack helped the Italian chauffeur load the bags into the cavernous boot. I asked the man his name, it seemed rude not to.

'Alfredo,' he told me with a wink. He was middle aged, stooped and a little dour, his silvery-black hair greased back off his fleshy face. I could tell Maud was disappointed. She'd probably been expecting Robert De Niro.

'Like in *Cinema Paradiso*?' I asked.

Maud glared at me. She was in a filthy mood. 'Stop wittering on, Alice,' she snapped. She pointed at the mountain of bags. 'Deal with the luggage.'

Jack and I helped Alfredo load the cavernous boot. Maud's cases were all Louis Vuitton, Jessica's were beige Gucci, and Gunella had two ancient tan leather travelling bags, which had probably been in her family for hundreds of years. Jack's plain black Nike hold-all lowered the tone a little, as did my Tesco's best lime-green suitcase with the wonky wheels.

Satisfied we hadn't left any of her precious cargo on the pavement, Maud climbed into the car and settled herself in the middle of the cream leather seat. Gunella joined her. They sprawled out on the back seat like starfish, legs stretched in front of them, taking as much room as was humanly possible.

'Where will I sit?' Jessica demanded petulantly. Gunella's half-sister was arresting, even with her straggly blonde hair, ripped jeans and plain white vest top. She had a heart-shaped face, wide-set eyes that looked like almonds and high, cat-like cheekbones. In fact she reminded me of a young Sophie Dahl, without the glorious peachy flesh. Jessica was muscular, tanned and flat chested. She was twenty-four and worked part-time as a model for a well-known Irish knitwear designer. She and Gunella may have shared a father, but they didn't look a bit alike.

Maud pointed rather rudely at the seat opposite her. 'Get in and close the door behind you,' she told Jessica. 'It's so sticky out there, I'm melting away.'

Jessica climbed in, sat down and crossed her arms in front of her chest, glaring at Maud and leaving the door wide open

'I'm melting, I'm melting,' Jack said, pretending to sink into the pavement, like the Wicked Witch of the West.

I grinned at him, impressed. The *Wizard of Oz* is one of my all-time favourite films.

'I have a feeling we're not in Kansas any more, Toto,' I said with a grin.

'Alice!' I heard Maud's voice from the bowels of the limo. I stuck my head in the door. 'For God's sake, stop messing about,' she clipped. 'The sooner we get out of this hellhole the better. I hate Naples; it's such a scruffy city. Pass me my vanity case. My poor skin is utterly dehydrated from the plane.'

I located it in the small mountain of luggage and handed it to her. She pulled out a water spritzer and began to spray herself.

'Can I have some?' Jessica asked. Maud scowled at her but handed it over wordlessly. Then she shut the door practically in my face.

'They're like grumpy teenagers,' I told Jack as Alfredo finally slammed the crammed boot shut. I think he'd heard Maud's 'scruffy' comment, judging by his scowl.

'You're very good to drive us, Alfredo,' I said to him, trying to smooth things over. 'I know it's a long way.'

He shrugged. 'It's my job. I like to drive. I listen to music, I watch the road. S'OK.'

'Can you listen in to the conversation in the back?' I asked. 'Do people ever . . . you know?' I lifted my eyebrows. I was in quite a giddy mood. Must have been the heat.

He laughed. 'All the time. I take picture and post on internet.'

I must have looked shocked because he added quickly, 'Only joking. And as long as seats are clean, you make fucky-fucky. I no mind.'

Jack gave a delighted chuckle. 'That's very kind of you, but I don't think there'll be any girl on girl action today. And I'm going to take a nap. But thanks for the offer.'

'*No problemo*,' Alfredo said cheerily and walked towards the driver's door.

'Don't look so worried, Alice.' Jack smiled at me and raised his eyebrows. 'As long as we've got plenty of bubbly on board, the girls will be fine.'

Almost two hours later, we arrived at Positano. Jack was right, once Maud, Gunella and Jessica had started tucking into the bottles of Prosecco from the limo's mini bar, our worries were over. By the time we had whizzed passed Vesuvius, Maud's mood had lifted and they were singing 'Que Sera Sera', Maud wafting her hand in the air along to the music, elegantly, like the Queen Mother; Jessica hiccupping and burping in a rather unladylike way.

I was a bit miffed by their lack of interest in the volcano after all my internet research. I'd woken Jack up to show him and to share my extensive knowledge. I'd found a live webcam of the volcano the previous week and had spent ages watching its craggy profile set against the pink-tinged sky.

'The left bit's still active,' I told him. 'Imagine. It could blow at any minute. It's the only European volcano to have erupted in the last ten years.'

'Really?' he sat up a little. 'Ten years?'

I think my date was a little off. 'The last hundred years anyway,' I amended. After my flight experience I didn't want to worry him. He smiled at me patiently, and then had a quick look before going back to sleep.

Jack and I sat facing Maud and Gunella for the whole trip, Jessica sandwiched in between us, like a skinny slice of ham. Jack probably had the right idea. He dozed for most of the journey, his head lolling against the head rest. I tried to ignore the three other women as best I could, which wasn't hard, as I seemed to be strangely invisible to them. I gazed out the window, taking in the landscape flashing by the limo's windows with all its colour and fizzy energy: lemon trees, olive groves, stone buildings with flaking exterior paint, leaf-green shutters and flat roofs edged in curved terracotta tiles that rolled over and over like a series of waves. Maud insisted on having the windows up and the air conditioning on full tilt, which was a shame. I quite fancied sticking my head out the window like a dog, taking in the new smells and feeling the gritty heat against my skin, but instead I just soaked it all up with my eyes.

'Positano,' Alfredo said a little later and I stared at the low wall and cluster of whitewashed houses to my right. The whole village was perched on the side of the cliff like a hanging basket: the road wound down towards the sea in tight hairpin bends.

'Hold on to your hats,' Gunella shrieked excitedly. 'We're going down.'

Jessica giggled and looked at Jack suggestively. He wiped the corners of his mouth with his thumb and forefinger and ignored her. As we drove down the steep hill Maud and Gunella slid off the leather seat and onto the dark-grey carpet.

'Oops,' Gunella said, scrambling back on to the seat.

Jack held out his hand for Maud and she gripped it and then seemed to sober up a little. 'Where are we?' she asked.

'Positano,' Jack told her.

Maud peered out the window. 'Where on earth is he going? Gunella, look out the window for God's sake and try to pay attention. Is this the right way to the villa? This is some sort of tourist hell.'

Alfredo came to a standstill in a small bustling square. A donkey was led past the window and Maud reared back.

Gunella laughed. 'We're in the village. Let's get out. We could go to a bar, Maud. There's a darling one overlooking the harbour.'

'I have no intention of going to a bar,' Maud said stiffly. 'I need to lie down. I'm exhausted.' She rapped on the driver's partition. 'You'll have to turn round,' she clipped. 'We're going the wrong way.'

'Back up to the top of the hill, my good man,' Gunella said. There was a click and the left passenger door opened and then banged shut. Jessica had scarpered.

'Where's she going?' Gunella asked, staring out the tinted window as Jessica ran down an alley-way.

Maud rolled her eyes. 'I knew it was a bad idea to bring Jessica. She's such a handful. You'll have to follow her, Jack.'

'Fine,' Jack said tightly. He picked up his rucksack. 'I'll meet you all back at the villa. I have the address.' He opened the door and climbed out.

'I'll help you,' I said, grabbing my handbag and climbing out after him. 'He doesn't have any Italian,' I added.

'Oh, for God's sake,' Maud said. 'He'll be fine. Get back in, Alice. I need you to unpack my bags.'

I pretended not to hear, running after Jack who had just disappeared round a corner in hot pursuit of Jessica.

'Alice!' Maud didn't sound impressed. 'Come back here.'

I felt like a child bunking off school. I turned and cupped my hand to my ear. 'Sorry, can't hear you.' And then I followed Jack. I could hear Alfredo's horn beep behind me, but I just kept running.

Chapter 21

Jack tapped his glass gently against mine. '*Cin, cin*. Here's to escaping. In more ways than one.' He took a sip of his rosé wine, his eyes resting on mine. I felt a shiver of excitement run up and down my spine. I still couldn't quite believe it. I was sitting on a quiet veranda under a midnight-blue Italian sky, drinking wine with my very cute, very single boss. Alone. And unless I was very much mistaken Jack was flirting with me. It was so peaceful here, the only noise was the easy bustle of the waiters at the work station behind us, polishing cutlery and glasses and chatting amiably, and the lapping of the sea in front of us. It was heavenly and with every sip of my wine I felt more and more relaxed.

It was hard to believe that only hours ago I had been in Dublin, my head fizzing with anxiety, giving frazzled instructions to Grace, in a last-minute panic about leaving Adam with her for three nights. I'd only just made the airport bus in Dun Laoghaire, standing in front of it and waving frantically as it pulled out.

'Do you think Jessica will get back to the villa in one piece?' I asked Jack. After a thorough search of the village, running down all the back streets calling her name, much to the amusement of the local 'lads' who called 'Jess-ee-ka, Jess-ee-ka' after us, we'd found her down at the small harbour, calmly chatting to a tall blond man.

'What are you guys doing here?' she'd said easily.

'Being your nursemaid,' Jack replied a little testily. He clicked a number into his mobile and handed it to her. 'Talk to Gunella, she's worried about you. Thinks you've been sold into white slavery.'

Jessica laughed. She walked away, spoke briefly to Gunella and then handed the mobile back to Jack. 'I'm going to get a taxi up to the villa later with Zane,' she said. 'He's dying to see the infinity pool. He's a medical student. From Texas.' She smiled at him. From the way Zane was looking at Jessica, it was more than the infinity pool he was after. But he seemed pleasant enough, and smiled back at her.

'That's right,' he said. 'I have ten days to do Europe. I'm off to Paris, France, tomorrow.' With his easy drawl and golden tan he was Matthew McConaughey's double.

'Isn't he sweet?' Jessica said. 'Then he's off to London, England. Anyway, Gunny said Maud's asleep, so they'll see both of you in the morning.'

It felt like a gift from the gods.

Jack and I had spent the late afternoon on the beach. We'd bought the cheapest swimming costumes we could find, which were still extortionately priced; Positano wasn't exactly the Costa del Sol when it came to shopping. Its narrow winding alleys held all kinds of expensive treats and surprises: a Gucci shop, a lingerie shop full of frothy lace creations, a shop selling arty silver jewellery.

From the look of the average tourist – Panama hats and linen shorts for the men, upmarket white linen dresses for the women, plus lots of Americans in their national costume: white runners, baseball caps, baggy shorts, university T-shirts and big, big cameras worn like Olympic medals – Positano wasn't your average package destination.

I'd insisted on buying the largest beach towel I could find, a bright red affair with a lobster on it, which at 42 euro was also the most expensive towel I'd ever owned. If I was going to change in front of Jack, I wanted as much coverage as possible. I shouldn't have worried. Ever the gentleman, he borrowed my towel and quickly pulled his new swimming shorts on, then ran down the beach, leaving me alone to change.

I was so glad I'd let Grace slather fake tan all over me, making my pale Irish skin a little less luminously white. I'd left my knickers on and put my arm across my breasts as she'd slapped on the acrid-smelling cream and rubbed it into my skin. She'd even made me exfoliate my knees, round my ankles and my elbows beforehand, ever the perfectionist.

As I eased my new swimsuit up my legs I admired my newly golden calves. The tan didn't quite hide the stretch marks on my thighs, but it helped. The swimsuit was cut a little differently to my own, but it seemed to fit all right. At least it covered my stomach even if it did plunge rather dramatically at the front.

I wrapped the towel round my body like a sari and moved Jack's bag and my clothes down the beach, dropping them on a white plastic sun lounger. Then I walked the few steps into the gentle surf at the edge of the water. It was cooler than I'd expected and it made my toes tingle, but as I was hot and sticky from travelling, it was delicious.

'Hey, Alice!' Jack waved. He was waist-deep in the water and I got a good look at his upper body, water dripping off his patch of black chest hair. In fact, Jack was surprisingly well built, with an almost washboard stomach. He hides that well under his work shirts, I thought. Normally I didn't like chest hair, it usually came hand in hand with a hairy back, but on Jack it looked just right.

'Are you coming in?' he said.

I realized I'd been staring at him. 'In a minute,' I said, willing him to turn away so I could run into the water without him seeing too much.

He turned and gave a few strokes, powering away from me. I quickly dumped the towel on the lounger and ran into the sea before he turned back. I waded deeper and then lurched forwards, shrieking a little as my chest hit the cool water.

I stood up, the water just under my breasts.

Jack was just in front of me, his eyes fixed on my chest.

I looked down. The swimsuit had shifted sideways, exposing my lily-white breasts to the world. I pulled the black material back over them, shaking my head. 'Sorry about that.'

He just laughed. 'Don't worry about it.'

'Race you to the blue boat,' I said, pointing to a small fishing boat to our right.

He won easily, even with my best splashy front crawl. We both held on to the side of the boat, catching our breath.

He surprised me by reaching a hand towards me and pushing my hair back off my face. 'I'm so glad you're here,' he said. 'It might just make the next two days bearable.'

After swimming we went for a walk, following the coast to the right, under a rocky arch and along the narrow coastal path. And there it was, Hotel Pupetto, a small hotel tucked into the side of the cliff, with its own private beach and restaurant overlooking the sea. Perfect.

And here we were still. And after a delicious pizza each and two bottles of wine, we were feeling no pain.

'Fancy a paddle?' Jack asked.

I nodded. He spoke to one of the waiters, grabbed the wine bottle by the neck and then offered me his hand.

'*Mia cara,*' he said.

'*Grazie molto!*'

'*Ah, parli italiano?*'

'*Solo un po.*' I smiled. 'Italian boyfriend. A long time ago. In London.'

We walked down the wooden steps towards the sea. The

beach was stony, but I threw off my flip flops anyway, and felt the warm stones under my feet.

'Alice, I hope you don't mind me asking, but how many boyfriends have you had exactly?'

I ignored his question and continued walking gingerly over the stones. Was he implying I was some sort of floozy?

'Sorry. Don't answer that,' he said, realizing he'd made me feel uneasy. 'I didn't mean it the way it came out. I'm just curious.'

'It's fine. A good few I suppose.' I shrugged. 'London is full of cute single men. Well, mostly single,' I added, remembering Roger, the married GP who'd told me he was on call just once too often. When his mobile was turned off one evening and I'd rung his house looking for him, his wife had answered the phone.

'What about Dublin?' Jack asked. 'Is it full of cute single men too?'

I gave a snort of laughter. 'Not exactly. Unless I've been missing something. But I haven't been back here all that long.'

'What brought you back?'

'Adam. I didn't have much of a support system in London. Grace lives over here and I needed her help.'

'I understand. But what about Adam's dad? Is he still around?'

'No. He's in London. He's not in the picture.'

'I'm sorry to hear that. Kids need their dads.'

'No, they don't!' I said a little too sharply. 'I mean, OK, yes, ideally it's nice for kids to have a mum *and* a dad, but life doesn't always work out that way.'

'I'm sorry, I didn't mean to sound judgemental.' He sighed. 'Look, there's something important—'

But I didn't want to hear it. 'Well, you are being judgemental. I loved Adam's dad, really, really loved him, but it wasn't enough. He rejected us. Both of us. I'm doing my best. I'm working my ass off just to keep my head above water. Do you think I want to be here, in fecking Italy with three rich cows who treat me like shit? I want to be with Adam.' I gave a snort. 'But if I don't keep this stupid job I won't get a mortgage and I won't get my own place and I'll be living with my sister for the rest of my life. How sad is that?' Tears ran down my cheeks and I wiped them away with my fingers. 'Now, if you'll just excuse me.' I walked quickly away from him, to the far end of the small beach, the sharp stones pricking into my soles, hurting me. But I didn't care. It took my mind off the hurt I felt inside. And the fact that I'd just made a complete fool of myself in front of Jack.

I sat down on a large rock and bent forwards, putting my head in my hands, the tears still flowing. I should have gone easy on the wine; my head was spinning a little.

'Alice?' I heard a crunch and looked up. Jack sat down on a stone beside me, staring out at the sea, the bottle of wine still in his hand.

'I'm so sorry. I'm such an idiot. I only said that because of Amelie.'

'Amelie? Who's Amelie?'

'My daughter.'

'Daughter? Are you serious?'

He nodded. 'She's six. I should have told you about her ages ago but . . .' he shrugged. 'To be honest, I didn't want you to think I was a pathetic single dad on the pull. Koo and Maud don't know about her. Unlike you, I wasn't brave enough to bring it up at the interview.'

'Why? Maud has children.'

'I wanted the job so badly. At the time I thought the board would see it as a disadvantage.'

'And you never said anything to Koo?'

'To Koo? No, why?'

'You two just seem close, that's all.' I paused. 'But they do know about Juliette?'

He stared out to sea. 'I told them about her at the interview. I thought it might win me a sympathy vote.'

I must have made a noise because he looked at me and added, 'I'm not proud of it. But it's the truth.'

'But why don't you tell them about Amelie now? I don't understand.'

'Because they'll think I've been lying by omission for two years, which I have. It's a bit of a mess.'

'I think you should come clean. Surely Amelie wants to see where her daddy works? And she could come to one of the hospital's fun days.'

He blew out his breath. 'It's too late. I know Maud and Koo. They'd always hold it against me.'

He'd obviously made up his mind.

'Just think about it,' I said gently.

'I will.'

'Anyway, tell me about Amelie. Where's she in school? Does she like it?'

As he talked about his daughter, his eyes sparkled. He was clearly a devoted dad. He showed me a picture of her, stored on his mobile. She looked just like him, apart from her cute button nose, piercing dark blue eyes and long dark hair held out of her eyes with two sparkling clips. As I listened, I thought about Adam. I wondered absently if Jack could feel the same way about a stepson. I tried to block the thought from my mind, but I couldn't help it. Jack was right, children needed a dad and I'd failed Adam in that respect.

When Jack stopped talking we sat in silence for a little while. Then he said, 'Want some?' and handed me the bottle of wine.

I took a gulp, spluttering as it went down the wrong way. Jack patted me on the back.

'Are you OK?'

'No!' I wailed. 'I'm a sloppy drunk and I'm always crying.' I pressed my fingers against my eye sockets to stop the tears, but it was no use. 'I'm sorry, I'm a mess.'

He put his arms round me.

'Come here,' he said into my hair. 'You're not a mess, you're wonderful.'

'What?' I hiccupped through my tears. 'You must be crazy. Or on drugs. Are you on drugs?'

He laughed and drew back a little. 'No. There's just something about you. The way you smile.' He pushed my hair back off my face. 'The way you hide behind your hair when you're embarrassed. The way you blush.'

I pressed my fingers into my cheeks and groaned. 'I hate that. It's pathetic.'

'It's sweet. And I love the fact that every day is like a new adventure for you. You still have hope.'

'What's the alternative?' I asked, rubbing my eyes. I'd stopped crying, thank goodness. 'To give up?'

He shrugged. 'Some people do.'

'How do they go on, then?'

'Maybe they have a kid, that's a good enough reason for getting up in the morning. Or maybe they just don't have the courage to stop it all; so they just crawl along, day by day until they die.'

'That's very cheery, Jack. Thanks.'

He gave a laugh. 'Sorry. I can get a little morbid at times. But I'm just saying, not everyone has your hope. You're lucky.'

'I don't feel very lucky.'

He smiled, his eyes creasing at the edges. 'You also listen to people. Even Maud likes you. And that's saying something.'

'She has a funny way of showing it.'

'Maud has her own problems. And Koo doesn't have a bad word to say about you.'

'Koo likes you too,' I said. '*Really* likes you.' I'd been keeping it in all evening but now I couldn't help myself.

He stared down at his hands. 'She told you.'

'About Portugal? Yes.'

He blew out his breath. 'It should never have happened. I came back from running one evening and she was waiting for me in the hall. I was hot and sweaty and dying for a shower but she pounced on me. I should have pushed her away, but I didn't. When she's got her mind set on something it's hard to say no. I hadn't been with anyone since my wife and I guess I wanted things to move on. I wanted to feel something again, anything.'

'Was it just the once?'

He shook his head. 'No. It happened a few times, but only in Portugal. On the night before we left I told her it had to stop. I felt terrible about Mac. She seemed to accept that.'

'But you still did it, knowing about Mac?'

'Yes.' He stared down at his hands. 'And I still feel guilty about it.'

'And what about Koo? Does she feel the same way or is she expecting another holiday fling?' I didn't want to break Koo's confidence, but I had to know.

He ran his hands through his hair. 'No. It's over. I made that very clear in Portugal. It was a mistake. The sex was good, but that was it.'

'I'm glad the sex was good,' I muttered. 'Bully for you.'

'Please don't be like that, Alice. We all make mistakes. Haven't you ever slept with someone and regretted it?'

'I suppose,' I said grudgingly, thinking about Roger. 'But maybe you'd better talk to Koo as soon as she gets here, make it absolutely clear that it's not going to happen again.'

He nodded. 'That's a good idea. I will.'

'Promise?'

'Yes. Now's please let's stop talking about Koo and talk about us instead.

'Us?'

'Yes. Us, you and me. Is there any chance we could . . . you know . . .' He shrugged. 'Maybe I could take you out to dinner when we get back?'

I was so startled I couldn't say a thing. My mind went into overdrive. Jack liked me; it wasn't just wishful thinking on my part. He really liked me.

'No,' he continued, taking my silence for rejection, 'of course not. What would you want with someone like me? Of course you're not interested. Ignore me.' He stood up and wiped his hands on the back of his jeans. 'I've been completely stupid.' He seemed horribly embarrassed. 'I guess we'd better order a taxi. I hope they can find the place, I don't fancy ringing for directions and waking Gunella from her beauty sleep.'

'You haven't been stupid.' I jumped up and stood facing him. 'Dinner would be lovely. In fact, dinner *was* lovely and I'd like to do it again.'

He grinned. I put my hand up and stroked the side of his cheek, brushing back his hair. 'And stop hiding behind your hair,' I added.

He leaned forward and pressed his lips against mine, his light stubble grazing my chin a little. His kiss was gentle yet firm and unleashed a rush of endorphins so strong that my knees went weak and I nearly lost my balance. He put his hands on my waist and steadied me.

'Thanks,' I whispered.

'It's a pity it's so rocky,' he said. 'I can't throw you down on the sand and ravish you.'

Ravish? I liked the sound of that. I pulled his shirt up and ran my hands over his back. 'We could always get a room,' I suggested boldly.

He smiled at me. 'Good thinking, Batman. Wait here.' He

strode towards the veranda and I watched as he spoke to one of the waiters. Minutes later he came back dangling a key on a finger, our bags slung over his shoulder, my sandals in his other hand. 'One of the beach-house rooms is free. They're bringing down another bottle of wine and some dessert. I hope you like *gelato al limone*.'

'Absolutely. Especially with that accent. Say it again.'

'*Gelato, gelato, gelato*. See that small white building over there,' he pointed, 'that's the beach house. We have our own private terrace too.' I winced as I followed him, the stones biting into my bare soles.

'Let me help you.' He scooped me up into his arms and I shrieked with delight, feeling like a Mills and Boon heroine.

'You'll do your back in,' I warned.

'It's worth it.'

Chapter 22

I was woken in the early hours of the morning by a strange noise – bangs, clicks and cheerful-sounding shouts. Then it suddenly dawned on me. I wasn't in Dublin, I was in Italy, in a beach house, with Jack. No rainy Irish weather, no Adam, no work. The noise outside was the staff putting out the sun loungers on the hotel's private beach.

Then I had a horrible thought and I opened my eyes. Maud! My heart began to race. What the hell were we going to tell Maud?

I looked at Jack; he was sleeping soundly on his back, one arm thrown above his head. He looked so peaceful. I wanted to kiss him, but after last night I wasn't sure where I stood.

You see, in the end, Jack had rejected me just like every other bloody man in my life. He'd done it in the nicest way possible of course, and his reasons were sound, but he'd still rejected me. It had hurt at the time and it still hurt now. Not to mention the embarrassment factor.

We'd stumbled into bed after our ice cream and a bottle of dessert wine, our mouths clashing, our tongues exploring. I'd ripped his shirt off, then unbuckled his belt and started to unbutton his jeans.

'Are you sure?' he'd asked quietly. I'd just pulled the denim down roughly and smiled at the growing bulge in his boxer shorts. Then I'd crawled down the bed, and started to lick him, slowly at first, using both my hands to cradle his balls. He moaned.

'Alice,' he said, his voice tight with desire, 'come here.' But I ignored him and continued until I felt the familiar lukewarm sensation at the back of my throat. 'Just like bursting a warm cherry tomato in your mouth,' Grace had told me back in our teenage days when I quizzed her incessantly about such things.

Jack had lain quite still for several minutes, his heart thumping madly in his chest, his eyes tight shut. Finally he opened them and said, 'That was incredible. You're incredible.'

I'd excused myself to rinse my mouth out in the white-tiled bathroom.

When I'd come back, he was lying in bed with the sheet pulled up to his waist. I stripped, trying to look as tantalizing as I could, holding in my stomach and wishing yet again I was wearing decent underwear. At least it was dark, the only light a pale glow from the moon outside seeping through the shutters. I hopped under the sheet in my bra and knickers.

'Would it be OK if I just held you?' he'd said. Presuming he was joking, I'd taken off my bra and leapt on top of him, smothering his lips with kisses and rubbing my body up and down his, my nipples caressing his hairy chest.

'I think we should wait,' he'd said, holding my waist firmly as I started to whip his chest with my hair. 'Did you hear me, Alice?'

Oh, I'd heard him all right, but I was ignoring him. I snaked my hand down his stomach but he grabbed it and pulled it up again.

'I'd like to wait,' he said again. 'There are things we need—'

'OK, OK, I get it,' I said, sitting back on my hunkers and

staring at him through my curtain of hair. 'Thanks for the blow job but you can fuck off now.'

'It's not like that.'

I snorted. 'You weren't exactly complaining.'

'I wasn't given the chance. Lie down beside me; I want to tell you something.'

I did as he asked, my arms crossed stiffly across my chest.

'I don't have any condoms,' he whispered.

My tension lifted a little. 'Maybe they have them at reception.'

He laughed. 'I'm not going to ask at reception.'

I sat up. 'I'll do it then.'

He pushed me back down. 'I know it's frustrating, but there's no rush. Maybe it's a sign that we should wait.'

I snorted grumpily, but he added, 'I want you to close your eyes and try to relax. Imagine you're lying at the edge of the ocean, on a tropical beach. The warm waves are lapping at your toes and moving up your legs. Very, very slowly.' His hand snaked up my legs and towards my inner thighs. It was delicious.

'Now turn over,' he said in a wonderfully smooth voice. This was more like it. Of course he wanted sex, he was a man, wasn't he? He obviously couldn't resist my womanly charms. Any minute now he'd be sprinting outside to beg one of the waiters for a condom.

'The water's moving up and up.' I gasped as his fingers grazed my buttocks. 'You have such beautiful smooth skin; it's like a baby's.'

My nerve endings were all dancing a tango and I tried to keep still. I could hear my blood thumping in my ears. His fingers stroked my back, smoothly and firmly. I reared my bum up a little, willing him on. But his hands stayed firmly on my back.

'Try to relax,' he said.

'I'd be a lot more relaxed if I had a bloody orgasm,' I muttered into the pillow.

'What?'

'Nothing, nothing.'

He started to massage my shoulders, rubbing away the knots of tension with his strong fingers. I began to sink into the mattress, deeper and deeper, my stress melting away.

The next thing I knew it was morning.

He opened his eyes. 'Hi, gorgeous,' he said giving me a warm smile.

Kiss me, I willed him. Kiss me. I was about to move my head nearer to his to give him a little hint, but then I remembered I hadn't brushed my teeth last night and my breath probably smelt of stale garlic and wine. Not to mention . . . the less said about that the better. I could feel my cheeks burn at the very thought of it.

'It's ten to eight,' I said, lifting my eyebrows. 'Maud said breakfast at eight sharp. I'll leave it to you to explain why our beds weren't slept in.'

He groaned and hit his head against the pillow. I sat up and pulled the sheet round me like a toga, exposing his rather magnificent erection, poking through the front of his boxer shorts like an erotic Jack in the box.

'Sorry,' he said sheepishly, grabbing a pillow to cover it up.

'What a waste,' I said.

'Excuse me?' he asked.

'Nothing,' I said. I gave a small nervous cough. Why was the morning after always so awkward, or was it just me? And we hadn't even *had* sex. 'I'm just going to have a quick shower.'

He grinned at me, and there went the eye creases again, along with my heart. 'Can I join you?' he asked.

And see me in the nip in broad daylight? Was he mad? I put

one hand on my hip. 'Why that would just be improper, Mr Wiseheart. You *are* my boss.'

As I closed the door behind me I heard him give a belly laugh.

Chapter 23

An hour later I was in Maud's dressing room in Villa Positano, a smaller bedroom she'd seconded for her clothes. Jack had obviously managed to cobble together some sort of plausible explanation, as she didn't say anything about last night's absence. In fact Maud was her usual self.

'Fold the tissue paper *neatly*, Alice,' she said in a this-is-so-tiresome voice. She was wafting about the room in a white linen dressing gown. When she stood in front of the window the material became see-through and I was trying to avert my eyes from her almost skeletal frame. At least she was wearing knickers. 'You'll need to reuse it when you're packing on Saturday. Please iron my white linen shirt, it's appallingly creased. Ask the housekeeper for the ironing board.'

'Maybe she'll do the ironing,' I suggested. I'm terrible at ironing and I didn't want to scorch one of Maud's expensive shirts.

Maud gave a deep sigh. 'I wouldn't trust her, she looks shifty. No, you do it. And when you're finished come and find me. After my shower I'll be having a meeting with Gunella on the veranda.' She'd already found a swimsuit after a rummage in one of the smaller suitcases and she'd made me lay it out for her on her bed. Her bedroom was just down the hall, past the palatial marble bathroom with its huge sunken bath.

The bedroom she was actually sleeping in wasn't huge but

it was like walking into a snowdrift. Pure white, from the walls and shutters, to the furniture and the heavenly sheets, which felt like silk. Grace would have been impressed, she was always going on about thread count – Villa Positano's were probably in the millions judging by the feel.

'I'll see you when you've finished.' Maud gave me a curt nod and walked out of the room, her dressing gown wafting after her like a bride's train.

I unwrapped Maud's three suitcases of clothes from their tissue-paper packages and arranged them in neat piles on the bed. To make it more bearable I pretended I was Grace on Christmas Day, carefully opening her presents (as I always ripped the paper off it wasn't a good idea to pretend to be me!). Halfway through the job, I heard voices outside. I stood against the wall and stuck my head out the window.

Gunella was lying on a 1950s style wooden sun lounger just below me, basting herself with sun oil. Jessica was sitting a few inches away from her in a skimpy white crochet bikini, her eyes hidden behind enormous sunglasses with silver frames that looked like something out of *Star Trek*. Maud was sitting at the far side of the pool, fanning herself under the shade of a big red sun umbrella. She was wearing the black Hermès swimsuit I'd laid out for her, a huge and very glamorous floppy white sun hat, and silver sandals with six-inch heels.

'Gunny, can we go to Antigua next time?' Jessica whined. She turned over on the padded cushion of the sun lounger, squashing her flat stomach and fried-egg breasts against the white linen. She kicked her legs up and crossed them at the ankles, a thin gold chain sliding down her calves. 'I mean really. The pool here is tiny. And there's no one decent to shag. Zane was a real disappointment; those preppy American boys are very repressed. I'm so boooored.'

'Shush,' Gunella warned. 'Maud will hear you. Just try to be polite.'

Jessica wriggled her body; she seemed fractious. 'So what if she does? We can't go to the beach, it's filthy and full of Italians, not to mention English tourists in their bloody Panama hats and creased linen suits. And that's just the women. They've all been watching far too many movies. That *Talented Mr Ripley* has a lot to answer for.' She sighed deeply. 'Positano is hardly the exclusive resort you made it out to be, Gunny. Don't know why I bothered.'

Gunella sighed. 'What's not to like? Just relax and top up your tan. You're such a spoilt brat sometimes.'

Jessica muttered what sounded suspiciously like, 'Fuck off, granny,' under her breath.

'Just look at this place.' Gunella waved her hand in an arc. Her sweep took in the miniature palms in their ceramic pots, the mirror-shiny Travertine marble patio and pool surround, the hot-pink and turquoise silk curtains which wafted at every ground-floor window, making the whole place look like an exotic Indian bazaar. Gunella was right, the Villa Positano was sheer heaven.

'Suppose it's OK.' Jessica clearly wasn't convinced. She rolled over, and propped her chest up with her arms. Her bikini bottoms were still damp from her quick dip in the pool, the outline of her carefully shorn pubic hair a dark shadow beneath the crocheted material. She arched her spine, planted a leg on either side of the lounger and threw her head back, her mouth falling open. Then she thrust her lower jaw forward and closed it, jutting her teeth over her top lip.

'What in God's name are you doing?' Gunella asked her.

'It's a yoga pose. Good for stress. Called the lion or something.'

'You look ridiculous. And close your legs for heaven's sake. Fabrizio, the waiter, is ogling you.'

'Really? How super. Is he fit?' she asked, perking up. She sat up, tossed her head and sucked in her already surfboard-flat stomach. Gunella was right. A rather tasty waiter was giving her a deliciously evil eye from the door of the pool house. He was tall and muscular, with dark olive skin. A Celtic bracelet tattoo peeped out from the bottom of his left shirt sleeve and one of his eyebrows was pierced.

'A bad boy, fabarooney!' Jessica said in a low voice.

'*Jessica*,' Gunella hissed. 'Behave yourself.'

He walked towards them, holding a round silver tray. It tinkled with glasses full of crushed ice drenched in a dark pink liquid. 'A morning Puccini, ladies?'

Jessica beamed at him, then rested the tip of her tongue on the upper lip of her generous mouth. 'Yummy! You are a darling,' she cooed.

His gaze rested on her chest. From the wanton look in his eyes, he was clearly a big fan of her au natural breasts. Jessica reached out a hand to take a glass, her skin purposefully grazing his. '*Grazie mille*. I'm Jessica and you are . . .'

'Alice!' Maud hissed. 'What the hell are you doing?'

I jumped and stepped back from the window.

'I was just checking the weather,' I said nervously.

She glared at me. 'I want you to accidentally tip this over Jessica,' she said.

I must have looked a bit sceptical, because she said, 'Now!' so sharply it almost cut me. I grabbed the glass of what looked like iced water out of her hand, ran over to the window and hurled it down.

The chilly liquid hit Jessica on the chest. She immediately screamed, 'Oh, for fuck's sake!' and leapt up, brushing shards of ice off her stomach. The waiter, sensing trouble, walked quickly away without looking round.

'You!' Jessica scowled up at me. 'What are you playing at? Are you simple?'

'Sorry, I tripped,' I said. 'But it's only water.'

'Water?' Jessica laughed nastily. 'It smells like pure gin to me. Aren't you supposed to be working? I thought you were Maud's maid or something.' She narrowed her eyes.

Maid? I opened my mouth to say something, but before I had a chance Maud appeared beside me, her hands clutching the top of the metal balcony. 'Alice *is* working. She's taking a red-wine stain out of a lace bra with iced gin. It's an old laundry woman's trick that has been handed down through the generations. Not that I'd expect you to know anything about brassieres, Jessica, you hardly need one. Or family tradition for that matter.' She looked the younger woman up and down sniffily.

'Gunny!' Jessica said. 'Are you going to let her talk to me like that?'

Gunella just smiled at her sister. 'You're asking for trouble if you mess with Fabrizio.'

Jessica scowled. 'Oh, for Gawd's sake, what's the problem? I was only talking to the man.' Jessica stood up, flounced towards the pool and jumped in feet first, her slim frame hardly making a splash.

I stared at Maud. 'Can you really use gin as a stain remover?'

She gave a hollow laugh. 'I have no idea. Now I'll be busy for a while and I don't want to be disturbed. Understand?'

'In here you mean?'

'Not in here, Alice,' she said wearily. 'This is my dressing room. I'll be in my bedroom. And please do get on with my unpacking. We're going to Capri later this afternoon and I'll need my white palazzo pants, my white linen shirt and my brown and cream Chanel sandals with the block heel.'

I felt like saluting her, but stopped myself. 'Yes, Maud,' I said curtly. 'Whatever you say, Maud.'

She looked at me a little crookedly but decided to let it slide. 'And ask the housekeeper to organize some nibbles and plenty of wine to take on the boat. White. Chilled. And champagne.'

'What kind of nibbles?'

She waved her hand in the air. 'Olives, prosciutto, oysters, lobster, quails' eggs, anything like that. You decide.'

Just as well I'd asked, nibbles in our house meant cocktail sausages and Ritz crackers with cheese spread.

As I walked down the stairs to talk to Nadia, the house-keeper, and to find Jack and complain about being treated like a servant, I bumped into Fabrizio. He was bounding up the stairs and gave me a wide grin, his white teeth setting off his bronze tan. God, he was stunning. I could feel my cheeks heating up.

'You Alice,' he said. 'Jack tell me about you.' He puffed out his chest like an ape and pointed to it. 'I Fabrizio.'

'Hi,' I said, a little flustered.

'I see you later, yes, on boat? You go to Capri?'

'I think so.'

'Capri is beautiful.' He kissed his fingers with a smacking noise. 'Good for lovers.' He smiled at me again, a wicked glint in his eyes and then continued up the stairs.

I lingered, wondering exactly where he was going. Maud was the only person staying on that floor. Gunella and Jessica were on the second floor, Jack and I on the ground floor. But he waited at the top of the stairs, still smiling at me. He waved me away with his hand and then put his finger to his lips as he walked down the corridor and stopped outside Maud's bedroom door.

Finally the penny dropped. The whole business with Jessica. Fabrizio and Maud. My mouth dropped open. Villa Positano was hopping with hormones. I hoped it would have the same effect on Jack.

After seeing Nadia, I went back upstairs to finish unpacking Maud's clothes. I tried not to think about what was going on in her bedroom. After a few minutes curiosity got the better of me and I went into the bathroom and pressed my ear against the wall, but I couldn't hear anything through the marble except rather sad and mournful opera. It sounded like *Madam Butterfly*. I tried holding a glass against the wall, like they do in films, but it didn't work. Coming out of the bathroom, Jack startled me.

'What are you up to?' he asked. 'You look very shifty.'

I shushed him, then grabbed his arm and pulled him into Maud's dressing room. 'Fabrizio's in her bedroom,' I whispered.

He grinned. 'Apparently they were at it last night too.'

'Who told you that?'

'Fabrizio himself. He's that kind of guy. Pity, he's definitely Koo's type.'

'Which is?'

'Up for it.' Then he realized what he'd said. 'Sorry, I didn't mean . . . you're different, Alice. Koo's . . .'

'It's fine,' I said through tight lips. 'Forget it.' I busied myself by folding up the white tissue paper, taking more care than was strictly necessary. He sat down on the bed beside Maud's small towers of clothes and ran his hand over a cream jumper.

'Don't get that dirty,' I said. 'It's cashmere.' I took it off the top of the pile of jumpers, gave it a shake and thrust a wooden coat hanger into its neck.

'Maud likes her jumpers on shelves,' he said mildly. 'Says they stretch on hangers.'

I glared at him.

'I'm just saying.'

'Well don't. And how on earth do you know that anyway?'

He shrugged. 'Floss I think.'

Maybe he'd been involved with his last assistant fund-raiser too; he talked about her a lot. Maybe I was just the next in line. God, I was so stupid. 'Hanging them is just fine,' I snapped. I'd come over grumpy all of a sudden. Jack and Floss, sexual frustration and the fact that I'd become Maud's skivvy, all combined to make me feel very ratty indeed. I picked up the second jumper, a sky-blue one, and gave it a hanger too. Then peppermint green. Jack just watched me.

'How many jumpers does one woman need?' he asked. 'We're only here for two more days and it's not exactly cold.' He stood up. 'Let me help you.' He picked up a white silk draw-string bag and pulled out a lacy purple bra. He put it up against his chest. 'Does it suit me?'

I snatched it out of his hands. 'Look, about last night . . .' I began, wanting to get it over with and needing some answers.

'Yes?' He cocked an eyebrow.

'Stop looking at me like that.'

'Like what?'

'Like you've seen me naked. Just stop, OK?' I could feel my cheeks burn. I turned away and hung one of Maud's silk dresses on the rail.

Jack stood behind me and put his hands round my waist. Then he put his chin on my shoulder. He smelt fresh, like the sea. He was obviously just out of the shower. 'Alice?'

'Yes?'

'Just breathe. I know Maud can be difficult and I know you're not exactly enjoying being her personal maid, but we'll have the whole evening to ourselves.'

I was glad my back was turned. 'Are you making fun of me?'

'Why would I do that?'

'Jack—' I began.

'Alice!' It was Maud. 'What on earth are you doing?' she demanded.

I jumped away from Jack as if I'd been scalded and banged my head on the edge of a wooden coat hanger, sending the rest of them clattering.

I turned. Maud was standing in front of us in her dressing gown, her hands on her hips, her cheeks flushed. This time she wasn't wearing any knickers. I noticed with a shock that she'd gone Brazilian and I winced. But there was something there, a dark shape, a familiar shape. My God, it looked like a boot. Italy! Wasn't that a bit footballers' wives?

'Alice?' she said again.

'Sorry,' I said, dragging my eyes away. 'Jack was helping me with—'

But Maud interrupted me. 'Why are my jumpers on hangers? They'll get all stretched. Oh, Alice, have you never dealt with cashmere before?' She sounded so disappointed and disapproving.

I'd had enough. Of Jack, of Maud, of everything. 'No!' I practically shouted at her. 'I don't own any cashmere jumpers, Maud. Or linen trousers, or silk dresses.' I flicked my hand over a polka-dot dress and it fluttered at my touch. 'Or Gucci shoes or Prada shirts. I have absolutely no designer clothes to my name.'

'But your Louboutins,' Maud said. 'And your suits.'

'All borrowed. I wanted to make a good impression. I'm doing my best here, but I don't have a degree in luxury fabrics and I've never worked in Benetton. Maybe you'd be better off with someone who does own cashmere jumpers, like that Flossy person you're all so obsessed with. Because clearly I'm not good enough for either you or your precious wardrobe.' I wasn't finished. 'Here's a novel idea,' I went on, 'you could travel light or even, and don't faint, Maud, pack and unpack your own clothes like the rest of us mere mortals. Now, if you'll excuse me.' I brushed past Jack and went towards the door. In the hall I stopped and shouted back, 'And it wouldn't hurt you to say thank you once in a while.'

'Alice!' Maud shouted after me. 'Alice, you're . . .'

But I was halfway down the stairs and I couldn't hear the rest of her sentence. But I didn't have to. I knew what she was going to say. 'You're fired.'

Chapter 24

In fact I was wrong. Jack found me in my room, throwing Petra's carefully chosen clothes into my suitcase.

'What are you doing?' he asked, standing just inside the door, his hand on the crystal door knob.

'What does it look like?' I blew out my breath. 'I'm such an idiot.' I shook my head. 'I should never have come on this trip in the first place; what was I thinking? I knew I'd be found out.'

'What are you talking about?'

'My whole CV was a fabrication.' I explained to him what Grace had done, exaggerating my qualifications, from the beer promotions to scraping a pass in my Leaving Cert. As it all came tumbling out I felt smaller and smaller.

'So you tweaked your job descriptions a bit,' he said. 'Is that what you're saying?'

'Yes.'

'At least you didn't lie. And your referees were both very complimentary.'

I cringed. 'They're friends of my sisters.'

He just smiled. 'Better than using enemies I always say.'

He was taking this very well.

'But I don't even like the theatre,' I blurted out, determined to tell him everything. 'Apart from musicals, I love musicals.'

'And the Polish?' he asked.

I shrugged. 'I do have some Polish. But I only have a few words of Slovakian and Czech. *Ahoj.*'

'Excuse me?'

'*Ahoj*. It's "hi" in Slovakian.'

'It's more than anyone else has.' He smiled at me gently. 'So you exaggerated. Everyone tries to make themselves look good on their CV. That's normal. You did a great interview, Alice, that's why we chose you because we thought you'd be the best person for the job.'

'But that wasn't me,' I explained. 'At the interview I mean. Grace groomed me for days, asking me test questions, drilling the correct answers into me. All that Beckett stuff, that was Grace.'

He laughed. 'Looking back, it does seem a little out of character, but it impressed Maud. And she loved your suit, she mentioned it several times.'

'Don't you see? Even my suit was fake. I don't own any decent suits so I had to borrow one from my friend Petra. She owns a second-hand designer shop.'

'And the shoes with the red soles?'

'Petra's too. I'm one big lie from top to toe. You have every right to fire me. So go on, break it to me and I'll get out of your hair for good.'

'What are you talking about? I'm not going to fire you.'

'You're not?'

He shook his head. 'No. And Maud said to say that you're right. She wants to talk to you. She's waiting for you in her dressing room.'

I felt a wave of nausea. I couldn't face Maud. Not after being so rude to her.

'I can't,' I wailed.

'Of course you can. She wants to apologize. I suggest you let her. If you want to hold on to your job that is.'

Rosewood Cottage flashed in front of my eyes. Rosewood

Cottage after I'd cleaned up the front garden, planted pink climbing roses round the front door. If I could just hold down this job for two more months . . .

'Yes,' I said softly. 'Yes, I do.'

My heart was hammering in my chest as I walked up the stairs. Jack was just behind me. He'd promised to stand outside the door, to give me moral support.

'Can't you come in with me?' I'd pleaded.

He'd shaken his head. 'No. Maud wants to talk to you alone.'

I took a deep breath to calm my nerves and knocked on the door.

'Come in.'

I walked in and was surprised to find Maud with a coat hanger in her hand. She picked up a red chiffon sun dress, shook it out and then hung it up.

'Don't look so shocked,' she said. 'Sit down.' She gestured at the chair in front of the dressing table. I turned it to face her. She sat down on the bed. Most of her clothes were now hanging in the wardrobe.

She looked down at her hands for a moment and then caught my eye. 'I owe you an apology. You're quite right; I always pack far too many clothes. I like to cover every eventuality; it's a nervous habit I suppose.'

She stared out the window and continued. 'I used to work in Brown Thomas, you know. In the designer rooms. I was a shop assistant before I met Nick. Happiest days of my life. I was completely broke of course, but I always had the most beautiful clothes, even then. The designers used to give me their samples. It was wonderful. I suppose I've always taken nice clothes for granted. I'm sorry if you feel I've been rubbing your nose in it, Alice, I honestly didn't mean to. I know you probably don't have the same,' she gave a little cough, 'allowance for clothes as I do.'

I must have wrinkled my nose because she quickly added, 'I don't mean to sound crass. I know what it's like to be on a tight budget. At least I used to. What I'm trying to say is that I'm sorry. I do appreciate you, even if I don't always say it. Please don't leave me, I mean, us. You can consider yourself relieved of packing duty. I'll get Nadia to help. Even if she does have shifty eyes.'

'Thanks.' I didn't know quite what else to say.

'So you'll stay?'

'I suppose so.'

'And Alice?'

'Yes?'

'That black Prada suit, the one you wore at the interview? It used to be mine.'

'What?' I said, confused.

'Magda brings all my old clothes to some sort of shop in Blackrock where they sell them on. I had the buttons changed to match a pair of shoes. I'd know that suit anywhere. Wore it several times. If you'd like any more of my cast offs,' she continued, oblivious to my discomfort, 'you could have a rummage through the bags before Magda drops them off. I always donate the money to St Jude's. But giving them to you would also be charity, wouldn't it?'

She just couldn't help herself. And to think I had just given her the benefit of the doubt.

'Thank you, Maud,' I said through gritted teeth, 'but that won't be necessary.' Think of Rosewood, I told myself grimly. Two more months. Two more bloody months.

'Where's Jessica?' Maud demanded at four o'clock. The trip to Capri had been delayed because of the stifling afternoon heat. If you opened your mouth you could almost take a bite out of the heavy air – I'd tried, making Jack laugh. We'd spent a very pleasant afternoon together drifting at the shady end of the pool. Maud, Gunella and Jessica had taken an afternoon siesta after their rather boozy lunch. Jack and I had shared some cold meats and cheese in the cool basement kitchen with Fabrizio and Nadia. Fabrizio had run off as soon as his mobile bleeped.

'My mistress calls,' he'd said with a grin. Nadia didn't seem all that amused. It turned out they were brother and sister and she didn't approve of his dalliance with Maud. Working at the villa was a cushy job, she explained, and Fabrizio was jeopardizing everything. 'Ruled by his trouser snake,' she'd said, making me laugh.

But now the heat was starting to wane so it was all systems go.

'Well, where is she?' Maud asked again, looking round the enormous living room as if she'd find her hiding under one of the huge white sofas.

'She's gone to bed with a touch of sun stroke,' Gunella said.

Maud pressed her lips together and bit the inside of her cheek. 'We'll have to go without her then. Everyone set?'

I smiled to myself. This was like some sort of military operation. We were only going on a short boat trip to Capri. On a luxury motor cruiser no less.

'Alice, have you got the bags?' Maud demanded. 'And the cooler boxes?'

'Excuse me?' I spluttered. She was treating me like a servant again and I wasn't having it.

'I have the food and the wine covered,' Jack said smoothly, giving me a wink. 'And Fabrizio will bring the bags down now.'

'He's taking his time.' Maud clipped towards the staircase in her Chanel sandals, megaphoned her hands and bellowed, 'FABRIZIO.'

No answer.

'Maybe he's outside,' Gunella suggested.

Maud walked outside and tried again. 'FABRIZIO!' We all followed her.

'I'll start packing the car,' Jack said. I stood under the portico in the shade, Gunella by my side as Jack swung open the boot of the silver Mercedes jeep.

Fabrizio came out of the pool room, tucking his shirt into his trousers.

'About time,' Maud said.

'Sorry, I fell asleep,' he said. He ran his hand through his tousled hair.

'Bags,' Maud said, her eyes flinty. He went up the stairs and came down with the bags slung over his back, like a pack mule. Jack and I helped him fill the boot with the bags and the cool boxes. Maud and Gunella just stood there, watching us work. I glared at them, but Jack caught my eye.

'You won't change them,' he whispered. 'Just let it wash over you.'

'How very Zen,' I murmured.

He smiled.

As Fabrizio helped Maud into the front seat of the jeep (you'd swear she was ninety from the way she was carrying on) Jessica tumbled out of the pool house looking slightly dazed, her hair standing out thick and wild, like a lion's mane.

'What the hell was she doing in there?' Maud glared at Fabrizio.

He looked at Maud defiantly, but said nothing.

'Do that again and I will insist Gunella fires you,' Maud told him succinctly. 'You *and* your sister, do you understand?'

He nodded curtly.

Jessica appeared beside the jeep, a white see-through kaftan thrown over her bikini bottoms.

'You seem to have forgotten to get properly dressed,' Maud said. 'Or did you leave your bikini top in the pool room?'

Unperturbed, Jess said, 'I'm not sure. Fabrizio, have you seen my bikini top?'

He opened his mouth to say something but Maud interrupted, 'Fabrizio, you're coming with us. Go and get changed. Do you have anything decent to wear?'

Fabrizio stared at her without blinking. 'Maud, I'm Italian.' He flounced off, Jessica gazing longingly at his bottom.

'Maybe I'll come too,' Jessica said.

'There's not enough room in the jeep,' Maud said. 'You're staying right here.'

'Gunny!' Jessica whined. 'That's not fair.'

Gunella shrugged. 'I did warn you not to mess with Fabrizio.'

Chapter 25

The *Elenora* was an amazing boat. As soon as I stepped on to the wide platform at the back of the huge motor cruiser belonging to Gunella's family, I felt like Princess Caroline of Monaco. I stared at the cabin's luxurious interior, the built-in curving leather sofas, the mahogany drinks cabinet, the green-felt card table, the spotless cream carpet.

Soon we were powering away from the marina towards the island of Capri. The multi-talented Fabrizio was at the helm and Jack and I were sitting to his right. We were outside on the flying bridge, perched above the cabin, the warm salty air whipping our faces and tangling our hair. Well, my hair to be more strictly accurate; Fabrizio's dark crop was so short it looked sprayed on, like an Action Man doll's hair. Jack looked great in a white T-shirt and khaki shorts, showing lots of strong and acceptably hairy leg.

I'd picked my outfit carefully. Petra had given me clothes for every eventuality and I was wearing a red cotton sun dress over white pedal pushers, teamed with neat white Keds. They had been filthy before Grace bunged them in the washing machine along with all kinds of sinister-looking bleaching products, but now they gleamed.

Maud and Gunella were lying on the deep leather seats on the back deck, Maud in the shade of the boat's awning, Gunella baking in the late-afternoon sun.

We passed a cluster of houses dangling over the sea. Some had arches covered in frothy dark pink bougainvillea; others had ancient-looking stone walls, held together by their thick carpets of ivy.

After a few minutes we stopped coast-crawling and Fabrizio turned the boat's bow towards the open water. As we gained speed her nose lifted out of the water and I shrieked as he opened the throttle and the *Elenora* powered into action, growling like a grizzly bear. I usually wasn't much of a speed fiend, but this was different, exhilarating, the throb of the engine under my bum, the warm air pinning my body against the back of the seat.

'There it is,' Jack shouted over the engine's drone. 'Capri.' He pointed at land in the distance. I squinted and watched as the island got bigger and bigger.

A little later we could see the busy harbour of the Marina Grande and Fabrizio slowed the boat, until her bow nestled back in the water. We were surrounded by boats of all shapes and sizes: small ferry boats packed with tourists clutching cameras; traditional wooden boats zipping away from a thin wooden quay; power boats dodging the swimmers.

I looked down; there was a thin film of rainbow-coloured oil on the water just beside us and I wondered if it was really suitable for swimming. It didn't seem to be stopping anyone; the beach to the far left of the harbour was teeming with people.

'Welcome to Capri.' Fabrizio stood up and waved his arms expansively. 'Quiet, no?'

I laughed. The place was hopping.

He steered the *Elenora* alongside the dock and we all scrambled on to land, Maud making a bit of a meal of it as usual.

Then we sat on a low wall and waited while Fabrizio took the boat into the marina. Maud crossed the road to wait in the shade. Jack and I eyed up the wonderfully over the top tourist shops with their swirling glitter 'snow' globes of the Grotta

Azzurra – the Blue Grotto – and models of the Certosa di San Giocomo, the fourteenth-century monastery in the hills. Tourists piled off ferry boats and gathered in knots, chattering and looking round; some walked up the main road, others immediately joined a heaving queue on the shoreline.

'What are they waiting for?' I asked Jack, pointing at the snake of bodies.

'Boats to the Blue Grotto.'

'Isn't that where we're heading? I can't quite see Maud and Gunella queuing with the proletariat.'

Jack smiled. 'I'm sure they have other plans.'

He was right. Fabrizio came back in a sleek black air-conditioned Mercedes and Maud and Gunella climbed in; they were off to hit the designer shops. Jack and I were dispatched with Maud's camera to take masses of pictures of the Blue Grotto.

To be honest, I was delighted. We could pretend to be tourists; scratch that, we could pretend to be lovers. Hell, with any luck we would be lovers. Holding on to that thought I stood in the queue and tried to ignore the couple in front of us. They looked like cartoon twins in their matching clothes. When I whispered this to Jack he laughed.

'What do we look like then?' he asked.

'Honeymooners?' I suggested.

'Really? Shouldn't we be doing more of this if we're honeymooners?' He bent down to kiss me, but our sunglasses clashed.

I giggled and lifted mine up. He did the same. 'That's better,' he murmured, moving towards me again. Our lips touched, zing, a fantastic, full-on kiss.

A few minutes later we heard a loud cough. '*Excusez-moi.* The queue has moved.'

We broke apart. There was now an acre of space in front of us and some irritated-looking people tut-tutting behind us.

Jack put his hands in the air. 'Sorry, we're on our honey-moon,' he said loudly.

'Jack!' I hissed, mortified. 'I was only joking.'

But the atmosphere became instantly less hostile, the word honeymooners moving down the queue like a game of Chinese whispers.

Jack grinned at me and said, 'Hi there, Mrs Wiseheart.'

I shook my head at him, laughing.

We stepped into a long wooden boat, like a fishing boat but with more seats. Jack squeezed my hand. 'Start taking pictures,' he said. 'Maud will expect loads of them.'

I turned on Maud's neat digital camera and took a couple of snaps of Jack taking snaps of the harbour.

He slapped my arm playfully and tried to shift me down the wooden seat into the Germans.

'Stop!' I giggled.

We pulled out of the harbour in a packed boat and chugged down the coast. It was a pleasant enough trip, but I missed the *Elenora's* comfy seats and powerful engine. This boat's engine was like a purring kitten in comparison.

The cliffs were rocky and rugged, with high-tide and sea-weed stains along the shoreline. If you looked up there were flashes of trees and plants clinging bravely to the cliff top – forest green and a lighter olive green.

Once we reached the grotto, we all climbed out into several tiny rowing boats. Ours was steered by a pint-sized Italian boy who looked about twelve.

'Lie down, lady and man,' the boy said to me and Jack. 'No heads cracked off please.' He gave us a toothy grin. We were hovering outside the tiny bullet hole of an entrance to the Blue Grotto and I wasn't feeling all that confident. I'd been expecting something a little more dramatic, live music, a bit of razzmatazz. But instead I was lying with my back against Jack, waiting for the waves to settle down so we could be rowed through the blowhole of an entrance by a child.

'This is fun,' Jack said wryly, shifting his body a little. His back was pressed against the wooden planks of the boat. At least I could use him as a cushion.

'We off,' the boy said and began to row towards the hole, pulling strongly on his short oars. I squeezed my eyes closed and then – pop – we were inside the cave.

I gasped. 'Wow!' It was lit with a heavenly blue light.

'The light is reflected from the floor by the white sand,' Jack said. 'Isn't it amazing?'

I nodded, speechless. It was like being in fairyland. Tears sprung to my eyes and I bit my lower lip to stop them.

'You like, lady?' the boy asked, a kind look in his eyes. 'Is beautiful, yes?'

'Yes.'

'My family find cave, many many years ago,' he said confidently.

Jack nudged me in the back. 'I bet they all say that,' he whispered.

Then the boatmen all started singing 'O Sole Mio' in unison, like an Italian barber's shop quartet. They didn't have the greatest voices in the world but they were obviously getting a kick out of it.

Jack joined in, his voice surprisingly good and I giggled to myself, savouring the moment.

'Did you enjoy that?' Jack asked as we lined up to leave the cave, all too soon.

'It was amazing.' Then I remembered something. 'But we're going to have to go back in, Jack.'

'Why?'

'We forgot to take any photos for Maud.'

We bribed the boy with a handful of lire. He took us straight back. This time we both saw the grotto through the view-finders of our cameras.

Back at the harbour, we found a café and sat outside, sipping stomach-clenchingly strong espressos while we waited for Maud and Gunella. I felt blissed out from the sun and the sea air.

'Good day?' Jack asked me.

I smiled at him. 'Can't complain. The company wasn't up to much though.'

He put his fingers in his glass and flicked water at me.

On the way back to Positano, Maud and Gunella finished their 'nibbles' in the cabin, shopping bags littering the floor under their feet, while Jack and I sat beside Fabrizio on the bridge. I, for one, was glad to be away from the other women. Maud had asked us to join them, but once we'd had a glass of champagne each and some posh food (give me cocktail sausages and crisps any day; Jack said the oysters were supposed to be slimy, but yuck!) we'd excused ourselves and left the pair of them to their quails' eggs.

Jack squeezed his thigh against mine. 'I could get used to this, Mrs Wiseheart.'

My stomach felt as warm and tingly as my slightly sunburnt skin.

When we got back to Villa Positano, Koo was drifting in the pool in an armchair-shaped lilo, sipping a glass of white wine. She was wearing over-sized sunglasses, a straw cowboy hat and a skimpy black swimsuit, which barely covered her nipples, let alone her full C-cup breasts.

'Gunny, Maudie!' Koo waved her fingers in the air and then dangled them in the pool again. 'This is the life. Hello, Jack.' She trilled at him. Then she noticed me.

'Alice,' she said simply. Was I imagining it or did she scowl at me? It was hard to tell through her dark lenses. 'Jessica has been filling me in on all the shenanigans. I hear the two of you went AWOL last night.'

I shuddered. Damn. Jessica was obviously getting her own back for the gin incident.

'Pay no attention to Jessica,' Jack said smoothly. 'We just went for a walk, to check out the Italian ambience for the ball. How's Mac, Koo? Did he settle into respite OK?'

'He settled in fine. But I'm on holiday now. Let's forget about real life for a few days. So what's the plan for tonight? I feel like getting royally sloshed and dancing on a table.'

As they discussed the options, Jack murmured to Maud, 'Just going inside to download the photographs,' and we slipped away.

Later that evening Maud and her posse headed into Sorrento for a night on the tiles, leaving me and Jack alone in the villa. Nadia had left some supper out – a large plate of antipasto and olive bread – and we'd eaten on the veranda and shared a bottle of red wine.

After dinner, Jack decided to take a dip. He stripped down to his boxer shorts and jumped straight in.

He splashed me. 'Are you coming in?'

'No!' I squealed.

He grinned. 'Go and get your togs if it makes you feel any better.'

After getting changed in the privacy of my room, I slid into the pool, the water caressing my body with a deliciously silky embrace.

'The water seems warmer,' I said as I waded towards Jack.

'It's on a timer,' he said. 'Warm in the evening, cool during the day. Whoever designed this place thought of everything.'

I was almost out of my depth so I swam the last few yards to the edge of the pool. I held onto the reinforced glass and looked down. The pool was perched on the edge of the cliff and staring down made me feel quite dizzy. Jack moved towards me and our shoulders touched.

'Isn't it stunning?' he said. We gazed down at the sea. I could just make out the other villas on the hill, their white walls and lit windows picked out against the velvety night sky. Below us was another swimming pool, its edges decorated in tiny spots, like fairy lights. Classical music drifted up from someone's garden. The air was filled with a heady aroma of bougainvillea mixed with the tang of the sea.

'Quite a view,' I said, 'and so peaceful without Maud around to bark orders at me.'

He gave a laugh. 'Let's forget about her. Tonight it's just you and me.' He brushed some stray hair off my face with his hand and my stomach gave a flippy somersault.

'Hey you,' he said gently. He kissed me. I kissed him back, hard, wrapping my legs round his body, holding on to the edge of the pool with one arm. Luckily he was a lot taller than me and could just about stand on the bottom. He pulled down the top of my swimsuit and ran his hands over my breasts, lingering on my nipples, drawing little circles around them with his fingers. I clung on like a limpet with my legs, throwing my head back as he kissed my neck.

I moved my hands down his back and rested them on his buttocks, kneading the firm muscular flesh under my fingers. He gave a throaty sigh and stopped kissing me.

'Alice, what are you doing to me?' he asked with a grin. 'Let's go inside.'

I nodded. 'Don't want to frighten the wildlife.' I pulled my swimsuit back up my body and watched as he walked up the marble steps and out of the pool. He offered me a hand and pulled me out of the water. Then he bundled up his clothes and headed inside. I followed him. Jack's bedroom was nearest so he pushed open the door and shut it firmly behind us. I carried over a chair and jammed it under the door handle, just in case.

'But what if Maud wants to join in?' he asked.

I slapped him on the arm.

'Hey, that hurt,' he said. 'You're in trouble, missy.'

'Oh yeah?' I pulled the top of my swimsuit down to my waist. 'You were saying.'

His eyes drank me in and he stepped towards me, whooshed me up into his arms and threw me down on the bed. Then he climbed on top of me and pinned my hands down with his.

'You're dripping all over the bed,' I said.

'It'll dry,' he said, his chest heaving. 'God, you're so beautiful.'

I smiled up at him. 'You can give me a back massage again if you like but this time I promise not to fall asleep.' I tried to roll onto my back.

'I'll give you back massage.'

'Give me your worst, Mr Wiseheart,' I said, and he obliged.

'Dear God,' I said, seeing stars in front of my eyes. 'Jack Wiseheart, who would have thought?'

And then . . . nothing.

'Alice? Alice, are you all right?'

I opened my eyes. The bedside light was on and all I could see was Jack's concerned face. He was crouched over me, his palm on my forehead.

Then it came to me, I'd fainted in the middle of having sex with Jack. How mortifying. 'How long was I out?' I asked.

'Not long. Maybe twenty seconds.'

'I'm so embarrassed.'

'Why?'

'Did you even . . . you know?'

'Did I orgasm you mean?'

I nodded.

'Just as you passed out. That's why I didn't notice for a few seconds.'

I slapped him. 'Charming. I could have been dying.'

He grinned sheepishly. 'I'm glad you're OK.'

'More than OK.' I blew air out of my mouth and bit my bottom lip. 'Bloody hell.'

'That was something all right,' he said. 'Now, I don't know about you, but I need a rest.' He lay down and snuggled into my back. Spoons, just how I like it. And that's how we woke up at six o'clock the following morning.

We made love again, this time at a more leisurely pace, with no fainting on either part. It was a glorious way to start the day. A little later I snuck back into my bedroom in one of Jack's shirts, flopped on my bed and fell sound asleep.

Chapter 26

The following afternoon, Maud, Koo and Gunella were determined to put together a mood board for the Amalfi Ball. They'd sent Fabrizio to Sorrento to print out yesterday's photographs and find some art equipment: poster board, glue dots, spray glue, felt-tip pens, multi-coloured paper and fashion magazines. Fabrizio had come back laden with plastic bags.

Even Maud was impressed. 'Well done, Fabrizio,' she said laying everything out on the enormous walnut dining-room table.

Maud put one of Jack's photographs of the Blue Grotto in the centre of the large sheet of card. God forbid she'd choose one of mine, even though they were just as good. The card was held down at each corner by a heavy solid-silver fork – Jack had checked the hallmark and pointed it out to me when the others weren't looking. She then surrounded the photo with sheets of turquoise blue paper, stuck down with the spray glue which smelt like hair spray.

'Don't sniff the glue, Alice,' Maud said. She missed nothing. Jack gave me a fake cross look and I tried not to laugh. We'd been working together all morning, discussing the charity auction, the upcoming St Jude's event, and batting suggestive looks at each other across the table, like a game of flirt ping pong. Unfortunately Koo had tottered in and out of the room in her swimsuit and heels, asking Jack questions, and reading my emails over my shoulder, which was really annoying and rather rude.

'We now have our central theme,' Maud said rather grandly. 'The Grotta Azzurra, otherwise know as the Blue Grotto.'

I thought it was a bit of a cheek, coming over all lady of the manor like that. She'd been too busy re-enacting *Lady Chatterley's Lover* with Fabrizio to actually visit the place.

'I've seen it several times, of course,' she said, looking pointedly at me.

Great, so now she could read my mind too! This just got better and better.

'The Mansion House will glow with blue light,' she said. 'Inside and out. Are you getting all this, Alice?'

Jack passed me a pen and a fresh foolscap pad and I began to scribble everything down.

1 Venue: blue light — inside and out

'The menu will be inspired by southern Italy. Wine from Regaleali and Donnafugata. Olives at the reception. Mini pizzas. The appetizers will be plates of antipasto: artichoke hearts, roasted red pepper, courgette. Simple peasant food, brushed with the best olive oil. Are you keeping up, Alice?'

I nodded.

2 Menu

I had no idea how to spell the wines but I scribbled them down phonetically and hoped that Jack could make sense of it all later. I was impressed. Maud had obviously been doing her homework. She'd visited several wine merchants this morning and had bullied seven different restaurants into giving her a menu, so she could 'borrow' some of their ideas. She'd also come back with six large boxes of *baci*, little Italian chocolates. They were to be tied into squares of blue chiffon with silver thread, like 'favours' at a wedding. 'You'll be doing that when we get back to Dublin,' she'd said earlier. 'I'm sure Magda will help you.' Because, of course, Magda and I had nothing better to do!

Maud also wanted cassata for dessert, and later in the evening, a cheese board at every table. 'The caterers will have to source provolone, scamorza and ricotta,' she said.

'How about mozzarella?' Koo suggested, 'or is it a bit Pizza Hut?'

Maud wrinkled her nose. 'I think so.'

'What about Brie?' Gunella said. 'I do like a good runny Brie.'

Maud and Koo just ignored her.

'Now the place settings,' Koo continued.

They went through these in great detail, from glasses and crockery, to napkins, cutlery, blue and silver table confetti (Jack had suggested this, but Maud had dismissed it as 'tacky' before changing her mind). I had no idea where I'd get it, but I put a huge star beside it to remind me to start sourcing it as soon as I got back to Dublin.

'Alice, any suggestions for the live music?' Koo said.

'Perry Como?' Gunella piped up, delighted with herself. 'Or Pavarotti?'

'I said live,' Maud said curtly. 'Alice?'

Since Maud had decided the ball's music was to be my department, I'd visited the venue – the Mansion House – and I'd thought about this carefully. 'A string quartet in the foyer playing Italian music as the guests walk in,' I suggested. 'Puccini and Vivaldi?' I added tentatively.

'Excellent,' Maud said. 'And?'

'A slightly more upbeat band at the reception. Playing foot-tapping kind of songs, with an Italian theme to get everyone in the mood, 'That's Amore', 'Que Sera, Sera', that kind of thing.

Gunella clapped her hands together. 'I love that one.' She

began to sing the chorus. She had a funny high-pitched singing voice, like Minnie Mouse.

'Gunella!' Koo said, 'stay focused. And after the meal?'

I bit the inside of my lip. They would either love this or hate it.

'Well?' Maud asked, impatiently.

'A Frank Sinatra tribute band. It would be something different, something people would actually enjoy and could dance to. The theme would be Italian-American crooners. Dean Martin, Sinatra, of course, Mario Lanza, and, especially for Gunella, Perry Como.'

'I like it,' Koo said. 'The Italian Rat Pack.'

Maud nodded. 'Not bad. I was thinking along the same lines myself. You can go ahead and book it all, Alice.'

I looked at her, my eyebrows raised.

'*Please*,' she said.

'And can we have a mouth that eats people's hand if they lie?' Gunella said. 'Like in that film?'

'What are you on about, Gunny?' Maud demanded. She looked baffled.

'Gunella's talking about *Roman Holiday* with Audrey Hepburn,' I said. 'They visit the Bocca della Verita. It's supposed to snap shut on your hand if you're a liar. It's one of my favourite films.'

'That's right!' Gunella said. '*Roman Holiday*. I love Cliff Richard.'

Cliff Richard? Poor Cary Grant would roll over in his grave. Jack winked at me, and I put my hand over my mouth to hide my giggles.

Two hours later we had the whole ball mapped out in detail, right down to the design brief for the visual-display company, who we'd target for press coverage, the ticket prices and who we'd invite as a celebrity guest to make the after-dinner speech. (When I say we, obviously I don't include myself, I was too busy writing to be of much use. Although I did try and make some suggestions.)

'Phew,' I said as I walked out of the room with Jack. Maud, Koo and Gunella were still inside, discussing their dresses for the night. 'That was quite intense.'

'But successful.' Jack patted his laptop, which was tucked under his arm. 'We can go online now and get cracking. You make a start on booking the music, I'll ring Carlo McCarthy's agent.' Carlo was the Irish-Italian television presenter we'd decided to invite as the celebrity guest.

I sighed. 'Now? My brain's exhausted.'

'We're here to work, Alice,' he said surprisingly loudly, 'let's get busy.' Then he closed the door to the dining-room and winked at me. He lowered his voice. 'But first we should have a quick private meeting in my bedroom. What do you think?'

'Vital.' I grinned at him. 'I'll meet you there. Give me two minutes.'

I sprinted into my room, flicked off my sandals and slipped my feet into Petra's Louboutins, shrugged my arms into a smart jacket and unbuttoned my shirt to the waist.

When I pushed open the door to his room, Jack was already undressed and lying on his bed, completely naked.

'Good afternoon, Mr Wiseheart,' I said. 'I see you were expecting me.' I walked towards him, my heels clicking on the marble tiles. I held a notebook and pen out in front of me. 'I believe you have some dictation?' I lifted my eyebrows and smiled suggestively.

'I have something for you all right, Miss Devine. Come here. And please leave your shoes on. This is a very formal office.'

Chapter 27

Later that night, after a quick shower and some furious teeth scrubbing, I wriggled into my best black lacy underwear and opened the door to Jack's room. We'd shared supper in the kitchen, followed by a romantic stroll into Positano, where we sat on the low harbour wall and watched the world go by. Maud, Gunella, Jessica and Koo were all in Sorrento having dinner with the mayor; Boothy had arranged it. Fabrizio was their driver for the evening, so Jack and I were alone in the villa and we intended to make the most of it.

I climbed into the bed beside Jack and nestled into him. 'Hi, sleepy head.'

'Alice!' A woman's voice rang out. 'What the hell are you doing?'

She rolled over. It was Koo.

I sat up instantly and stared down at her. I could just make out her smirk in the moonlight. 'What the hell are *you* doing? Jack's expecting me.'

Koo gave a hollow laugh. 'We could always share him. Ever had a threesome?'

'No,' I said through tight lips, 'and I don't intend to either.'

'Don't get all defensive,' she said. 'I was only joking. But you will have to run along now. I sent Jack off for a bottle of champagne; he'll be back any minute. I won't say anything about your visit. It'll be our little secret. And I do like the underwear, by the way, very sweet.'

'Look, Koo, I don't know what's going on here. Jack really is expecting me. I think it's you that should leave.'

She laughed. 'Oh, Alice, you are naive. Jack and I have an understanding. I did try to warn you.'

'But Jack said—'

'Of course he did. He was just trying to get into your lacy knickers. He really is insatiable. He had Flossy too. Did he mention it? Probably not. But he's such a dear; I have to forgive his little indiscretions. He does love his little secrets. Has he told you about Amelie?'

'Yes, he has.'

'At least that's something. Such an adorable child. Looks just like her dad. Apart from that darling button nose. She got that from Juliette.'

'You've met Amelie?'

'Yes. We've spent such fun days together, just the three of us. You're way out of your depth, Alice. Just leave Jack and I to it.'

The bastard. He said Koo and Maud had no idea he had a daughter, let alone met her. To think I'd trusted him.

'I'm sorry,' I murmured. I jumped to my feet and scuttled out of Jack's room. I felt like dirt. What must Koo think of me? I was going to remove his testicles with one of Nadia's kitchen knives. I grabbed a shirt in my room and then went looking for him. He was in the corridor, fully dressed, holding a bottle of champagne by the neck.

'I was just coming to look for you.' He noticed my face. 'What's wrong?'

I just shook my head and walked away, so angry and upset I couldn't even speak to him.

'Alice?' He ran after me. As I passed his bedroom door, he caught up with me and grabbed my arm. 'What's going on?'

I opened my mouth to tell him exactly what I thought of him

but at that moment Koo walked through his bedroom door stark naked. She had an amazing body and I couldn't help but stare at her sexy curves and her horribly impressive breasts. No wonder Jack couldn't say no.

I just shook my head at him. 'I thought you were different. Let go of me.'

He looked at Koo. 'What are you playing at, Koo? Get dressed for heaven's sake.'

'Waiting for the champagne,' she said. 'I'll just go back inside, will I, darling? Clearly you and Alice have things to discuss. I know I've turned a blind eye to all your previous dalliances, but this has to stop. Say *ciao* to your new little fund-raiser and come back inside.'

'Get the hell out of my room,' he told her. 'You asked me to get you some champagne from the cellar, well here it is.' He thrust the bottle at her. 'And the next time you can get it yourself, spiders or no spiders. If this is some sort of joke, it's not funny.'

Koo just took the bottle off him and shrugged. 'Good try, but Alice isn't that stupid. And I'm not leaving. You jumped out of bed before I even climaxed.' She went back into his room and slammed the door behind her.

'I trusted you.' I began to hammer my fists against his chest, tears pricking my eyes.

He grabbed my hands. 'Listen to me, Alice, Koo's crazy. I talked to her earlier, told her I wasn't interested, that there was someone else now. I thought she'd taken it well, but clearly not. She's obviously cooked this whole thing up to get back at me. You have to believe me.'

'No! I thought you were different, but you're just the same as everyone else.' I ran into my room and shut the door.

'Alice,' Jack said through the wood, 'let me in.'

'No, go away.'

He opened it anyway. 'Please. This is all a big mistake.'

'Really? Then how does she know about Amelie? She says she met her, Jack. She described her perfectly. Explain that.'

He looked confused. 'I can't, but you have to listen to me.'

'No, I don't. You're a lying scumbag. Go back to Koo. She's welcome to you.'

The following morning we had a torturously early four a.m. start. I hadn't slept a wink. Nor had Maud, Gunella or Jessica apparently, from the looks of them. I couldn't bear to so much as glance at either Koo or Jack, so I had no idea how either of them were. They'd probably made up and had wild, champagne-fuelled sex. I was trying not to care, but I did, deeply. I thought Jack and I had had a real connection. It just goes to show, when it comes to matters of the heart, you can't trust anyone.

As soon as we sat down in our aeroplane seats Jack said, 'Alice, now that we're finally alone can we please just talk about this?'

I glared at him. 'No, we can't, especially not in a packed plane. And don't try to hold my hand either. You're on your own this time, turbulence or no turbulence.'

A few minutes of stony silence later the air-hostess told us there was a free seat in first class and did one of us want to join our 'friends'.

'He can go,' I said, climbing out of my seat to let Jack out. 'They're his friends, not mine.'

'Fine,' Jack clipped. 'I was going to say we're both happy where we are, but as we're so clearly not . . .' He climbed out and then stood in front of me, our faces almost touching. I could smell stale alcohol on his breath. 'I'll happily drink Scotch in first class. Maybe Koo would like to join the mile-high club.'

'I'm sure she's already a member,' I snapped.

He followed the bemused air hostess wordlessly down the aisle without turning round.

When the plane touched down in Dublin I was incredibly relieved to be home, even if it was drizzling. I'd spent most of the last three hours on my own and I was dying to see a friendly face. Since things with Jack had gone belly up I'd felt dreadfully homesick and I couldn't wait to see Adam. Jason had offered to take the kids, including Adam, this morning, so Grace was collecting me from the airport. I couldn't wait to talk to her.

Chapter 28

As soon as I saw Grace's drawn face anxiously scanning the crowds passing through the arrival gate, I knew something was wrong. Immediately I thought of Adam. Please God make him all right, I prayed. If he's all right I'll never, ever go away again. And I'll be celibate for the rest of my life. And I'll go to church, and not just at Christmas.

'Alice!' Grace waved and ran towards me. She threw her arms around me. 'I'm so glad you're back.'

'Is Adam OK? Tell me he's OK, Gracie'

She pulled away and gave me a smile.

'He's fine, stop worrying. You'll see him in an hour as long as the traffic's not too bad. 'And you've got some colour; you look great.'

'I don't feel great,' I admitted, although I was relieved that there was nothing wrong with Adam.

'Are you sick?'

'Nothing like that. My heart's just bruised.' I sighed. 'Nothing new. I'll tell you about it in the car. Where are you parked?'

As soon as we sat down in the car she turned towards me. 'I was on *Joe Duffy* this morning.'

'Really? Did you ring them?' The *Joe Duffy Show* is a phone-in radio show on RTE 1. Listeners can ring Joe with their tales of outrage and injustice. Jason's a huge fan.

'No!' she wailed. 'But they were talking *about* me, all right.'

'I don't understand.'

'Neither did I until Jason rang me in a rage.'

'At you?'

She gave a wry laugh. 'Funnily enough, no.'

'You'd better explain.'

And explain she did. In my absence Grace, or more precisely 'Grace the Cougar' and her 'Afternoon Delight' Bebo page, had become quite the celebrity. It had been picked up by some of the tabloids, as well as the *Joe Duffy Show*, before Grace even knew it existed.

It had all come to a head yesterday morning when Jason rang Grace from his jeep.

'Grace, do you have a Bebo page?'

'What are you on about? Is this some kind of joke?' She'd been up all night with Eric who had a soaring temperature and was in no mood for being trifled with.

'Someone has set up a Bebo page using your details. It says you're looking for young men for afternoon delight. It has some clips,' he coughed, embarrassed, 'of your voice. Something to do with a frube. And a very grainy photo of you taken with a mobile-phone camera. In your underwear.'

An icy shiver ran down Grace's spine. Oh, dear God.

'Gary!' She screamed. 'I'll kill him. But why would he do such a thing?'

'Who's Gary?' Jason said sharply.

She said nothing.

'Grace?' His voice was firm. 'I can only help you if you tell me who Gary is.'

Grace fixed on the word 'help'. Had Jason said 'help'?

'I'm sorry,' she whispered. 'I'm so, so sorry. Gary is a guy I've been seeing.'

'Is it serious?' Jason sounded so horribly wounded that she felt terrible.

'Serious?' She gave a disgusted snort. 'Not now! But none of this makes sense.'

'You must have done something to upset him. Either he's pretty angry or he has a sick sense of humour. The Bebo page must have taken him hours.'

'You've seen it?'

'Yes. That's why I'm ringing you. I had a look on one of the lad's iPhones. It was in the *Irish Sun* this morning and Joe Duffy's talking about it right now.'

'I'll ring RTE,' Grace said frantically, 'and the papers. I'll tell them it's all lies. I'll sue!'

'Are you at home?'

'Yes.'

'I'm a few minutes away from you. Don't ring anyone. I'm just going to make a quick call to our solicitor. Do nothing, understand? If you ring while you're in this state you might say something you'll regret. Just sit tight, I'm on my way.'

Grace couldn't help herself; she flicked on the radio and tuned in to RTE 1.

Joe Duffy's voice rang out loud and clear. 'We'll be coming back to the price of petrol in Cork in a few minutes, but now we have Imelda on the line. Imelda, what do you make of all this cougar stuff?'

'I think that woman should be ashamed of herself.' Imelda said in a tight voice. 'Luring young men into bed. In the afternoons! She should be cooking dinner for her husband and children, not licking ice cream—'

'Frozen yoghurt, I believe it was, Imelda,' Joe Duffy interrupted.

'Yoghurt then, off young men's private parts. And what's this cougar thing anyway? I don't understand. There were no animals involved in procreation in my day.'

Joe Duffy gave a chuckle. 'It's a term for older women who like younger men, Imelda. Like wild cats, you know, cougars. They live in South America, mainly.'

'And what's the name for older men who like younger women?' Imelda asked. 'Are they panthers then? It's all very silly.'

'Sure, they're just normal,' Joe said. 'Now, what's that? Wait for it listeners, my producer tells me Grace's husband is on the other line. He has a very interesting angle on all this. Hold onto your hats. He'd like to be called Rick to protect his anonymity. Rick?'

'Hello, Joe. Can you hear me?'

'Loud and clear. You have something to say I believe?'

'I do. I've been on to our solicitor and the Bebo page is being taken down as we speak. Grace had nothing to do with that page, and we'll sue anyone who either prints or broadcasts anything from it.'

'Oh, right.' Joe seemed rather taken aback. 'Who *is* responsible then?'

'We have a good idea, but the guards will be looking into it properly. That's all I have to say on the matter. It's clearly just a nasty prank that has got out of hand. It's a warning to everyone: internet bullying comes in all shapes and forms, and it's not just teenagers that get hurt.'

'Good point, well made, Rick. We'll leave that story there now, as you've requested. Thank you for clearing all that up for us. Imelda, Imelda, are you still there?'

'I am. That poor woman.' Imelda sounded genuinely shocked. 'Why would someone do such a thing?'

Grace clicked off the radio. Why indeed? She rang Gary's mobile. It was turned off. She felt so dirty and so used. What on earth had she done to make him hate her so much? Or had she been taken in by a twisted and cruel person?

*

'What happened once Jason arrived?' I asked Grace. We were still sitting in her car. We were in danger of going way over our allotted time for leaving the car park but I was glued to my seat.

'Jason drove over to Gary's to have it out with him, but he's disappeared. His flatmate hasn't seen him for three days. It's so frustrating.' She turned and looked at me.

'I don't know what to do. Luckily Jason's call has nipped the media coverage in the bud. No one knows it was me, thank God.'

'And Jason?'

'What about Jason?'

'How does he feel about it?'

Grace sighed. 'He's been really good. It can't be easy for him. I don't know what I would have done without him. He stayed the night last night.'

I raised my eyebrows.

'On the sofa. Don't get too excited. But you know, he seems calmer. Almost like the old Jason.'

'Did he tell you about all his thyroid problems?'

'Yes. We were up most of last night talking.'

'And?'

'I don't know. Somewhere along the line I think we stopped being a couple and became just parents. And then there's Gary of course.' She shrugged. 'It's all a bit of a mess.'

'At least you're talking,' I said eagerly.

She smiled at me gently. 'I know how much you like Jason, but don't get your hopes up; some things are beyond fixing.'

'But there's hope?'

She laughed. 'You're such an optimist, sis. If only I'd seen Gary for what he is. I still can't understand why he'd do such a thing.' She went quiet, lost in her thoughts.

'There's something I should tell you about Gary,' I said. 'But you have to promise not to kill me first.'

'What?'

'Promise first.'

'Fine, fine, I promise. Go on.'

I took a deep breath. 'Arvin is Gary's stepdad.'

'*What?* He can't be.'

'Well, he is. I called into his house and met his wife, Maureen, who also happened to be Gary's mum. I wanted to ask Arvin's advice about the whole Gary thing. I was stupid, I see that now. But—'

Grace's face went pale. 'Why didn't you tell me this earlier?'

I shrugged, feeling foolish. 'There was never a right time. It all happened the night before I went away; I didn't want to leave you to deal with the news on your own.'

'Then this whole Bebo thing is *your* fault,' she said firmly.

'*My* fault? Why? Why is it my fault? I haven't done anything.'

'You should have told me.'

'I know and I'm sorry. But they're not blood related. I was going to tell you today.'

Grace hit her skull against the head rest. 'OK, this is all starting to make sense. I bet Arvin put Gary up to it.' She gripped the steering wheel. 'Where does Arvin live?'

'Bray,' I said sheepishly. 'I'll come with you. But won't he be at soccer training this morning? This is all sounding very weird. Am I missing something? Why would Arvin want to hurt you?'

'Damn.' Grace punched the steering wheel, ignoring my questions. 'We'll go to soccer training instead. I'll tell you the whole story. About me and Arvin. We're family; no more secrets, OK?'

She gave me a loaded look and I turned away. I got the feeling she was talking about Adam's dad, but I ignored her dig.

'But first,' she said, 'we'd better get out of this car park.'

*

As we drove down the M50 towards the N11, Grace began. 'Some of this you know, some of it you don't. Arvin was in third year in college, I was in fourth year. When the following October came round I was working at the *Southside Gazette* and Arvin was still in Trinity. It made everything a bit awkward; I wanted to go out with my new workmates, Arvin was still drinking in the college bar with his rugby buddies. I guess I wanted to be a grown-up and Arvin was still very much a student, but we muddled along for a while. Meanwhile I was still very friendly with Rita. Remember Rita?'

I nodded. Of course I remembered Rita. She wasn't the kind of girl you'd forget easily. She was loud and infectiously funny.

'Rita had repeated second year so she was still in college too. She hung out with Arvin and the rugby gang. One night we went out for a pizza, just me and Rita. I guess I was being a bit quiet so she asked me what was up and stupidly I told her. Arvin was having problems in the bedroom department and—'

I laughed. 'In the bedroom department? You mean he couldn't get it up?'

'Yes. And stop laughing. The poor guy was mortified. He'd get to a certain stage and then, when he tried to . . . well, you know, pouf, it just disappeared.'

I held back my giggles. It was pretty funny. 'And what did Rita say?'

'Like you, she thought it was amusing at first. We talked about it for a while and she gave me some advice.'

'What kind of advice?'

'Alice! I'm not going into it. Anyway, it was all nonsense, none of it worked. But Rita told some of the guys in the bar and they started calling Arvin LD.'

'LD?'

'Limp Dick. Every time he walked into the bar they'd put up their little fingers and then bend them over. Arvin thought *I'd* told everyone; he was pretty cut up about it. I swore it wasn't me, but he wouldn't listen. He said I'd betrayed him and we broke up.'

'But she's the one who told everyone, it was hardly your fault.'

'No, it *was* my fault, I should never have discussed it with her, I knew she had a big mouth, I just didn't think. And Arvin . . . After that, Arvin didn't do so well. Actually he tried to . . .' Grace blew out her breath and clutched the wheel tightly. 'He took some pills.'

I gasped. 'But someone found him, right?'

'Yes. I found him. Look, I'm going to have to pull over. Give me a second, OK?' She pulled on to the hard shoulder and stared straight ahead of her, still clutching the wheel.

'Oh, Gracey. Are you all right?' I asked.

'I've never really talked about this before. Jason knows a bit about it, but no one else. It's all such a mess.'

'What happened to Arvin?' I said gently. 'Surely it must have been more than just the teasing in the pub.'

'I think that was the catalyst. He'd been feeling low for quite a while and it tipped him over the edge. He dropped out of rugby – and he loved rugby with a passion. He went from being really fit to being a couch potato; all he'd do was sit in his bedroom and watch his portable telly. I tried talking to him but he just shut me out. Overnight he went from being one of the most respected guys in college to being a joke. He just couldn't take it. I rang his parents from the hospital and they flew over and took him home. I don't know what he told them, but they refused to speak to me after that first phone call.'

'Back up a bit,' I said gently. 'You found him? On your own?'

'Not exactly. One of his friends rang me at work. He was worried about him. Arvin hadn't turned up to lectures or seminars and he usually took his studies pretty seriously. So I went to his rooms and banged on the door. His roommate was away on a geography trip and when I asked around no one had seen Arvin all day. So I got one of the porters to let me in. We found him slumped against the couch in his living room. There were several large bottles of paracetamol on the table and a bottle of vodka. As soon as the porter saw that he called an ambulance.

'Arvin looked terrible, his face was so pale, almost grey, and there was all this white foam at the side of his mouth. I tried to wake him up, but he was so out of it I couldn't. I kept talking to him while I waited for the ambulance, telling him I was sorry, that I loved him, to hang on, that everything would be OK. I went with him in the ambulance. They pumped his stomach.' She paused. 'If he'd been left for another half an hour he would have damaged his liver so badly he wouldn't have made it.'

'But he did make it,' I said gently.

'Yes. As soon as his parents arrived later that night I left the hospital. I wrote to him, telling him how sorry I was, but he never replied, so maybe he never got the letter. Or maybe he hated me so much he didn't want anything more to do with me. Maybe he still hates me. Maybe that's why, you know . . . the Bebo thing . . . maybe he and Gary—' She broke off.

She looked so distraught I put my arms round her and held her tight. 'I'm so sorry,' I said. 'That doesn't sound like the Arvin I remember; he wouldn't hurt a fly, but who knows? People do crazy things when they're upset. Would you like me to drive?'

'Please.'

Grace stared out the passenger window the whole way to Bray and I could see she was crying. I left her to her thoughts. I could understand why she'd tried to track Arvin down on Google, but not why she'd considered playing with his emotions again. Surely that was a bit cruel? But Grace clearly felt she had unfinished business there, and we all do crazy things sometimes. I thought of Ned in London and wondered if he and Betty had got married in the end. Tears started to prick my eyes too.

As we walked towards the soccer pitch, I squeezed Grace's shoulder. 'Are you sure you want to go through with this?' I asked. 'What are you going to say to him?'

'I'm going to apologize. I'm going to tell him . . . oh, I don't know. I just need to talk to him.'

'And the Bebo site?'

'I just want to know one way or the other; whether he still hates me that much.' She shook her head.

As luck would have it we almost walked straight into Gary. He was sitting in the boot of his electric-blue hatchback, lacing up one of his soccer boots. He looked up and his face paled.

Grace grabbed my arm. 'Is that the face of a guilty man or what?'

'Grace,' he said nervously, 'come to watch the boys' match? It won't be on for a little while.'

'It was you, wasn't it?' Grace said in a steely voice.

'Ah, here now.' He sucked in his teeth. 'I had nothing to do with that. It was Antonia.'

'Antonia?' Grace demanded, narrowing her eyes. 'Who the hell is Antonia?'

'My girlfriend. She's a bit unhinged. Mum told her about you.'

'Girlfriend? I'll give you girlfriend, you two-timing slime. You'd better start explaining or else.' She picked up his second boot by the laces and started swinging it over her head.

Gary put his hands over his head and cowered. 'Jesus, woman, calm down.'

'Don't tell me to calm down.' She smacked him in the ribs with the boot and he yelped.

'Grace! That hurt,' he said, trying to grab it off her.

Then she kicked his leg. He grabbed his shin with both hands. 'OK, OK, I'll tell you if you stop attacking me.'

Grace's eyes sparked. 'You dragged my good name through the mud, you little prick. So get talking.'

'Alice called over to the house and apparently my mum recognized the name, Devine. Alice went a bit shifty when Mum asked was she related to you, and I think Mum was a bit shaken by the whole thing. She's very protective of Arvin and didn't know what to think, Alice dropping in like that. Anyway Antonia was in the kitchen, waiting for me. Mum had invited us over for dinner and I was running late.

'Antonia asked her was she OK and Mum told her all about Arvin's depression in college and everything that had happened. You should have told me you'd been involved with Arvin, Grace.'

'It didn't seem relevant when I met you,' she said. 'I didn't know you were related then. Plus you said he'd disapprove of us seeing each other because of the age gap, remember?'

He shrugged. 'True. But you still could have said something.'

Grace looked irritated. 'Stop stalling; finish the story.'

'OK. Antonia was already a bit suspicious about you. I'd told her you were just one of the soccer mums, but I don't think she believed me. She stole my mobile and must have found the photos and voice files. She was the one who made that Bebo page. She wanted to get back at me and I guess Mum's story hadn't helped.'

Grace lifted the boot over her head again. 'You can tell your girlfriend that I've decided to pack you in for a real man. I presume she dumped you?'

He looked sheepish. 'No. I promised her there'd be no more women; we're getting married.'

'That's pathetic,' Grace said. 'Who'd want to be married to

a serial cheater? She must be mad.' Grace threw his boot and it landed at his feet.

'I guess she loves me,' he said.

Grace just snorted.

There was a shout from the soccer pitch and Arvin waved at us.

Grace quickly asked, 'Does Arvin know about us?'

'Arvin?' He looked genuinely surprised. 'I'd hardly tell *him*. I got in shit trouble for messing around with another yummy mummy last year.' Then he realized what he'd said. 'I mean—'

'That's fine.' Grace put her hands up. 'Don't.'

'I see you've found Gary.' Arvin smiled at me and Grace. 'Shane's already on the pitch. Jason dropped him over earlier. I hadn't realized you'd married Jason, Grace. I always liked him. Hey, Gary, Grace was my first Irish girlfriend, how about that? Way back when.'

Gary opened his mouth to say something but I dug my heel into his shin. He yelped.

'So sorry, Gary,' I said turning towards him and then giving him a glare and a tiny shake of my head. Thankfully he got the message.

Gary coughed. 'Isn't it a small world all the same?'

Grace said, 'Arvin, can we talk?' She took his arm gently and they walked down the pitch, their heads together.

'What's all that about?' Gary asked.

'Two old friends catching up. And if you ever, ever say a word to Arvin about Grace I will hunt you down and kill you, do you understand?'

'He'd kill me himself if he ever found out. Her secret's safe with me.' He looked after Grace wistfully. 'Shame. She's a real goer once you get her started.'

'Gary,' I said, disgusted, 'she's my sister. And what about your fiancée?'

He looked at me with a glint in his eye and grinned. 'Hey, you're single, aren't you? I don't suppose you'd—'

'No!' I cut him off instantly. 'Stick with Antonia. I have enough man trouble of my own thank you very much.'

Gary put his second boot on and ran on to the pitch. 'You know where to find me if you ever have an itch,' he shouted at me, running backwards and almost colliding with a six-year-old.

I smiled. 'In your dreams.' That was one itch I would not be scratching.

I watched as Arvin gave Grace a bear hug. She buried her head in his chest, her shoulders heaving.

Chapter 29

On Tuesday I was back to work at Maud's house, which meant I could legitimately avoid Jack most of the day. I sent him a short email asking him for the caterers' quotes for the Amalfi Ball and confirming that our designer had everything she needed to start working on some roughs for both the invitations and the press release. Jack had already sent me an equally curt email:

> Alice
> Carlo McCarthy can do the ball. Please send him the St Jude's press pack and print off some pages of the website for him. Please send c/o his agent, details below. Please let Maud know. He will waive his fee for the event.
> Jack

The excessive use of 'please' made me wince. But he was the one in the wrong, not me. From now on we'd have a strictly professional relationship. Of course, what I actually wanted to do was to scream at him, slap his face and generally maim him, but he *was* still my boss. Less than two more months, I kept telling myself. Hang in there.

Besides, I had more pressing problems on my hands, namely staff mutiny. Magda was not a happy camper and

Maud had told me to sort it out. Maud's clothes were yet again at the centre of the argument.

'Tell Magda she must iron everything,' Maud said through tight lips. We were sitting in her study going through the final details for her drinks party tomorrow night. It had a summer solstice theme, with yellow cocktails and yellow food. Don't ask. 'And wash all my white linen. That Italian woman . . .'

'Nadia,' I said.

'Yes, yes, Nadia. I have no idea what kind of washing powder she uses but it doesn't smell right. Magda will have to wash everything again.'

'I'll tell her,' I said. 'But she's not going to like it. She's in the middle of polishing the hall floor for your party.'

'About the party,' Maud swept on, ignoring me, 'keep an eye on the waiting staff. Last time I found them sitting down in the kitchen gossiping while they should have been working. The caterer said they were waiting for the hors d'oeuvres to come out of the oven, but honestly. There is to be no sitting down on the job, is that understood?'

'Quite,' I said. 'Appalling behaviour. I don't know what this country's coming to.'

Maud narrowed her eyes. 'You're in a very peculiar mood this morning and I don't like it. Snap out of it.'

I bit the inside of my lip. At this stage I had so many little cuts in my gums they looked like minced meat. She was about to leave the room when I remembered Jack's email.

'Carlo can do the ball,' I said. 'And he'll waive his fee for the evening. Jack was talking to his agent this morning.'

'Excellent. And tell Magda to check the linen tablecloths for the party. They may need to be starched. I'm going to the airport now. You can get me on my mobile if you need me.'

'The airport?'

'I'm collecting my son. He flew back with one of his

classmates. And do remind Magda to go shopping this afternoon for his tea. Seb has very particular tastes.'

Her face seemed to soften a little when she mentioned her son so I asked, 'What age is he?'

'Seven.'

'And he's in boarding school?' I knew this, of course, but I just couldn't help myself.

'Just get back to work, Alice. My son is none of your concern. And for your information my husband started boarding at five. All the best schools take them young.'

I'd clearly touched a nerve.

'I didn't mean anything by it,' I said. 'I'm just surprised. I'm sure he loves boarding school. Harry Potter and all that. Mallory Towers, midnight feasts, tuck shops—'

'I'll be back by four,' Maud cut me off. 'Tell Magda to have Seb's room ready and the bed turned down.' She walked out of the study and I heard her run down the stairs and bang the front door behind her. Seconds later Mikey, the gardener, who doubled up as her driver, sped out of the gates.

I put my face in my hands. I'd never remember the list of things she'd told me to tell Magda. I should have jotted it all down. I'd never learn.

Magda walked into the room.

'What she want now?' she asked. Her face was glowing with sweat and she didn't look happy. 'I to clean toilet with toothbrush? Or maybe cut lawn with nail scissor?'

I smiled. 'Nothing quite that extreme, I promise. Look, I'll help you with the clothes. She wants you to rewash them. She doesn't like the smell of the washing powder Nadia used in Positano.'

'She crazy. I spray with Febreeze.'

'OK,' I said a little doubtfully, but I wanted to keep Magda onside. 'What else? Oh yes, something about linen tablecloths.'

'I do that already.' Magda wiped some wisps of hair back off her face. 'That all?'

I racked my brains. 'Seb's room.'

'I already turn down bed. She never go in his room. Stupid woman. Pah.' Magda put her thumb and forefinger almost together and scrunched up her eyes. 'I this close to walk out. Understand?'

My heart began to race. 'Please don't, Magda. She's just extra manic because her son is coming home.'

'Son.' Magda snorted. 'What kind of woman send baby away? He only seven. Not right. She heart of stone.'

'She said her husband started boarding at five.'

'I no surprised. Look what happen to him. I tell you, boarding school bad news for Seb. He hate it. Anyway, I finish floor and then do clothes.'

'Can I help you?'

She patted my hand. 'No, you good girl. I know you busy.'

When Maud's car pulled up later, its wide wheels crunching over the gravel, I stuck my head out the study window and stared down through the branches of the chestnut tree. Magda was standing on the gravel, waiting. A neatly dressed blond-haired boy dashed out of the car and gave her a hug. Mikey opened the door for Maud, who stepped out and walked towards Seb, pulling him away from Magda, then said something to her and walked inside. Magda trailed behind them. Seb turned round and pulled a face at his mum's back and Magda winked at him.

I moved away from the window and walked on to the landing. I didn't want to miss anything. Seb dashed up the stairs to his bedroom on the first floor. Then I heard him say 'Ace, Mummy. You're the best,' with a slight Home Counties accent. He ran back down the stairs with a pair of roller blades, knee pads and a helmet under his arm.

'Oh, no, Seb,' Maud said, 'they're far too dangerous. Where on earth did they come from?'

'They present from me,' Magda said firmly. 'He ask for them for ages. I get knee pad too and helmet. Keep him safe.'

'I suppose.' Maud didn't sound all that convinced.

'Please, Mummy? All the boys at school have them. Please?'

'All right. Alice will watch you.'

'Who's Alice?' Seb asked.

'My new assistant.'

I heard Magda add, 'New slave,' and Maud said, 'That's quite enough, Magda. I don't know what's got into you and Alice today. Are you both riddled with PMT?'

'What's PMT?' Seb asked.

'Never mind that. Alice!'

'Coming,' I shouted down the stairs.

Ten minutes later I was sitting on one of the metal garden chairs, watching Seb speed around on his roller blades.

'Don't tell Mummy but I've been practising at school,' he said. 'My best friend Charlie lets me borrow his.'

'Good for you,' I said. 'Do you play soccer? My nephew loves soccer. He's nearly five.'

'No. We play rugby. And cricket in the summer.'

'Do you like rugby?'

'Not really. I'm not very fast you see. And a lot of the boys are much bigger than me. But I like cricket.' He swung his arms back and pretended to hit a ball with an imaginary bat.

Just then Maud came outside. 'There you are, Alice. Come and talk some sense into Magda. She's being utterly unreasonable.' I stared at Maud. She had Josh on her hip. I'd never seen her carry him and it looked strange. He was happily sucking on the long ribbon tie from the neck of her cashmere jumper. He had no trousers on and his vest was flapping open at the bottom. From the look of his sagging rear he needed a nappy change and fast.

'Where's Janny?' I asked.

'Ask Magda,' Maud snapped rudely. She really was in a delightful mood.

'Hi, Josh,' Seb waved at his little brother. 'Look at me. Wheee.' He pushed himself off the garden table and went whizzing down the garden path.

'Careful, Seb,' Maud said. 'And no skating until we come back outside, understand?'

'OK, Mummy.'

'Follow me, Alice,' Maud said, not waiting to see if I was actually behind her. She stood outside the door of the laundry room. 'Now explain to Magda that she can't leave, she has a contract and so does Janny.' Magda was leaning against one of the huge top-loading industrial-sized American washing machines. Her arms were crossed in front of her chest and she looked stern. She reminded me of a 1950s photograph I'd once seen of a young Russian woman driving a tractor.

There were two washing machines in the room and two matching tumble dryers. It seemed crazy for one household, but Maud insisted on fresh bed linen every two days, all ironed and starched. As I'd gathered by now, Maud wasn't exactly sane at the best of times.

'Go on,' Maud told me, 'tell her in Polish.'

'I good English,' Magda said. 'I understand.'

I was mightily relieved. I had no idea what the word for contract was in Polish.

'I no stupid,' Magda added, 'and I no washing holiday clothes again. They perfect. Not dirty.'

'Tell her they smell funny,' Maud said. 'Tell her she *has* to do them again.'

'That it! I have enough. You do them yourself.' Magda picked up a bundle of freshly laundered towels and threw them at Maud. 'You do bloody washing. You do floors. You do baby. You do Seb. You do cooking. I quit! And Janny quit too.'

'You can't quit,' Maud said. 'You have a contract.'

'This what I think of stinking contract.' Magda pretended to spit on the floor. 'We work hard. You pay Janny nothing. Janny have degree. She clever girl. I clever too. You no speak Polish. I speak Russian, German and English and I clean toilets and say, "Yes, Maud. No, Maud" all day. I sick of being your slave. You not nice woman, Maud. You make advantage of person.' She brushed past us both and walked down the corridor towards her room.

'If you're not happy, then leave,' Maud shouted after her, clearly rattled, 'and you can find somewhere else to live. And I'm not paying you this for this week's work, either.'

Magda spun round. 'You not throw us out. We stay till we get other job. Or I go to newspaper and tell how you treat us. I tell how much you pay Janny. I tell them you no look after son. I tell everything. About how Nick treat you *and* about his girls. I see what happen when you away. When you in Italy I see that voman from the telly, O—'

'Stop!' Maud shrieked, cutting her off. 'That's the most appalling thing I've ever heard. And it's all lies. Besides, no one would be interested.'

'Plenty be interested. Nick always in paper. You always in paper. And I keep everything, Maud. I give them Janny's contract. You pay Janny two hundred euro a week. That not right. Alice say not right.'

Maud looked at me. 'Alice?'

I had to say something and I knew where my loyalty lay. 'She has a point, Maud,' I said. 'It's not a lot, and Janny's brilliant with Josh.'

'It's more than most au pairs get. Plus I pay for her English classes. She should have told me she had good qualifications . . . anyway it's none of your business.'

I'd never seen her look so annoyed and that was saying something.

'But you just asked me to talk to Magda for you.'

'Go and check on Seb and stop annoying me. And as for you, Magda, you and Janny can stay for one more week, do you understand? After that, I want you both out.'

Magda said, 'Two week, and a month pay each.'

Maud stared at her through narrowed eyes. 'Fine.' Then she said, 'Alice, what did I tell you?'

I spun on my heels and walked quickly down the corridor. 'I'm going, I'm going,' I muttered. The woman was unbelievable.

'Goody,' Seb said as soon as he saw me. He was sitting patiently on one of the garden chairs, rolling a foot backwards and forwards in front of him. Any normal seven-year-old would have been speeding up and down the patio, despite what they'd been told, but not Seb. 'Can I skate now?'

'Of course.' I gave him a smile. 'But go easy.' As I watched him I picked at a hangnail distractedly and my mind began to wander. I was already dreading Maud's party tomorrow night; without Magda on hand to help it would a nightmare. Maud was already in a dark mood; I'd be blamed for anything that went wrong. Feelings or no feelings, I had to alert Jack. I dialled his mobile.

He answered immediately. 'Alice? What is it now?'

I ignored his prickly tone; I was in no humour for it. 'Magda's just walked out and she's taking Janny with her. Maud's in a stinker. And Seb's back from boarding school. It's mayhem here. I just wanted to warn you.'

'Thanks.' He softened. 'What about Josh? Who's looking after him?'

'He's currently on Maud's hip.'

Jack whistled. 'That should be interesting.'

There was an almighty scream and then a splash. 'Have to go. Seb's just skated into the pond.' I threw down my mobile and ran towards Seb. I waded into the pond and pulled him out by the arm. 'Are you OK?' I asked him, depositing him on the grass, bending down beside him and pulling stringy green pond weed off his leg.

He grinned. 'I was going really fast, wasn't I, Alice?'

'What the hell is going on?' Maud strode down the garden, her hair flying behind her like Boudeccia. Josh was crying, his face red and puffy.

'I skated into the pond, Mummy,' Seb said before I could stop him. 'It was ace.'

Maud glared at me. 'I told you to keep an eye on him.' Josh kicked his little legs. 'Take Josh instead. I'll deal with Seb.'

I peeled Josh off her, put him down on the grass and whipped his soaking nappy off, then I let him crawl towards his brother. Seb began to tickle him under his arms and Josh giggled.

Maud stared at me frostily. She looked down at her side. Her jumper was soaking wet. She pressed her fingers against the damp patch and then smelt them, wrinkling her nose. 'I'm going upstairs to change,' she said. 'Please get Josh a fresh nappy. You know where his room is. Seb, put your wet clothes in the laundry room.'

'OK, Mummy. I'm starving. What's for tea?'

Maud's face went blank. Then she muttered 'Hell' and walked quickly towards the house.

Half an hour later I was cooking fish fingers in the kitchen. I'd sent Mikey down to the local convenience store with a short shopping list: fish fingers, potato waffles, eggs, cheese, milk, Smarties. Magda hadn't had a chance to shop since Maud had come back from Italy, and the fridge was practically bare.

Maud wasn't impressed with my fish-finger suggestion, but Seb assured her he was well used to fish fingers; in fact he had them every Friday in boarding school. I fed Josh scrambled eggs with toast soldiers and cheese cut into heart shapes (more to amuse myself than anything else, besides, I thought he could do with a little love) and he was munching away happily enough.

At five o'clock I called Maud. She'd been running up and down the stairs for the last hour, putting linen tablecloths on the dining-room table, polishing the vases for the flower delivery in the morning, ringing the caterers, ringing Jack to give him an earful about the rudeness of the caterers. They'd refused to send extra catering staff to babysit – as they weren't qualified or insured to work with children – and had suggested trying a nanny agency instead. It was all fun and games at Shelbourne Lodge.

'What is it?' Maud said, wiping her hands on her black trousers and following me into the kitchen. She'd tied her hair back with a brown and white spotted scarf, making her look quite girlish.

'I have to go now,' I said. 'Josh has eaten a good tea and once Seb finishes his peas I told him he could have some ice cream with Smarties. Is that OK?'

She sighed. 'I suppose so. As a special treat. But where are your clothes, Seb? You can't sit around in your boxer shorts and T-shirt. It's not right.'

I smiled at him. 'Sorry, my fault. He was starving so I said he could get dressed after his tea.'

'I'll overlook it just this once, but you'll have to stay and help me put Josh to bed.'

'I'm sorry, Maud, but I have to put my own son to bed.'

'I'll pay you,' she said, looking slightly panicked. 'Name your price.'

'It's not that,' I assured her; although I did wonder how high she'd go if pushed. 'I won't see Adam tomorrow night because of the party and he's a bit unsettled because I was away. It's just not possible.'

'Jack will have to do it then. Ring him.'

'Jack?' She wanted Jack, a highly qualified fund-raising director, to help put her toddler to bed, was she mad? I stared at her.

'Please,' she added.

'You want me to ring Jack for you?'

'Yes.'

'Ring him yourself, but to be honest I think it's a mistake. You'll manage. Now I have to go or I'll miss my train. I'll see you in the morning. I'll come an hour early. At eight. OK?'

'Fine,' she clipped. 'Don't be late.'

As I stomped down the road to Sandymount train station her parting words rang in my ears. 'Don't be late.' I'd offered to come in a whole hour early and she told me not to be late. God she was infuriating.

Chapter 30

By six o'clock on Wednesday evening I was utterly exhausted. I'd spent all morning trying to iron out last-minute problems with the Especially For You charity auction, the next event on the St Jude's calendar. First the printer had rung to say they'd run out of the handmade paper with the damson red ticking thread that we'd ordered for the programmes and would a wine red ticker thread do instead? I'd said yes without checking with Maud. Damson, wine, it was all the same. Only Maud would notice and it would be too late by then for her to complain. Then Maurice, the auctioneer, rang to say his wife had just gone into hospital two weeks early with her twins. He'd have to ask one of his colleagues to do the auction instead. This one, I ran by Maud.

She said, 'Yes, yes as long as they're good-looking and competent, in that order.'

I'd checked out the auctioneer's website; the woman he'd suggested looked very competent, but with her cropped brown hair she also looked like a lay nun. But then I spotted another auctioneer, a man in his forties with olive skin and dark shiny hair shot through with grey. In fact he looked like an older Fabrizio.

'Maud would like Alan Verdi if he's available,' I told Maurice.

Maurice laughed. 'He'd be ideal. He's actually based in our

London office at the moment, running commercial property, but I'll see what I can do.'

'Hang on a sec.' I put my hand over the receiver and relayed this information to Maud, who was standing beside me. She grabbed the phone out of my hand.

'Hello, Maurice. We'll pay Alan's air fare. Business class. And put him up in the Shelbourne for the night. He'll be on the top table with Nick and all his business cronies.'

Maurice rang back ten minutes later to say Alan would be happy to do the auction. One less thing to worry about.

The day had started reasonably well. Luckily Janny had Josh in a very structured routine. Walk in the morning, lunch, long nap in the afternoon, bath, followed by bedtime at seven. Maud had sent Mikey out with the buggy in the morning (he wasn't too thrilled; he'd worn his dark glasses even though it was overcast); Seb was happy curled up on the sofa, watching one of Shane's Pixar DVDs. I'd thrown a handful into my bag this morning, along with some sweets and a large container of frozen lasagne from Grace's freezer. Hopefully it would defrost by teatime. I'd instructed Mikey to buy some salad ingredients and some bread for lunch.

'Janny's not very happy with you,' he told me as I helped him zip the rain cover on to the apple-green Phil and Teds buggy, just in case.

'Why?' I asked.

'For making things too easy for Maud.'

'Does she want Maud to suffer?'

He gave a laugh. 'Na! She wants her job back. She loves that kid.' He nodded down at Josh, who was happily kicking his legs in the buggy.

'Where are Magda and Janny today?' I'd seem them skulk out the side door just after nine. I'd called after them, but I don't think they'd heard me.

'They've gone into town to check out some of the job agencies.'

'I see. So Magda's serious about leaving.'

'Unless Maud apologizes and gives Janny a hefty pay rise, yes. And you know what her highness is like.' He hiked a thumb up the stairs and rolled his eyes. 'No hope.'

At two the Paradise Catering jeep arrived, followed by the O'Brien's off-licence van. The wine, spirits, glasses and mixers were carried inside by two polite older men from O'Brien's, together with a whole box of gleaming metal cocktail shakers. A small blonde woman with flushed cheeks climbed out of the driver's seat of the jeep. She was wearing a white shirt, black trousers, black ballet pumps and a dark red wrap-around apron with a large pocket in the front. She pulled a notebook out of the pocket and checked something before smiling at me. 'You must be Alice,' she said with a slight American accent.

'That's me.'

She held out her hand. 'I'm Minnie. And this is my sister Adelaide.' She whistled. 'Nice pile.'

Adelaide jumped down from the passenger seat and gave me a grin. 'Excuse my sister. She lived in New York for years and she can be a bit direct.'

'Hey.' Minnie dug her sister in the ribs. 'Thanks, sis. I wonder what you say about me when I'm not around.' She checked her list again. 'So, mixed hors d'oeuvres from six and then hot buffet at half past seven. Lots of yellow food to tie in with the sun theme.'

'That's right. And Maud's a stickler for time-keeping, just to warn you. So she really does mean half seven. Nick, her husband, gets indigestion if he eats too late.'

'No problem,' Adelaide said smoothly. 'Show us the kitchen, and where you'd like us to serve up and we'll get organized.'

*

'I'm not doing that tomorrow,' Mikey grumbled as he helped me rearrange the garden furniture near two chrome outdoor heaters. I took the catering company's glass pub-style ashtrays out of a battered cardboard box, gave them a quick polish with a piece of kitchen roll (Maud had insisted) and put one on each table. Maud couldn't abide cigarette smoke in the house, so this was to be smoking central.

'What?'

'Taking Josh out. I felt a right tit. What if one of me mates had seen me? They might think it was me and Janny's or something.'

'You and Janny? Hey, Mikey, you're a lucky man.'

He shifted around a little uncomfortably. 'I don't know about that, she's fierce bossy.'

I laughed.

'What are you two sniggering about?' Maud asked. She looked stunning. Her hair was hanging loosely down her back, glittering like a sheet of copper in the late-afternoon sun. She was wearing a gold crochet dress over a matching silk sheath and her make-up artist had given her dramatic smudged-brown eyes, with sweeping fake eyelashes and bee-stung coffee-coloured lips. I had no idea how she'd eat without removing her lipstick, but, unlike me, she probably wasn't worried about that. I'd seen her eat a scone and a square of chocolate at lunchtime, which was probably her ration for the day.

Mikey stared at her. I could tell he was impressed.

'You look amazing, Maud,' I said, meaning it.

'Thank you,' she said shortly, as if it was her due. 'Alice, Mikey can finish up out here, I need you to read Seb a story and put Josh to bed.'

'Where are they at the moment?'

'One of those catering women is keeping an eye on Josh, and Seb's in his room.'

I smiled to myself. Maud had us all under her thumb.

'Darling!' Koo swept out of the kitchen's French doors in a dramatic conker-coloured floor-length dress. It was slashed down to her belly button at the front and just above her bum at the back. A thick brown leather belt cinched her waist and she wore strappy brown Greek-style leather sandals, their laces snaking up her calves. Her hair was piled on top of her head and, unlike Maud, her make-up was subtle for once, her lips glazed a delicate petal pink.

'What do you think?' Koo gave a twirl. 'I'm not sure about the make-up though, it's a bit casual.'

'Takes years off you,' I said, 'you don't look a day over forty.' It was the first time I'd seen her since Italy and the way I'd been treated by both Koo and Jack still stung.

'I wasn't asking you,' she said. 'And for your information I'm only in my mid-thirties.'

She stared at me. I didn't have the energy to take her on, not tonight. 'I'd better go inside,' I murmured. 'Put Josh to bed.'

At quarter past seven my nerves were shot. Maud hadn't let up for one second.

'Door, Alice. Coats, Alice. Drink for Mr Lambay, Alice; white lemonade now, not tonic, understand? Diet if they have it. Tell the caterers they have ten minutes to go.'

Jack arrived at twenty past seven and I was fit to murder him. 'Where the hell have you been?' I hissed at him as soon as I opened the door.

'Nice to see you too,' he said walking in, passing me so closely we almost touched. I breathed in the familiar lemony aftershave and my stomach lurched with longing. 'You can do the door now,' I said. 'I'll be in the dining room. They're just about to serve the food.'

'Look, I'm sorry, I just couldn't get away. Something came

up.' He looked me up and down. 'You look stunning by the way.'

'Thanks,' I said, pleased that someone had finally noticed, even if it was the biggest philanderer in town. The only other person who'd noticed was Nick, who'd pinched my bottom when I walked past him, then laughed in my face when I'd glared at him.

My dress wasn't as dramatic as Koo's or as unusual as Maud's, but I liked it. Petra had dropped it over last night. It had been slightly too big round the chest but she'd sewn in a few tucks and now it fitted almost perfectly. It was an Italian dress, funnily enough, midnight-blue chiffon with delicate silver beading on the straps and bodice. She'd also found me a pair of almost matching blue satin shoes with peep toes. The heel was a little high for running around, but so far I was coping. I'd gone over my hair with Grace's GHD hair straighteners this evening to make it look 'done' and I'd given myself sparkling peacock-blue eyes, and dramatic red lips.

I was glad I'd made the effort; this was a seriously glam party and everyone looked like movie stars: pink satin Marilyn Monroe dresses, black beaded cocktail numbers, achingly fashionable cap-sleeved fitted dresses worn with skyscraper heels. I'd even spotted two hats, one an over-sized Trilby with a feather that screamed Philip Treacy, the other a miniature fuchsia felt beret, perched on the side of a woman's 1950s style bob. The men were equally dapper: three-piece suits, charcoal-black suits, pointed-toed patent-leather shoes. Even Jack had scrubbed up well, in a pin-striped suit, sky-blue shirt and dark pink tie.

There was a photographer from *Gloss* magazine snapping away, a tiny, doll-like woman who wove in and out of the crowds with her huge camera, jotting down people's names in a spiral-bound notebook. The cocktails were going down a treat, and Koo was certainly enjoying them. Every time I passed her she had a fresh glass in her hand and waved it at me animatedly.

'Isn't this *fun*?' she kept saying. 'I'm having so much *fun*. Such a shame you have to work, Alice.'

The dining room, sitting room and hall were teeming with people, all chatting animatedly. I heard snippets of conversation as I buzzed past the clumps of party goers.

'Do you really think he's gay? Surely not. Although there was that incident with Singer, do you remember?'

'Bratislava is so over, property wise. Moscow is your only man.'

'We were thinking of the BVIs for our next cruise. Or maybe Antigua again, but the English harbour gets so terribly busy during race week . . .'

When I went into the kitchen to check on Minnie and Adelaide, Nick was surrounded by a throng of men, all admiring his sharks.

'Maudie hates them of course,' he said and then guffawed, 'but a man has to have his little hobbies.' He slapped Adelaide on the bottom as she walked past with a large steaming dish of rice for the flame-heated side server. She nearly dropped it.

'Can I help you carry anything through?' I asked, following her into the hall. When Nick was out of earshot I whispered, 'Sorry about that. He's a pig. He pinched my ass earlier.'

'One of the perks of the job,' she said wryly. 'Don't worry, I've had worse. And thanks, but this is the last dish of rice. We'll start serving now. Can you let Maud know?'

I stood at Maud's side, waiting for a lull in the conversation. She was discussing art prices with Gunella and a large, tubby man with a pink face and tiny eyes. His stomach was so big his tie only reached halfway down it, bobbing about like a child's school tie.

'Maud, I think Alice wants you,' Gunella said.

'What is it now?' Maud asked.

'The food is ready to be served,' I said meekly.

'Is that all? Announce it then. And be polite.'

'Me?'

'Yes, you. I'm hardly going to do it.' She waved her hand at me. 'Go on.'

Luckily Jack was still in the hall. I braced myself to talk to him, 'Jack, I have to announce the food's ready. Do I just shout it out or what?'

He gave a laugh. 'Maud would love that. Don't worry, I'll do it.'

'Thanks,' I said gratefully, forgetting for a second how appallingly he'd behaved. I watched as he went halfway up the first flight of stairs, a fork and a glass in his hand. He hit the glass several times and gradually people stopped chatting and looked up at him.

'Ladies and gentlemen,' he said, 'the buffet is now being served in the dining room. Thank you.'

He walked back towards me, stopping to pluck two cocktail glasses off a waiter's round silver tray. 'Now we can both relax,' he said, handing me a glass. 'Garden? We should talk.'

'What about the front door?'

'Most people are here by now, but just in case . . .' He had a word with a passing waiter. 'It's fine, he said he'll keep an eye on it. Quick, while they're all queuing up for food. Maud's in the dining room playing the perfect hostess, she won't miss us.'

Once outside, I said, 'I presume you want to talk about Magda or work, because otherwise I have nothing to say to you.' My palms were sweaty and I could feel my heart thumping in my chest. I so didn't want to discuss Positano. It was all too upsetting and I still felt such a fool for trusting him.

There was a lone male cigar smoker sitting on the bench beside the pond. It was the Humpty Dumpty man. 'Will I tell him the food's ready?' I asked Jack.

'He's probably out here to get some peace. That's Ralph, Gunella's husband.'

'No! He's ancient.'

'He's younger than he looks; nice man really. A bit hen-pecked by Gunella and his daughters. Lives down in Wicklow most of the time.'

'Gunella has daughters?'

'Three of them. All in college in England. Mad into horse riding and shooting. Trixie, Cass and P.'

'Look,' I said cutting to the chase. He was being far too chatty for my liking. From now on I wanted to keep our relationship strictly business. 'We have to persuade Magda and Janny to come back. It's a nightmare. Maud wants me here tomorrow and Friday to look after her children. It's not on. The charity auction is next week and I haven't even finalized the menu yet. Or briefed the auctioneer, or—'

'It's all under control, stop worrying.'

'That's not the point. Maud's driving me nuts.'

'Look, just hang in there for a few more days. I'll sort something out for next week, I promise.' He put his hand on my arm but I pulled it away.

I said, 'If we could just get Maud to apologize.'

'Alice, it's not really any of our business.'

'Do you have any idea what she's been paying Janny? Two hundred euro a week. It's criminal. And she pretends to be this wonderful, charitable person. It's a joke.'

'Don't get involved.'

'I have to stand up for what's right. With the amount of hours Janny does, that's way below the minimum wage. We have to say something to Maud. She can afford it. If she stopped buying so many bloody clothes—'

'Alice, if you say anything else about Janny's wages to Maud, she'll fire you on the spot. She won't have you or anyone else judging her. She needs respect, especially from her staff. In case you haven't noticed, she gets little enough of it from Nick.'

Now my blood was boiling. 'I'm supposed to be working for St Jude's, remember, not Maud. And I have to stand up for what's right. I'm sick of being treated like a second-class citizen just because I have to work to pay my way. I'd rather live with my sister for the rest of my life than stand back and let her treat Magda and Janny like dirt. They're people too, Jack, people who also deserve our respect, whether Maud sees that or not. So what if she does fire me? There are other jobs. I have morals, you know, unlike some people.'

'Listen to me. I know you do and I admire you for it. But getting yourself fired isn't going to help anyone, least of all Magda and Janny. And I want you to stay.' He sighed deeply, his eyes flashing with emotion. 'Dammit.' He grabbed the tops of my arms, pulled me towards him and kissed me.

I pushed him away and wiped my mouth with the back of my hand. 'What the hell was that for? You had no right to do that. What about Koo? You're some piece of work.' I stormed off towards the back door.

'Come back. You've got it all wrong, listen to me. Why won't you believe me? Koo's lying, Alice!'

'Hello, old chap,' Ralph said as Jack ran towards me, stopping him in his tracks. 'How fortuitous. I wanted to have a dickie in your ear about that auction thing. Want to buy Gunny a present for her birthday. Something special. What should I go for do you think?'

Inside, Maud cornered me in the hall. 'I want words with you. Look!' Maud pointed at Odette Cunningham, who was poured into a red lycra dress. Odette was standing beside Nick, hanging on to his every word. Maud grabbed my arm and marched me through the front door. 'Odette Cunningham is here. In my house. And Nick says she was invited. *And* I spotted Dick

Toylin and some of his crooked business cronies. Dick's involved in a planning tribunal at the moment and he shouldn't be here. Nick is having conniptions. What did the invitation file say?' She shook me a little. 'Tell me.'

'Let go of me.'

She loosened her grip on my arms and I took a step back. 'It said invitation list, gold,' I said.

'Gold?' Her eyes sparked as though they'd been hit by a blacksmith's hammer. 'That was the old list, you bloody fool. The updated one is called Platinum!'

'Maud, the invitations were gold, so I just presumed—'

'Never presume. Always double check. You have no idea what you've done. No idea. Now go into the kitchen and make yourself useful clearing up. And stay out of my sight.'

I was on the verge of telling her where to stick her job, but she walked away before I picked up the courage. As soon as I got into the kitchen Minnie handed me a plate piled high with strawberry meringue roulade.

'I heard that. Ouch! Welcome to our world, babe,' she said, shaking her head. 'We have to deal with women like Maud all the time. You look like you could do with some sugar.'

'I hate that woman,' I told her. 'I really, really hate her. In fact, I think I'm going to kill her.' I held up the dessert fork and made a *Psycho* 'Eek, eek, eek,' noise.

Minnie laughed. 'She's something all right. And that husband of hers. Caught him in here earlier with a blonde woman. They were all over each other.'

'She wasn't wearing a red dress by any chance?'

'Actually she was. A little spray-on number.'

I started to feel faint. I'd obviously managed to invite Nick's mistress to the party. No wonder Maud was seeing red, literally. I was such an idiot. 'Can I help you?' I asked, going right off my dessert.

'No. Go and sit down. You look exhausted.'

I walked through the double doors which led into the small sitting room overlooking the back garden. I closed them behind me, sat down on the sofa facing the lawn and then, feeling utterly wiped, lay down, curling my feet up and pulling one of Maud's cashmere throws over me. Then I stared out the window. Jack was still beside the pond, talking to Gunella's husband. He was listening to Ralph, really listening to him as if he was the most interesting man on the planet, which he clearly wasn't. If I didn't know the real Jack, I'd think he was the kindest person I'd ever met. Instead of a big, fat liar.

Just then I heard voices and the double doors opened and closed again.

'Maud, you have to calm down.' It was Koo. I was about to sit up when I heard her say, 'It wasn't Alice's fault. It was her first week and your files *are* a bit cryptic. It's Boothy you should be angry with, not Alice. He's the one rubbing your face in it. But it's not just that, is it? It's the summer solstice – Hal's birthday.'

Who on earth was Hal? I was glued to the spot. If they found me I'd just say I was taking a nap and incur Maud's wrath for sleeping on the job. It was worth the risk.

'Don't,' Maud said, her voice breaking. 'I can't think about that now.'

'But you have a party every year on Hal's birthday, the summer solstice – 21st of June. You know that and I know that, and Boothy must know that too. I don't know why you put up with him, Maud, I really don't.'

'We're married. And the boys need their father.'

'Seb is only here because his boarding school finished early. Otherwise he'd still be locked up in that damn kennel for little boys. Nick barely acknowledges Josh at the best of times. When Hal died something happened to him. He changed. Maybe one day he'll learn to love Seb and Josh like a real dad, but you have no excuse. Your sons are growing up and you don't really know either of them. They need you. Things can't go on like this. You're becoming a bitter person and I hate it. You've always been strong, but if you could just hear the way you talk to Magda and Alice and even Jack. I'm telling you this because I love you.'

Maud made a low guttural noise and I heard the slap of a palm meeting skin.

Koo said, 'Ow! Jesus, Maud!'

'Let go of me!' Maud said. 'I hate you.'

'You can hit me all you like, I can take it.'

'How can you be so cruel?' Maud wailed. 'It's not true. I love my children.'

'It's been five years since Hal died, five years. His room is still sealed up like some sort of mausoleum. He's gone, Maud, but you have Josh and Seb to think about now. Please get some counselling and drag Nick along too, if he'll go.'

I could hear Maud making a strange mewing noise. Then she began to sob.

'That's right, my darling, have a good cry. You need it. Let Hal go, Maud. You have to let him go and get on with your life.'

'My baby.' Maud moaned. 'It was all my fault.'

'No, it wasn't. He was a terrible fellow for climbing; you couldn't take your eyes off him for a second.'

'He was reaching for the tree,' Maud said, her voice broken and ragged. 'He loved that tree. I should never have left the room. I had no idea he could climb up his chest of drawers like that. Or open his window.' She gave a heart-wrenching sob.

'Shush, now, shush,' Koo said soothingly. I imagined her stroking Maud's long hair. 'That's it, have a good old cry. It happened, Maud, and you can't do anything about that. But Hal would want you to move on. He was a happy little fellow, and he loved Seb, remember? Seb and Josh have to be your priorities now. You have to let go.'

For a few minutes, the only sound was Maud crying. After what seemed like an age Koo said, 'Ready to go back out now?'

'My eyes,' Maud murmured.

'I'll fix you up in the kitchen. My bag's in there.'

I could hear the door to the kitchen open.

'For Christ's sake, Boothy!' Koo screamed. 'The caterers could be back at any second. Odette, get out of this house. Now!'

'You have no right to tell me what to do, Koo Ryder,' came a woman's breathy voice. 'Nick?'

'I'll take you home, Odette,' Nick said. 'Let's get out of this madhouse. And what's wrong with your eyes, Maud? Did someone punch you?'

'That's it,' Koo said, her voice full of venom. 'If you don't kill him, Maud, I will. Do something.'

There was a deathly silence.

'Right,' Koo said. 'Get out of here, Nick, and take your slapper with you. Or you'll have me to deal with. It's the 21st of June. Have some fucking respect.'

'I didn't realize—' Nick began.

'Liar! Shut it,' Koo said. 'And get out!'

A few minutes later all was quiet. I peeped over the back of the sofa just to make sure. Koo had left the door to the kitchen open so I could see the room was empty. I jumped up quickly. Then I recovered my bag and coat, which I'd left under the kitchen table. It had been quite a night and I was finally going home. I'd leave a note for Maud and sneak out.

I scribbled 'Maud, see you at nine a.m. Couldn't find you to say goodbye. Alice' on the back of a stray invitation and propped it against an empty champagne bottle on the kitchen counter.

I walked into the hall, turned sharp right and focused my eyes on the door, willing no one to notice me.

'Alice!'

It was Maud. The bloody woman was everywhere. I rushed towards the door, hoping she'd think I'd gone momentarily deaf. Then BANG, I tripped over the large bucket she had left by the front door for donations to St Jude's. It fell over with a clunk and I bent down to rub my throbbing ankle.

'Alice, what are you doing? That money's for sick babies. I know you're broke, but really.' Maud stared at me, Koo just behind her.

I stood up, bank notes spread under my feet like autumn leaves, coins still spinning on the marble floor. 'Maud,' I said, lifting my chin up to eyeball her, 'I've been busting my ass for you all day; I've been feeding your children, for God's sake. Do you honestly think I'd steal money meant for St Jude's? No wonder Magda left you, she's right, you're an appalling person. I know your life's not exactly perfect, but whose is?'

'How dare you?' Maud said, angry red spots appearing on her cheeks. 'I won't be spoken to—'

Koo stepped forward and put her hand on my arm. 'Go,' she told me, her eyes kind for the first time all night. 'I'll pick up the money. I saw you knock it over; of course you weren't trying to nick it. I know that, and so does Maud. Don't you Maud?'

Maud just stood there glaring at me with her arms crossed tightly across her chest. 'Maud,' Koo said. 'I'm ashamed of you. Apologize to Alice right this minute or I'm leaving too.'

'But . . .' Maud was flabbergasted.

Koo continued. 'Alice didn't deserve it. Go on, apologize.'

'Sorry, Alice,' Maud said tightly. 'I'm having a very bad day.' She left it at that, but I caught her gaze and there was such deep despair in her hazel eyes that it hurt just to look at her. After finding out what she'd been through in the last few years, I decided to be the bigger person and accept her apology but I held my thumb and forefinger an inch apart. 'I'm this close to leaving, Maud. I can't take much more of this. I'll be in the office tomorrow if you need me. You'll have to look after your children yourself. I won't leave you high and dry or anything, but I think you should start looking for another PA.'

'We'll discuss it tomorrow,' Maud said. 'I'll ask Mikey to drive you home. You've had a long day.'

'Thank you.' You see, I told myself, I try to hate the woman and then she goes and does something nice. It's infuriating.

'You look like hell,' she added, 'and those cheap heels can't be comfortable.'

On second thoughts . . .

Chapter 31

'Nice car,' Grace said as I walked in the door. She peered out at Mikey, who was turning Maud's Mercedes in the drive. 'And who's he? Cute. Don't tell me you scored.'

'Hardly.' I smiled at her. 'That's Maud's driver.' I waved at him and he beeped the horn and waved back.

Grace lifted her eyebrows. 'He seems to like you.'

'Grace, would you stop, you're obsessed. He's with Janny.'

'Shame. How was the party anyway?'

I pulled a face. 'Horrible. I don't want to talk about it.'

'Please? Shane drew stick men all over the kitchen walls while I was changing Eric's clothes. That was the highlight of *my* day. Oh, that and Jason calling in. He wanted to see the boys.'

'Course he did.' I tried not to smile.

'Stop looking at me like that,' she said.

I followed her into the living room and we both flopped down on the sofa. She flicked off the television and gave me her full attention. 'So, go on, who was at the party? Anyone famous?'

I mentioned a few names, Odette of course, and a couple of models and businessmen. She was very impressed and pretended to recognize the names, even though, like me, she'd probably never heard of half of them. Then I told her how I'd fallen over the donations bucket. She laughed and I hit her.

'Grace, stop, it's not funny, I was mortified.' And finally I told her about Jack and how he tried to kiss me in the garden.

'God, that man is some piece of work,' she said.

'I know. And then Maud caught her husband in the kitchen with Odette Cunningham no less.'

'No! But from what you've told me about Maud, she probably deserves it.'

'I suppose, but I overheard something really tragic. Maud had another son called Hal. He fell out his bedroom window a few years ago and died.'

Grace's hand went to her mouth and she gasped. 'Oh my God, how horrible. The poor woman.'

'I know. It kind of puts things in perspective though. No wonder she's so grouchy most of the time. She blames herself you see.'

'But it was an accident, right? She didn't push him or anything?'

'Grace! She's not that bad. Of course not, she was in another room at the time.'

'Sorry, that was an unforgivable thing to say, ignore me. I don't know how you'd get over something like that. If anything happened to Eric or Shane . . .' She sucked in her breath and then shook her head. 'It must be so hard for her.'

'It's all very strange. She's very odd around Josh and Seb, nervous, even though I'm sure she loves them. I think she's scared of losing them too. And remember what I told you about Nick and Josh and everything? She's completely messed up. She was unbelievably rude to me this evening, but I couldn't really say anything because of Hal. Today would have been his birthday.'

Grace said, 'I'm dying to meet this woman, Alice. She sounds fascinating.'

'She's not fascinating at all,' I said passionately. 'I have to work for her, remember? It's no bloody picnic I can tell you.

I'm seriously thinking of packing it all in. No house is worth what she puts me through on an hourly basis.'

'But you're doing so well,' Grace said. 'Think of Rosewood. Only a few more weeks.'

'I'm exhausted. I feel like murdering the woman, tragedy or no tragedy. And this business with Jack isn't helping. I have to see him all the time and I really liked him, Gracey. Why does nothing ever work out for me? Why am I so cursed with men?' I started to cry, hot angry tears. I knew I was just feeling sorry for myself, I knew I was tired and I'd had a pretty gruelling day, but I couldn't help it. I felt so low.

Grace picked up one of my hands and stroked it. 'Not all of them. What about Adam's dad? He didn't hate you, did he? It was just bad timing.'

Then I started to really wail. 'No, he didn't hate me. But he didn't love me enough to leave his girlfriend, even when I told him I was pregnant. The truth is I wanted him so badly, I got pregnant on purpose, but it didn't make any difference. He said it didn't change a thing; he told me to have an abortion and to leave him alone.' I started crying again.

Grace looked shocked. She said nothing for a moment, than 'Stay there, I'll go and get you some tissues.' Seconds later she handed me a whole box of them, which was just as well; I had a mixture of tears and snot running down my face. I blew my nose and said, 'Thanks.' And then, 'Sorry.'

'No, I'm sorry,' she said. 'I had no idea. No wonder you want nothing more to do with him. But sometimes life's messy, and we just have to make the most of it. Adam is a great little lad, a real credit to you.'

'But it was such a stupid thing to do. What was I thinking?'

She shrugged. 'There's no point looking back, and you wouldn't wish Adam away, would you?'

'No, of course not. He's the best thing that's ever happened to me.'

Grace smiled. 'Well then. And you'll always have me. I'm here for you, no matter what. You can count on it.'

'Thanks, sis,' I said through my tears.

She put her arms round me and held tight.

Chapter 32

Thursday. I was all alone in the office. Jack hadn't even bothered to ring me in person; he'd left a garbled message on my office phone, claiming there was some kind of emergency at home. He's probably off bonking Koo in a five-star hotel, I thought ungraciously as I opened the charity-auction file on my computer. It was blissfully quiet for a couple of minutes until the phone rang.

'Alice,' Maud barked down the receiver, 'Seb wants scrambled eggs for his lunch. How do you make them?'

'Maud, it's only ten in the morning. Can I ring you back later? I'm on the other line.'

'Is it important?'

'Yes. I'm talking to Colin Farrell's agent about the auction.'

She sighed theatrically. 'Ring me back as soon as you've finished. My children's nutrition is important too, you know.'

I clicked back on to the other line. 'Sorry about that. Now, about the auction. The prize would be dinner for eight in a private room in the Mermaid, hosted by Colin. What do you think?'

'Colin's on for it,' said the actor's surprisingly down-to-earth London agent. 'But no press, OK? Just a private dinner.'

'Absolutely. It'll go to the highest bidder, obviously, but we will stress the fact that it's a private dinner; strictly a press-free zone.'

'In that case, I can't see any problem. Colin's a big fan of the hospital and he likes to do what he can to help. Let's talk dates.'

I put down the phone with a huge grin on my face. Dinner with Colin Farrell had been one of my ideas, and we'd managed to track him down through Jack's twin sisters, who had been at school with Colin's sister Claudine. In fact we were using several of my ideas.

The 'Especially for You' bit in the auction's title was mine, inspired by the Jason and Kylie song from years ago, not that I'd told Maud that, of course. Jack had grinned when I'd suggested the phrase and hummed the song under his breath, but I'd thrown him a flinty look and he'd kept his mouth shut. Although I was still livid with him, I was determined to be civil at work. It was difficult not to snap at him, frustrated by my feelings, but most of the time I managed to keep myself in check.

We were going to auction a whole host of things money couldn't buy like art lessons with uber cool Irish painters Graham Knuttel and Guggi; writing lessons with Maeve Binchy and Marian Keyes; a pair of one-off shoes designed by Eileen Shields; a unique cashmere coat designed by Lainey Keogh; the chance to be featured in various magazines and newspapers in what they called their 'furniture' pieces – 'My Favourite Car', 'What's in My Handbag', 'My Glorious House', 'My New Boobs', that kind of thing. That one was Jack's idea, he said it would appeal to vain, rich people who wanted to boast about their assets in the national press.

The auction was in less than a week, but I still hadn't heard back from Alan Verdi, our auctioneer. He was on holiday in Athens and wouldn't be back till Tuesday. He'd emailed me all right, but I hadn't talked to him in person. It would be just my luck if he had a stutter or, even worse, a monotonous voice. To induce people to bid and keep bidding, we needed style, charisma and a great sense of humour, someone who could inject the whole proceedings with real oomph. And in Jack's absence it was my job to pin down and vet Alan.

Maud rang at eleven – scrambled eggs again; at twelve – looking for the cheese grater; two – asking how to fix the DVD. Luckily Seb discovered she was trying to put the new disc on top of the old one.

'How was I supposed to know?' she'd grumbled. 'I never watch DVDs or television.' No wonder the woman's so odd, I thought. Imagine living without your *Grey's Anatomy* fix.

I needed to get the final wording for the auction programme to the printers by five so I stopped answering the phone after three. At ten past five I listened to the messages. All but two were from Maud. I groaned and then rang her.

'Alice!' she shrieked. 'Where have you been? Are slug pellets dangerous?'

'Slug pellets?'

'Yes, yes. If a child eats them, are they dangerous?'

'Maud, calm down. Who ate them and how many did they eat?'

'Josh and I don't know. Maybe two or three. Blue ones.'

That didn't sound good. 'Is he awake?' I asked.

'Of course he's awake. He's been sick several times. All over my ivory cashmere. I can't get the blue mark out of my sleeve.'

'Where's Mikey?'

'Just beside me.'

'Tell him to go and get the box of slug pellets.'

'Why?'

'Just get on with it! This could be serious, Maud. You may have to bring Josh to hospital to get his stomach pumped. Do you understand? My friend's son swallowed toilet cleaner at about the same age, that's how I know.'

Maud gave an anxious squeak and then I heard voices. Seconds later Mikey came on the line. 'Jesus, I'm so sorry,

Alice. I had no idea Josh would be crawling round the flower beds on his own. Janny doesn't let him near the beds; she says cat poo can be lethal.'

'It's not your fault,' I said. 'Tell me what it says on the front of the box.'

Mikey began to read. 'Advanced slug killer. Based on ferrous phosphate. Safe for children and pets. Kills only slugs and snails.'

'Thanks, Mikey,' I said with relief. 'Don't worry, Josh'll be fine. Can you put Maud back on?'

'Alice,' Maud said and I could hear the terror in her voice, 'will I call an ambulance?'

'No. Just keep an eye on him. It's good he got sick. Most of it's probably out of his system and luckily the pellets aren't lethal. But they could have been. Maybe you should ring your GP just to double-check what exactly ferrous phosphate is. But I think it's safe enough. And Maud, it's not Mikey's fault. He's just doing his job. Josh shouldn't be in the garden on his own.'

'I only took my eyes off him for one second,' she protested. 'I was watching Seb go backwards on his roller blades. I don't know how other mothers do this. I'm hopeless.'

'You're not hopeless, you just need more practice. One kid's hard enough, two's a real handful. Look, don't take this the wrong way but I think you'd better start looking for another nanny and housekeeper. Maybe Nick could—'

'That's fine, Alice,' Maud clipped. 'We have everything under control now. I'll see you tomorrow.'

'Tomorrow?'

'Yes, Jack said he could spare you, and as you said, I clearly can't cope on my own.'

'But I didn't—'

'Oh, don't bother, I know what you meant. Be here at nine, please. And don't be late.'

'But I still haven't got hold of Alan Verdi, and we've had

some last-minute table cancellations, I have to ring the reserve list and fill the places. After all the effort we've put into the auction, the last thing we want is empty tables. Then I have to do the press release, get details to all the photo desks—'

'That's not my problem. Maybe you should manage your time a little better. I have to go now. My children need me.' She put down the phone, cutting me off.

'Thanks for saving my child's life,' I said to the buzzing line. 'Stupid cow.'

I rang Grace and told her I'd be late. If I didn't make a start on the press releases they wouldn't go out tomorrow. I didn't want Jack to think I wasn't pulling my weight. I put my head on my desk and banged it gently against the wood.

'I'll do it,' Grace said later that evening when I moaned about having to help at Maud's the following day. 'I'll mind her kids.'

'What?' I stared at her. 'Are you serious?'

'Absolutely! I'm dying to meet this woman and see her house. You can come with me and introduce us. Once Maud's happy you can run into the office.' She held her hands palms up. 'That way everyone wins.'

'And the boys?'

'They'll be at school in the morning and I'll see if Petra can take Adam. And Jason can cover in the afternoon. It'll be fun.'

'Fun? Are you delusional?'

She just smiled.

Chapter 33

Maud opened the door. Her hair was scraped back off her face and she had no make-up on. There was a greasy-looking smear on her cheek and she had Josh on her hip. 'About time,' she said, handing Josh to me before I'd even had a chance to step inside the door, 'I desperately need a shower. I put him on the floor in the bathroom but he started to brush the walls with the toilet brush. I tried putting him in the bath but he turned the taps on and soaked himself. How do mothers stay clean?'

'They have showers when their kids are in bed,' Grace said. 'Or in your case when the nanny is on duty.' She stuck out her hand. 'I'm Grace, Alice's sister. I'm a highly experienced child-care professional and cook, and I've come to help you today. Alice is going to show me the ropes and then go into the office. I presume that's OK with you?'

Maud looked at me and then back at Grace, who in fairness looked ultra-efficient in her smart navy trousers and my white linen shirt. Maud seemed surprised by Grace's firm, no-nonsense tone. 'Yes,' she said, 'but don't you work in the media?'

'I'm on a career break from that,' Grace said smoothly, giving Maud a confident smile.

Maud smiled back. 'It would be quite a relief to have a professional on board. Alice is fine, but it's not the same, is it?'

Professional, my ass, I felt like saying; Grace is a professional bullshitter, but I bit my tongue. In Grace, Maud was about to meet her match and it would be very, very interesting.

'Alice, show Grace the kitchen. Seb's in the back garden on his skates. Mikey's keeping an eye on him. I really must have a shower. I'll see you in a little while.' She gave Josh a kiss on the top of his head and started to walk up the stairs. 'You could make a start on the washing too, Alice,' she added. 'I tried to do some last night but . . . well, see if you can sort it all out. I'm not very good with machines.'

'I'll have a go,' I said.

'Thank you,' she said. Probably for Grace's benefit.

'She doesn't seem all that bad,' Grace whispered as we walked down the stairs to the basement.

I rolled my eyes. 'You just wait.'

When I was sure Maud was in the shower I gave Grace a quick sneaky tour. 'This is the dining room,' I said, handing Josh another biscuit to keep him quiet. I didn't have to worry about crumbs on the carpet and marble floors, they were already grubby with roller-blade marks, foot prints and what looked like popcorn. Maud obviously hadn't found the Hoover yet.

Grace whistled under her breath, her eyes out on stalks. She ran her fingers over the mahogany table and gazed up at the huge crystal chandelier. She was even more impressed by the sharks in the kitchen. She shook her head a little. 'I didn't really believe you about these fellows,' she said knocking on the glass. 'But look at them. Scary but magnificent. Shane and Eric would love them.' They swam quickly towards her, obviously expecting a feed. Then it dawned on me. Magda usually did that, they were probably starving, but I had no idea what they ate. Maud would have to ring Nick; they were his sharks, surely he'd know.

After introducing Grace to Mikey, and playing with Seb and Josh in the garden for a while – reminding Grace to keep Josh out of the flower beds just in case – I went to look for Maud and tell her about the sharks before I left.

I caught her coming out of the bathroom in a towel, another one wrapped round her head like a turban. She wasn't impressed. 'What are you doing up here?'

I explained about the sharks and she said, 'Yes, yes, I'll ring him,' and walked into her room, banging the door behind her so hard it bounced open a little. I went into the study, remembering Jack had asked me to look for a copy of the auction programme from the year before last. Maud kept all the programmes in a big concertina file and I knew exactly where to look. I found it and was about to walk back down the stairs when I heard Nick's voice on the speaker phone. I decided I might as well find out how to feed the sharks from the horse's mouth so I stuck around.

'The sharks!' Nick said, and he sounded rather agitated. 'You pulled me out of an important meeting because of the sharks?'

'Yes,' Maud snapped, 'I don't mind if the buggers die, but I'm sure you do. They cost a fortune, remember?'

'Die? What are you on about?'

'They haven't been fed since Magda left.'

'Why the hell not?'

'Because they're not my sharks, Nick. You know how much I detest them.'

'What about your girl? Alicia?'

'Alice. She's hopeless. She doesn't have a clue about anything, let alone feeding sharks.'

After all I'd done for her. The bloody cheek!

'You'll have to ring the fish shop,' Nick said. 'The feed is delivered every week; that's all I know. Magda used to deal with everything.'

'Where's the fish shop?'

'Oh, for fuck's sake, Maud, I don't know. Somewhere in Dun

Laoghaire I think. And another thing, what's Seb doing home? It's only June. He's not supposed to be back for another month.'

'They're renovating the dorms. The boys doing exams were allowed to stay. Everyone else had to go home. So I thought it was best if Seb—'

'I'm not paying school fees this month if he's not in bloody school. I'll get my lawyer to ring them later. Fucking disgrace. I've a good mind to send him straight back and see what they do about it.'

'You can't do that,' Maud said, 'it would really unsettle him. He doesn't seem to like boarding all that much, Nick. Can't we rethink things? Maybe he could be a day boarder in Castle Park. It's only down the road. Or he could try—'

'Maud, we've talked about this before. Boarding school was the making of me. And I want Seb and Josh to have the same advantages I did.'

'What about what I want? Doesn't that count? I miss him. And I've coped with Josh this week, haven't I?' She obviously hadn't told him about the slug-pellet incident then.

'Yes, you've coped admirably, Maud. But I do wish you'd stop waiting for Magda to change her mind. Go and hire someone else. I don't know why you like the damned woman so much. I think she's creepy. And as for missing Seb, get a grip, woman, he's not a baby. Josh will be joining him in less than three years. And that will put an end to all this clucky hen nonsense. If Hal had had a nanny like I suggested—'

I gasped. Luckily Maud gasped at the same time, so she didn't hear me.

'That's a hateful thing to say. Hateful! What *is* wrong with you?'

'I'm sorry, you're right, forgive me.' He sounded contrite.

Maud took advantage of his softer tone. 'Please say you'll be home at a decent hour. Seb's dying to see you.'

'I'll try, but I'm not promising anything. Now, I have to go. The minister's on the other line.'

'We need to talk. I keep trying to tie you down, but you're always so busy. I've put up with all your indiscretions; I've never said a word. But I won't let you play with our children's happiness. I'm serious about Seb. He hates that school. How can I be a proper mother if he's never here? And it's not just me, Josh misses him too. We need to spend time as a family, the four of us. Nick, we've been through so much together—'

'We'll talk later, I promise. The minister won't wait, I have to go.' The line went dead and I scuttled down the stairs.

Back in the garden, Grace looked over and smiled at me. 'Josh needs changing. Where do his nappies live?' I showed her his beautifully decorated nursery in the basement, with the white wooden cot and matching furniture, and coordinated egg-shell-blue silk curtains, blind, and lampshade.

'Why is his room down here in the basement?' she asked.

'It's beside Janny's room,' I explained. 'If he wakes during the night Janny looks after him.'

'Wow,' Grace said. 'I've read about women like Maud, but I've never met one. I wonder if she's ever changed a nappy.'

'Yes, I've changed a nappy,' Maud said from behind us.

Grace and I jumped. I wondered how much Maud had over-heard. But I was starting not to care.

'It's Nick who insisted, not me,' Maud said. 'He gets to work every morning at six so he needs his sleep. But I'm going to move Josh upstairs as soon as his new room is decorated. Brothers should be close to each other, don't you think?'

'My two share the same room,' Grace said. 'They try to kill each other most of the time. But they're close all right.'

Maud nodded. 'Good.' It was only then I noticed she had something in her hands. 'Alice, is this ruined do you think? Or can the dry cleaners do anything with it?'

She handed me a cream cashmere jumper which had a

large brown scorch mark down the front. 'I washed it by hand,' she said, sounding pathetically pleased with herself. 'I found the Woolite in the laundry and washed it in the sink, following the directions. It wasn't all that hard actually. And then I put it on top of the Aga to dry.'

I winced. 'I can ask them,' I said gently. 'But I think it's a goner. I'm sorry.'

She sighed. 'Oh, dear. It's one of my favourites, a present from Koo. And I seem to have broken the toilet; and the washing machine.'

At lunchtime I arrived at the office to find it empty. Jack had obviously popped out for a sandwich. I sat down at my desk and thought about my rather bizarre morning. Grace had been utterly amazed at Maud's lack of domesticity. 'She can't even screw the teat on a bottle properly,' Grace told me. 'Josh got milk all over himself when he tipped his bottle up, poor mite. And what was she thinking putting a nappy down the loo? Or putting half a packet of washing powder in the washing machine? No wonder the laundry looks like Santa's grotto. She's nuts.'

'I did warn you.'

'You have to feel a bit sorry for her. She hides it well, but you can see she feels a bit of a fool.'

Jason had rung round and found a plumber to fix the toilet and drain the washing machine and Maud was apparently very impressed. So far, Grace could do no wrong.

'Has she been rude to you?' I asked.

'Not once.'

I gritted my teeth. How galling.

I was about to knock off for lunch when the door to the office opened and Koo walked in.

'Can I talk to you, Alice, alone?' She looked around. 'Where's Jack?'

I shrugged, pretending to be nonplussed at her appearance. In reality I was so angry with her, and so fed up and frustrated with how Maud was treating me, my blood was racing through my veins.

'I have no idea,' I said. 'I presumed the pair of you were shacked up somewhere cosy, pouring champagne over each other's private parts and licking it off.'

She grimaced. 'Don't be like that.'

'Like what? Look, Koo, I've had it up to here with this job, and having to work with your little boyfriend isn't exactly helping my mood.'

'That's what I wanted to talk to you about. He's not my boyfriend. That business in Italy, I set the whole thing up.'

'*What?*' I collapsed back into my chair, shocked to the core.

She sat on Jack's desk and looked at me. 'I was jealous. I'd been watching him flirt with you for weeks. It was obvious he was crazy about you. And then when he gave me his, "Sorry, Koo, I've met someone special and it's all over" speech, I knew it was you he was talking about. I just cracked. It was a horrible thing to do and I'm so sorry. I really wasn't thinking straight.'

'Why are you telling me this now?'

'You've been so good to Maud all week, helping out with Seb and Josh, arranging for your sister to come in; not to mention that whole business with the slug pellets. I guess it made me feel guilty. You're a nice girl, Alice, you deserve someone decent, someone like Jack.'

I shook my head. 'It's too late now, the damage is already done. But what about Jack and Flossy? Was that a lie too?'

She nodded. 'Yes, complete fabrication. I've never met his daughter either. I went through his mobile one day and found photos of a little girl who looked just like him. Then I read his text messages from her and put two and two together. It's despicable, I know. I'm sorry; I don't know what to say.'

I glared at her, my blood still racing. 'You're right, what you did was appalling and if you're looking for forgiveness, you can forget it. I think you should apologize to Jack for tramping all over his good name. You have no idea what you've done, no idea. We might have had a chance, me and Jack, but now we're barely speaking to each other.'

'I have to meet Maud for lunch, but I will ring Jack later, I promise.' She paused and then said, 'Give him another chance, Alice, he's a good man. I feel so awful about all this.'

'It's not that simple and I don't really want to talk about it, especially not to you. Would you mind leaving?'

I managed to hold back the tears until she closed the door behind her. What a mess; and what a bloody waste. I couldn't go on working with Jack, not after everything that had happened. Why hadn't I believed him?

I was still waiting for Jack at two. And at three. At ten past four he walked in with a big smile on his face. I had no idea what to say to him so I went straight into work mode.

'I've sent out the press release for the auction,' I said brightly, 'and I've spoken to all the picture desks. We have to ring most of them back on Thursday morning, but they've all agreed to send a photographer as long as something bigger doesn't come up.'

'Excellent,' Jack said. He sat down on the edge of my desk. 'I have someone outside who's dying to meet you.'

'Unless it's Alan Verdi, I'm not interested.'

'No, it's Amelie.'

I nearly fainted. My poor nerves couldn't take much more. First Koo, now this.

He continued, undeterred. 'She had a bit of an accident yesterday, that's why I wasn't—'

'Daddy!' A young girl came skipping into the office. Her right arm was in plaster but she was still smiling. Her dark brown hair hung in two paint-brush pigtails; she had a button nose, olive skin, and big, sky-blue eyes. Eyes just like Jack's.

'Are you Alice?' she asked me.

I nodded at her, dumbstruck.

'Daddy said you were pretty,' she said.

Jack beamed at her and then back at me. 'Koo rang me to apologize,' he said. 'I know how it must have looked, but she says she's spoken to you and sorted everything out. In the circumstances I was hoping we could start over. So I brought Amelie in to meet my new—'

'Jack,' I said. 'Please! I can't do this.'

'Amelie, me and Alice are just stepping outside the door for a second, OK? We have some work stuff to discuss. You can draw at my desk.' He handed her some pens and a notepad.

'OK, Daddy,' she said easily.

In the corridor he stepped towards me, arms outstretched to give me a hug. 'It's all over now. Come here.'

I backed away. 'No. I meant I can't do this at all. I'm so sorry I didn't believe you in Positano, but it doesn't change anything. I still need to be on my own at the moment.'

He looked at me for a long moment, before dragging his eyes away.

'I see,' he said. 'Then I'm sorry for bothering you. I'll drop Amelie home now.'

I felt hollow. 'OK,' I said. Then I remembered. 'What happened to her arm?'

'She fell out of a tree. She was climbing with her cousins; she goes there after school during the week. I was at work but I should have been there.' He seemed upset.

'It was an accident,' I said gently. 'These things happen.'

'I owe her so much. She gave me back my life; I wouldn't be here if it wasn't for Amelie.'

I wanted to tell him I knew how he felt, that Adam had saved my life too, but I didn't. 'I'm leaving St Jude's,' I said instead. The bank had rung earlier and they'd finally accepted my mortgage application. As soon as I could find another job I was out of this mad house.

His face fell. 'Is it me?'

I shook my head. 'It's Maud,' I said truthfully. I'd had enough of Maud to last a lifetime.

'I'm sorry to hear that,' he said. And then without another word he and Amelie left.

Amelie waved at me with her good arm and hand. 'Bye, pretty Alice.' She giggled, her eyes crinkling at the edges. I smiled back. She was the spit of her dad. I'd been waiting for this day, for my Rosewood Cottage day for so long. Now it had finally arrived and knowing I could leave St Jude's, leave Jack, I felt not happy but bereft.

Chapter 34

On the way home I called into Shelbourne Lodge. Maud met me at the door, she looked frantic.

'Finally!' she said, dragging me inside by the arm. 'I need you to nip into town and buy some shirts for Nick.'

I'd finished work for the day and she was still giving me orders.

'Now?' I asked. 'Why didn't you ring me while I was actually in town, Maud?'

'I didn't know I'd need them until a few minutes ago. That darling plumber friend of Jason's fixed the washing machine – one of Josh's socks was stuck in some sort of tube thing – but Nick's shirts are ruined. He needs three each day and he's down to his last two.'

'Three? Isn't that a bit excessive? Where's Grace?'

'In the basement.'

I walked past Maud and down the hall towards the basement stairs. I had no intention of going back into town, but I was trying to delay the news. 'How's Grace getting on?'

I waited at the top of the stairs for Maud to go ahead of me. She had this thing about going down stairs first; probably something to do with keeping people in their place. It was hardly because she was self-conscious about her bum; unlike mine hers was boyish, as flat as a cliff face.

'She's quite . . . how can I put this delicately?' Maud said.

'Bossy?' I suggested. 'Bullish? Stubborn?' My goodness was that a smile? Had Maud actually smiled at something I'd said.

'Let's just say assertive,' Maud said. 'She's brilliant with Seb. She's very organized, Josh is bathed and ready for bed and Seb is drawing pictures for Koo at the kitchen table. In fact, I was thinking of offering your sister Janny's job.'

I stifled a laugh. 'I think you'll find she has her hands full at the moment. But it's a nice thought.'

'Oh.' Maud's face dropped. 'I guess I'll have to start ringing the agencies then.'

Just then I heard a bang and the chatter of voices. Polish voices. Magda and Janny walked in the back door, their arms full of shopping bags from Penny's and the two-euro shop.

'I see you've both been busy,' Maud said rather caustically.

'Presents for our family,' Janny said. 'Clothes mainly. They're much cheaper here. A friend from our village is going home next week and she's promised to take them with her.'

Maud's face was a picture. 'You speak English. I don't understand.'

Janny just smiled at her. 'I have fluent English, Russian and German. You presumed I was a stupid little teenager with no qualifications, didn't you? I'm twenty and I have a degree in international tourism and business studies. I have three interviews lined up next week for hotel work.'

'I'm sorry,' Maud said, clearly taken aback. 'I didn't know . . . Magda never said.'

'That's OK.' Janny turned to Magda and said something I didn't catch in Polish.

'Wait,' Maud said to Magda, who had just turned to walk away from us.

'Maud,' Magda said, 'I nothing to say to you. I find new job soon. Sorry we still here. We be quiet as mouses.'

'It's not that,' Maud said. She gave a little cough. 'Magda,

I'm sorry I had no idea how much work you do. The washing alone must take you hours.'

Magda gave a snort. 'I tell you about washing. You no listen.'

'And the floors. What was I thinking? White marble is a nightmare with children. I've ordered some rugs and they'll be here next week. Is there anything else that would make your life easier?'

Magda's eyebrows lifted. 'Internet. You give me computer and I do shopping on internet.'

'Done,' Maud said. 'I'll get Nick to buy a laptop for the kitchen. Seb can use it too. He'll need it for school.'

I looked at her in surprise. So did Magda.

'He no go back to bored school?' Magda asked.

Maud laughed. 'No, I've enrolled him in Willow Park in Blackrock. I haven't told Nick yet,' she added, a thin line of worry creasing her forehead. 'So don't say a thing to Seb.'

'He be happy boy,' Magda said. 'This good thing you do, Maud. But I no say I come back.'

'Please? I'll give you a pay rise. How about ten per cent? And an extra day off a week?'

'I think about it,' Magda said, but from the slight smile on her lips it was almost certainly a yes.

'And Janny, what about you?' Maud said.

Janny shook her head. 'I need to stretch myself a bit. I was thinking of going back to college in Dublin. But maybe I could work for you part-time. I do miss Josh, but you'll have to pay me properly.'

'Of course,' Maud said. 'Whatever you think is fair. I was paying you au pair's rates, Janny. I'm sorry if it wasn't enough. I do apologize. I'll back-date the pay to when you started. We can talk about it later.'

'Hey, thanks. That will be a great help with the college fees.

And I can't wait to play with Joshie again.' Janny smiled, clearly delighted.

'So Magda?' Maud said. 'What do you think? Will you come back too?'

'Maybe.' Magda seemed to be enjoying keeping Maud in suspense. 'Now we go wrap presents. I tell you later my decide, OK?'

Maud watched them walk towards their bedroom, shaking her head.

'There you are, Maud.' Grace bustled out of the kitchen and then spotted me. 'Hi, Alice. Nice day at the office?' She smiled at me and gave me a wink.

Grace continued, 'Now, Maud, I'm going to show you how to separate the washes.'

'It won't be necessary, thank you,' Maud said. 'It looks like Magda's coming back.'

Grace snorted. 'And what happens when Magda's on holiday and you run out of baby clothes?' She smiled at her. 'Jeeze, I thought I was stubborn. Come into the laundry, will you? It's not all that difficult. Just don't put red baby socks in with Nick's white shirts again, OK?'

I watched from the doorway as Maud nodded once and stood with her back against one of the dryers, listening to Grace explain about colour transference, hot washes, cool washes and detergent overload. Science geek that she was, Grace made it all quite interesting. Even I, who had had intimate relationships with several different washing machines, learned something.

When I walked back into the kitchen, leaving them to it, Koo and Seb were dancing to the radio, Koo bumping Seb's bum with her own, Seb giggling like a girl. Josh was investigating the saucepan cupboard. Koo stopped dancing and handed me a large glass of wine. 'Hello, stranger.'

I bristled but took the very welcome glass off her all the same. 'What's this for?'

'Life, summer, children, dancing in the kitchen.' She shrugged. 'Does there have to be a reason? And I guess it's another apology. Have you talked to Jack yet?'

'Yes.'

'And?'

I shrugged. 'Nothing's changed.'

'Alice! Give the guy a chance. You owe him that much at least.'

'I don't owe him a thing. I haven't done anything wrong. And I don't want to talk about it, remember? It wouldn't have worked out anyway, it's all too complicated.' I didn't have the energy for all this. I was fed up with the whole stupid situation and wanted to forget it had ever happened.

'For what it's worth, I think you're making a mistake. Guys like Jack Wiseheart don't come round all that often. Once in a lifetime if you're lucky.'

'Koo! Would you please stop.'

She put her hands up. 'Fine, fine, I'll drop it.'

No doubt bored with the conversation, Seb ran into the garden and began to hit the pink roses with a bamboo stick.

'Should he be doing that?' I asked.

Koo hollered out the door. 'Seb, go and hit something else. Your mum likes her roses. Hit those big cactus things instead. They were Boothy's, sorry, your dad's idea. Give them a good whack from me too.'

'What are you saying about my husband?' Maud asked, joining us, Grace behind her.

Koo grinned. 'That he's an idiot and doesn't deserve you.'

'Why's he called Boothy?' Grace asked. 'I've always wondered.'

'He was caught having, you know,' Koo whistled twice, 'in

a VIP booth in Molly's Bordello. Years ago. They had curtains in those days but one of the waitresses caught him at it.'

'No!' Grace's eyes widened. 'Really?'

Maud's cheeks began to turn as pale as her marble floors. She poured herself a large glass of white wine, cupped it in her hands and stared out into the garden, as if distancing herself from the conversation.

'Was it you, Maud?' Grace said. 'In the booth, I mean.'

'Grace,' I hissed, but it was too late.

Maud swung around. 'What was that? I was miles away.'

I gave Grace an almighty dig in the ribs.

'Nothing,' Grace said. 'Ignore me.'

Koo said, 'She didn't speak to me for, what was it, Maudie, seven months?' She took a cigarette out 'Don't worry, I'll go outside to smoke it. I was working in the club a couple of evenings a week at the time and Boothy came in one night. Said he'd split up with Maud, that she'd dumped him. I felt sorry for the bugger. We had too much champagne and one thing led to another.' She stopped for a moment and tapped the filter of the cigarette on the box. 'He can be very charming when he wants to be. Thing is, they hadn't split up at all. In fact, she'd given him an ultimatum; no more women or you lose me. Isn't that right, Maudie? Stupid pig decided to teach her a lesson. A no one tells Nick Hamilton-O'Connor what to do kind of lesson. So he seduced me, his girlfriend's best friend. I was flattered. Drunk and flattered. Young and stupid.' Koo put the cigarette back in the box. 'The following week, after one hell of a row, he proposed to her. Stupid bastard said I'd come on to him. And Maud believed him. Didn't you, Maudie? It was only several years later, when one of his mistresses appeared at the front door demanding to see him, saying she'd go to the press unless he returned her calls, that Maud realized he hadn't changed: he'd lied to her all along, and their marriage was a sham. She decided that one day she'd leave him. And you will, won't you, Maudie? One day. After he's slept with the whole female population of Ireland.'

'You're despicable,' Maud said. 'Shut up, just shut up. I can't believe you've just—' Maud picked up Koo's bag and threw it at her. The contents spilled all over the floor, a bubble pack of pills, a battered Gucci wallet, several grubby tissues, crumpled-up prescriptions, and enough make-up to fill a MAC counter.

Koo was undeterred. She bent down and picked up her things. 'What's wrong, Maud? Can't take the truth?'

Maud's nose wrinkled. 'You had sex with him. In Molly's. It's disgusting.'

I could see Grace's face stretch with surprise.

'Yes, I did,' Koo said, 'and I'm sorry. It should never have happened. And you've made me pay for it over and over again. But that was years ago. I can't sit around and watch you make a fool of yourself any longer. Boothy doesn't love you, and he certainly doesn't deserve you. He's only capable of loving one person, and that's himself.'

'That's not true,' Maud cried. 'He loves me in his own way. I know he does.'

'Odette's pregnant, Maud. And this time it's for real. One of the gossip columnists rang me looking for a quote. They were very coy about the father, but the whole of Dublin will soon know it's Boothy's baby. Now, for the love of God, will you please throw the bastard out?'

Maud gave a whispery gasp and dashed out of the room.

Koo lit a cigarette with shaking fingers.

'Why did you say all those things in front of us?' I asked, shocked. 'She must be mortified.'

Koo stood at the back door, drew on her cigarette heavily, the tip surging red, and blew the smoke outside. 'Because you and Grace are real. This way maybe she'll do something about her farce of a marriage. I'm sorry, I know it was low, but I need your help to make her see. She respects you both so much.'

'*What?*' I said. 'Are you deranged?'

Koo looked at me. 'Come on, you're both so accomplished. Look at Grace, knowing all about plumbers and washing machines. And you're an amazing cook, Grace. That salad you made for lunch was delicious.'

Grace smiled. 'Thanks.'

'And you're so capable, Alice,' Koo continued. 'You can turn your hand to anything. Plus you're both so good with children. It seems to come naturally. I think Maud envies that. After losing Hal, her confidence was almost completely destroyed. She wouldn't so much as pick Josh up for weeks. She said she was jinxed. And Boothy was a pig about it, said she was a danger to herself and the children. Made Maud get a full-time nanny for him.'

'Magda told me what happened,' I admitted. 'Don't let on to Maud, though, Magda would kill me. But it wasn't Maud's fault; it could have happened to anyone.'

'Try telling Boothy that.'

'I have to ask you something,' Grace said. 'Why do *you* call him Boothy? Maud doesn't. It seems a bit odd in the circumstances.'

'To remind us both of what he's capable of.' Koo pulled on her cigarette again, a column of ash falling on the floor. She ground it into the terracotta tiles with her toe. 'He almost destroyed our friendship. Almost. Men always underestimate the power of female friendship. There's no bond quite like it. I bet there's very little that would come between you two for instance. Is there?'

'No,' Grace said. 'We're in it for the long haul. Even though she is a pain in the ass most of the time.'

'Hey!' I said, strangely touched.

Koo smiled. 'I've known Maud since I was seventeen. She's

a few years old than me and so glamorous, so beautiful. She took me under her wing. And now, twenty years on, we know each other inside out. She knows I haven't a sou to my name and I'm about to lose my house; I know how scared she is of leaving Boothy. Such is life. I guess I love her.' She gave a crooked smile. 'Plus she gave me her old car. Boothy nearly had a fit.'

'Where did you meet her?' Grace asked.

'We worked in the old Brown Thomas store together, in the designer rooms. Maud used to model the clothes for rich husbands and sugar daddies who wanted to buy something for their women. Boothy took one look at her and dumped his long-term girlfriend. Rumour has it they had rampant sex in the private changing room, but Maud swears it was just a kiss. They got married six months later; but they didn't have kids for a while. It didn't suit their lifestyle. They were always jetting off somewhere exotic.'

'Did you find a rich husband too?' Grace asked.

'Grace!' I said.

Koo just laughed. 'Not in the Boothy sense of the word, no, but we're comfortable. At least we were when he was still working; it's not so easy now. Mac's one of life's good guys. It's just a shame we didn't have more time together before his stroke.'

Seb ran in from the garden. 'Is there any food? Where's Mum? And why is Josh's mouth all black?'

Josh was sitting on the tiles outside, eating the ash from one of Koo's cigarettes.

'Maud's going to kill me.' Koo looked at Seb. 'You don't need to tell her about this, do you?'

'My birthday's soon. Will I get a big godmother present?'

'That's blackmail.' She rubbed his hair backwards and it fell back down in layers, like a field of wind-blown grass. 'Good lad. You're learning. It'll work wonders with the old man.'

'What's for tea?' Seb said. 'I'm starving.'

'I'll have a look,' I offered. Grace dealt with Josh's face and I opened the fridge door.

'Ham and cheese sambo do you?' I asked him.

He nodded eagerly. 'Wicked. Thanks, Alice.'

Maud walked back into the room, her eyes still a little red.

'Hey, Mum,' Seth said. 'I'm having a sambo. What's a sambo?'

She smiled at him. 'A sandwich.'

He ran over and threw his arms around her waist. 'A sambo. Ace. Mum, do I have to go to summer camp next week? I'd much rather stay here with you. And maybe I could have a friend over to play. Are there any boys my age on this road?'

'No, I don't think so, pet. I'm sorry.'

His face fell.

'My friend's boy, Josep, is about your age,' I said. 'He's great fun. Very smart. Although he does have a bit of a thing about torturing worms and snails, I'm afraid.'

Seb grinned. 'He sounds ace. Can I have Josep to play, Mum?'

'Yes, of course you can. And you don't have to do that rugby camp if you don't want to. I'll talk to your father.'

'Will you?' Koo asked pointedly. '*Talk* to him.'

'I will,' she said. 'In my own time. I promise.'

'When you do, I'm here for you,' Koo said. 'Whenever you need me. Understand?'

Maud nodded. 'OK. Now, tell me you haven't finished all that wine.'

'Course not,' Koo said. 'But we might need another bottle soon. Alice is tearing into it.'

'I am not!' I grinned. 'Don't listen to her. There are steaks and chicken wings in the fridge. Do you have a barby, Maud?'

'I'm not sure.' Maud shrugged. 'I think so.'

Magda and Janny walked into the kitchen, carrying several

dirty mugs and plates each and a rubbish bin crammed with old takeaway boxes and wrappers. No wonder I hadn't seen much of them, they'd obviously been holed up in their room, watching telly and scoffing Chinese food.

'What you doing in kitchen?' Magda asked Maud, her eyes saucers of surprise. 'You cook? You no go out?'

'We're having a barbeque,' Maud said. 'If we can find the barbeque that is.'

'In shed.' Magda held her arms out as wide as they would go. 'Can't miss. Silver, big as car. Has wheels too.'

'Magda . . .' Maud began.

'Is OK,' Magda said. 'I help. No problem.'

'I was going to ask if you'd care to join us.' Maud bit the inside of her gum and danced from one foot to the other, like a child needing the loo.

Janny gave a laugh. 'Are you serious?'

Maud smiled, actually smiled. 'Yes. So, how do you like your steak?'

'You real serious?' Magda asked, her nose wrinkling a little just like Maud's.

'Yes.' Maud met her gaze. 'I'd like you both to join my friends and I for a barbeque. Why ever not?'

Magda said, 'We staff, that why not.'

Maud shrugged. 'Staff, Magda, not slaves.' She gave a wry smile. 'Things are going to change around here from now on. You have my word.'

'But Mister Nick—'

'Forget about him. He's out with his mistress.'

'What's mistress, Mummy?' Seb asked.

'Someone with the morals of an alley cat,' Koo said, 'the opposite of a friend.'

'Koo,' Maud said sharply.

'We'd be delighted to accept your kind invitation,' Janny said rather formally. 'Wouldn't we, Mum?'

'*Mum?*' Maud stared at Magda. 'When were you going to tell me, Magda?'

Magda shrugged. 'We all have secrets. Reech lady, poor lady. We all same.'

Janny laughed. 'Mum, would you stop with the poor nonsense. If you went back to Poland, you could buy a palace with all the money you've saved. Maud, you pay her far too much you know.'

Maud coloured a little. 'She deserves it.' She picked at the nail on her index finger, clearly embarrassed. 'I'm starving, can we please eat?'

Koo laughed. 'Does this mean you're finally going to stop that bloody diet of yours?'

'Yes,' Maud said simply. 'Fuck the diet.'

'Mum!' Seb said.

'I'm sorry, darling.' She pressed her hands over his ears. 'And fuck my fucking shit of a husband. How dare he? Odette Cunningham.' She spat out the name, like a round of machine-gun fire. 'She looks like a cheap hooker, I could vomit just thinking about it. And she has no knuckles on her right hand, did you know that? Dreadful woman and hardly skinny either.' She snorted. 'I've been starving myself for fifteen years and for what? For nothing. I'm forty this year. Forty! I'm going to eat what the hell I like from now on. Hips and thighs here we come. Up to a point, of course. Nothing trashier than a flabby stomach.'

Koo hooted with laughter. 'Quite right too, Maudie. Now quit gabbing and go and fetch some more booze. Let's see how many bottles of Nick's best vintage vino we can get through. It will serve him right.' Her eyes lit up. 'In fact, I have an idea.'

Chapter 35

'Where are you, Koo? We need you.' Maud tapped her Gucci-
ed foot impatiently, her mobile phone pressed to her ear over
her hair, presumably to stop her perfect blow dry from being
ruined. We'd slipped into the hotel manager's office for a last
minute pow wow before the 'Especially for You' auction
kicked off and Koo was still nowhere to be seen. We'd abandoned our auctioneer, Alan Verdi, who was utterly charming
and most attractive, right down to the unusual silver 'badger'
streak down the middle of his otherwise dark hair, but he
seemed happy to chat to people at the drinks reception. He
also seemed quite taken with Maud, his eyes following her
round the room. He'd certainly be wondering where she was
now.

'What?' Maud demanded. 'In the car park? What are you
doing out there? Oh, I see,' her voice softened. 'I'll be straight
out.'

She clicked her mobile off. 'Follow me,' she said without
preamble. 'Trust Gunella to be away when we actually need
her,' she muttered under her breath.

Gunella's husband had decided to surprise her with a trip to
Paris for her birthday, much to Maud's annoyance.

'Where are we going?' Jack whispered to me as we made our
way into the lobby and out the heavy glass doors. Jack's long
legs kept up with Maud's strides, but I had to half walk, half

trot along in my heels, pulling my fitted skirt up with my hands, feeling pretty silly.

Outside, it was still balmy. We wound our way through the lines of Mercedes and Lexus cars and jeeps, and past the taxis spilling out their dolled-up charges at the door. Almost everyone called a greeting to Maud and she gave them all a smile and a wave.

'Lovely to see you,' she called 'So glad you could make it.' 'Don't you look amazing?' But her voice sounded flat.

Koo was slumped over the steering wheel of her Mercedes. Maud pulled open the door and knelt down beside her. 'Koo, I'm so sorry.'

Koo looked up. Her mascara was streaming down her cheeks. She looked like Alice Cooper on a bad day.

Jack touched my bare arm, his cool hand making my skin tingle. 'Should we leave them to it?'

I shook my head. 'Maud might need us. We'd better stay put.' To be honest, I also wanted to find out what was wrong with Koo.

'I'm going to lose Mac,' Koo wailed. 'They don't think he'll make it this time.'

'Where is he?' Maud asked her.

'Vincent's.'

'Then he's getting the very best treatment, Koo, you know that. The doctors will take good care of him.'

'The doctors can't do anything. He's in a coma. You don't understand, Maud; this time it's different.'

Maud stroked Koo's hair. 'Mac's as strong as an ox. He'll pull through.'

Koo shrugged off her hand and turned the key in the ignition. 'I'm going back to the hospital. I need to be with him.'

'But what about the auction?' Maud twisted her chunky engagement ring round and round on her finger.

Koo looked up at her. 'You *are* joking? Mac's dying and

you're worried about your bloody auction. That's just great. Thanks a lot.'

'I didn't mean it that way.'

'How did you mean it?'

'I really think we should—' Jack whispered in my ear.

'Shush,' I told him, rooted to the spot. I half expected him to leave me there, but he stood beside me, not moving an inch.

'I just hate doing these things on my own, you know that,' Maud said. 'I need you by my side, Koo. I can't do it without you.'

'What about Nick?' Koo asked.

'*She's* here.'

'No! Where's she sitting?'

'At his table,' Maud admitted. 'Beside him.'

'What a nerve. Bloody fool of a man. You have to do something; he's parading her in public. People will talk.'

'Do what?'

'Maud,' Koo gave a wry laugh, 'I don't have time for this right now. But here's a suggestion, you could start by telling him about Seb's new school, and that you want to look after Josh yourself some of the time.'

Maud's face crumpled. 'I'm not very good with toddlers.'

'Don't talk rubbish,' Koo said. 'You coped fine when Magda and Janny were on strike. You can do it again. God, sometimes I wonder why we're still friends. Grow up, Maudie. And guess what, you could even get a job like the rest of us mere mortals.'

Jack gave a little gasp. 'Now she's done it.'

'I think Koo's right,' I whispered back. 'It would stop Maud obsessing about the small stuff. And it would keep her off your back too.'

Koo must have heard me because she looked over. 'What do you think, Alice? Should Maud get a job? Look after her own kids? Clean her own house?'

'She's not the best at housework,' I said carefully, not wanting to tell any tales out of school. After all, she had almost flooded her house with soap suds, and blocked the loo. I looked at Maud. She was staring straight ahead, her eyes glassy, avoiding my gaze. I felt a wave of sympathy. I added, 'But she's great with the kids, and they adore her.'

Maud looked at me in surprise. 'How can you say that, Alice? I nearly killed Josh with those slug pellets.'

'You're exaggerating,' I assured her.

Koo's mobile beeped. She whipped it up. 'Yes?' She listened for a moment, and then said, 'I'll be there straight away.' She clicked off her phone. 'That was the hospital. Mac's woken up but his heart's in trouble. I have to go.' She slammed the gear stick into reverse and we all stood back as she pulled out, eyes wild.

'Good luck,' Maud shouted after her. 'Good luck? What the hell am I saying?' There were tears in her eyes. 'What am I doing, Alice? Why am I here? I'm no use to anyone.'

She was still looking at me. Shit, she wanted an answer. Jack was looking at me too.

'The show must go on,' I said firmly. 'Maud, you make your speech and then Jack and I will take over. You should be with Koo. She needs you.'

'You're right,' Maud said, 'of course you're right. I don't know what I'd do without you. Thank you.' And for once I think she actually meant it.

Half an hour later, when everyone had finally taken their seats, Maud was standing at the podium on the stage, in front of a sea of expectant faces. Jack and I were flanking her for support in Koo's and Gunella's absence. I looked down at the crowd. Each table sat fourteen people, all dripping with silk ties, expensive suits and dresses, the women's ears and necks flashing with diamonds. If a highway man burst into the room with a swag bag, he'd come out a very rich man.

Alan Verdi was sitting at the top table with Nick and some of his business friends, and their much younger wives and girlfriends. Jack and I were standing rigidly, Jack's hands to his sides, mine clenched in front of my stomach, trying to hide my paunch. All the other women here were freakily thin, apart from Odette of course.

Men with ruddy cheeks were quaffing champagne like it was about to run out; beside them blonde, unsmiling women were fiddling with the spaghetti straps on their dresses and yawning discreetly behind perfectly manicured hands.

I spotted Nick leering at Odette's ample chest. For a man who liked his women thin, he had a funny way of showing it. Or was his interest in Maud's weight a power thing, yet another way of controlling her and making her feel inadequate? How could Maud bear it? I caught her looking down at him and then quickly glancing away, the notes in her hands shaking.

'Ladies and gentlemen,' Maud began, her voice shaking a little too. The room was still alive with chatter and the tinkle of glasses. She coughed. 'Ladies and gentlemen,' she tried again. Still noise.

Jack took his silver Cross pen from his pocket, held a water glass up to the microphone and tapped it. 'DING, DING, DING. Pray silence please for Maud Hamilton-O'Connor,' he said. Instant silence and a few giggles.

'Shit,' he whispered to me as he slotted in beside me, Maud taking his place at the podium. 'Did that sound a bit strange?'

'Not at all,' I whispered back, trying not to laugh. 'Pray silence for our esteemed leader.'

'You're a cruel woman.' He smiled at me, so he obviously didn't mean it.

Maud cleared her throat with a tiny cough and then began: 'Ladies and gentlemen, thank you all so much for being here. Your kind patronage means the world to all of us at St Jude's.'

Her hands began to shake furiously. 'I was supposed to be introducing my committee member now, Koo Ryder, but she can't be with us I'm afraid. She's . . . she's,' Maud stammered, 'otherwise detained.'

'Otherwise detained?' I hissed at Jack, a little too loudly.

Maud looked over at me.

'Sorry,' I mouthed silently.

Her eyes lingered on mine, a strange expression on her face.

'Actually she's in St Vincent's,' she said, 'with her husband, Mac. He's not at all well—' She broke off and stared down at the crowd. Her hands dropped limply to her sides. She stood like that, silent, for what seemed like an age, but must have only been half a minute.

An embarrassed hush spread through the room. There were a few coughs and a titter of laughter from Nick and Odette's table.

Jack switched the microphone off. 'Maud,' he said, 'are you all right?'

'I'm sorry,' she said. 'I can't do this.'

'What about the auction?' he asked.

'You and Alice are more than capable.' She squeezed his arm. 'I'm so sorry. Koo . . .' There were tears in her eyes.

'We understand,' I said, 'and we'll do you proud, Maud, I promise. Tell Koo, tell her . . .' I didn't know what to say.

'Tell her we're thinking of her,' Jack said helpfully.

Maud gave a nod and ran off the stage and out the double doors at the back of the room. Nick watched her with interest, but didn't follow her. Odette said something in his ear, and he patted her hand and smiled. Bastard! The crowd began to chatter, the noise level rising quickly.

'Now what?' Jack asked.

I pointed at the podium. 'It's all yours. I'll be right beside you.'

He stepped up. Of course he did. He was that kind of guy. I

knew he hated public speaking, he'd told me so himself, and his face and neck were turning mottled red. But he still did it. He flicked the microphone back on.

'I'd like to welcome our auctioneer, Alan Verdi, to the stage,' he said, sounding surprisingly confident.

Alan walked towards the stage to a warm round of applause and stood beside me. As Jack introduced him, Alan asked me in a low voice, 'Is Maud all right?'

'Not really,' I whispered back. 'Her best friend's husband is dying. She's gone to the hospital to be with her.'

His eyes showed genuine emotion. 'She's a good friend.'

'Yes,' I said. 'Yes, she is.'

Mac died at nine p.m. from heart failure. Koo slept in Shelbourne Lodge that night. The following day Maud insisted that she stayed on for a few weeks, until she felt stronger. Nick wasn't impressed. Maud also told him that Seb would not be going back to boarding school and he threw a complete wobbler. He said he wasn't having it, so she said she'd had quite enough of his bullying and his womanizing and asked him to leave, very calmly apparently.

I got the abbreviated version from Jack who'd spoken to Maud first thing in the morning. It had obviously been an eventful night for all concerned. Poor Koo was speechless with grief. She was wrapped up on the sofa and Magda was feeding her weak hot whiskies with plenty of sugar.

Maud told Nick it would be a quiet, civilized break up as long as he fully complied with her lawyer. She promised not to be unreasonable; she only wanted enough maintenance to run the house and look after the children. I did wonder if 'running the house' included cashmere jumpers and designer shoes. If he didn't comply, Maud threatened to tell the press all about his slightly iffy offshore accounts and foreign investments. And as part of the agreement, he had to donate the sharks to the aquarium in Bray; that was Magda's idea – she'd always felt sorry for the poor animals.

Koo wanted Maud to clean him out, sell his car, his wine cellar, his golf clubs and his designer suits on eBay but Maud wasn't having any of it.

'I don't want revenge,' she'd said. 'I just want him out of my life for good.'

Mac's funeral was packed. I recognized dozens of faces from the social pages and the media: ladies who lunch, their cleavage covered up with pashminas; television personalities; news readers; actors; musicians; and several politicians. It was impressive.

'Mac was quite the man about town in his day,' Jack said in a low voice. We were standing together in the back pew of the large Protestant church in Ballybrack, Mac's childhood parish, the parish he'd never left even after moving house several times. We slid into seats near the aisle, so we could hop out if either Koo or Maud needed us. 'Church warden too. He used to drag Koo along to morning service every Sunday.'

I smiled. 'Really?' I couldn't imagine Koo in church.

Jack nodded. 'She says she used to nod off halfway through the first reading, but the singing always woke her up. Mac loved belting out all the hymns. He had a great voice: tenor.'

'Did you know him before the stroke?'

'Yes. He used to sing with the college choral society. I was standing beside him when we did the *Messiah* one Christmas in St Patrick's Cathedral.'

I stared at Jack. 'You sang in a choir?'

'Still do.' He gave a laugh. 'Don't look so surprised. There's a lot you don't know about me.'

The organist began to play slow, sombre music and we stopped talking and turned to watch as Koo walked up the aisle clutching Maud's arm, following three tall men in their forties and early fifties. They all had long, angular faces, and one of them looked eerily like Ronnie Wood.

'Koo's brothers?' I asked Jack.

He nodded. 'They all live abroad. London, Chicago and somewhere in Europe; Prague I think. Koo's the only one still in Dublin.'

As Koo passed us she turned her head a little and gave us a tiny nod. Even today she looked stunning. Jack mouthed 'Hi' and I gave her what I hoped was a supportive and sympathetic smile, my eyes welling up as soon as they met hers. She was wearing a tiny black top hat perched on her curls, held in place with hairpins, and her eyes were covered with the hat's thin black veil. Her long black coat had tails at the back and as she walked you caught glimpses of her black leather on-the-knee skirt, black fishnets and black patent boots with dagger heels. Pure Koo! But even through the veil I could see her eyes were red and puffy from crying, her skin doughy from lack of sleep.

All the anger I'd felt towards her had melted away the instant I'd heard about Mac's death. It was then I realized just how much I had to be grateful for: Grace and her boys, Adam, Roz and Josep; and how lucky I was, despite my disaster of a love life.

Today Maud was wearing a plain black cashmere coat over a black dress and T-bar shoes with a neat heel. Her face was rigid, her lips pressed together in a line, her eyes red and glittering. When Maud, Koo, and Koo and Mac's families had slid into the top pews, the rector, a friendly-looking man, began the service. As I mouthed the opening hymn, 'The Lord's My Shepherd', tears rolled down my cheeks and fell onto the hymnal, leaving dark spots on the thin paper. I always cried at weddings and funerals.

Jack sang with his eyes closed, his voice clear and perfectly in pitch. He knew he had a nice voice and he wasn't ashamed to share it with the world. Why would he be? The stupid thing is I can sing too. Not like Jack, but I don't have a bad voice. As I listened to him sing about walking in death's dark vale, I opened my mouth and belted out the last verse with all my might. It was louder than I'd intended but it didn't matter.

> *Goodness and mercy all my life*
> *Shall surely follow me;*
> *And in God's house forevermore*
> *My dwelling place shall be.*

My eyes smarted with tears as I sang, but I kept going.

'Alice Devine,' Jack said quietly at the end of the hymn. 'Now there's a surprise.'

'There's a lot you don't know about me,' I said.

'I look forward to finding out in that case.'

I leaned in towards him and whispered, 'Are you flirting with me at a funeral, Mr Wiseheart?'

'Maybe.' He smiled. 'I don't think Mac would mind. He used to flirt with all the girls in the choir.'

Maud hosted the funeral lunch at her house. Minnie and Adelaide were doing the catering again, and they, Magda and Janny had everything in control, so I sat in the small living room off the kitchen with Jack, on the very sofa where I'd first heard about Hal.

'I'll be sorry to leave Maud in a way,' I said staring out the window.

Maud was running after Josh in the garden. She whipped him up into her arms and then sniffed his bottom and handed him over to Janny. I smiled. Some things would never change.

'I never thought I'd hear you say that,' Jack said, 'but she does kind of grow on you.'

'Like a fungus,' I said, remembering.

He grinned. 'Like a fungus.' He took my hand. I pulled it away. 'Alice, just let me hold your hand, OK? Nothing more.'

Wordlessly I gave him back my hand. His palm was warm and inviting and I gave his hand a squeeze.

We sat there for a few minutes, staring out into the garden. 'So where do we go from here?' he asked. 'I know what you said before, and I promise this is the last time I'll mention it. Have dinner with me. Please?'

'Yes,' I murmured.

'Yes? Oh, Alice—'

'Don't get too excited, it's only dinner. I'm so sorry about Italy. I should have believed you. But Koo was—'

'Hush,' he said. 'Life's too short to worry about the past. Let's just concentrate on the future. Our future.'

He grabbed me round the waist and kissed me firmly on the lips, my whole body relaxing into his embrace. It was like coming home.

'Jack!' I pulled away after a few seconds and a few more kisses. 'We're at a funeral lunch.'

He pushed my hair back off my face and smiled down at me. 'I think Mac would approve,' he said, before kissing me again.

Later that evening I told Grace about what had happened.

'I'm so pleased for you,' she said. 'I hope it all works out this time, sis.'

'So do I. And what about you? How are things with Jason?'

'Not bad. He's been a great help with the boys.'

'And?'

'And nothing.'

'Gracey!'

'OK, OK, we're talking. Trying to work out what went wrong between us and why. I know his thyroid had something to do with his moodiness, but he still shouldn't have run off to

London like that.' She sighed. 'And then there's the whole business with Gary of course. We've both made mistakes. Maybe we can work things out, maybe not.'

'But there's hope?'

She smiled. 'You're such an optimist, Alice, but yes, I guess there is. Now, enough already. I want to hear all about this dinner date next week with Jack. Most importantly what are you going to wear?'

'I'm sure Petra will have something,' I said with a laugh, 'as long as she's sure it's not Maud's this time.'

Chapter 36

THREE MONTHS LATER

Maud and Koo surprised everyone by going into business together, a designer boutique called KuMa. Thanks to Alan Verdi, Maud's new 'friend', they found an ideal premise in Donnybrook. Alan had moved back to Dublin and the couple had been spotted around town together, much to Nick's disgust. Alan was nearly ten years younger than Nick and a lot fitter.

'Maud? *Working?*' I asked Jack when he told me the news.

'Don't sound so shocked. Koo's worked on and off all her life. And Maud's more a sleeping partner; she'll help Koo with some of the buying and she's promised to send Magda or Janny over whenever Koo needs an extra hand.'

'That sounds more like it. And how are Magda and Janny?'

'Good. Janny's doing some of Maud's paperwork and the shop accounts. Maud's very impressed. Magda misses the sharks though. She goes out to the aquarium every month to visit them.'

I laughed. 'I do miss Magda.'

'And Josep and Seb have become great buddies.'

I grinned. 'I thought they might.' Maud got quite a fright when she found Roz chatting away in Polish to Magda in the kitchen. Roz told me all about it. Luckily I'd warned her about Maud before Josep's first play date.

'Don't worry,' Roz had said. 'I'm sure she'll get over it. And it's not about her, is it? It's about her son. Maybe in time she'll see that.'

To give Maud credit, she did. Josep soon won her over with his impeccable manners and bright, sunny smile. She didn't know he was also teaching Seb to swear in Polish, much to Magda's delight.

'And how's the new job going?' Jack asked.

I'd stayed at St Jude's for five weeks after Mac's funeral, until Jack had found someone to replace me. He'd taken on a twenty-two-year-old, Tony Packen, who was straight out of college and dead eager. The job description had been tweaked a little, Tony wouldn't have to work for Maud, not officially anyway, although she had summoned him to cut the grass at Shelbourne Lodge when Mikey and Janny were on holiday.

Thanks to one of Jack's sisters who was married to the head of news, I was now working as a trainee producer cum girl Friday on the morning show at East Coast FM in Bray. I loved it. I'd only been there two weeks, but I was already reading the traffic reports and bantering a little on air with the presenter, Declan.

To top it all I was very close to being the proud owner of Rosewood Cottage. There was some sort of legal hold up and I hadn't got the keys yet, but thanks to Grace, the end was almost in sight. She has a brilliant manner with solicitors. 'Just do it and get back to me when it's finished,' she told them curtly. 'No more excuses.'

In fact, Grace and Jason gave me the last few thousand euro I needed for the deposit. Jason had savings put aside to upgrade his jeep but Grace managed to persuade him he didn't need a new one, that the old one was just fine. And I'd completely underestimated Maud. She gave Grace five hundred euro in cash for helping her out when Magda and Janny were on strike. Grace put it straight into my hands, to help towards the deposit, bless her.

On my last day in St Jude's we all went out for lunch – me, Jack, Maud and Koo. In Patrick Guibauld's, one of the swishest restaurants in Dublin. It was amazing. And the staff were so nice, not toffee-nosed at all. They didn't bat an eyelid when I spilt my water all over the table.

Jack gave me a beautiful silver necklace as a going-away present, a tiny butterfly hanging on a delicate chain. From Tiffany's no less. I squealed when I saw the turquoise box tied up with a cream ribbon.

Maud and Koo gave me a very generous voucher for Brown Thomas. 'To buy things for your new house,' Koo said, and another voucher for Maud's beautician.

'Get her to sort out your eyebrows,' Maud said in a low voice. 'And, darling, for heaven's sake get a facial, I can see your open pores from here.'

I just smiled at her. Nothing could dull my mood that day. 'Yes, Maud,' I said. 'Whatever you say, Maud.'

Koo laughed into her wine and Maud scowled at her.

'I'll miss you, Alice,' Koo said. 'Keep in touch.'

'I will,' I promised. Then I looked at Maud. 'And will you miss me, Maud?' I asked her, the three glasses of wine making me feel bold.

She held my gaze. Her eyes seemed softer, less tortured. 'Yes,' she said finally 'and no.'

I laughed. 'You're priceless.'

'And you, Alice, are an incurable snoop. You'd make a great spy.'

The day after my farewell lunch, I finally got the keys to Rosewood Cottage. As I turned the key in the lock, Adam on my hip, Grace by my side, I braced myself for the smell of cat pee. I pushed open the door but – nothing – just a slight mustiness. I looked down. The carpet had been ripped up, leaving bare wooden floorboards.

Grace followed my gaze. 'They'll come up nicely with a sand and a coat of varnish.'

We stepped into the living room. The curtains had disappeared and again, the carpet had been ripped up. I found an envelope propped on the mantelpiece. I handed Adam to Grace and opened it. I pulled out a card with a black cat on the front. Inside it read, in sloping handwriting:

Good luck in your new home. I asked the estate agent to arrange a bit of a clear out for you. Fresh start and all that. I wasn't allowed to bring Barney with me – he's my cat. Any chance you could adopt him? I believe you have a boy, he might like him. If not, Mrs Peters next door will take him, she's been feeding him for me. Hope you are happy in Rosewood Cottage – take care of the old girl for me. I'll miss her.

Kind regards,

Jack Shulman, ex-owner of Rosewood Cottage

I smiled to myself. Jack. So that's what the J on the house contracts stood for. I looked out the window at the freshly weeded concrete patio. A black cat was lying on the slabs, sunning his belly.

'Miaow,' Adam said.

'That's right.' I reached over and rubbed his head. 'Miaow. Looks like we have a new pet.'

Tears sprung to my eyes. I loved cats. And this fellow was just perfect.

'What's wrong?' Grace asked.

I shook my head. 'Nothing. For the first time in my life, absolutely nothing.'

Epilogue

'What do you want for Christmas?' Jack asked me as we played hunt the animals in Dublin Zoo with Adam and Amelie. We were watching the sea lions, the only animals we could actually find. It was a cold but sunny October day and the other critters were all hiding in their dens, refusing to cooperate.

We'd been seeing each other for nearly two months now and so far, so good. I'd told him about Ned, and how Grace had pretty much saved my life; and he'd just given me a hug.

'We all make mistakes,' he'd said. 'Look at me for God's sake; I'm a mess. I still think you're amazing.'

Adam had taken to Amelie from the very first time they'd met in an Italian restaurant. The moment she'd let him dip his crayon in her milk he knew he'd met a kindred spirit.

'Christmas?' I said. 'It's not even Hallowe'en yet, Jack.'

'I know, it just feels Christmassy today, don't you think?' He stomped on a large mound of crispy leaves.

I laughed. 'You're such a child. So what do *you* want, then?'

'Just you. Naked. With a big red ribbon around your waist.'

'Stop!' I bumped my shoulder against his.

'There's something else I'd like,' he said, his neck turning red.

'Yes?'

'A December wedding. Will you marry me?'

My heart soared, I tingled all over and I could tell I was blushing furiously. This wasn't how I'd imagined Jack's marriage proposal. I had been thinking more along the lines of Paris in springtime, on the top of the Eiffel Tower.

'What do you say? I'm dying here, Alice.'

'To be honest I've never really wanted a big wedding with all the palaver.'

'A woman after my own heart. I'm thinking sun, sand, peace and quiet . . . Barbados maybe. Just us and the kids. And our sisters; they'd kill us otherwise.'

'No Maud or Koo?'

'No Maud or Koo, that's a promise.'

I smiled. 'In that case, Mr Wiseheart, it's a yes.'

And then he kissed me.

Acknowledgements

This has been a funny kind of book. It started off life as something completely different and ended up – well, right here, in between these gorgeous Robyn Neild covers. It wasn't the easiest book to write, but I cried when I finished the final edit, sad that I wouldn't be spending any more time with Alice, Grace, Jack, Magda, Koo and, yes, even and most especially my rather mad charity queen, Maud.

This book is set in the world of charity fund-raising. There are thousands of women all over Ireland and the UK who do tireless voluntary work for hospitals and other charities, and I'd like to congratulate my mum, Melissa Webb, who has been working as a volunteer for the National Children's Hospital and the Rotunda Hospital for over thirty years now. Last year she was awarded an honorary doctorate for all her work (along with Robert Redford, and yes, she met him, swoon!) and we're all very proud of her. At last we have a doctor in the family!

I'd also like to point out that Mum is nothing like Maud Hamilton-O'Connor in the book – she's a very kind, thoughtful woman and she doesn't live in a palace of a house or have a fountain on the drive like Maud, which is a shame as it would be fun to paddle in!

I always go on far too long in my acknowledgements, and

302

these ones won't be any different, ha – I might be run down by a bus any day now and I have a lot of people to thank!

First up: so much love and thanks are due to my family for their ongoing support. To my parents; to my fiancé (yes, we got engaged recently – much excitement) Ben, my children Sam, Amy-Rose and Jago. And, of course, my sisters, Kate and Emma, who give me lots to write about – only joking, girls!

My dear and most fab friends, Tanya, Nicky and Andrew. We all met in our teens and have been great friends ever since. Here's to many more years together.

My dear writing friends, especially Martina Devlin, my chief sounding board and bottle washer (that would be champagne bottles!), Clare Dowling, Martina Reilly, Marita Conlon-McKenna, Catherine Daly and Vanessa O'Loughlin. I would be a very sad and lonely writer if I didn't have you guys to moan to and exchange writerly woes with. Also to the gang at Irish Pen and all the other Irish Girls, my writers in crime, for all the entertaining and enlightening social events.

To my amazing au pairs, Anna and Christina, who took such good care of my children while I was writing this book. *Ahoj*, girls!

To Ali Gunn, my agent.

To Imogen Taylor and Trisha Jackson, my editors at Pan Macmillan, for all their hard work on my behalf. I've been very lucky to have the same editorial team for eight years now and it's been a real blessing. This is the first book I've worked on with Trisha in her new editorial role, and I hope it's the first of many; she has a great eye and is always a delight to talk to. Editors like Imogen and Trisha also make the technical and business side of being a writer (dealing with cover copy, edits, cover illustrations and things like that) a relatively stress-free experience, which is a real skill. Thanks also to Liz Cowen and her team.

And of course, to the lovely Cormac Kinsella, who does my

PR in Ireland, and David Adamson, the best and kindest rep in the world.

To all the booksellers in Ireland and the UK who have supported my books over the years, especially the gang in Eason and Dubray. Maria, David and Susan deserve special mentions. Thanks for all the help and advice, guys and dolls!

And finally to you, the reader. This is novel number eight, and some of you have stuck with me the whole way from book one. What a journey! God bless your patience, and thank you so much for all the encouraging emails and letters; they make it all worthwhile.

I love hearing from readers and promise to answer every single email and letter, so do write. My contact details are on my website: www.sarahwebb.ie or you can email me at sarah@sarahwebb.ie or sarahsamwebb@gmail.com.

Happy reading!

Much love,

Sarah XXX